THE ACCIDENTAL
CORRUPTION

KOS PLAY

aethonbooks.com

THE ACCIDENTAL CORRUPTION
©2023 KOS PLAY

Aethon Books

www.aethonbooks.com

Print and eBook formatting by Josh Hayes. Artwork provided by Cyan Gorilla.

Published by Aethon Books LLC.

Aethon Books is not responsible for websites (or their content) that are not owned by the publisher.

ALSO IN SERIES

[1]

I WAS HOMELESS. Armed with nothing but a letter from my mom and Lavender's word that she was sending someone to pick me up, I sat in front of a 7-11 drinking a Slurpee.

The only good news was that my connection to Kalli was strong enough to communicate across dimensions. I heard her voice in my head as I sighed loudly. *Don't worry Mel. Just think of this as your next big adventure. Besides, you can come visit anytime.*

Memories of the random family in my mom's house made me worry that teleportation may be difficult. I was spared from having to answer when a rather loud horn startled me.

Looking up, a smile spread across my face as a familiar cab that had been magically converted into a Hummer pulled into the parking lot. I climbed to my feet and called out to him, "Lou! Long time no see."

The driver waved a stubby arm out of the window and grinned, honking the horn again for good measure. "It has been a while, Mac! Welcome back to Earth."

I climbed into the back seat after he pulled around in front of me. "How did you know I was on another planet?"

Lou looked back over his shoulder. "Lavender told me. She is my new biggest customer. She got me started in the magic business, and now I'm driving for witches and wizards full time. Also, I don't know what you did to my cab, but I don't need to put gas in the tank no more."

He turned back around and pressed a red button, which caused the seatbelt to wrap around me like the vines of an aggressive plant. When I struggled with my bindings, he chuckled. "Lavender made a few modifications. Safety first. Stop struggling, and it won't hurt you."

When I relaxed, the seatbelt loosened up enough so I was comfortable, and Lou took off. I felt Kalli's excitement through our connection. *I can't believe that's really Lou. Tell him I said hi.*

———

The drive to Lavender's house was fairly uneventful. Lou made some small talk, but I mostly chatted with Kalli. She was busy with her family and got distracted a lot. Even though she told me not to, I was sorely tempted to teleport back to Gaia. It felt as though Earth held nothing for me anymore.

When we arrived at the gate to Lavender's property, it swung open allowing Lou to proceed toward the house. I leaned forward for a better view of the picturesque drive. "That's new. She didn't let you in last time."

Lou grinned over his shoulder at me. "That's because I didn't work for her last time. This time I can take you all the way to the front door. Full service."

When we arrived, there was a trio of people waiting for us. I recognized Lavender in her sparkling gown, looking every bit the supermodel. At her side were a couple of kids I couldn't place right away.

My mouth fell open when I inspected the boy.

Name: Eddison Thompson III
Class: Warlock
Level: 12
Affection Level: Proud

Lou stopped the Humcab and walked around to open the door for me. Only then did the seatbelt release me, and I was able to climb out. Eddie smirked at me as I inspected the younger girl at his side. She appeared to be nine or ten years old.

Name: Sylvia Moreheart
Class: Affectionist
Level: 2
Affection Level: Loving

Something about the girl felt strangely familiar. She had short blonde hair arranged in a pixie cut and amber-colored eyes. Sylvia also seemed to know me because she ran up and wrapped me in a hug as soon as I got out of the vehicle.

The instant we made contact, I felt a spark of energy and mana seemed to radiate from her entire body. The mana flowed over and through me, both washing away my fatigue and making me smile at the same time.

She looked up, her eyes like saucers. "Do you remember me, Melvin?"

I turned to Lavender mouthing the word *help*, not remembering where I knew the kid from.

The enchanter gave me a lopsided grin and said, "Don't look at me. She's yours. You made her."

My ears began to ring as Kalli shrieked, ***Melvin Murphy! What is she talking about?***

I covered my ears with my hands as I attempted to reason with my girlfriend.

Give me a break! The kid's like ten years old. I would have had to have had her when I was six.

I felt Kalli's mouth fall open and saw everyone staring at her in the throne room. Apparently, she was in the middle of something and had jumped to her feet in outrage. She answered with a short, ***Oh.***

Lavender chuckled, likely having witnessed our internal conversation somehow. "Okay, fine. I'll help you out. This here is Sylvia. She was supposed to die last year, and you prevented that. To top it off, you also awakened her. So, here she is. A newborn mage. You are going to have to take responsibility and raise her. She now bears a great role in the future of this universe. You do as well for the role you chose."

It suddenly dawned on me how I knew the kid. She was dying of cancer, and I had awakened her in the process of saving her. With tears coming to my eyes, I knelt in front of Sylvia and stroked her hair. "I knew it would grow back quickly."

She blinked at me. "It grew back so fast. I had to get twelve haircuts since then. I don't mind, though. We gave my hair to the other sick kids."

"She's a healer," Lavender pointed out from behind her. "She can heal wounds when she hugs someone. And she just loves to hug as you can see. Right now, her power isn't quite at the level yours is at. She can't cure cancer or anything fancy like that."

"So, what do I have to do?" I asked, wondering how I was going to take responsibility. "I don't know the first thing about raising a kid."

"No, silly." Sylvia giggled, letting me go. "You are going to teach me how to use my magic."

I nodded absentmindedly. It was true that I could heal. Sylvia knew firsthand as I had healed her. Nodding at the kid, I said, "Sure. I'll teach you what I can."

"Great!" Lavender said, clapping her hands together. "Now that that's settled, let's go inside."

———

The inside of Lavender's cottage was just as large as I remembered it. A red carpet lined the halls, and a grand staircase filled the entryway. Lavender led us down one of the halls to a sitting room with several chairs around a lit fireplace. "Make yourselves at home. I will have some food brought out shortly. You kids take a few moments to get reacquainted."

The moment she was out of earshot, Eddie's smile faded, and he muttered, "I still haven't forgiven you for what you did to me."

I yawned, gazing into the fire. "Well, your family did kidnap Kalli. What did you expect me to do?"

"I don't know," Eddie replied, glaring at me. "Maybe you could have trusted me to do the right thing and help you."

Eddie was just too young to understand the situation I'd been in. There was nobody in that house I would have trusted while Kalli was locked up in the basement. I sighed and said, "Look, I'm sorry about what happened to you. You have to understand. Kalli was in danger."

He folded his arms and turned his back on me. Sylvia chose that moment to sit on my lap. "Lavender tells me you went to another world. What was it like?"

I smiled at the kid as Eddie peeked back at us, obviously interested in my adventures. "The sky was green. That's the first thing you notice when you go to Gaia. That's what it's called by the way. There is also a big planet called Luna in the sky that has rings. You know, like the ones on Saturn."

Sylvia's eyes widened as I told her stories about villagers with the plague and of the many different races I had met. Unable to contain a fit of the giggles, she asked, "Are trolls really that stinky? And they like it that way? I can't believe it."

"I'm not joking!" I laughed. "It's really bad. Kalli had to give their leader a bath to get them to trust us. Her name is Esha."

"The leader is a girl?" Sylvia asked, her voice full of wonder.

I nodded as Lavender returned with several plates of stew. Sylvia hopped off my lap and made her way to a small table where she sat across from Eddie. Lavender set two bowls down for them, and then made her way over to me with another. Once we were all served, she sat in a chair next to mine.

The stew was delicious. I knew better than to ask Lavender where she got it from. She watched me eat for a while before saying, "Let's get down to business. I've been watching you. I see a great deal of what goes on in the universe, but I must admit some things are hidden from me. In your battle with Lady Mardella, did you use the ring on her?"

I swallowed hard. She had directly warned me not to do it, and I had inadvertently trapped her within the ring and released Malric, whoever he was.

Admitting to using the ring felt like the equivalent of saying I opened Pandora's box, so I lied, "No. I started to but remembered what you told me."

Lavender heaved a sigh of relief. "I am very happy to hear that. You don't want to know what could have happened if you misused that ring."

"Can you tell me more about the ring?" I asked, running my finger over the glowing blue gemstone.

She watched me closely as I caressed it. "Not a whole lot is known about the ring. Like many artifacts, it chooses its owner. They say that the stone in that ring has existed since before time itself. Little is known about it because only its owner can ever truly know what it's capable of. I have heard that this particular ring calls to its owner. As I warned you before, do not heed its words."

I bit my tongue as I nodded silently. If Lavender knew who Malric the Magnificent was, she wasn't telling. I figured it was best I not mention it either. After all, he was probably out enjoying his newfound freedom on some tropical planet somewhere. Surely, he wouldn't use his second chance to live a life of evil.

After giving me plenty of time to reply, Lavender went on. "The true reason I brought you here is that you are not progressing fast enough. There will come a time when your chosen manipulator class will not be enough. As you have seen multiple times, you are weak when it comes to combat. We are going to have to remedy that."

"How?" I asked, taking a bite of stew. "It's not like I haven't been trying to improve."

She smiled deviously. "Nothing so crude as that. We are going to power level you. We have made a world specifically for that purpose."

Meanwhile, in a galaxy far, far away...

Malric tended to her wounds. It was an interesting body, capable of both physical combat and magic. While Malric had never been a woman, he was quite scrawny in his past form, so the difference wasn't all that great.

Unfortunately, the body was wounded. She had been stabbed in the back quite literally. Time was needed to make a full recovery. Once that was complete, Malric planned to make full use of her second life to get revenge. Revenge against a certain man. A man who had robbed her of everything oh so long ago.

[2]

Lavender walked down a maze of corridors after making sure that the other two kids were in their bedrooms. For such a large house, I noticed a lack of servants or helpers. It was amazing that she kept the place as spotless as she did. I decided that it must be magic.

Kalli was preparing for bed over on Gaia, too, washing up in the bath chamber I still remembered fondly. She sighed as she felt my eyes on her. *Always peeping, aren't you? I don't know if I'm ever going to get used to sleeping alone again.*

I felt the same.

At least we can still share our dreams.

When we got to the door at the end of the maze, Lavender held out a key that looked like it was from a video game. On one end was a red gemstone that looked like a ruby, and on the other was a three-pronged key.

Lavender smiled as I took the key and said, "I am giving you this suite so you can feel a little more at home while you stay with me. Please, don't take Sylvia or Eddie here. The last thing I need is them getting lost in, well, your restroom. You see, this room is special. I think you might appreciate it. Have a good night."

She said that last word with a wink before spinning on her heels and marching off into the darkness. I slid the key into the lock and twisted it. At first, there was a click followed by a loud rumbling sound as a rather intricate lock disengaged.

The bedroom didn't disappoint. It was a close call between the queen's suite in Castle Celestea and the room I found myself in as to which was more glamourous. The big difference was the fountain in the corner of the room that looked like a waterfall flowing over a rainforest. I stood mesmerized for several minutes before deciding to check out the rest of the room.

The canopy bed in the center of the room was much too large for just me. Several fluffy chairs made up a sitting area, and there was a very large television on the wall that seemed out of place. Thus far, I hadn't seen any electronics at all in the rest of the mansion.

Then my eyes found what I was looking for. Lavender had said something about the restroom and it being off-limits to the other kids. I made my way over to the door and found it also to be locked. Fortunately, the room key worked on the lock and, after another showy display of the lock clicking into place, the door swung open of its own accord.

Then Kalli screamed. I found myself in a very familiar bath chamber, complete with Kalli sitting on a commode. She screamed, "Help! There's someone in the privy with me. Melvin, come quick!"

Out of reflex more than anything, I teleported to her side. Then, realizing she had seen me on the other side of the room, I started laughing.

She glared up at me and growled, 'That's not funny!"

I walked back over to the open door and stuck my head through, having trouble registering that my body was halfway between worlds. Kalli finished her business and walked up behind me. "Is that…?"

"Yeah!" I announced, holding the door open for her.

She smiled, giving me a quick hug before walking into my room. "This is Earth? I'm back on Earth? Well, that solves a lot of problems, doesn't it?"

I matched her smile and followed her into my room. "So, which room shall we sleep in?"

Kalli made her way over to the massive bed in my new room. "Well, we haven't slept in your room yet."

———

Our dream started off the same as it did every night. Kalli stretched out in my lap as I did my best to massage her shoulders. She sighed heavily and tilted her head back to look up at me. "I don't think I want to be a princess anymore. It's too much work."

I kissed her on the nose, causing Kalli to giggle. "Don't think about it like that. You're a princess by birth. Do it the way you want to. Don't let your mother bully you. Remember, the people love you. Almost as much as I do."

She laughed. "They love me that much, huh?"

I grinned, "You're impossible not to love. I'm so happy Lavender gave me that room. I didn't know how I was going to live without you."

"Geez, Melvin," Kalli replied, rolling her eyes. "We were only apart for a few days."

I pouted, sticking out my tongue at her. "It felt like forever, and you were a whole dimension away."

Kalli sat up, suddenly reinvigorated. "So, what shall we dream about tonight?"

———

With the sudden freedom from both contracts and drama in our lives, Kalli and I let loose in our dream and had no business waking up as rested as we did in the morning. I opened my eyes to find Kalli snuggled up next to me. She smiled when she saw me and whispered, "Five more minutes please."

As I was in no hurry to get up either, I pulled her close and basked in her aura. It wasn't until thirty minutes later that we actually dragged ourselves out of bed. A loud knock on the door announced we were probably late for breakfast.

When I checked, the presence of two trays on the floor was the only evidence that somebody had been there. A note accompanies the food.

Melvin and Kalliphae,

I trust the two of you enjoyed last night's surprise. It makes me happy to accommodate young love. You two share a bond that is more special than either of you realize.

Please, feel free to take your time getting ready. When you are prepared to join us, follow the light in the halls. I will explain your training when you both arrive.

Lavender

Kalli read the letter over my shoulder and smiled. "I guess I'm getting trained, too. Mother won't be happy, but I'd rather train with you than balance another book on my head."

I chuckled, remembering some of the things I saw her mother make Kalli do. Breakfast was bacon and eggs and just as delicious as the stew had been the night before.

After quickly washing up, we were both excited to see what Lavender had planned for us. We noticed the lights as soon as we left the room. The red carpet seemed to come to life as brilliant red colors sparkled and flashed in the thick fibers and rippled their way down the hall. Before we knew it, we were running to keep up.

By the time we made it to our destination, Kalli and I were both out of breath. I looked up to find several people I didn't expect to see waiting patiently with Lavender.

Sylvia giggled and announced, "You were right, Melvin. Trolls do stink."

Esha huffed at the tiny human attached to her leg. "If you dislike my odor, why do you insist on clinging to me?"

"Hugs!" Sylvia cried out as she held on for dear life. The troll was trying to throw her off. "I am going to hug away the bad smells!"

By the look on Esha's face, it appeared the affectionist was pulling it off. A goblin peeked her head out from behind the troll. "Boombrix is here as well to assist with the training. She brings booms and bangs to make your foes run in fear."

I smiled, happy to see the new additions to the group. Sensing the unspoken question, Lavender explained, "Wendy has taken Joe to Japan to meet her parents, and Rundell has decided to focus on school and spend more time with his family. These three from Gaia have agreed to help out in the meantime."

"Three?" Kalli asked hesitantly. "I only see two."

"I'm here, too," Shiviria chirped from a chair on the far side of the room. Her icy blue hair flipped over her shoulder as she jumped to her feet. "Please, don't be mad. I wanted to come, too."

Kalli rushed over to hug the girl. "Of course, I'm not mad. I'll bet Mother is going to freak out when she finds both of us gone though."

Shiviria shook her head, frowning as Sylvia wandered over and wrapped both of them in a hug. "Don't worry about mother and father. Lavender spoke to them."

"How did you manage that?" Kalli asked, raising an eyebrow at the enchanter.

Lavender covered her mouth, laughing quietly. "I have my ways. I can be very persuasive when I feel the need to be. In any case, I told them Shiviria won't be leaving the house. That seemed to placate them."

"Then, how are we going to train?" I asked, getting more curious.

The enchanter laughed again. "Don't underestimate this house."

———

We stood in front of a door. It wasn't exactly the front door, even though it looked a lot like it. Lavender stood next to it as though she were unveiling a new creation. "What you are about to see is the culmination of life's work. Several very talented magicians have created a world where everything is both real and imaginary at the same time. To make it even more special, we have managed to create a digital overlay allowing non-magical folks to experience it as well. To them, it's a video game. For you, it's going to be a training ground. Allow me to introduce you to the wonderful world of Eternal Legacy Online."

Then the doors swung open revealing a spiral staircase in a dreary gray tower. I laughed and said, "It doesn't quite live up to the hype."

Lavender huffed dryly and replied, "Very funny, wise guy. Go check it out."

We descended the stairs quickly and stepped out into Homestead. It was night, which made no sense to me considering we just had breakfast. The kids all ran ahead, checking out the various restaurants and shops on Main Street.

"I feel different," I said, probing myself with mana.

Lavender nodded and patted me on the back. "Good observation. That's because you check your body at the door when you enter this world. Don't worry. Your physical bodies are in limbo. In here, you are a manifestation of your mana. That will come in handy when you die."

"We are going to die?" Shiviria asked nervously, looking like she was having second thoughts.

Going to comfort the girl, Lavender explained, "Don't worry, child. Death is only a setback here. That's what makes this place a perfect training ground. When you die, you will just respawn."

Shiviria looked slightly less afraid. "What does respawn mean?"

Lavender smiled warmly at the girl. "It's just what they call it when you return to town. When a monster defeats you, it will feel like you teleported back home. It doesn't even hurt."

After waiting a moment to be sure everyone was okay with it, Lavender continued the tour. "This is Homestead, home of the cast members. That is what the NPCs like to be called."

I stopped short. "NPCs can think in this game? Are you saying they are sentient?"

Lavender paused, looking back at me. "You've met the game master. She calls herself Aya. She runs this place. The cast members are her children. Please, treat them with respect."

I nodded. "Of course. I wouldn't treat them any other way."

We followed Lavender to a two-story building with a restaurant on the ground floor. Upon entering, I saw a familiar face. I waved and said, "Hey! I remember you from that restaurant in Occanside! Your name is Phylis, right?"

The woman looked up, a little surprised to see me. "Oh, right. Yes. My name is Phylis. I do run that restaurant."

"So, you're a human, right?" Kalli confirmed.

Phylis shook her head. "No, I am a cast member. We use bodies that are a combination of android and magic when we need to go out in the real world."

I looked back at Lavender. "Wow. That's neat. How does that work?"

The enchanter gave me a knowing smile. "There are many different kinds of magic that you don't know about yet. Your friend Joe is on the path that leads to the creation of android technology. There are also classes known as technicians and artificers. Most innovation is a combination of a vast array of talents. If you wish to learn more, you should visit the Technician General Bureau at its home base in Poland. They are currently experimenting with artificial portals using scientific magic. "

"What is that?" I asked, both amazed and confused at the same time.

Lavender rubbed her chin. "Hmm. I guess you can call it artificial mana. They refine the mana of the living into a form that can power the devices they create. Some of them say that their goal is to break the universe, but they are mostly harmless from what I've seen."

"Were there any technicians involved in the creation of this world?" Kalli asked.

Lavender nodded, sitting at one of the tables. "Yes. A man called Roland Yin created Aya. He is not affiliated with any mage guild and the person he answers to is also not awakened. She is a very powerful woman and I advise you to steer clear of her."

"So, what next". I asked.

With a grin on her face, Lavender motioned to the seats next to her. "The reason I brought you here is to make it your respawn point. Then you are going to begin your training in The Shadowlands."

[3]

THE PORTAL ROOM was filled with multiple columns of various colors. Lavender directed us to an ominous portal with a black light. "This is the one for you. It leads to The Shadowlands. Players of ELO can't go there yet, so you won't run into them."

One by one we stepped into the portal. When it was my turn, I noticed it felt similar to teleportation with the exception that we did not pass into the void space between worlds. When I stepped out, I asked, "This is different from teleporting, isn't it?"

Lavender nodded her approval. "This is true. The reason for that is this world exists in the space between matter. It's the same magic that made your fanny pack and normal bags of nil space. The only difference is that we've created a world in here rather than using it to store things."

The world we stepped out into felt like nothing I had ever experienced before. A sinister cloud covered a wilting land in a shroud and ominous sounds echoed in the distance.

Shiviria shuddered and clung to her sister. "This place is scary. Are you sure it's safe, Kalli?"

Lavender stood in front of us and announced, "Listen up, children. None of you have anything to fear. While there will be scary monsters,

16

and you will have to fight them, none of them will hurt you. This is the safest place for you to learn combat."

When nobody moved, Lavender sighed and moved back to the still-open portal. "If any of you want to turn back, now is the time."

Shiviria and Sylvia looked at each other as they hid behind Kalli. She knelt and whispered, "It's okay to be afraid. This place is spooky. Lavender promised that nothing here will hurt us. How about you watch the first couple of battles and decide if you want to jump in later?"

Sylvia nodded and said, "I'll hug you if you get hurt."

"I'd like that," Kalli replied, giving the kid a hug for good measure.

Lavender moved out of the way and said, "Now that we've settled that, let's start with something basic. Prepare yourselves."

As if on cue, a rumbling sound could be heard coming from the darkness. The ground shook around us as the first monster came into view.

Name: Kong Ding
Class: Monkape
Level: 50
Affection Level: Simulated

My heart jumped in my chest as I saw the level of the first monster. "Level fifty? Are you sure this is something we can handle? Kalli and I are the only ones above level ten!"

Lavender nodded. "That's right. You've been lucky so far. On multiple occasions, you have fought monsters that are higher level than yourself and emerged victorious. This time, you have to learn how to do it on purpose."

Willing my armor to coat my body, I stepped in front of Kalli.

This isn't going to be easy, is it?

Kalli gently touched my back, a sensation I felt through the armor.

Don't worry, Mel. Just do your best.

Kong Ding yawned as he towered over me, unimpressed by the armor-clad Whac-A-Mole in front of him. I summoned my mana blade, which finally managed to make the monster rear up. It balled its hands into massive fists and brought them down on me.

I held the sword up, hoping to skewer the monster. It pulled its claws apart at the last second, slamming them both back together around me in a massive *clap*.

"Melvin!" Kalli screamed as the shockwave of the attack hit her.

Kong Ding pulled his paws back and flung me through the air like a boulder. Kalli raised her hands in the air, and a wave of fire rushed to greet me. The flame caught me in a soft embrace and lowered me to the ground in front of Kalli.

She cupped my face in her hands and asked, "Are you hurt?"

I felt for damage. While I should have been hurt, the attack felt more like roughhousing with friends than anything else. Still, a health bar appeared in front of me to display my damage to the group.

HP: 30%

"I'll fix it!" Sylvia announced while tackling me to the ground in a massive hug.

Not only did it feel good to be hugged by the kid as her mana seeped into me, but it also repaired the video game damage.

HP: 85%

Lavender issued instructions from over by the portal. "Melvin, the purpose of this exercise is to learn teamwork. You need to learn to rely on your friends and not rush in all the time."

Kong Ding seemed to be waiting patiently, so I turned back to the others. "All right, everyone. Huddle up."

We formed a circle and leaned in. I was secretly happy Sylvia gave Esha the hug bath and erased her smell. Kalli smiled at me and asked, "Okay, Mel. What's the plan?"

I looked at all of the eager faces. It was suddenly up to me to figure out a strategy. "Okay, what can everyone do?"

Kalli rolled her eyes as I looked at her first. Realizing she wasn't helping, she said, "Fire. I can make fire."

"I can do ice," Shiviria announced excitedly. "Just wait until you see how much better I've gotten since you awakened me."

"I give warm hugs!" Sylvia grinned, demonstrating on Shiviria.

"Hey!" Shiviria shrieked, trying to pull away.

"I'll go in first," Esha said, flexing her biceps and ignoring the two young girls who were rolling around on the ground. "I can take a hit from that thing, no problem."

Boombrix held up a familiar-looking bomb. "Boom has these. Just say the word, and she will make big booms all over the furry monster."

Turning my attention to Eddie, I asked, "What can you do? You're the last one, Eddie. Don't be shy?"

Eddie glared at me before looking at the two girls his own age. "It's really cool. Just wait and see."

Shrugging, I started moving people into position. "Okay, that's the plan. Esha and I will go in first. Kalli, Shiv, and Boom provide ranged support. Sylvia heals anyone who gets hurt and, um, Eddie can surprise us."

"That's right!" Eddie grinned at Shiviria, ignoring me completely. "I'm totally full of surprises."

Without waiting for me to give the word, Esha broke our huddle and charged at the giant ape. When she was halfway there, it threw something large. Esha ducked, and I raised the mana blade. The moment it made contact with the large orb, it broke apart and a murky brown substance splattered all over us.

I dipped my finger in it and sniffed. It didn't smell bad. Wiping my hand on my pants, I muttered to myself, "I'm going to pretend that's mud."

Lavender chuckled. "That's probably a good idea."

Shiviria, who got a face full of the stuff, asked, "Ew, what is it?"

Lavender continued laughing. "You don't want to know."

"Ew!" all three girls screamed at once.

Prepared to support Esha, I charged in behind her. When I was about halfway there, something sailed over my head. It bounced off

Kong Ding and exploded. The blast knocked back both the monster as well as Esha.

"Watch out for friendly fire!" Lavender called from behind us.

I jumped in front of Esha, bringing my greatsword to bear. "Are you okay?"

The troll grunted, pulling herself to her feet. "I can keep going. That didn't hurt at all."

"There's no pain," Lavender reminded us. "Keep your eyes on the health gauge."

Looking over at Esha, I noticed that her health bar dipped into the yellow.

HP: 50%

"Melvin, look out!" Kalli screamed.

I brought my sword up just in time to parry a massive fist as Kong Ding attempted to smash me into the ground again. Jets of fire and ice sailed over my head and scored a direct hit on the ape's face.

Using the distraction, I swung my sword in an attempt to strike the monster in the torso while its defenses were focused up high. My blade made contact but didn't have the desired effect. While Kong Ding roared in outrage, it did not fall.

With a powerful swipe of its claw, it sent me sprawling. Before I could collect myself, Esha was back in the fight rushing forward to take my place. Above us, a dark cloud crackled with what seemed to be electricity. Only there was no light coming from it. The darkness seemed to rain down sporadically on the ape, causing it to roar at the sky.

"Got you!" Eddie called out from somewhere behind Kalli.

I had just managed to get to my knees when I felt two arms wrap around me. Turning, I was surprised to see Sylvia so close to the monster. Her smile was like sunshine as she chirped, "Don't worry. I got you!"

I hugged her back as I noticed my HP return to full. Getting an idea, I called out to Esha. "Pull back when I say to."

She grunted but nodded. Then, I instructed Kalli and Shiviria to hit the ape with another coordinated attack. Their fire and ice blasts seemed to work well together.

Just as their attack was about to land, I called out to Esha, "Now! Pull back."

The troll dove out of the way, and I shouted to Boombrix, "Boom, make it rain. Throw a bomb!"

The goblin didn't hesitate. I watched as her bomb flew toward Kong Ding. Just as it was about to hit, I sent a wave of flame right into it. The effect of the magic combined with the explosive blasted the ape ten feet back, where it landed with a *thud*.

"Now!" I screamed, readying my mana blade. "Let's finish this thing."

Together, Esha and I rushed in and pummeled the fallen monster. Eddie added his dark thunder attack, which caused us both some damage as well as the boss.

We managed to polish off the last of its HP before it managed to get back to its feet. Esha and I were still walking back to the group when Lavender clapped. "Not bad for your first fight. You all did very well. However, I see a lot of weak points you need to work on. For now, let's split you up into groups. Kalliphae and Shiviria, I want you two to work together to see if you can come up with ways to combine your ranged attacks. While it's great to work together, you were still casting separate spells. I see potential there. Boombrix, how about you try working with Esha. You want to make sure that your bombs are helping her, not hurting her. Come up with a system that works for you. Melvin, I want you to work with Sylvia. I know you enjoy playing with that sword, but you are an all-around type of fighter, and I think we should focus on your strengths. As a healer at your core, you will best serve the group by keeping everyone alive. That will be even more important out in the real world."

"What about me?" Eddie whined as he watched everybody get into groups.

Lavender smiled at the kid. "Don't worry, Eddie. I saved the best for you. I am going to work with you personally. Since you are using a weather-based attack, you would be best suited to compliment Wendy. Since she isn't here, I am going to teach you a new spell that will work better with Kalliphae and Shiviria."

Eddie's frown turned into a smile as he realized Lavender was about to teach him something new. As I turned to accept yet another hug from Sylvia, Lavender called over her shoulder. "By the way, Melvin. Why don't you figure out how to heal people from a distance. If you need a reference, just think about Kalliphae's favorite spell."

[4]

THE SHADOWLANDS LIVED up to their name. Shrouded in eternal darkness, the world around me looked like a post-apocalyptic wasteland.

In stark contrast to her surroundings, Sylvia sat cross-legged next to me with a smile on her face that seemed to light up the world around her. She leaned in and gave me yet another hug and whispered, "My parents want to meet you. I told them that you cured me with magic but, don't worry, they promise to keep it a secret."

I was only half-paying attention while looking at my hands and trying to focus the healing aspect of my mana into a corporeal form. Thus far, my healing had always been to inject the patient with my mana and correct problems when I discovered them. It was an active process that required a hands-on touch. How was I supposed to make that airborne? I couldn't exactly touch everyone in the middle of combat.

"Melvin? What do you think about that?" Sylvia asked tentatively, leaning closer to get my attention.

"What?" I asked, dropping a blob of mana on the ground.

"Will you come meet my parents?" she asked, trying to will me to say yes with her biggest smile. "They want to thank you in person. "Daddy has lots of money. He says he will buy you a car if you want."

I laughed out loud at the thought of someone buying me a car. Several years ago, I would have given anything for someone to get me one. With the ability to edit a rock into virtually whatever I wanted, my desire for physical things was pretty low.

Still, the kid was waiting for an answer. "Sure. I'll meet your parents. I hope they aren't mad that I pretended to be Make-A-Wish."

Sylvia giggled. "No. They weren't mad at all. I heard Justin Bieber was mad that someone impersonated him. He wasn't in California, though, so he didn't get in trouble. Did you really kill a baby?"

Recalling that incident made me feel sick to my stomach. "I was too late. There wasn't anything I could do. I tried."

The kid frowned and hugged me again. "It's not your fault, Melvin."

Even though she was little, I felt like I was being comforted by an adult. Shaking my head to clear the negative thoughts, I said, "Let's work on our healing. I need to figure out how to make mine airborne."

Sylvia smiled. "Me, too! How can I hug people without touching them?"

I rubbed my chin and laughed when I came up with an idea. "You could always blow them a kiss."

Just then a powerful explosion blinded us. I rubbed my eyes, trying to see what happened. What I saw was amazing. Brilliant blue and red light swirled together as Kalli and Shiv's magic collided. The ice hissed and steam rose as cold embraced heat.

"Whoa," I gasped, watching the girls work.

SMACK!

Something hit me on the cheek, sending a tingling sensation down my spine. I turned to find Sylvia giggling profusely. I touched my face and asked, "What did you just do?"

She beamed at me. "I blew you a kiss. Did it heal you? Did I do good?"

I groaned out loud and sent my frustrations over to Kalli.

I just got outdone by a kid.

Kalli laughed at me as she focused on her spell. *I know! I saw that.*

Looking up, I saw tears in Sylvia's eyes. "Did I do it wrong? I'm sorry."

I held up my hands and tried my best to smile. "No! You did it perfectly. I was just jealous because you figured it out before me."

She smiled again, and that infectious happiness returned. "I can show you how I did it if you want."

The kid was amazing. She managed to create a new skill with just a few words from Lavender.

When I nodded to her, Sylvia took a few steps back and placed her hand on her lip. Then, she removed the hand and blew me a kiss. "Muah!"

SMACK!

I felt her mana strike my face again, sending the same singling sensation through my body. Unlike Kalli or Shiviria, whatever Sylvia was doing was invisible. I made my way over to the kid and asked, "Do you mind if I check your mana while it's inside of you?"

"Like you did when you cured me?" she asked with a smile. "Sure. I remember what that felt like."

Wasting no time, I placed my hand on the kid's arm and probed her with my mana. Just as I thought, I sensed light mana flowing through her channels.

Moving deeper into her body, I was astounded when I came to her core. What was once a feeble heart-shaped core was four times larger and shone like the sun.

Sylvia wiggled in my arms, making me realize I was mesmerized by her core. I heard her voice echo in the distance as I extracted myself. "How much longer are you going to hold my hand? It's getting tired."

I let her go and said, "Sorry about that. You've grown a lot since the last time I saw you."

She nodded in excitement. "I've hugged a lot of people since you cured me. Mostly in the hospital. It always makes them feel better. Lavender says I'll level up fast once I get bigger."

"Okay, now it's time for me to try," I announced, cracking my knuckles as I climbed to my feet.

"Yay!" Sylvia cheered me on. "Show me, show me, show me!"

Picturing the flame hand spell "**Pvruzth**," I pointed my hand at Kalli. Only, rather than changing the element to fire, I focused on corralling my natural element into a steady stream that I could channel through the air.

The spell went everywhere. Rays of light that only I could see spread in every direction and dissipated harmlessly. Groaning in frustration, I turned to look at Sylvia, who watched me quietly. "How did you control where your kiss went?"

"I blew it to you, silly," Sylvia said with a giggle. "Everyone knows that."

I couldn't help but laugh when faced with the kid's logic. It worked because she knew it would work. Was that the reason Lavender paired me with her and not because we both were healers?

Forgetting everything I knew about the world, I imagined my mana flowing like water from a fire hydrant and channeled another spell at Kalli. The pyromancer was taking a break, chatting with her sister when my spell hit.

The force of the blow lifted her off the ground. Kalli let out a pained grunt as she tumbled through the air. Realizing my error, I teleported to her and did my best to catch her. The collision was so strong that Kalli knocked the air out of me, and we both crashed back to the ground.

"A little warning would be nice next time," Kalli wheezes, rubbing her stomach where the spell had hit.

I felt her pain through our connection and pumped some healing into her the old-fashioned way as I said, "I'm sorry. I wanted to surprise you. I guess I need to fine-tune it."

Kalli ran a finger over a tender spot on my chest, causing me to wince. "Don't forget to heal yourself. Thanks for trying to catch me, at least."

Everyone stopped what they were doing to watch me as I trudged back to Sylvia. She gave me a curious look when I arrived and asked, "What did you just do? Is Kalli okay?"

"I used too much pressure," I muttered as I refocused my efforts.

The problem was that if I used the wrong concept my mana became an attack. I needed something gentle. Something soothing. I began by making my mana into a ball and passing it from one hand to the other. The good thing about light was that it was much faster than any of the other elements. The problem was that it liked to spread off in every direction.

Giving mana the density and nature of water turned it into an attack. I needed something that broke the rules, similar to Sylvia's kiss. If water was too much, I needed something that wasn't. Something pleasant.

I turned to Sylvia and asked, "Do you mind if I try something on you?"

She looked nervously at Kalli, who was still rubbing her belly where the mana blast hit her. "Will it hurt?"

"I don't think so," I replied.

Sylvia bit her lower lip but nodded anyway. Channeling more mana to my hand, I willed it into a fine mist and sent a tiny stream of it toward Sylvia. She spluttered and held up a hand to block her face. "Eww, what is that? Why does it feel wet?"

I adjusted the spell and instructed my mana to flow like a gentle breeze. "Try healing wind."

Sylvia's hair blew back as my mana washed over her. She giggled and said, "That feels good."

The problem with wind was that it wasn't very effective over a great distance. Being like the wind meant that actual wind had an effect on it, essentially blowing my spell off course the farther it traveled.

After more trial and error, I made a finger gun and pointed it at Kalli, shouting, "Healing laser!"

A beam of light only I could see shot from my finger and went straight into Kalli's hip. She yelped and glared at me. ***Stop using me as a training dummy!***

But it worked.

She stuck her tongue out at me. ***No more!***

Sylvia counted off spells I invented on her fingers. "So, that makes Regenerating Wind, Cure Bomb, and Healing Laser. What's next?"

The laser was nice, and it worked at range, but it was too small. I needed something bigger. I scratched the back of my head while I thought. "It needs to be a beam."

"What do you mean?" Sylvia asked, trying to blow kisses at Kalli.

Kalli didn't seem to have as much of a problem with Sylvia testing spells on her as she did with me. It must have been something about kids being adorable or something.

Focusing my mana like a spotlight, I shone a beam of healing mana on Kalli. She glowed in my eyes as my mana bathed her in light. Kalli looked up at me when she felt the effect. Then she shrugged and gave me a thumbs up.

"I think it worked," I said, taking a moment to celebrate.

———

A short while later, Lavender showed back up with a rather pleased-looking Eddie. "I trust you all made some progress. Are we ready for monster number two?"

After getting an affirmative from everyone, Lavender made her way over to me. "Look, Melvin. I want you to try something during this next fight. I know you just focused on learning to heal, but I want you to start thinking about fights like a manipulator. Look for opportunities to edit."

Her latest advice went against everything she told me in the past. "Didn't you tell me to hide what I am?"

Lavender chuckled. "Well, that cat has been out of the bag for some time, Melvin. It's no big secret that there is a manipulator in the world. Another thing that is known about you is that you are a world traveler. Be wary of people you don't know trying to get you to smuggle them off Earth. In some cases, that is a crime."

"It never occurred to me that teleporting between worlds could be against the law," I replied, worried that there was a warrant out for my arrest somewhere.

Lavender gave me a reassuring smile as she replied, "Don't worry. While rare, there are exceptions in the law for gifted mages who possess abilities like yours. Few are aware of how you did it, but your passage has been approved."

"Well, that's a relief." I sighed, turning my attention back to training. "So, how do you want me to edit things during battle?"

"Use your imagination," Lavender replied. "You used it to great effect on some occasions. Just always be mindful. That is a sign of a good leader."

I grinned. "This is going to be fun!"

[5]

ERROR: WORLD EDITOR MODE UNAVAILABLE
ERROR: YOU DO NOT CONTROL THIS TERRITORY

I FROWNED AT THE ERROR. "Um, Lavender. The System says I can't edit anything."

Lavender's angry voice replied, "Not that kind of editing. Try editing a rock like you normally do."

"Oh!" I gasped, realizing what she meant.

The second monster that emerged from the darkness was a giant. A tall lumbering man with a combover stomped his way toward us wielding a club that was at least as tall as he was.

The first target for editing was obvious.

Item: Fool Smasher
Components: Wood, Essence of Grurk
Item Rank: C
Item Level: 1
Item Owner: Grurk

While I could have just deleted it, I wanted to do something to confuse the already dumb-looking creature.

Item: Very Large Rubber Snake (Edited)
Components: Rubber
Item Rank: F
Item Level: 1
Item Owner: Grurk

While the edited snake came out a lot smaller than intended, it did have the desired effect. The giant paused when the rigid staff in his hand went limp on him. Seeing the snake's head bobbing in his grubby fist made him drop it and jump back. The ground quaked around us as Grurk landed hard, nearly toppling over.

"Now!" Esha roared, rushing in with a goblin riding on her back.

A pair of shiny projectiles flew through the air toward the lumbering giant, fueled by the cries of a goblin. "Go boom stick make boom-boom!"

BOOM!

With a thunderous explosion, the giant toppled over backward, making the ground shudder once again. A flash of light came from behind me as swirling reds and blues orbited around one another as the attack sailed toward the downed Grurk.

"My turn," Came Eddie's triumphant voice as a wave of smoke mixed in with the girl's attack.

Angry thunder crackled and sparked from the cloud, looking like the electrical discharge over an erupting volcano. The combined spells smashed into the downed giant, kicking up a massive cloud of dust.

Did we get him? Kalli sent through MateChat, along with a feeling of satisfaction over her new spell combo with Shiviria.

The answer came in the form of a thrown rubber snake. It sailed through the air directly at Kalli. However, I was quick to react.

DELETE

The snake vanished, the sound of it swishing through the air dying along with it. Kalli, who had just ducked, tossed me a quick smile when she realized what I'd done. *Thanks.*

The sound of Esha clashing with the giant drew our attention back to the battle. The troll was barely half the size of the giant and was getting pushed back. On closer inspection, I noticed that Boombrix was missing.

Kalli, can you guys attack again? Esha is going to be in trouble at this rate.

Kalli grunted in response. *We're working on it. That attack took a lot of mana. Remember Eddie and Shiv are still little.*

Heaving a sigh, I materialized my mana blade and started to move forward. Lavender stopped me with a shout. "Remember the rules, Melvin. Healing and editing only. Your role is support."

I groaned, trying to think of another plan. At the rate we were going, the giant was going to win. Next to me, Sylvia was blowing a steady stream of kisses at Esha with remarkable accuracy.

I needed to edit something. Anything. Other than throwing a rock at the giant and changing it into a boulder, I was drawing a blank. Then I noticed what Esha was holding.

Item: Short Sword
Components: Bronze
Item Rank: C
Item Level: 1
Item Owner: Esha

I didn't really think about equipping people properly. Boombrix had her bombs, but Esha was practically naked. The least I could do was edit her weapon.

Item: Imitation Excalibur
Components: Dragon-Forged Steel
Item Rank: B
Item Level: 1
Item Owner: Esha

The edit didn't go exactly as planned. I meant to name the weapon Excalibur, but it ended up being an imitation, and a B-ranked one at that. Esha, on the other hand, was ecstatic. She roared triumphantly when the sword grew in her hands and swung it wildly at the giant.

Another thing that I noticed was that the troll wasn't a very proficient fighter. Her class, empress of Wrotor, didn't lend itself to any proficiency in combat. About the only skill I knew the troll to have was her stench.

However, that was a problem for another day. I needed to focus on the present. Esha was doing her best to take on the giant by herself with only Sylvia healing her.

I tried targeting the ground behind Grurk.

DELETE

Unfortunately, I didn't have much control over my skill. The ground beneath both Esha and Grurk vanished, causing them to both cry out in shock as they fell into the crater I created.

"Esha!" I screamed as I ran toward the pit.

"Melvin, wait!" Lavender commanded, causing me to stop in my tracks once again. "Hold your position. You aren't allowed to rush in. Remember, nobody is going to die here. Use this to learn and better yourself from your failures."

After waiting helplessly for any signs of life, I heaved a sigh of relief when Esha crawled over the lip of the crater. I immediately hit her with a healing beam, shining a strobe light of mana on the troll.

From the distance, I couldn't feel its impact, but I had the benefit of watching her health increase as I focused my mana on her.

40%

60%

80%

Then the giant's head popped up. Esha just managed to roll out of the way as a tiny green goblin tossed something into the pit. A series of explosions made me stagger.

BOOM!

BOOM!

BOOM!

Grurk faltered and struggled to climb from the pit. A dark storm cloud grew above him with the dark lightning I saw Eddie produce earlier. Then, just as the lightning hit, a bolt of fire and ice struck the giant in its head, causing it to fall over backward.

Esha, back at one hundred percent health, jumped into the crater with her newly minted Excalibur replica pointed at the giant's throat. Moments later, the battle was over.

Lavender clapped from behind us and said, "Good job. That will be all for today."

―――――

Lavender pulled me aside once we returned to her house. "Melvin, do you understand why I am doing this?"

Admittedly, I was feeling a little singled out. "I don't know. Why won't you let me help Esha out when she gets in trouble? We both know the armor will protect me."

Lavender sighed, sitting on a red velvet couch and patting the spot next to her. I sat as she began to speak, "As I am sure you have already deduced, I can see many of the things you do in the world. What you don't know is that I can also see things in the distant past as well as the future. Your storybooks refer to people with my gift as an oracle or a fate."

I got excited as I thought of all the possibilities of knowing my own future. When I reached out to touch her, she stopped me. "Trust me when I tell you that you don't want this. I know you have the ability to absorb bloodlines through touch, but what you would find inside of me is very different. There are certain things that exist outside of the System."

"What do you mean?" I asked, not understanding how anything could escape the System.

Lavender took a deep breath, giving me the impression she was about to spill some great secret. "Many of the things you understand are spelled out for you by the System. You can see traits and abilities and see value in them. You also know that when you cast certain spells, you can do magic. Think about it like this. When you use your mana to cast a spell without saying the word, don't you have more control? This is working outside of the System."

I absentmindedly tossed an invisible blob of mana from one hand to the other as I contemplated her words. "That makes sense. It still doesn't explain why you don't want me to absorb your skill. It sounds so cool and useful."

The enchanter threw her head back and laughed. It wasn't a humorous laugh. "If you only knew the curse that comes with knowing your own future. To see your own demise and stand helpless to do anything except slowly marching toward it is a difficult way to live. I wish to spare you more than anything. Especially with who you are."

"Who am I?" I asked, frustrated that multiple people knew a lot more about me than I did. "Why won't anybody tell me? Does this have something to do with my father?"

Lavender was silent for a while, appraising me as we sat together on that comfy red couch. "I cannot tell you everything, Melvin. I can't even tell you why. What I can tell you is that your father has been around for a very long time. He is among a handful of mortals alive before the System. Your father had a hand in the System's creation. That is all I can say."

I glared at Lavender. While it was a revelation that the System was created rather than just something that always existed, the fact that my father had something to do with it was mind-blowing. "Can you tell me where he is?"

She shook her head, so I continued questioning, "Can you tell me where my mother is?"

Again, she shook her head. I sighed. "Can you tell me why she left?"

Lavender refused to make eye contact with me when she replied, "She likely went to see your father. I came to that conclusion because I cannot see where she is. Your father emits an aura that makes him invisible to my ability."

Rubbing my chin, I asked, "Do you know where he is?"

She stiffened as she answered. "Yes."

My eyes widened. "Then tell me!"

Lavender shook her head. "No! What would you do if I gave you that information? You'd seek him out. That's what you'd do. That would be suicide as you currently are. This is why you need to grow."

"Are you saying that I need to fight my dad?" I stammered, the dream of my dad wanting to meet me dying just as it began.

Lavender placed a hand on my shoulder, but I pulled away from her. She spoke softly, trying to soothe me. "Melvin, I doubt you will have to fight your father. I don't think he is that kind of a person. The truth is that you're more likely to end up doing battle with your siblings than you are with him."

"Siblings?" I asked, thinking about Maya and Kiki. "Why would I want to fight them? I love my sister."

Lavender hesitated again. "I don't know how to put this gently. There are hundreds of people with the M bloodline out there right now. Your father has recently begun fathering children in multiple dimensions. To this day, I don't understand his intentions. I do know that you're…"

"I'm what?" I balked as she trailed off. "What am I? Don't you dare say special. Give me some details."

She sighed again. "You're the key. I am not going to do something so uncouth as to spout a riddle of a prophecy, but I will tell you that you are the one that is going to unravel the mystery of your father. As a matter of fact, my fate is tied to you directly."

"Perhaps it will make better sense to me if you just show me," I began. "What could it hurt if I had the ability to see what happens before it happens?"

Lavender scooted away from me again as I reached out to touch her. "You aren't thinking this through. First off, having the ability to see the future and be powerless to change it is not an advantage. This is the first lesson that every seer learns. You also share a bond with Kalli. Would you truly wish such a fate on her?"

For the first time since the conversation began, I hesitated. While it seemed like a good idea, I wouldn't want to subject Kalli to any of the side effects. I didn't want to know the future that badly.

Possibly having seen the future or just sensing that I had come to a conclusion, Lavender stood up. "I suppose that will be all for now. You can come to me should you have more questions, but I am afraid there are certain things I cannot tell you. Knowledge comes with a price, after all."

[6]

MY HEART DROPPED when I got back to my room and found that Kalli was gone. She noticed and whispered through our connection, *Why don't you just come over to my castle?*

I grinned widely as I made my way toward the restroom.

My princess is in another castle!

That house is not a castle! Kalli replied with a giggle.

I chuckled, realizing she didn't get the joke. It was a little strange to enter Gaia through the bath chamber, but I didn't care. I had a way to return to Kalli's world after all.

She wasn't in her bedroom. I could tell through our connection that Kalli was in the throne room with her mother. I arrived just in time to catch the tail end of an argument. "…not allowed to go traipsing off onto some strange planet. To make matters worse, you dragged your sister along."

"But mother…" Kalli began, using a line that so many children on Earth tried.

It never worked, as it didn't in this case. "That'll be enough of that. While you were off with your boyfriend, you missed some important events that took place here on Gaia. As you know, we have been accepting a great number of refugees from all over the world. One of them is perhaps someone you know."

"Who?" Kalli asked, a nervous look appearing on her face.

"Send them in," the queen mother commanded, standing beside the throne and motioning for Kalli to sit. Then, in a quieter yet no less controlling tone, she said, "Take a seat, young lady. You wanted to be the queen. It's time to learn what that means."

I smirked at Kalli from the back of the room.

You wanted to be queen?

Kalli scrunched up her nose as she gave me a look of annoyance. *No! Mother is still bitter that the castle chose me.*

Behind me, the doors swung open, and an entourage strutted into the throne room, stopping in the middle of the room to kneel. Kalli's expression of shock matched mine as we both recognized Lady Hellquist.

She looked down at Kalli's feet, unmoving in the sudden silence. Kalli gaped at her for a minute before clearing her voice and saying, "You may rise."

"Thank you, your Majesty," Lady Hellquist began, straightening herself along with the people behind her. "I would like to thank you and the queen mother for granting us this audience."

Kalli glared at her mother momentarily before returning her attention to Lady Hellquist. Her voice was dripping with sarcasm when she spoke, earning her a reproachful look from her mother. "And just what brings us the pleasure of your visit today?"

Lady Hellquist stiffened. "Your Majesty, our private business with you has become public knowledge. As a result…"

I cut her off. "You're talking about the contract and how you basically sold her, right? Let's not sugarcoat things here. Be very clear about what you did."

Celestea motioned to one of the guards standing by the door. I recognized the stocky dwarf. He took one look at me, and then looked back at the queen mother, shaking his head.

Lady Hellquist cleared her throat. "Very well. Yes, I am speaking of the contract. Your Majesty, as you well know, we entered into that deal as your request and lived up to our end of the bargain. It is hardly fair to—"

Kalli cut her off with a wave of her hand. "I am well aware of how you do business. Is the old man you tried to marry me off to here today?"

Lady Hellquist looked over her shoulder at a bald middle-aged man with a wispy mustache. "He is, your Majesty."

Seeing the man Kalli was betrothed to made my skin bristle.

Do you mind if I turn him into a frog? Or perhaps a newt.

Kalli covered her mouth in embarrassment as a giggle slipped out.

No! That would be funny though. What's a newt?

It's kind of like a salamander.

She was still confused, so I promised to show her later. Suddenly, the bald man spoke, "Your Majesty, I offer my most sincere apology for the way our family treated you regarding the contract. You see, when my wife passed and left me without an heir, we felt you were an ideal solution to the problem. We had no way of knowing you were royalty. I would have given you a good life. Better than that of..."

"A peasant?" I yelled at him. "That's what you were going to say, wasn't it?"

The man looked over his shoulder at me, shaking his head rapidly. "No, my Lord. It was my understanding that she was an orphan. I was going to give her a family. She would have wanted for nothing."

I had no words, so I looked to Kalli.

Please, tell me we can throw him in the dungeon. As a matter of fact, let's throw them all in there. Or maybe the ring? I can lock them all up in my ring!

Ever so slightly, Kalli shook her head. *No need to do all that. I can handle this.*

I sighed and answered the man, "The fact that you see her only as an orphan shows me that you were never worthy of Kalli. You're lucky she's nicer than I am."

Then Kalli spoke, "What is it that brings you here today?"

Lady Hellquist continued, "Well, you see, your Majesty, word of our private business has recently become public, and it has had a negative impact on our town. Several of the townsfolk have moved away, and we lost the stipend we once received for the orphanage."

Lady Hellquist froze when Kalli stood suddenly. "You got money for us? Some of the littles died because there was no food. What did you spend the money on?"

"Well, there was rent, and…" Lady Hellquist stammered, cowering before Kalli, who motioned for the guards.

I had never seen Kalli so mad. With tears in her eyes, she shrieked, "How dare you come in here and ask for favors when your greed caused so many to suffer. I never once hated you, even for my contract. But this…this!"

Kalli stopped talking as she seethed at the noble who was suddenly looking much older to me. Lady Hellquist dropped to her knees, mimicked by the rest of her entourage. "I beg your forgiveness for my selfishness. I know I cannot change my actions in the past, but I do wish to make amends. Tell me what I can do, and it will be done."

"I'll tell you what you can do…" I began.

Kalli gave me a look, and I immediately shut up. Walking slowly up to Lady Hellquist, she knelt beside the woman. "If you truly mean that, then you will do what I am about to suggest. I want you to surrender your land and your title. Come to Celestea as a refugee and find yourself a place among my people. This will make life better for your town, and those who wish to stay. While you will become the peasant you seem to hate, I can guarantee you they will treat you better than you ever treated us."

I was proud of Kalli. Lady Hellquist had no choice but to either accept the deal or go back home with her tail tucked between her legs. Kalli turned to give me a weak smile, feeling my emotions. The experience was bittersweet for her. While Lady Hellquist was given the opportunity to be humbled, all Kalli could think about was a small child's lifeless body that she helped bury.

Finally, a young boy climbed to his feet and spoke, "I cannot speak for the rest of the family, but I plan to accept your generous offer."

Kalli forced a neutral expression on her face as she replied, "Very well. How are you related to the Hellquists?"

"My name is Magnus," the boy said with a bow, moving closer to Lady Hellquist. "This is my mother. I was supposed to marry you. They didn't ask me either."

Kalli stared at the kid. "I've never seen you before."

Magnus sighed wistfully. "They shipped me off to boarding school when I was old enough. I only returned when the school kicked me out."

I laughed at the kid, a little jealous that he was engaged to Kalli. "What did you do to get kicked out?"

Magnus threw his head back and sighed. "The contract. Everything it touched is tainted. Once the headmaster discovered what my mother did, they expelled me immediately. You might say we are pariahs now. She will never admit it, but you are doing us a favor by giving us asylum."

Lady Hellquist glared at her son but said nothing. Radiating annoyance, Kalli spoke to Lady Hellquist, "What is your answer?

She looked over her shoulder helplessly at her brother and another man who I assumed to be her husband. "Well, I couldn't possibly make such an important decision without having a conference with the entire family. Would it be possible to give us a letter granting us a temporary pardon so that we can survive while we come to a decision?"

"Hah!" Kalli laughed. "The last thing I will ever do is exchange any documents with you ever again. Be gone and do not return unless you are prepared to accept my offer."

The guards took that as a cue and surrounded the Hellquists, urging them toward the door. Kalli held up a hand, stopping them. "Wait! Magnus may stay if he wishes."

I don't like him!

Kalli turned sad eyes on me. *He's just another victim in all of this.*

He was engaged to marry you!

She stuck her tongue out at me. *Not really. That was his mother's doing. You can't be jealous of a little. I won't allow it. Besides, you know I love you, right?*

I was forced to smile, unable to resist the warmth she sent through our connection. Kalli was right, and it was my job to comfort her after the trauma she just endured.

I know. I'm sorry.

Kalli smiled weakly and returned to the throne. The guards were just closing the doors when there was a ruckus in the halls. "Wait! I must speak to the queen. It's of vital importance. Or Lord Melvin. I hear that the emperor has returned!"

I recognized the voice. "Hey! That's Guinny's dad. Let him in."

As the doors swung open, I suddenly realized I didn't know the man's name.

Name: Gulliver
Class: Miner
Level: 1
Affection Level: Determined

He marched into the throne room like he owned the place. Then he turned and stomped over to me. "You made a promise to me, m'boy! I mean no disrespect, but I expect you to honor it."

I stared at him, trying to remember our conversation. Then it dawned on me. Kalli and I both spoke at the same time. "Guinny!"

He nodded emphatically. "Not just her. Everyone from Hudholm was relocated to who knows where. Nobody seems to know where. Please, find her!"

———

Meanwhile, in Poland...

TGB HEADQUARTERS

A group of men and women in business suits sat around a table. In the middle of the table was a tablet propped up on a stand. From the tablet, a voice spoke, "Give me an update. Where are we at on the artificial portal project?"

A bespectacled woman looked down at a clipboard and replied, "We believe we have sufficient mana to test the device. Several locations have been chosen, but I personally think the Biolowieza Primeval Forest to be the most ideal location. It is just remote enough to not arouse suspicion while also meeting the parameters you set for the experiment."

There was silence for a minute. The members of the council were used to waiting for the tablet to respond. The Administrator was a busy man after all. "Very good. What is the next step?"

The woman hesitated, looking across the table for support before speaking. "Well, sir, all we need is your approval, and we will begin transporting equipment on site. We have already extracted mana from the prisoners, so there will not be any delay in that regard."

"Enough mana for how many attempts?" the voice queried.

The woman looked helplessly at the others, all of whom averted their eyes. "Well, one attempt, sir. We only have enough mana to try this one time."

"Well, then," the voice replied coldly. "You had better not fail then. You have my permission to proceed with the experiment."

[7]

OUR QUEST TO find the missing Hudholm citizens began in Dabia. Teleporting through the Thief's Corridor made travel easy. A quick trip through the sewers, and we were ready to be seen by King Thomas.

When we arrived at the castle, we were met by a familiar face. The groundsman looked me up and down before sneering at us. "I don't recall sending for a chambermaid."

I chuckled at him and replied, "That was just a disguise. My name is Melvin, and we are here to see the king."

"What makes you think you can just walk in the front door and demand an audience?" Rolfe asked.

Kalli stepped forward, mimicking a smile I was used to from her mother. "Would it help if The Queen of Celestea requested the audience?"

"It would," Rolfe responded. "Were the queen here."

Kalli sighed and introduced herself. "My name is Kalliphae Celestea Murphy, heir and rightful Queen of Celestea. King Thomas will acknowledge me. Please inform him that I wish to speak with him."

Rolfe looked over his shoulder before shaking his head. "No, I'm sorry. More proof is necessary than just your word for me to disturb the king."

"Are you saying that the king refuses to see his people when they wish to speak with him?" Kalli asked incredulously.

The way Rolfe looked down on us made me all but positive that the king refused to see anyone that didn't come equipped with a noble title. It probably didn't help that the last time he saw us, we were mucking out noble's bedside commodes. "Come back when you have proof that you are someone of importance. Until then, these doors shall remain closed."

Without giving either of us a chance to reply, he slammed the door shut.

DELETE

Rolfe gaped at me as the door he had just shut vanished without a trace. I grinned at him. "Is that enough proof for you?"

———

We got our audience with the king along with what I decided to call an honor guard. Armed knights marched on either side of us as we wound our way up to the second floor of the castle.

Kalli glared at me. *You know, Melvin, there was a diplomatic way of dealing with that!*

I shrugged at her, forcing myself to not laugh out loud.

What? He asked for proof. I hear it's called forceful negotiation.

King Thomas's eyes widened when we arrived. He waved off the guards and said, "That won't be necessary."

Rolfe stamped his foot when the guards turned to leave. "But, your Majesty, these two…"

"That will be enough, Rolfe," the king cut him off. "Leave us."

The groundsman paused to glare at us before pulling the doors closed, leaving us alone with the king and his attendants. Giving us a weary look, he turned and sat on the throne. "I take it you've come to talk about the Hellquists? I assure you, we intend to forfeit their land

and titles. It was brought to my attention that she visited you. If there is any…"

"It's not about that," Kalli interrupted.

King Thomas stared at her for a few minutes before continuing, "Ah, I see. The queen explained to me that the past incident with the contract is in the past. You do not mean to…"

"It's not about that either," Kalli cut him off again. "Also, please understand that I am the queen. My mother is just an advisor. I don't see any reason to bring up the contract. I am fully aware of the fact you were enthralled by Lady Mardella when you purchased it, so I won't hold it against you. I am here to ask you about the citizens of Hudholm Summit and what you did with them."

The king was at a loss for the moment. "Which citizens? I do not believe I am familiar with Hudholm Summit."

"You should be," I replied. "It's part of your kingdom, isn't it?"

One of the advisors whispered in the king's ear, and he nodded. "Oh, yes. The mining colony. That town was evacuated after an incident with trolls. I am told there was an attack."

I was forced to laugh, earning me a look of reproach from the king. "Do you mean when Lady Mardella attacked and kidnapped Wendy? We just want to know where you evacuated the people."

King Thomas turned to ask a whispered question. We waited patiently while he received a reply. Then he cleared his throat and said, "Alas, we do not have any information about that as Lady Mardella gave the order."

Kalli and I exchanged a look. Knowing what I wanted to do, she shook her head and turned back to the king. "Do you know if they were relocated within your kingdom?"

The king turned to his attendant and nodded. The man then spoke to us directly, "We can't say with any certainty where the citizens were reassigned to. The Purple Lady was secretive about where she placed resources. While it's completely possible they were assigned to one of the other camps or townships, Lady Mardella could have also reassigned them to the high house or other nations."

We can solve this by just asking her.

Kalli shook her head again, not meeting my eyes. *Absolutely not! We aren't talking to her unless we exhaust all other options.*

It took me a few minutes to think about it while Kalli grilled the attendant. Then an idea hit me.

We can ask Alariel. She is Lady Mardella's daughter, after all. She might know something. Besides, didn't Kiki say she was going back to the high house with her? If Guinny is there, she might know.

Kalli stopped talking mid-sentence and turned to me. *How do we get in touch with them? They left the group when you went back to Earth.*

I guess we will have to go there.

Returning her attention to the king, Kalli put on her diplomatic smile. "King Thomas, how does one travel to the high house? We would like to pay Melvin's sister a visit."

———

I was on a boat and loving it. The same couldn't be said for Kalli. She looked miserable. I held her hair back as she puked over the side of the boat for the third time. When she came up for air, she gasped, *I really hate boats. You need to figure out a way for us to fly back.*

The wheels in my brain were already turning.

I can send you home once we're done with Kiki. You know, the same way I sent you back to Gaia in the first place. With any luck, you'll end up in the castle. Even if you end up in that village or the monastery, it will be easy to get home from there.

Stop talking! Kalli groaned in my ear as she continued to retch. *I'm trying to focus on not being sick, and your voice is making it worse!*

As I stood over her, I began to wonder if there was anything I could do for Kalli more than just hold her hair and tell her I hoped she felt better. I had cured cancer after all. Putting on my doctor's hat, I took out the M-Phone.

NO SERVICE - OUT OF SERVICE AREA

I fumbled through the preloaded apps until I came to a medical encyclopedia.

LOADING - MEDIMANCERSAURUS (FREE VERSION)

I clicked through the loading screens.

THIS APP WOULD LIKE TO SEND YOUR LEVEL INFORMATION TO THE DEVELOPER FOR QUALITY PURPOSES

NO!

WOULD YOU LIKE TO UPGRADE TO THE FULL VERSION? (1 GOLD)

NO!

I wondered if muggle phones had so many popups. I'd likely never know because I'd never owned one. Once the app finally loaded, I looked up information on seasickness.

SEASICKNESS (Also known as motion sickness)

The sickness originates in the inner ear where the balance mechanism in all humanoid beings resides. Caused by the vessel's erratic movement up and down as well as side to side while the room itself remains relatively motionless. Mixed signals are sent to the brain causing the release of stress-related hormones that can cause nausea, vomiting, and vertigo.

Since I had a place to start, I pushed my mana into Kalli's ear. She gurgled at me as she tried to both vomit and chastise me through Mate-Chat at the same time, *Melvin, stop that! It feels weird.*

I pressed on while explaining what I was trying to do.

Give me a second. I think I can help with your sickness.

Kalli dry-heaved and tried to catch her breath but didn't stop me. The first thing I noticed was that no mana flowed through her ears.

Before I continued, I checked my ears and found my mana channels there.

The first thing I needed to do was redirect Kalli's mana so that it matched mine. At least for the ears in any case. It was a relatively easy task. I added a slight detour as her mana passed by them anyway. As I traced her mana, I noticed that while it flowed all through her brain, eyes, and mouth, it had bypassed her nose and ears.

Once I connected her ears, something changed in Kalli. She paused for a second and tested her body. Realizing she no longer felt the need to be sick, she sat up and kissed me on the cheek. *Wow, what a difference. I feel light on my feet.*

I wanted to be grossed out because she was just throwing up, but I was too focused on her mana to worry about it. Using my body as a guide, I followed her mana through her body, making adjustments when it missed important body parts.

Kalli squirmed in my arms with her eyes shut as she traced what I was doing with her mind's eye. It was a little awkward when I got to certain areas, but Kalli didn't stop me, so I finished by making sure our mana channels matched completely.

When I pulled back, Kalli was staring at me in wonder. *Do you always feel like this?*

I wanted to understand what she meant, but she felt the same to me as she always had.

I don't know. You feel normal to me.

She smiled and stood, taking a deep breath. *Can you smell it? The sea has its own smell, and it makes a sound like a song. I also feel so...so...um, good. That's the only way I can describe it. It's almost like I've been asleep all this time, and now I've awakened. Do you think that's why they call magic people awakened?*

So many thoughts swirled through my head. Had Kalli's mana channels been stunted? Was I special? The only way to tell would be to do the same experiment on somebody else.

Kalli, do you think Kiki or Alariel would want...

Kalli shook her head and giggled. *No! You're only allowed to experiment on me. No other girls.*

I raised an eyebrow at her.

Then boys?

She laughed. *Why? Did you want to?*

It was my turn to shake my head.

No! You're the only one for me.

Kalli sat next to me again, her sickness long forgotten. *Good!*

———

We both gaped at the sight before us. An active volcano stood on the horizon. That wasn't the impressive part. Between cascades of lava that flowed down the sheer walls of the summit stood glamorous buildings nestled in between them.

"The high house," a voice behind us announced.

I turned to see the captain of the ferry. He was a grizzled old man I would have expected to see on one of those dangerous job shows back on Earth. "You kids are lucky. Not many are granted permission to even see this place let alone visit. I've been making this run daily for the last twenty years and this is the first time I've ever transported anyone.

I whistled when I looked at the lava flow dangerously close to one of the structures. "Why would they build so close to a volcano? Aren't they worried about what might happen when it erupts?"

"Hah!" The man laughed. "I thought you were magical. Those mages up there aren't worried about anything that good ol' Gaia can dish out. From what I've heard they feed on that thing like leeches. Suck the life right out of that lava, I tell ya."

I didn't bother to answer. While I knew perfectly well what magic was capable of, the idea of channeling a volcano had never occurred to me. Kalli shivered next to me in excitement. *Do you think Kiki is up there?*

I followed her gaze to one of the towers.

She should be. That's where they said they were going.

[8]

THE STRUCTURES BUILT into the volcano were much larger from up close. Bursts of light flashed in the mountainside as something ran up and down veins of glass leading from one structure to another. Upon close inspection, the volcano itself appeared to be manmade. Or at least made by magic.

Nobody greeted us as the ferry docked in one of the many berths in the harbor. I looked at the captain who was busy tying the boat off with the crew. "Do we wait for someone to come to get us?"

He tipped his head back and laughed. "Sorry, kid. That's above my pay grade. My job ends here. We shack up in those shanties for the night and head back to the mainland in the morning. There is a no questions asked policy about how they unload the cargo. If you have business with the folks up there, you're on your own."

I stepped off the boat and held out a hand to Kalli to help her.

Look's like it's just the two of us.

Kalli smirked at me and took a bounding leap onto the dock, ignoring my hand. Once she was ahead of me, she grabbed it. ***Well? Coming?***

After a moment of shock, I snapped my jaw shut and took her hand, laughing.

Lead on.

———

At first glance, the glass tubes that terminated at the base of the mountain had no entrance or controls of any kind. However, when we approached, a disembodied voice spoke, "Greetings travelers. Present yourselves for identification."

Not knowing what else to do, we walked slowly up to the closest tube.

"Scanning."

"Bloodline confirmed."

"Welcome, Lord and Lady Murphy of the M bloodline. Please, enjoy your visit."

In front of us, the outer shell of the glass tube liquified and melted away, leaving an entrance for us to climb aboard. I raised an eyebrow at Kalli, not offering my hand this time.

Shall we?

She nodded and preceded me into the elevator. The walls of the chamber reformed around us, and we were launched up through the tube as though a giant were sucking on a straw. Moments later, we shot into the first building, popping out of the tube and floating a couple of feet in the air before landing softly on a dais in front of a reception counter.

Kalli staggered a few steps before composing herself. *I'm glad you did what you did on the boat because that would have made me sick.*

I lurched and coughed a few times.

I still might be sick.

The person behind the counter was unlike anything I had ever seen before. The best way I could describe her was part human, part ostrich. Resting atop the torso of a woman was a long feathery neck with a tiny avian head on the top. The result was a woman who looked down on us as we approached her podium. "Welcome, Lord and Lady. I trust your travels went well. Would you like to be shown to our guest wing or would you like to conduct business first?"

"How do you know about us?" Kalli asked hesitantly. "Also, why do you know me as Lady Murphy and not Queen Celestea?"

The ostrich lady held up a device and a red line scanned Kalli. "Ah, yes. You are the queen of a primitive country. Unfortunately, that title does not grant you access to this facility. As renowned members of a dominant bloodline, you are both granted full access to everything on the island."

Wondering what kind of people occupied the high house, I decided to inspect the woman.

Name: Scuawk Struthio
Class: Receptionist
Level: 2
Affection Level: Weary

I rubbed my chin at my findings and asked, "How many unawakened work here?"

Scuawk scoffed at me, her large neck leaning over the desk until she was towering over us. "What are you getting at? Are you saying that I am not worthy to serve you? Well, I'll have you know…"

I held up my hands in defense. "Wait! I'm sorry, I didn't mean that as an insult. We are looking for some unawakened friends, and I was hoping they might be here."

Scuawk blinked and suddenly began laughing hysterically. "Friends, you say? You are friends with the unawakened? Well, that's something I've never heard before."

"What's so funny about that?" Kalli asked, frowning at the bird lady.

She thought the next part to me. *I don't think I like her!*

Unlike Kalli, I had a feeling I knew exactly how Scuawk felt. "Miss Scuawk, how would you like to be awakened?"

"Well, every chick dreams…" she began, choking back her laughter. "Wait, how do you know my name?"

I chuckled, and she pulled her head back. "I know everything about you. You know about my bloodline so you should know at least that much."

Scuawk looked sad when she sighed. "Very well, Master Murphy. Your joke was truly entertaining. Will it be the guest quarters or straight to business?"

I could tell that Kalli was starting to feel bad for the bird. I placed a hand on Squawk's feathery hand resting on the table. "I was serious. I can awaken you if that's what you want."

She froze as she looked down at my hand, regarding it as one might a snake. I gave her a minute before clearing my throat. Scuawk jumped and said, "I, um, yes. Yes! I would, please. I mean, please do that. Awaken me. Please!"

Kalli giggled at the excitement we both saw in Scuawk's face. I nodded and, without wasting any time, passed my mana into her. Inside, her mana channels were similar to the many other people I had awakened. I wasn't sure if birds would be different as I never attempted to awaken any.

There was something strange about my mana that I hadn't seen before. Black impurities bobbed along the surface of the otherwise pristine white mana.

It didn't take me long to arrive at her core. A nest hung in the darkness filled with what appeared to be multi-colored feathers. I jump-started it with my mana and watched in awe as the feathers came to life and began to glow. Then they rose and swirled around the nest in a multicolored tornado.

Again, the black specks invaded my handiwork, making the colorful display of her core somehow dirty. I tried to push the thought from my mind as I tugged a string of her newly formed mana through Scuawk's channels before extracting myself. I emerged to see the ostrich lady stiffened, her feathers all puffed out.

"So, this is what it feels like," she whispered, waving a hand in front of her face. Then she fell to her knees, her head still somehow above the desk. "I swear myself to you, Lord Melvin. If there is any way I can ever repay your kindness, just give the command. If you need companionship—"

"He has all the companionship he needs!" Kalli barked, causing the Scuawk to recoil. "I mean, he doesn't need that. You don't have to do anything for us. It was a gift."

"Oh, but she does," a tired-sounding Maya said from a doorway. "You see, you've tainted her. She will forever be loyal to you, which means she no longer has a place here. I assume that won't be a problem considering you have an entire country to keep her in. I assure you she is one of the very best receptionists I've ever had. Very discreet."

I stared at my older sister as she strutted into the room. "Maya! You don't have to fire her. I was just…"

"Actions have consequences," she interrupted. "You can't just go granting favors for other people's servants. What would the world come to? Besides, I am giving her to you. Consider it a gift."

"She not an item!" Kalli roared, scowling at Maya.

Maya tutted and patted Kalli on the head. "Relax. I am not calling her that. She is a servant though. You need to remember that. Even though you may choose to govern in a certain way, that doesn't mean that others will always have the same customs. With that said, we treat everyone with the utmost respect here. Isn't that right, Scuawk?"

I turned to notice Scuawk kneeling with her head bowed. When Maya addressed her, she nodded vigorously. "Yes, my Lady. It is the greatest honor to serve the high house."

Maya smiled at the bird lady, motioning for her to rise. When she did, she continued, "Please, tell these two about the perks of serving in the high house."

"Of course," Scuawk squawked. "Receiving an appointment to the high house is a most unbelievable honor. Not only is the selected given a life of luxury but their entire family for three generations either way is granted an estate and all that comes with it here on the island. We don't even need money because everything is provided for us. All I have to do is work at this desk three days a week. I don't mind giving that all up to serve you. It will be an honor."

Kalli still refused to meet Maya's eyes, indignant that the woman had patted her on the head. I couldn't take my eyes off Scuawk, my new receptionist.

Do you think we can give six generations of her family a good life?

Kalli snapped out of it and sighed. ***I don't know, Melvin. I mean, we can give her family a place to live and make sure she has everything she needs, but she seems pretty spoiled here even if she is a servant.***

I sighed, deciding to worry about that another day. Turning back to Maya, I said, "The reason we're here is that we're looking for Kiki. Actually, you might be able to help, too. Are you familiar with a town called Hudholm Summit? Mardella relocated some people from there, and I need to find them."

Maya rubbed her chin, and then nodded to Scuawk. The ostrich lady stiffened before turning to a device on her desk. "Oh, right. Yes, my Lady. Let me see, Hudholm Summit. Spelled H U D H O L M. Got it. Evacuated. Citizens relocated. Troll revolt so it seems. Hmm. Well, depending on who you need to find, they could be anywhere. I see that the old mayor and her daughter were given a place in Lady Mardella's private villa."

"Guinny! Look up Guinny," Kalli exclaimed, before thinking better of it and adding, "Oh, and make sure everyone else is okay. If anyone got put in a bad situation, please make arrangements to let them come to Celestea."

While Scuawk hammered madly at her console, Maya spoke to Kalli, "I promise you that we will make sure everyone from Hudholm is treated with respect and decency. If you wish to relocate all of them to Celestea, I will see that it's done."

Kalli scowled at Maya, but I could tell her expression was starting to crack. I turned to Maya and asked, "Is Kiki here? I wouldn't mind seeing her."

Maya blinked at me in surprise. "No. She isn't here, Melvin. Didn't you speak to her in your guild chat?"

I wanted to slap my head. I forgot all about the guild. So had Kalli, apparently. She laughed nervously and admitted, "I actually turned that off because of how many people talk in there. I forgot Ki was part of the guild."

Turning guild chat back on, I reached out to my sister.

Kiki, are you there?

Her reply came instantly, **It took you long enough, dork! I've been trying to get your attention ever since you left Celestea. Your friend Guinny is here at the manor.**

The manor?

Kiki explained, **Actually, it's Alariel's house. More of a cabin in the woods actually. A very big cabin. It's neat, though. There's a big garden in the back, and it's so beautiful. You should visit sometime.**

Kalli said the same thing I was thinking, **Um, Kiki, is Mardella there?**

The thought of Malric inhabiting the body of Alariel's mother and taking Ki hostage made my skin crawl. I heaved a sigh of relief when she replied, **No, she's not here. Mardella hasn't been seen since you fought her. Alariel is worried. Remember, it's her mother after all.**

Scuawk startled me when she chirped, "Ah hah! I found her. She is at the summer manor of Lady Mardella!"

[9]

IT TURNED out we had traveled to the high house for nothing. On the bright side, we were able to get in touch with Guinny, and Kiki invited her to the guild.

Maya waited patiently while we made arrangements in guild chat. When we finished, I turned to her and said, "Thanks for reminding us about the guild. That saved a lot of time. We still need to find the rest of the villagers from Hudholm to make sure they didn't get split up like Guinny and her father did."

Maya nodded. "It will be done. In the meantime, I invite you to stay here for a few days. You did travel all this way after all. There are a few things I want to tell you about. Will the two of you please consider staying?"

Kalli gave me a nervous glance. While I could tell that she was uneasy, I sort of wanted to ask a few questions myself. *I don't know about this, Mel. We hardly know her.*

I think I want to stay. There is so much that we don't know about my bloodline. Maya might even know who my father is. Don't worry. I can send you back.

Kalli bit her lip and shook her head. *No! If you're staying, then so am I.*

Still feeling bad about making Kalli stay, I replied to Maya, "We will stay for a while. I wanted to talk to you more anyway."

A small smile tugged at Maya's lip. "Excellent. Scuawk, please prepare the VIP suite for our esteemed guests."

"Yes, my Lord," Scuawk acknowledged, hammering at her console furiously.

"Come this way," Maya motioned to the passage behind her. "I'd like to give the two of you a tour on our way to the guest wing. I can only imagine what you've seen on Gaia so far, but I'll bet some of the things we do here will still impress you."

———

"As a pyromancer, you should appreciate our artificial heat source." Maya winked at Kalli when we walked through a glass tube overlooking the central vent of the volcano.

I stared uneasily into the lava bubbling hundreds of feet beneath us. "You made this? The volcano wasn't here first?"

Maya laughed. "Heaven's no. Wouldn't that be convenient, a volcano appearing precisely where we want it? Also, natural volcanoes are way too unpredictable. We control everything here."

Kalli pressed her hands up against the glass to get a better view. She obviously didn't have the same problem with heights that I did. "How did you make a volcano?"

"Magic," Maya said, snapping her fingers for emphasis. "We know where the lava is and how it moves. It was a simple matter of making a hole and controlling the pressure. Too little results in not enough energy for our needs and too much means we blow up. We employ a full team of Geomancers to regulate it."

"What else do you have?" I asked, eager to get off the bridge.

Maya smirked at my question. "You want to see some toys, don't you? Very well. I'll show you my private collection."

From there, we didn't stop as much to sightsee. Maya walked with purpose through marble-lined halls with elegant designs on the walls.

She said nothing as she hurried to guide us to our destination, leaving Kalli and me to chat in private.

Do you think we should make a volcano in Celestea? I bet Joe can rig it to give the entire queendom electricity.

Kalli hesitated for a second before shaking her head. *That's a disaster waiting to happen. They need a whole team of Geomancers here to control it. You heard Maya. If we do it wrong, I can see a volcano destroying everything.*

She had a point. My philosophy usually was to blow it up and ask questions later. It was something I needed to work on.

On the surface, a volcano looked like such an easy thing to create. The high house also had the advantage of being the most sophisticated place I'd seen on Gaia. It even said air conditioning.

Eventually, we ended up in a long hall that reminded me of a fancy hotel. Every room had a number and a strange device on the doorknob that pulsed with light. Maya noticed me looking at it and said, "That's a mana reader. If a room is coded to you, nobody else but you can enter. Go ahead. Try it."

I reached out and grabbed the glowing handle. Something in the cool metal tugged at my mana, drawing it from my palm.

ERROR: UNKNOWN MANA
THE OWNER OF THIS ROOM HAS BEEN NOTIFIED

Maya smiled as I recoiled. "As you can see, it's very secure. Don't worry about the System message. I've already informed the occupant of what happened."

"Thanks, I think," I replied, rubbing my hand where the door had drawn out my mana. "Did you do that to discourage me from trying to open any doors?"

"Very perceptive," Maya smirked as she started down the hall again. "Truth be told, these rooms are mostly just living quarters for guests and lesser families. Come, let me show you what your life will be like someday."

At the end of the hall was another cluster of glass tubes. Maya stood under the scanner and one of the tubes opened up. "This leads to my villa. It's on the other side of the volcano and has a view of the sea."

The instant we entered the tube, we were shot sideways in an arc that passed beneath several of the other structures built into the volcano. Just when I thought I was going to be sick again, we were there.

From the platform we arrived on, Maya's villa towered above us while waves crashed against a rocky shore far below. Multiple stories tall, the entrance was lined with pure white Roman columns that spanned the entire building. As Maya strutted to the door, several topless male servants ran out and knelt along the path.

Maya laughed when she saw the shocked expression on Kalli's face. She nodded at the unspoken question and said, "Yes. They are servants and, yes, that's what I use them for. Don't get me wrong, they all signed up for the job and enjoy their lot in life. If you don't believe me, you are free to ask them."

Kalli huffed and did her best not to look at any of the servants. "No. I'm fine. I don't need to talk to them."

She added another more private message for me. *You aren't allowed to have servants. Not ever!*

The thought of servants reminded me of the man from my dream for some odd reason. I couldn't help but compare the shirtless men to the women standing beside the man on the throne.

Don't worry. I'll never want anyone like that. You're the only girl for me.

A smile appeared on her face as she replied, *Good.*

The interior of the building was just as glamorous as Lavender's house. The major difference was that everything was white. From the carpet to the textures on the walls, there was no color. Maya shrugged and explained, "My magic has a lot to do with the color white. It became something of a theme. You have heard I am called The White Lady, right?"

"That's right. You're a shimmer mage," I said, remembering her class from when I inspected her when we first met. "What does that mean exactly."

"Oh, my," Maya looked away, acting bashful. "Way to call a lady out. Just kidding. I suppose a demonstration is in order."

She guided us to a large room with a circular mat in the middle, reminding me of a karate dojo. Stepping into the circle, she said, "Don't blink. You'll miss it."

I tried my best not to blink, which is notoriously hard when you actively try not to do it. A foggy haze formed around Maya, which made my eyes water. I wasn't sure if I blinked or not but, moments later, Maya had vanished.

Suddenly, I felt a chilling sensation run up and down my spine as a high-pitched voice came from nowhere. "That is called Shimmer Frost."

Judging from the feeling I shared through my connection with Kalli, the spell had hit her as well. She shivered and spun, looking for her attacker. Then the air around us crackled, and I felt like I was standing beside an oven. Maya appeared in front of me and announced, "That was Shimmer Friction. I can do more than that, but I don't want to hurt you. There are also other applications of my magic that aren't attacks, but I can tell you about that another time. You wanted to see some toys, right? Follow me."

As we walked, Kalli and I chatted silently.

How did she do that? Do you think I can Shimmer?

Kalli giggled and shook her head. *I don't know? Can you?*

The truth was, I wasn't sure. I couldn't see her or her mana. I just felt the effects of it. There had to be something in the name, Shimmer. Or perhaps it had something to do with the haze she left behind when she vanished. It was like a mirage or some kind of optical illusion.

The room Maya led us to was filled with pedestals that reminded me of the artifact museum back on Earth or the pedestal where I found the ring in my dream. Each one had a placard describing what was on it.

I bypassed that and went to inspect the first one.

Item: Crown of the Eternal King
Components: Gold, Platinum, Ruby, Emerald, Sapphire,
Cursed Mana
Item Rank: S
Item Level: 50
Item Owner: Halifax

Maya walked up behind me as I looked at the gaudy crown. "That one has the hidden effect of making its wearer immortal. The only problem is that it also comes with a curse. Whoever wears this crown will constantly find themselves fighting to defend it. They usually die quick painful deaths."

I started toward another pedestal when Maya stopped me. "No. Come over here and check these."

Item: ??? ??? ?? ??????
Components: Mana, ???
Item Rank: S
Item Level: 1
Item Owner: ???

The item looked a lot like a torch, but the flame was frozen. I exchanged a glance with my sister and asked, "What is it?"

She shrugged. "I'm not sure. A lot of artifacts only respond when they recognize a master. I'd offer to let you try to claim one, but then I'd have to charge you if it took to you."

I looked down at the ring on my finger and wondered if I was going to get a bill from the man in my dream. Maya noticed my gaze and asked, "Do you mind telling me where you found that? I noticed you have a few artifacts of your own. Do you collect them as I do?"

Shaking my head, I tried to explain. "Actually, I just sort of stumbled on these by accident. The armor is from a museum back on Earth. It said it belonged to M and I touched it. Now, it won't come off. The ring is another story. I sort of found it, but I don't remember where."

The truth was that I didn't know where, but it felt dangerous to tell

Maya about the man in my dream. She nodded quietly as I explained before continuing the tour.

It turned out that Maya had seven relics that weren't a part of the System, though none of them recognized her as owner. At one point, she reached out and gently touched my ring, whispering, "How did you get it to choose you?"

I pulled my hand back, trying to think about what happened when I encountered the relics for the first time. "Have you tried imbuing it with your mana?"

Maya gave me a puzzled look. "How do you mean?"

"You know." I struggled to find the right words. "Push your mana into it. I know you absorb traits by, um, you know, doing it, but it's also possible to probe things and people with your mana."

After laughing at my nervous response, Maya rubbed her chin and asked, "Do you mind if I try it on you?"

Kalli stepped between us. "I don't know if I'm comfortable with that. Especially out here at your, um, house. Why don't you practice on one of your servants?"

Maya laughed at the way Kalli said *servant* and turned to face her. "What would I possibly gain from that? Doing so would be like probing a rock. True, they make excellent eye candy, but that is about all they're good for. I'm sure you understand. You must be surrounded by people who wish to please you that have nothing of value to offer."

Kalli glared at the white lady. "Everyone has something to offer! How can you look down on people who love you? Or do you actually force them to be here?"

Maya sighed, smoothing her robe methodically. "I mean no disrespect, and I apologize if it comes off that way. I was merely making an observation that the unawakened have a certain role in life, and it's our responsibility to make their lives better and not the other way around."

Kalli suddenly turned her attention to me. At first, I wondered what I had done to upset my girlfriend, but then I realized that I was excited to see what my sister's mana felt like and Kalli had noticed.

Maya must have sensed the shift because she said, "Look, Kalli, may I call you that? Would it make you feel better if I tried it on you instead? I am sure Melvin can tell me what to do."

Kalli backed away and I could feel how nervous she was to suddenly be on the spot. "It's Kalliphae, and, um, I don't know. Only Melvin has ever…"

I rushed over to Kalli, placing myself between her and Maya. "Look, we can do this some other time. Perhaps we can see that room you promised us now?"

Not to be deterred, Maya motioned to one of the relics. "What if I allow one of you to try to claim one of my treasures as payment?"

Kalli's eyes sparkled as she wandered over to a dark corner of the room. "What about this one?"

[10]

I COULD FEEL her excitement as Kalli gravitated toward a pedestal hidden in a far corner of the room. Maya held out a hand, and I thought I could hear an audible whimper from the woman. "But that's…"

She backed off when I turned to look at her. "Oh, never mind. A deal's a deal. Remember, though, only one of you gets to try and claim something. You still owe your part of the deal if she picks."

Kalli hesitated. She had already reached out and was inches away from the relic. *Do you mind, Melvin? I feel drawn to this one. Like it's calling to me.*

I took a few steps over to her to see what caught Kalli's attention. Resting on a cushion was a necklace with a ruby pendant attached.

Item: ?????? Of ??????? ?????
Components: Mana, ????, ???, Flarium, ????
Item Rank: S
Item Level: 1
Item Owner: ???

I felt her excitement.
Go for it!

Then she picked it up. Maya let out a gasp as a brilliant red light flooded the room. When my vision cleared, I noticed Kalli was wearing the relic, and the whole thing looked almost liquid as a sea of flames rippled over the ruby. The effect made the relic look somehow alive.

"That was unexpected," Maya sighed, leaning close to Kalli to see the relic. "I believe that particular relic was originally from Luna. There are stories about it being a part of the ring that broke off and fell to Gaia. How did you get it to respond?"

Kalli absentmindedly stroked the ruby, and her eyes had a dream-like state as she answered. "I don't know. As soon as I touched it, I was wearing it. One second it was sitting on the pillow, and the next it was around my neck."

She tossed me a quick glance as she spoke, *Did you feel that, Mel? It feels like my mana. My flame. I don't know how to explain it.*

The truth was that I could feel it through our connection. I felt how the mana imbued in the relic sampled Kalli's before embracing it and somehow finding its way around her neck.

That was amazing. It's obviously a fire relic. I can't wait to see what it does.

I wanted to touch it, to see if it would accept me as it did my girl-friend, but something told me that wasn't a good idea in front of Maya.

She cleared her throat, interrupting our private conversation. "Now that you've relieved me of one of my most prized possessions, how about you fulfill your end of the bargain. Since the relic recognized Kalliphae, I am going to insist that you demonstrate your mana technique yourself. No offense, but it's always best to learn these things from the source."

After getting a quick nod from Kalli, I walked with Maya over to a bench. Taking her hand, I explained the way it worked. "I am going to demonstrate by pushing my mana into you. From there, I will inspect your mana channels as I move to your core. I don't know if you'll be able to do it, but the least I can do is demonstrate."

Maya nodded and said, "Carry on."

I began by pushing my mana into her. Immediately after penetrating her, I could tell that she made full use of her mana channels. Strange mana that seemed to hum pulsed through her with strange vibrations that reminded me of bees.

I threaded my mana through hers on my way to Maya's core. I heard her voice echoing in the distance as I made progress. "I can feel you inside of me. It's strange, being invaded by another person's mana. We are definitely related. I can feel that much."

Then I arrived at her core. Or what I assumed to be her core. White mist hung in the air, swirling around a void that only manifested itself by displacing its surroundings. I continued toward it with my mana. As it had been a while since I touched the core of a fully awakened person and even longer since I did so with a high-level mage, I was completely taken by surprise when the feedback sent me flying across the room and crashing into a display case.

NEW TRAIT ACQUIRED: [SHIMMER]

The ceiling spun above me as I struggled to sit up. Kalli rushed over to my side, cupping my head in her hands. *Are you okay?*

I was only able to nod as Maya growled from across the room. "You bastard! What is this? Did you just give me an MTD?"

Shaking my head to clear it and wondering what it was she had just said, I asked, "Can you say that again?"

Maya stomped over to me. "An MTD. Mana transmitted disease! I thought this was a safe mana transfer, but apparently not. Also, what the hell is wrong with your mana?"

Suddenly, I remembered the black specks in my mana. Was that a disease? When had it first happened? Did I pass it to Kalli? She began to panic as she read my mind.

Maya noticed our expressions and said, "Relax, both of you. It's not the end of the world. I'm not dying or anything. There's just a taint that wasn't there before. We are going to have to see a specialist to figure out what it is."

Kalli had a look of concern on her face. *You're a healer, aren't you? Can you cure it?*

I hadn't thought of that. Ignoring Maya's question, I reached inside of myself and examined my core. It looked dirty with the tiny black particles all over it. If the night sky was a black canvas peppered with pinpricks of light, then my core was the opposite. It still shone brightly, but now it was tainted with thousands of black spots. That and the barbed mana wrapped around it which represented my oath to Kalli.

I was fortunate to receive an error when I attempted to **DELETE** the taint.

ERROR: YOU CANNOT DELETE YOUR OWN CORE

Realizing that whatever poison I had picked up had become a part of me, I focused on trying to filter my mana and remove the impurity. Again, nothing I did had any effect.

I was made aware of the fact that Maya had approached me when she placed a hand on my shoulder. "Well, I suppose now that you've already infected me, I might as well do what I paid for. I think I get the general idea of what you did."

That brought me back to my senses. "Ahh, oh, okay. You want to try it on me, right? Well, I'm ready when you are."

For the first time in my life, I felt someone other than Kalli invade my body with their mana. The experience was different too because when Kalli did it, I also felt it from her perspective. Maya's mana felt as though foreign vibrating mana was coursing through my veins.

I knew she was in my mana channels as I guided her. "Just follow that, and it will lead to my core. If your ability works anything like mine, just the act of touching it should activate your absorption trait."

"Oh, wow!" Maya gasped as she caught sight of my core. "It's so bright. Did mine look like that? Wait, what is that chain around your core?"

I decided to answer her questions in order. "Your core looked like a black hole surrounded by a cloud of white mist. I knew something was in there but only because it left an impression in the mist."

Before I could answer her second question about the chain, I felt a kick, and Maya went sailing through the room, crashing into another artifact display.

Stumbling to my feet, I called out to her. "Are you all right?"

She sat up suddenly and laughed. Kalli frowned at her. "Seriously, are you okay? Do you want me to call for help?"

Maya struggled to breathe through her laughter for a few moments and explained, "Well, if you think about the way I normally do this, that climax was a little more explosive. Still, the result is the same. Except for maybe the org... Well, never mind. In the end, it worked. What does Track Scent do?"

I laughed. Of all the traits for her to get, she would have to get that one. "It makes you smell better."

She sniffed herself. "Did I smell bad before?"

"No, no, no." I chuckled, unable to control myself. "I mean it makes it where you can smell things and know where they are."

It was Maya's turn to laugh again. "I knew that. I was only teasing you. Kind of worthless when you really think about it."

"So, what does Shimmer do?" I asked, unable to resist showing off what I got.

She stopped laughing and rubbed her chin. "So, you got that one, huh? I hate to break it to you, but it doesn't do a whole lot by itself. How good are you at shaking? That's the only clue you get."

"No fair!" I whined, shaking my butt for emphasis.

"Keep practicing, kid," Maya said with a smirk. "It took me a decade to master that, and I'm not giving you any shortcuts."

———

Promising to talk more in the morning, we retired to our suite for the night. It was there that I finally had a chance to look at Kalli's new relic. While I didn't expect it to jump off her neck when I touched it, I was a little disappointed that it didn't seem to react at all.

Did you figure anything out about it yet?

Kalli pried my hand off the pendant and frowned at me. ***That isn't*** *the top priority right now, Melvin. What are we going to do about this disease? It seems to have spread to me, too.*

While that shouldn't have been a big surprise considering the way we were connected, I still felt a surge of shame when she informed me. I ran my finger along her arm and pushed my mana inside to see for myself. She let out a sigh as she felt my mana and whispered, "I don't like you letting other people touch your core. Promise me you won't do that anymore."

I nuzzled her with my nose. "I promise."

Immediately after entering her mana channels, I saw the black particles. The corruption was the same as mine. Outside of spreading to whoever I touched with my mana, it didn't seem to be having any adverse effects on us.

I don't know what it is. Do you feel sick at all?

Kalli shook her head. *No. I feel fine. It just feels, I don't know, icky.*

It was definitely becoming something we needed to deal with.

Maybe Maya will know what to do. We should ask her tomorrow.

Okay, let's ask her about it first thing tomorrow. Kalli replied, rolling over to face me, kissing me softly. *What do you want to do in the meantime?*

Passing up a prime opportunity to make out with my girlfriend, I stroked her collarbone before shifting my attention back to her relic.

I'm really curious about what this does.

Then Kalli ignited.

———

Meanwhile, in Poland…

"Be careful with that!" the bespectacled woman hollered for the tenth time.

For the life of her, she never understood why the administration chose to pay minimum wage to low-level workers, and then trust them to haul around billions of zloty worth of equipment.

Somehow, she found herself supervising the cretins by herself. She was brought out of her thoughts when one of the workers approached. "Um, excuse me, Miss Boszczyk. This unit requires power. Where do you want us to plug it in?"

Miss Boszczyk slapped her forehead in frustration. "Nimbicile. As I've told you a thousand times, I brought a battery."

"I don't think you understand ma'am," the worker tried to reason with her. "This is heavy equipment and won't run on…"

She held a hand up and waved his comment off. "Who is in charge here? Do I pay you to think?"

"Well, no, but…". He tried again.

"But nothing," she roared back. "Just set it up and let me worry about plugging it in. Once you finish you can all go."

"But it isn't safe to…" She had to give it to him. The man was persistent. Probably worth a whole lot more than he made.

"Look," she said, her tone softening. "You may stay if you like but understand that this has nothing to do with safety. What is your name?"

He took off his hat to introduce himself. "My name is Antoni, ma'am."

She smiled, getting a sinister idea. "It's a pleasure to meet you, Antoni. I might have a special job for you after all."

Antoni looked back at the equipment, rubbing the back of his head. "Um, what exactly does this stuff do anyhow?"

A smile found its way onto Miss Boszczyk's face. "We are going to rip the time-space continuum."

[11]

I SHOULDN'T HAVE WORRIED. Kalli was fireproof after all. However, that didn't stop me from panicking when she spontaneously combusted. It wasn't the friendly kind of fire either. There were green flames everywhere, and they hurt!

The fear that Kalli was in trouble inside that fireball overrode my fear so I scooped her up and ran around looking for anything I could use to put her out.

Why didn't we explore the suite when we got here? This place is too big!

I thought out loud in my panic. Kalli was much calmer than I was. *Could you put me down? I need to figure this out.*

When I didn't immediately find what I was looking for, I targeted the nearest object, which was similar to a bear skin rug and transformed it into a pool.

Item: Plastic Pool (Edited)
Components: Water, Plastic
Item Rank: F
Item Level: 1
Item Owner: Murphy

A geyser of steam rose from the shallow pool as I dropped Kalli in it. She yelped, and I felt her pain as her bottom smacked the hard floor of the shallow pool, which wasn't enough to douse the flame.

I stood there in shock as Kalli slowly climbed to her feet and pouted at me through the raging inferno. *That hurt!*

All I could do was stare at the phenomenon. While I was used to Kalli being on fire, it felt different. It was something else. Something I felt the first time I saw her relic awaken. The flames felt alive.

Are you okay? Can you control it?

Kalli slowly waved her arms around, inspecting the new flame that danced with her before gasping and pointing to something behind me. She screamed, forgetting to use MateChat. "Melvin, the bed!"

I spun to find the bed in flames, which filled the room with smoke. Pointing at the bed, I did the only thing I could think of.

DELETE

The fire had spread from the bed to a nearby nightstand a curtain.

DELETE

DELETE

I ran around the room **DELETING** anything that smoldered before turning back to Kalli. She watched me from the pool, wearing the green flame as one would a cloak.

Can you turn it off?

Huh? Kalli gaped at me. *Oh, the fire. Right. Let me try. I think this will... Right. Yep. That worked.*

I watched in awe as the flame receded into the pendant. Kalli reached up to gently touch the ruby for a moment, and then she noticed and rushed over to me. *Mel! You're burnt.*

Ow! That hurts!

I squealed when the adrenaline left and the pain kicked in. We both looked down at my arms, which were already healing. I poured some mana on it to quicken the process.

Kalli ran her finger over my angry red skin and whispered, "I'm so sorry. I didn't mean to hurt you like that."

I shook my head, also speaking out loud. "Don't worry about it. I was just worried that your relic might be cursed or something. Why did it do that, anyway?"

She shrugged, reverting to MateChat. *Well, you were talking about it so I decided to feed it some mana. I guess it liked it because, the next thing I knew, I was covered in Luna Fire.*

Luna Fire?

Kalli giggled and walked over to the window. I had conveniently deleted the curtain and Luna was visible in the night sky. *Yeah. I call it Luna Fire because it's green like Luna.*

I followed her gaze up to Luna. It was far away, but I could still remember the replica of Celestea Castle where the gods lived. And the apparatus filled one of the rooms. I only turned when I felt Kalli's eyes boring a hole in the side of my head.

What?

She only replied after thinking about it for a moment, *I need you to take me there.*

I looked back up at the planet in the sky.

Why?

Kalli shrugged. *I don't know. Something about Luna is calling me the same way this relic did. I can't explain it. It's just a feeling I have.*

That brought up another question. If Kalli was feeling things about relics and planets, why wasn't I sharing those feelings? Were there some parts of us that we still didn't share?

I'll take you but the only way I know of getting there is through the basement in the castle. It will have to be when we go home.

She nodded and rested her head on my shoulder. *So, lover boy, where are we going to sleep tonight?*

The room was a mess. The bed was gone, the only trace of it ever having been there was the ashen shadow left behind by the fire. The smell of smoke was overwhelming even though the room had some kind of magical air conditioning.

In the end, I had to get creative. Just like the queen suite back home, we discovered another room with an in-ground bath. All it took was a little creativity, and I was able to edit a hammock big enough for two and strung it between two pillars over the water.

Kalli climbed in after me and kissed me on the cheek. *This reminds me of the time we slept together in the dungeon. Do you remember?*

I smiled and kissed her back.

Of course, I do. That was the day you taught me how to poop in a dungeon.

She scowled at me. *Really, Melvin? That is what you choose to remember?*

Not only that. I also remember how much I love having you next to me.

Kalli smiled and nestled in closer. *Me, too.*

———

After a fun filled night of making out in our dreams, we were startled by a loud scream.

SPLASH!

I got twisted in the hammock and Kalli plummeted a few feet into the warm water of the bath. She struggled so much that water splashed everywhere, including on me. Then, suddenly, I got a steam bath as the girl ignited once again and the top layer of water was vaporized.

Ow! Hot, hot, hot!

Kalli reigned in the green flames. *Sorry, Mel. I sort of overreacted. Who thought it was a good idea to place a hammock over a pool of water?*

"Hello?" a voice called from the main room. "Are the two of you decent in there?"

"Yes!" Kalli shouted back. "We're decent."

A man wearing a black suit with a bowtie bowed as he entered the room. "Good morning, young miss. Might I inquire as to what happened in the bedroom? Was there a fire?"

Kalli's face reddened as she apologized. "I am so sorry about that.

Something happened unexpectedly with my magic, and I sort of caught fire. We can pay for the bed if necessary."

"I assure you that won't be necessary, my Lady," the man said in a dull voice. "Assuming nobody was injured, there shouldn't be any problem. Lady Maya has instructed me to summon the two of you for breakfast. Please, make yourselves ready, and I will escort you there."

So much for breakfast in bed. I sighed.

Kalli looked up and saw that I was still imprisoned in the twisted-up hammock. *I am not getting back in that thing!*

Fair enough.

DELETE

SPLASH!

I came crashing down on Kalli as the hammock I was tangled in vanished without a trace. She kicked me in the stomach as she struggled to surface. We both emerged gasping at the same time.

The man in the suit smirked. "Well, then, I will be waiting outside when you are ready."

———

We found him in the hall after we made ourselves presentable. Kalli was still annoyed with me. *I can't believe you did that!*

Sorry! I was all knotted up in that thing, and it was the only way to get out.

She stuck her tongue out at me. *You could have, I don't know, asked me to move out of the way first or something?*

Oh...

As we walked in silence, I decided to inspect the man in the suit.

Name: Wallace Penderskew
Class: Concierge
Level: 4
Affection Level: Studious

I grinned at Wallace and asked, "Would you like to be awakened?"

The concierge shook his head mournfully and replied, "I'm afraid not, Master Murphy. We have been instructed to stay away from your mana. Until you get that MTD taken care of in any case."

"You know about that?" I gasped, looking at Kalli in alarm.

"I'm afraid everybody does, my Lord," Wallace said in his matter-of-fact tone. "What with Miss Scuawk hospitalized and all."

"She's in the hospital?" I echoed as the news kept getting worse.

I was beginning to lose my appetite. Kalli attempted to comfort me by wrapping her arm around my shoulder. "Don't worry, Mel. I am sure they have a top-notch hospital here. I mean, it's the high house after all."

The good news was that Kalli was no longer angry at me. I decided to take that as a win.

———

"Good morning, sleepyheads," Maya chirped as we entered the dining hall. "I was going to let the two of you sleep in but, when I heard there had been a fire, I decided to have Wallace wake you. I trust you slept well?"

Kalli answered before I could come up with anything. "We slept well, thank you. Your hospitality is most kind."

Maya smiled in response before motioning to a pair of chairs next to her. "I wasn't sure what the two of you like, so I had the chefs prepare a little of everything."

She wasn't joking. The long table was lined with every sort of dish I could think of, and some that I couldn't. Picking up something that looked like chicken, I asked, "What's this?"

My question earned me a smirk from Maya. "Can't you just inspect it? Very well, that is what we call Thunderbird. It's especially good when battered in rueberry paste and deep-fried. Now, I get to ask a question. What do you know about our father?"

I had been about to take a bite of the Thunderbird when she asked, "I know nothing about him. I was actually hoping you could tell me something. Do you think we have the same father? Isn't there a chance we're cousins or long-lost relatives separated by generations?"

Maya took a bite of blue toast with pink jelly as she thought about it. "That is true. There is the possibility that we have different fathers, but let me ask you, did your mother get pregnant with you at a young age? Did your father disappear before you were born and never come back? This seems to be the story that every M Class person has. That's what we call the family with the M Bloodline."

"How many of us are there?" I asked, realizing Maya wasn't just talking about me, her, and Kiki.

She gave me a knowing smile as she replied, "There are twenty-three of us on Gaia, not counting you and Kiki. I estimate there are hundreds of them spread across the universe. There are rumors from the other realms of brothers and sisters who fight among themselves to garner father's favor."

"His favor?" I asked, taking a bite of something that I hoped was bacon. "So, some of us have met him? And there are so many here on Gaia. Will I meet any of them?"

She nodded absently as she continued to eat. "Yes, yes. You will meet them. Not all reside in the high house, but those who are here would like to meet you as well. Many are significantly older than you, so be prepared for that. We have an accord here on Gaia, so please be warned that hostile action between siblings is expressly forbidden. All shenanigans must be taken off-world."

Kalli set her fork down. "Are there people here who might want to hurt Melvin?"

Maya shook her head. "Heavens no. As I said, many of our family here are quite old and quite content to just enjoy their endeavors without engaging in acts of aggression."

"How old is old?" I asked, wondering if my mom had hooked up with a wrinkled grandpa. "Dad would have to be even older than them, right?"

Maya chuckled at my question. "Well, our best guess would make him at least one thousand years old. I asked my mother once before she passed, and all she would tell me was that he didn't look old. However, that could be an illusion or perhaps he has some kind of longevity magic. Then again, none of our siblings look their age either, so there's that."

"When can I meet them? I asked, eager to question the rest of the family.

"Tonight," Maya replied. "First, we need to sort out this MTD."

[12]

THE HOSPITAL TURNED out to be just a house. The section of the volcano where it was located was part of a cluster with many other mid-sized homes. It was nothing like Maya's villa, though it still hung off the sheer wall of the volcano.

"Why are we here?" I asked Maya when we arrived at the cramped entryway.

Maya nodded to the man who stood at the door waiting for us. "As I said, we need to deal with the MTD. Jorvais, I think I have the source here."

Jorvais appeared to be in his twenties. His slick black hair was pulled back into a ponytail and pockets on his robe were the only thing that set it apart from typical wizard's attire. When he approached me, he took my hand and pressed two fingers against my wrist. "Hmm. Ah, yes. I see. Come with me, kid."

Maya's voice sounded harsh as she scolded him, "Jorvais, he's my brother. Know your place."

Jorvais stiffened momentarily as he walked back to the house. "I see. Sorry, my Lord. Please, come this way."

As we followed, Maya whispered in my ear. "Be patient with him.

He is probably the best healer on Gaia. If anyone can sort this out, it will be him."

The inside of the Jorvais home was split between an infirmary and a private home. Just inside the door, a lobby of some sort was set up, complete with rows of hard plastic chairs as well as a receptionist's desk.

To the right, stood a door leading to a room that looked like a sitting room. We followed Jorvais to the left where low-laying cots lined the walls. Half of them were occupied by people in various states of sickness.

I immediately noticed Scuawk at the back of the room. Her neck was too long for the bed, so they had pushed two of them together. She did not look good.

"I am so sorry, Scuawk," I said when I made my way over to her.

She gave me a weak smile. "Please, take care of my family. I am done for."

Jorvais stepped past me and leaned over the embattled bird-woman. "Relax, Miss Scuawk. I won't let you die. Not on my watch. We just need a little time to sort you out."

Remembering how I cured the plague, I inspected her for any traits that might tell me what ailed her. There was nothing. No traits or abilities. She was newly awakened after all.

I was about to examine her with my mana when Jovial grabbed my arm and marched me over to a bed, making me lay down. "So, Master Murphy. I am told that you are a bit more robust than our fine-feathered friend. Please, pardon me but you might feel a little pressure."

I never understood why doctors said that. Pressure was codeword for raging pain. Also, by a little, he meant a lot. As the doctor held his hands high above my body, something emanated from him and into me. It burned as it passed through my skin and interacted with my mana.

Looking down, I saw black streaks visible just under my skin that all seemed to intersect in my chest. A non-magical doctor might think that central location was where my heart resided, but I knew better. That was my core.

When whatever it was made contact, it got rejected and everything exploded out of me, throwing Jorvais into the far wall. Kalli, who had been speaking to a child across the room, rushed over, screaming at the doctor. "That hurt! You're hurting him. Melvin, are you okay?"

That was one of the few times I regretted my connection to Kalli. I was causing her pain, and we both knew it.

I can try to block the pain from you if you want.

Don't you dare! She gave me a glare that was mixed with concern.

"My apologies," Jorvais said as he made his way back. I noticed blood streaming down his forehead that he seemed to be ignoring.

He gently nudged Kalli out of the way and took a brush from one of his many pockets and proceeded to swab the wall where I noticed a sticky substance. "What's that?"

Giving me a knowing nod, he explained, "This is the disease. Rather, I should say this is your mana tainted by something. Your regenerative skills are remarkable. You have already returned to full health after taking my probe. Please, excuse me while I run some tests."

Just like that, he swept from the room and was gone. Kalli stayed with me for a few minutes before returning to check on the sick kid.

The fact that I was a carrier of some unknown disease frustrated me. There were people in the room that I could likely have cured if I wasn't damaged. Maya noticed me looking at the other patients and said, "Don't worry about them, Melvin. As far as Gaia goes, this is where they can get the very best treatment. We accept patients from all over the world, regardless of status. Jory even travels when the situation calls for it."

I sat up in the bed and fixed my sister with a hard stare. "Exactly where was he when the entire dark land was infected by the plague? Surely, you were aware."

An uncomfortable look crossed Maya's face as she hesitantly replied, "You have to understand, there are politics involved. Even here in the high house. We knew that territory was quarantined, but our hands were tied. Taking action might have caused a war within the high house."

"Was Mardella that powerful?" I asked, fidgeting with the ring absentmindedly. "Was the mighty White Lady scared of her?"

Maya scoffed, as she replied in an annoyed tone. "Hardly. We only learned of Mardella's involvement in the end when you defeated her. A creature known as the Puppetmaster has existed on Gaia for a very long time. He, she, they worked in the shadows and produced dark champion after campion to threaten balance in the world. Some on the council believe it is a necessary evil that exists within the world to prevent any one nation from becoming too strong."

"So, you just let thousands of people die?" Kalli asked with tears forming in her eyes. I could feel that she was upset by the revelation. "How can you be so cruel?"

Maya frowned, turning to face her accuser. "Listen, Kalli. It's not that simple. We can't become involved in every war. We don't have the…"

"Then we will do it," I spoke over her, nodding to Kalli who beamed at me. "This is going to be a new era where innocent people don't need to suffer while those with power do nothing. I don't know how strong I'm going to get, but I'm going to do what I can to help people."

"And I'll help you do it," Maya said, folding her arms. "You may think me heartless right now, but just wait until you are put in a situation where something truly awful happens in front of you and you are powerless to stop it. Sometimes that very action you wish to take will make something even worse happen."

"Like what?" Kalli asked, marching over to Maya. "Give us an example."

Maya sighed and sat on my bed. "Listen, you two. If a war were to erupt in the high house, it would spill out into the rest of the world. Millions of innocent lives would be lost. There is history."

"Ah hah!" Jorvais announced, running back into the room while holding a vial of red liquid that bubbled menacingly. "You do not, in fact, have a disease."

"Then what's wrong with us?" Maya asked with a look of confusion on her face.

"You have all been poisoned," Jorvais replied.

The good news was that I didn't have an MTD, but the problem was that the poison was unknown, and we didn't have the antidote. We sat around a conference table as Jorvais explained his findings. Kalli voiced the question that was on my mind. "Will Scuawk die?"

He shook his head. "Fortunately, she was brought to me right away. Any longer and I believe she would have succumbed to the poison. However, she will have to remain under my care indefinitely until we can find the antidote. This poison taints your core, which causes it to spread all throughout your body."

"Why aren't we affected by it?" Maya asked.

Jorvais smiled at her. "I am sure you are already aware of the answer to that question. Your bloodline prevents you from taking any lasting damage. While I still don't fully understand it, your regenerative abilities are significantly more potent than anything I've ever heard of. It's likely that you're just out healing the poison."

"So, we're fine?" Kalli asked hopefully.

"Not exactly," Jorvais replied. "I recommend that none of you touch another living being until you have this poison cleared up."

Maya looked furious. "Nobody? Not even physical contact?"

I began to laugh as I realized Maya's dilemma. "Too bad, sis. No servants for you for a while."

She huffed and taunted me back. "It is a shame. You're fortunate enough to have already infected your partner. You can touch her all you want."

"No, he can't!" Kalli replied.

I can't?

She stuck her tongue out at me. ***Not all you want! No.***

Jorvais cleared his throat to get our attention. "Let's get back on track here. I am a very busy man. Antidotes are not my specialty. You either need to seek out an alchemist or find the original, provided there is one."

"When did you first start to feel bad?" Maya asked, clasping her hands on the table.

I had to think about it for a moment. When did I first notice the black specks in my mana? Could it have been some residual corruption from when I dealt with that vampire, Carmilla? No, I had awakened a ton of people since then and none of them dropped dead. It was more recent. Then it hit me.

"Mardella! That blade of hers," I spat the words out. She had got me after all. "The blade must have been poisoned."

Everyone was silent until Kalli jumped to her feet. "That's great!"

"What?" Maya asked, staring at the pyromancer.

"She lived here, right?" Kalli explained. "That means the antidote might be right under our nose."

"Oh," Maya replied, rubbing her chin. "That is possible. She does have an estate here. We can look into it, but she hasn't officially been accused of a crime. We can't simply march in and—"

"What do you mean she isn't accused of a crime?" I choked out the words. "She nearly killed me. She tried to make me marry her daughter. She kidnapped Wendy. I'm pretty sure she was behind the death of Stephanie. I can go on. Where do I go to press charges?"

Maya just sighed. "Melvin. It isn't that simple. If you publicly accuse her, there will be an investigation, and then a trial. That's saying she even turns up. Think about the repercussions for her daughter and our sister in the meantime."

"What if I just make an antidote?" I asked, looking for something to edit.

Not finding anything, I fished around in my fanny pack and pulled out a small rock. Then I went to edit it into an antidote. The problem was that I knew next to nothing about antidote creation. Did I just call it an antidote and hope for the best? I tried to search for antidotes on the M-Phone and hundreds of different results popped up. All of them had unique names.

Looking up at Jorvais, I asked, "Would you happen to know the name of the antidote? I can edit one if I know what it's called."

He laughed. "Ah, yes. You are the resident manipulator, aren't you?

To be frank, if I knew the name of the poison, I could whip up an antidote myself. This is why we need the cooperation of its creator. It's difficult to guess if we don't know the specifics of what went into it.

"Oh, wait! What about Kiki?" I thought out loud. "Can't Alariel let us into her mother's estate?"

Maya rubbed her chin thoughtfully. "Why, yes. Yes, she can. I suppose we can send for them. I believe they are enjoying their honeymoon at the summer cabin. If you wish, the two of you can accompany the airship out there and pick them up. There is a chance the antidote could be there, too.

"Let's do that!" I exclaimed. "I always wanted to ride an airship."

———

I stood at the front of the ship as it sailed majestically through the clouds.

Come over here, Kalli. There's this scene from a movie I want to reenact.

Kalli stood as far from the side of the airship as she could. *I'd rather not. Is there something you can do with your mana to make me less afraid of heights?*

I looked at her in confusion.

But you flew on the phoenix all the time.

She shook her head. *That's different. I was in control.*

I wasn't sure what to do, so I walked over to her and hugged her. Kalli was trembling as she nestled into my arms. *Just do this until we land, and I'll be fine.*

———

Meanwhile, in Poland...

It actually worked. Miss Boszczyk hadn't expected that. The more elaborate experiments never did. It was her job to test, document, and report. Now, she was stuck with a dilemma. The device had punched a hole in the very fabric of the universe. The only problem was that she had dismissed everyone but the worker, Antoni.

Then there was another problem. The portal had let off some kind of a pulse that fried all of her electronics. Not only did she lose all of her precious data, but she couldn't even call the result in or request assistance.

"What do you want to do, ma'am?" Antoni spoke, bringing her out of her thoughts.

She looked at the brave worker who stayed. "Well, we succeeded. Do you see the anomaly over there? It's a door to another world. We are on the brink of changing everything."

Either that or it was the beginning of a horror film. Miss Boszczyk couldn't decide which. Antoni motioned toward the Jeep they arrived in. "Would you like me to drive back to town and…"

She looked at the Jeep. It was probably fried, too. "There's no time for that. I need you to test it."

"What?" Antoni froze, looking at the portal. "How would I do that, ma'am?"

Miss Boszczyk fixed the man with the best smile she could muster. "Consider it like a door. I want you to walk through."

He took a few steps toward the portal, stopping just short of coming into contact with it. "Is it safe, ma'am?"

She considered how to answer. In theory, it was very safe. Exactly like a door. Of course, she had no clue how long the gate would last once the machine stopped functioning. There was also a myriad of other unknowns.

Miss Boszczyk dug through her duffle bag and pulled out a metallic hazmat suit. "Put this on, and it will be perfectly safe."

Antoni tugged the bulky garment over his worker's attire. Then he returned to the portal and reached out to touch its shimmery surface. The portal rippled just like a pool of water.

He took his gloved hand back and examined it before waving to Miss Boszczyk. "It didn't hurt."

"Very good," Miss Boszczyk replied, impatient to get results. "Now, step through!"

He turned and took one long step. The surface of the portal parted as he passed through it, and then he was gone. Once it had done its job, the portal closed.

"Great," Miss Boszczyk groaned. "Now, I have to walk back by myself."

[13]

I HAD zero experience with poison. After multiple attempts to purify my mana, I took to the M-Phone for advice. Conveniently, the Medimancer app was still open, so I looked up topics on poison.

Poison: A substance capable of inducing illness or death when absorbed into the blood.

Poison wasn't in my blood. It was my mana that was affected. I tried another search.

Mana Poisoning: Artificial substance introduced to the body that corrupts mana. Typically curse-like in nature, mana poisoning is generally challenging to reverse.

Scrolling further down, I found a section about antidotes.

Generally, when poison that affects the soul is introduced, an antidote is prepared at the same time as a safeguard. Other methods for mana cleansing include curse breaking and divination.

Kalli had stopped trembling by that point and looked over my shoulder. *Can you do any of that stuff?*

I don't even know what it is, let alone if I can do it.

We got distracted as the airship passed between a pair of high mountain peaks. Since it was Maya's personal sky yacht, the only other person aboard was the captain, and he hadn't said a single word to us.

I don't think I've ever been here before, Kalli informed me as we sailed past the snow-frosted peaks.

It was strange to feel as warm as I did when there was snow twenty feet on either side of us. Once we cleared the mountains, the airship began descending into a lush valley that was littered with trees. In the distance was the cabin. Of course, I could hardly call it that. It looked more like a resort with interlinked buildings made from notched logs.

———

Kiki and Alariel stood waiting for us when the airship touched down. A cradle stood on one of the rooftops that the airship glided into smoothly.

"Welcome to the summer cabin," Kiki announced as we made our way down the gangplank. "Normally, I'd hug you but not while you're sick."

I laughed at her. "Since when have you ever hugged me?"

She shrugged. "Maybe I was about to start. Who knows?"

Alariel smiled from behind her. "I've taken the liberty of checking Mother's study. I'm afraid there doesn't seem to be anything that looks like poison or an antidote."

"Should we just go back to the high house, then?" Kalli asked, looking back at the ship.

"No!" Kiki snapped. "You just flew all the way out here. You don't get to leave before you check out the cabin. It is so awesome here. Just wait until you see the moose."

Alariel laughed and hip-checked Kiki. "I told you before, they aren't called moose here. They are called bramblers."

"Well that's a stupid name," Kiki replied. "I am going to call them moose."

We all laughed as Alariel led us inside. The interior of the cabin was a stark contrast to the rustic design of the outside. Exquisite lilac rugs lined the sleek hardwood floor in the hall we entered from the rooftop. Paintings of various people with purple hair lined the walls. It was definitely a family retreat for Alariel's family.

"Can we look around?" I asked as Alariel guided us with purpose. "Maybe Mardella has a hidden chamber or something where she hid all the cursed items. I saw it in a movie once."

"That's unlikely," Alariel called over her shoulder. "I practically grew up here. I know every inch of this place. It's more likely that anything evil is in one of her other houses. This is where she kept things she didn't care about. Like me."

Kiki took her hands. "She cared about you in her own twisted way. At least she didn't sell you like my mom did."

It was fairly obvious that we weren't going to find any antidotes at the cabin, so I asked, "How many other houses does your mom own?"

Alariel, who had been whispering to Kiki, replied, "I'm not sure. Four that I know of. There is our private suite in Dabia, the high house, this cabin, and the castle. I always thought she had more, though. There were times when she would disappear for weeks, and I had no idea where went."

Kiki raised a finger in the air. "Perhaps she's there now. In one of the secret hideouts."

"Where do you think she was most likely to have hidden something?" Kalli asked, speaking for the first time since we landed.

Alariel looked through a window in the direction of the mountain pass. "Well, your best bet is going to be the castle. We have already searched here, and Kiki can tell you that our suite in Dabia isn't very big."

Kiki laughed. "If you call seven rooms not very big, then, sure."

"Well comparatively," Alariel conceded. "I also doubt you will find anything incriminating in the high house. Our family is not the most powerful on Gaia, and she wouldn't hide anything incriminating where it could be seized. So, that leaves the castle. It's also the only place where certain areas were off-limits to me."

"How do we get there?" Kalli asked. "Can we take the airship?"

Alariel laughed. It was a high-pitched sound somewhere between a shriek and a squeal. "That's complicated. You see, those loyal to Mother still live there. Even if they let me bring guests, they wouldn't just let me have full run of the place."

"Can we sneak in?" I asked, getting excited about the prospect.

She stared at me as though I were insane. "Well, it is possible. I mean, nobody would expect someone to try to sneak in, so it's not exactly guarded. I can't go with you, though. I'll give you a map and guide you in group chat. That's the best I can do."

While a part of me wanted to continue the quest for the antidote, there was another part of me excited to check out the cabin in the woods.

"What do you want to do first?" Kiki asked in excitement. "There is an awesome hot spring out back. Or we can play some magical games. There are a few things on Gaia that I know we don't have back on Earth."

I grinned at the two girls. "I was little curious about what kinds of games you two were playing out here."

"Hah." Kiki said with a smirk. "I'll bet you were. But, no, you only get to know about the PG rated games little brother."

That was how we ended up going to the hot spring. While Kalli was able to transform her dress into a bikini, I was forced to borrow a pair of shorts. While my artifact armor could transform into swimwear, it always felt like a murky black paste that got stuck to my skin.

By the time I made it out of the dressing room, three beautiful girls were waiting. Kiki smiled and said, "Took you long enough. How long does it take to put on a pair of shorts?"

The truth was, I was nervous. While I was used to being around Kalli, I suddenly found myself outnumbered and outgunned. It was Kalli who took pity on me. "Let's just get in already."

Taking her cue, I decided to do a cannonball.

SPLASH!

When I came up for air, I saw three glaring soaking wet girls. Kiki stuck her tongue out at me and shouted, "Jerk!"

Then she jumped in right next to me, sending a mini-tsunami cascading over me. She came up laughing. "Just kidding."

Kalli and Alariel took the stairs and entered the water. Alariel gave Kalli a sidelong glance before motioning to the two of us. "You can tell there are related, can't you?"

Kalli giggled. "Yep. You sure can."

The water in the hot springs was hot. Bubbles also came from somewhere, which made the springs feel like a hot tub back home. There was also a strange aroma in the water. I looked at Alariel and asked, "What's that smell?"

She sniffed the air for a moment before explaining. "That's magic. We scent the water to erase the sulfuric smell that this place has naturally. Smells nice, doesn't it?"

"I'm trying to figure out what it smells like," I said as I sniffed the air. "It reminds me of a new car smell."

Alariel gave me a puzzled look. "I'm not sure what this new car you speak of is, but the magic is designed to smell like cured leather."

Melvin? Are you there? We need you.

It was guild chat.

Esha? Is that you?

The troll's voice replied again, **Yes, my Lord. It's me. We have a problem back here.**

What kind of a problem? Can Celestea help you?

Esha sounded frustrated when she replied, **Humans don't understand our language. It is difficult to communicate.**

But I've seen you talk to them.

She replied, **That only works when we are in your presence, my Lord. Or Empress Kalliphae.**

Then I remembered the first time I met the trolls. The humans in Hudholm also couldn't speak to them. Deciding to leave the language problem for another day, I attempted to refocus the conversation.

Tell me what happened.

She sounded almost like she was laughing when she replied, **Our patrols discovered a human wandering the wilderness. We found him wearing a strange suit of armor, and none of the humans in the City Under the Mountain can communicate with him. We have citizens that speak Dabian and Celestean, and neither of them can talk to him either. I am suspicious he may have been up to something. Would it be possible for you to return?**

I looked to Kalli who gave me a small nod.

We will be right there.

Alariel smiled and said, "We can coordinate your visit to Mother's castle after you sort whatever that is out. Let's form a group so we can discuss details in private."

ALARIEL MORIN WOULD LIKE YOU INVITE YOU TO JOIN A GROUP

I grinned at Kiki. "She took your last name!"

Alariel blushed, and Kiki slapped me on the back. It really hurt because I wasn't wearing a shirt and her hand was wet. "Of course, she did. Did you forget we got married to satisfy your contract?"

Alariel gave Kiki a scandalized look. "Is that why you did it?"

"That wasn't the only reason." Kiki amended. "You know how I feel about you."

I waded over to Kalli and wrapped my arm around her. It seemed like they were going to argue, and I was anxious to find out about the mysterious visitor. Without warning, I folded mana over us and warped to Kalli's home point. We arrived with about fifty gallons of water in the throne room in Celestea Castle. Unfortunately for us, the throne room was in use.

"Kalliphae Celestea, uh, I refuse to say your last name!" Celestea screamed in outrage. "What are you wearing, young lady?"

It was Kalli's turn to scream as she realized she was still wearing the bikini. Spending two seconds scowling at me, she ran from the room, leaving me and her mom in the flooded chamber.

Redirecting her ire at me, Celestea shrieked, "What is the meaning of this? Where did all of this water come from, and why are the two of you half-naked?"

"Sorry," I muttered, beginning to follow Kalli.

"Wait," she called after me. "I, um, need your help with something."

I stopped in my tracks. It was rare for the queen mother to recognize my existence, let alone ask me for help. "What can I do for you?"

"It's Orpheus," she began. "He's sick. My daughter tells me you can help. Please. He is a valued member of this family and I fear he isn't going to make it."

Poison!

I thought the thought before I realized it, which shocked Kalli.

What? Who's poisoned?

Orpheus.

She gasped. **Oh, no!**

———

After changing clothes, Celestea led us over to Orpheus's chamber. He didn't look well. His eyes were sunk in, and his body was covered in sweat. Even though he was awake, he appeared delirious and didn't recognize us.

I looked at Celestea and said, "We need to get him to the high house. They have a doctor there that can help keep him stable while we look for an antidote."

"Antidote?" she asked, a frown forming on her face. "Do you think he's been poisoned?"

"Yes," I explained. "Most likely by me when I saved his life after the battle with Mardella. I didn't realize her sword was poisoned at the time."

She looked at me apprehensively. "Then why aren't you dying?"

Kalli placed a hand on her mom's shoulder. "That's complicated, Mother. You see, we have a special trait that makes us stronger than the poison. It can't kill us but, unfortunately, we're still infected."

I would have tried to help him, but I wasn't one hundred percent certain he was poisoned. I'd have to leave that diagnosis to a professional. Since we didn't have a fast way to return to the high house, I reached out to my sister in group chat.

Kiki, can you send us the airship? We think Orpheus is poisoned.

It's on the way. She replied immediately. *When the two of you left so suddenly, we decided to send it so you can go to the castle when you're ready.*

Turning to Celestea, I explained, "The high house is sending an airship to transport him to the infirmary there. My sister, Maya, will take good care of him."

Kalli stared at me. *Are you sure, Mel? You didn't even ask her.*

While I didn't know my sister well, I had a good feeling that she would help.

I think it will be fine. We need to find the antidote more than ever now. Let's go see this strange human so we can be ready to go when the airship arrives.

[14]

"It isn't safe," the man in the HAZMAT suit repeated for the tenth time.

I sighed. "It's safe. You can come out. Nobody here is going to hurt you."

He eyed the trolls in the distance as he backed away from me. "But, the radiation. Miss Boszczyk said I would be safe so long as I wore this. Those green people over there don't look so well."

"Are you talking about the trolls or the goblins?" I asked, slightly amused.

"Trolls?" he asked, his panicked breathing fogging up the suit. "Do you mean like Harry Potter?"

I laughed, more out of relief than anything else. "If it makes you feel any better, I'm also from Earth."

The man grew even more frantic, trying to look everywhere at once. "Is that why the sky is green? This isn't Earth?"

"Nope. This isn't Earth" I chuckled. "This is Gaia. How did you manage to travel to another world without realizing it?"

"I don't know," he admitted reluctantly. "Miss Boszczyk activated the machine, and this strange glowing mirror appeared. Then she asked me to climb through, so I did and here I am. Will I ever be able to go home? I have a wife and kids."

"Relax," I said, trying to get the man to calm down. "I'll make sure you get home. First, I need to ask you some questions. Let's start with your name. My name is Melvin. What's yours?"

He adjusted the baggy head covering before replying, "My name is Antoni. Are you sure it's safe to take this off? It's getting hot in here."

"Sure, it's safe," I replied. "I'm pretty sure you're the only person on Gaia wearing one of those."

He tugged at the back of the HAZMAT suit, contorting himself as he struggled to get free. I lent him a hand, and he finally emerged through a flap in the back. He wiped the sweat from his brow and said, "That feels much better. Now, how do I get home? I want to make it home in time for dinner."

"We can feed you," I said, not wanting him to go just yet. "I still have a feel more questions for you."

He raised an eyebrow at me. "Questions? Like what?"

"For starters, who sent you here?" I asked, wondering if some new threat was about to reveal itself. "What part of Earth did you come from?"

Antoni's accent gave me the impression that he wasn't from America, but I couldn't quite place it. He seemed just as curious about me as well. "I am from Teremyski." When he didn't get a response, he continued, "That's in Poland. Where do you live? You said you are also from Earth, right? You sound American."

"That's right," I explained. "Is being American a bad thing? I'm from California."

Antoni shook his head. "Not at all. I was just making an observation. How do you speak Polish so well?"

I grinned at him. "It's magic. I'm speaking English. You just hear me in Polish. I wonder what my accent sounds like to you."

"Magic?" Antoni asked, scratching his head. "Isn't that just a fairytale?"

"Kalli?" I said, turning to give her a nod. "Want to show him some magic?"

She rolled her eyes at me. ***You know you can show off just as well as I can.***

Then she did it anyway.

"Pvruzth."

Antoni cringed involuntarily as flames sprang to life in each of Kalli's hands. She made the fireballs that I had only seen her use in my dreams and soon they were orbiting around her. She winked at Antoni and said, "I am a pyromancer. I control fire."

He stared at her for a few moments before whispering. "Are you a goddess?"

I cut her off as she was about to answer, "Yep. She's totally a goddess, and also my girlfriend."

Kalli rewarded me with a face full of fire. "No! I am not a goddess. I *am* his girlfriend, though I have no idea why right now. Oh, and don't worry, I didn't hurt him. My flame is only hot when I want it to be."

I brushed the flame from my face and grinned at Antoni. "See, she loves me."

Kalli scoffed and stuck her tongue out. Antoni look around the cavern. "Can everyone here use magic?"

He backed away from a group of goblins that was wandering by as he spoke. I laughed and explained, "Well, that's tricky. Not everybody can do magic like Kalli. People have specialties but that just means they are awakened. Do you know if you're awakened?"

Antoni looked clueless. "What is awakened?"

"Well, that answers that," I muttered, wondering how much I should explain to the guy. "How about you tell me how you made it to this world. Who is the lady with the machine? Do you work for her?"

He hesitated for a second before answering, "I work for, uh, the TGB. It is my responsibility to haul and assemble heavy machinery. Things the scientists don't want to bother with. They do all of the fine-tuning. They push the buttons."

"What is the TGB?" I asked. "That sounds like the government."

Antoni laughed. "No! We don't work for the government. The TGB is a private organization. Very private."

Kalli tried to help by asking, "What does TGB stand for?"

Antoni stiffened as he replied, "I'm afraid, that's, uh, confidential. Please. I am not permitted to speak about the administration. I could lose my job."

"If I take you home, will you show me where the TGB is?" I asked, wondering if I could bypass his confidentiality agreement by visiting his office.

His eyes widened as he took in my proposition. "Do you mean to tell me you only intend to take me home if I show you where I work?"

I nodded. "That's right. I need to know who just poked a hole in my empire and sent a low-level grunt through in a HAZMAT suit. It seems like the only responsible thing to do."

"I am not a grunt," he complained, looking visibly annoyed. "Coming here was an accident. I just want to return to my family. Please."

I turned to Kalli.

I'm going to go with him. I'll teleport back to you once I figure out who sent him.

Kalli nodded. *Don't take too long. We need to get Orpheus to the high house.*

If the airship arrives before I'm back, take off without me. I can teleport to you no matter where you go.

Kalli surprised me when she leaned into me, wrapping her arms around me. Then she kissed me. *Be safe over there. We don't know anything about this guy.*

All too soon, she let go and hurried off. It took me a minute to recompose myself.

I'll be careful and come back in no time.

I didn't expect her to answer, but she did. *You'd better!*

Turning back to Antoni, I asked, "Are you ready to go home?"

"Now?" he asked, looking like he wanted to climb back into the HAZMAT suit. "How do you travel between worlds?"

"Magic," I explained, walking over to him and taking his hand. "Are you ready to go home?"

He gasped for air and redoubled his efforts to climb back into the suit. I started helping him as he asked, "Will it hurt?"

I grinned, thinking back to my first time teleporting. "Well, you might feel sick. It's okay to throw up. Try holding your breath, and it will feel a lot better."

Antoni answered by fumbling with the flap until it was sealed. Taking that as a sign that he was ready to go, I said, "Think only of your home." And then I folded our mana over the both of us.

Walking through the void was becoming second nature for me. It was strange following a person I didn't know to his point of origin. I just had to have faith that his soul knew where it was going.

———

BOOM!

The ground shook around me as we appeared. Something had exploded right next to us. I looked at Antoni in shock and asked, "What is this?"

He was on his hands and knees, trying to crawl behind a wall while splattering his suit with his own sick. "I don't understand. Why did you take me here?"

"Where is here?" I screamed. "I took you to your home!"

"This is Krakovets," he gurgled, gasping for breath. "I have not lived here in a long time."

"Why is there a tank?" I asked, sliding next to him behind the wall.

"I don't know," he replied, unzipping the hood from the suit. "The war wasn't supposed to have spread this far west."

"War?" I asked, wondering what I just teleported into.

"Do you not watch the news?" he growled, peeking out over the wall.

"You still didn't explain why we ended up here," I yelled back. "My spell is supposed to take you to your home."

He turned back to give me a hard stare. "I grew up in Ukraine. This hasn't been my home for many years."

BOOM!

I groaned as the building across the street was annihilated by another blast from the tank. Gunshots rang out as unknown people retaliated.

"We need to get out of here," I barked, reaching out to grab Antoni. "I'm going to have to take you back with me. It isn't safe for you here."

"No, wait!" Antoni shouted, clearly agitated. "You can use magic, right? Can't you do something about that tank?"

I looked back over the wall to discover the barrel of the tank swiveling in our direction. It was now or never. Fight or flight. Those were the options.

Item: T-72A Tank
Components: Iron, Steel, Petroleum, Gun Powder, Rubber
Item Rank: C
Item Level: 1
Item Owner: Puntin

DELETE

ERROR: TARGET OCCUPIED
CONFIRM DELETE Y/N

I crossed my fingers and prayed that I wasn't about to kill someone.

YES.

For a moment, nothing happened. I was afraid the tank was going to open fire, and I wasn't sure if my armor could stop a tank blast. Then it wasn't there. It was gone, vanished, deleted.

A distant yelp was all the proof I got that the operators weren't deleted along with the tank. I didn't bother to stay to find out if they suffered any injuries. Grabbing Antoni, I twisted my mana over the two of us and thought only of Kalli.

———

Kalli shrieked when we appeared in front of her. She lunged at me and wrapped me in my second hug of the day. *I was so worried. Stop rushing into danger.*

I pulled her closer.

There was no way I could have known that was going to happen.

Antoni poked me on the shoulder. "Um, guys. I hate to break up your reunion, but does this mean I never get to go home?"

I laughed, letting Kalli go. "No. It just means we have to go through the bathroom."

"Um, what does that mean?" Antoni asked, looking at me like I had gone mad.

———

It was Celestea's turn to shriek when the three of us arrived suddenly in the throne room. When she recovered, she scolded us, "You two need to stop doing that, and what is this thing?"

"Sorry. No time," I croaked out, dragging Antoni out of the throne room. "We need to be back by the time the airship arrives."

The three of us raced through the castle toward the queen's suite. When we entered the bath chamber, Antoni gasped. "You call this a water closet? The two of you must be very rich."

"It is a castle, after all," I explained, pulling open the door to Lavender's house. "We need to go through here."

———

We found Lavender waiting for us in my bedroom. "Welcome back, everyone. I see you've encountered the TGB."

"You know who they are?" I asked, not really surprised that Lavender kept it from us.

She yawned. "Yes, I know of them. They are a group of scientists with an unquenchable thirst for knowledge. As you have seen, they are starting to make progress in interdimensional travel."

"Is that all?" I asked, looking at Antoni with renewed interest.

Kalli repeated her question from earlier. "What does TGB stand for?"

Lavender replied, "It's called the Technician's General Bureau. It's run by a very curious individual."

———

Meanwhile, in Ukraine...

A man watched the surveillance video from a rural city. He twirled a long pointy beard in his fingers. "Very interesting. Another one has appeared. A most worthy prey."

[15]

"CAN YOU HELP ANTONI GET HOME?" I asked, feeling sorry for the man in the HAZMAT suit.

Lavender nodded. "Yes, I will have him home in no time."

I chuckled and motioned to a wardrobe in the corner of the room. "Let me guess. There's a portal in there that leads to Poland."

"Don't be absurd. That portal leads to Quackenglokt. The home of one of your professors," Lavender said, taking a slip of paper from a bag that looked like a fancy purse. "I took the liberty of purchasing him an airline ticket to Warsaw. I take it you can handle things from there, correct Mr. Peresada?"

The HAZMAT suit rustled as Antoni shifted uncomfortably. "Er, yes, that will do. Excuse me, Miss. How do you know my name? Have we met?"

Lavender shook her head, the amused smirk never leaving her face. "No. We have never met. Just consider me mysterious. For now, these children must be getting back to their adventure in another world. How would you like to join me for a cup of tea?"

Antoni continued to fidget before Lavender took him by the hand and guided him to the door. Before she left, she winked at us. "Carry on, then. Don't do anything I wouldn't do."

———

I wonder if there's anything she wouldn't actually do.

We stood at an airship landing I didn't know existed in Celestea. Beside us, Orpheus lay on a stretcher, coughing occasionally but otherwise motionless.

Kalli heard my thoughts and gave me the stink eye. *There are plenty of things a lady wouldn't do, and you're not allowed to do any of them.*

I laughed.

Do you mean like peeing standing up?

Kalli gagged. *Ew! Enough about that. Have you come up with any ideas for breaking into Mardella's castle?*

I do have one idea, but you might not like it.

She raised an eyebrow. *What is it?*

Well, I can ghost you. I don't think I can do it to myself because I might not be able to undo it. Do you remember what happened to Eddie when we first met him? Nobody but me could see or hear him. I can do it to you and you can sneak in. Also, if anything goes wrong, I can teleport to you in an instant.

Kalli frowned. I could tell she was nervous about the idea. Nobody wanted to be ghosted. However, she steeled herself and said, *Try it now. I want to know what it feels like.*

———

"Sir, will Lady Kalliphae be long?" the captain asked, speaking to me for the first time.

"She's here," I replied. "Feel free to take off when you like."

He must have been used to mysterious things happening because he just nodded and spun on his heel. Then we were airborne. I leaned over the rails as we passed over the villages of Meltopia. Or was it Celestea? It was weird being both a queendom and an empire at the time time. I chose not to question it. The people were happy and that was all that mattered.

Beside me, Kalli watched Kalliville pass beneath us. ***Being ghosted isn't so bad. I mean it might suck only being able to talk to you if it was permanent, but it's fine for a little while.***

Travel by airship was much faster than any other form of transportation on Gaia but it still took us half a day to get to the high house.

Maya met us at the airship landing in front of Jorvais' infirmary with a couple of attendants to help manage Orpheus. "Welcome back. Where is your mate? It's odd for you to be traveling solo."

I grinned. "She's around. Can you really not see her?"

Her smile betrayed her. "I can. It was just a little odd for you to hide her like that. I was curious so I thought I'd play along."

"She can see me?" Kalli asked. "Won't that make the plan fail if people can see me?"

I shook my head. "No. Only people from our family can see ghosted people."

Maya corrected me. "Not just our family. There are others. On Gaia, I would say less than ten people would be able to do so. Ghosting is an advanced form of invisibility, so normal methods of detection will not work. That's because it was designed to isolate offenders from the awakened community. Do you mind telling me why you ghosted her?"

"We are going to sneak into Mardella's castle to look for the antidote," I explained. "Can you offer us any assistance?"

Maya shook her head. "While I have no great love for the woman, I cannot move against her without direct provocation. I am aware of the fact that she has wronged you but outside of formally charging her, we have no recourse. I can assure you that she lacks the skill to see through a ghosting."

"Can you give us a ride there?" I asked, motioning to the airship.

"Of course," she replied, getting a small nod from the captain. "Alcobar here will take you there, no problem. I'll even give you a map of the area. Just give us a little time to load supplies."

———

By the third airship voyage, the novelty was starting to wear off. One thing I noticed was that Gaia was much bigger than I thought it was. We passed by several villages and at least one major town on the way to Mardella's castle, and I didn't recognize any of them.

Alcobar finally spoke with us as we got close. He emerged from the cabin and pointed to a small hill on the horizon. "We will drop you off there. It's several miles from the castle, but to get any closer would alert them to your presence. Once I drop the two of you off, I have been instructed to make a delivery and hopefully distract the guards. I wish you luck on your quest."

"Thanks," I replied, realizing Kalli couldn't say anything. "Don't wait for us. We will teleport out when we are finished."

He looked around for Kalli, then shrugged, marching back to the cabin. The airship flew low for the final leg of the journey, hidden from the castle by the hill in front of us. When we got there, the airship hovered five feet above the ground and stopped.

Kalli and I didn't wait for confirmation before jumping to the ground. No sooner had we disembarked than the airship rose majestically to the sky and proceeded toward the castle.

It looks like we're on our own now.

Kalli gave me an uneasy smile. ***Don't worry. It'll be fine.***

I nodded, wishing I felt the same confidence as she did. The dense forest forced me to summon my mana blade to cut a path. In the distance, we could hear calls of animals or monsters that were unfamiliar to us, though none showed themselves.

After a while, I got tired of swinging the blade around, so Kalli took over and used her flame to burn the thick shrubs and vines. I was impressed with how much control she had over fire, incinerating only what she needed.

When she needed a break, I decided to just start deleting large swaths of forest, careful to leave the canopy so that nobody could track our progress from above.

———

Finally!

I heaved a theatrical sigh of relief when we emerged from the forest. That left only an empty field between us and the castle. The airship concluded its business and took off at some point while we were making our way through the forest.

So much for a distraction.

Kalli shook her head. *It'll be fine. I'm sure his visit served a purpose.*

Mardella's castle looked more like a dungeon, murky gray turrets and embattlements hung low to the ground surrounding an inner keep with only a solitary tower rising into the sky. The whole thing looked dreary as though it were meant to be evil.

I turned to Kalli, giving her hand a squeeze.

Are you ready to do this? You just say the word and I'll teleport right to you.

Kalli thought about it. *Just make sure you're paying attention if I get in trouble.*

I edited a pebble into a toilet. Kalli crinkled her nose. *What are you doing?*

I shrugged.

Well, I needed something to sit on. Besides, I kind of have to go.

She wrinkled her nose. *Whatever. Just be sure to delete that when you're done.*

Then, she took off in the direction of the castle.

———

I sat on my throne in the forest with my eyes closed, watching Kalli as she approached the outer wall of the castle.

Do you know how you are going to sneak in?

Kalli stuck out her tongue at no one in particular. *Oh, please. I used to do stuff like this all the time back at the monastery. When you're an orphan there's nobody to tell you to be careful. Honestly, I sometimes thought they preferred I'd break my neck. One less mouth to feed.*

Wow, that nun didn't seem like she was that mean.

Kalli laughed. *No, she was always fair with me. That was just what I imagined in my head when I climbed trees or high walls.*

As I watched, Kalli rubbed her hands together and started to climb the outer wall, digging her fingers into divots in the stone. The going was slow, but Kalli slowly made her way to the top of the enceinte.

The castle wasn't guarded at all. Not a soul was in sight no matter which way we looked. *Do you think the place is abandoned?*

I don't think so. Alcobar was docked here earlier. He had to have met with someone. Keep your eyes peeled.

She nodded and pressed on in silence. One thing ghosting couldn't hide us from was closed doors. Kalli had to open them, and that could arouse suspicion. The first one didn't cause any issues. She slipped into the castle undetected as there was still nobody in sight.

That luck quickly ran out as we started to hear a creaking noise in the distance. Whenever Kalli made her way through the halls, the noise was never far off. She pressed herself against the wall and held her breath, listening for any sign of whatever made the noise.

Every time, nothing emerged from the shadows. Then, Kalli pressed on, her heart thundering in her chest. *I have a bad feeling, Mel. Do you think we should leave?*

A part of me wanted to. I couldn't stand the fact that Kalli was in danger. Just when I was about to tell her so, we both caught sight of a stairwell leading down. She paused. *Should I check it out?*

Every bone in my body screamed, "No!" but I bit my tongue.

Okay, but be ready to teleport if you run into anything.

We both held our breath as she descended. It was abnormally dark as if the stairwell was intentionally left without any light source. We were fortunate that Kalli shared my traits because without God Eye, she would be blind.

Again, we heard noises but when Kalli stopped to see what made them, nothing was there. At the bottom of the stairs stood another door. Kalli frowned. *This is worse than that dungeon we did back on Earth.*

At least you could see the monsters in the dungeon.

As I said the words, I couldn't help but wonder why the place seemed abandoned. Where was everybody? What were all those noises? Before I had a chance to think, Kalli opened the door.

CREAK.

The door made the loudest sound yet as it swung open. Kalli cringed and hid in a corner, trying not to make a sound even though the ghosting already did that for her.

We both waited with bated breath for something to happen, but nothing did. If anybody was in there, they either hadn't noticed or they were waiting for us to proceed into the trap.

This is a bad idea. You should go back up the stairs.

Kalli shook her head. ***No. I have a gut feeling that something is down here. Trust me. I'll be careful.***

I didn't like it one bit as she picked herself up and peeked through the door. The lower level wasn't a jail as I had suspected. It was a long hall connecting a series of rooms. The first several contained stacks of rolled parchments and walls lined with dust-covered books.

Then we came across a room filled with cages. The cages weren't built for humans. Each cage contained the carcasses of various monsters and animals. I wondered if Mardella's absence caused their demise.

At the end of the hall, we found what we were looking for. Only, the room wasn't empty. Beady eyes looked back at us through the darkness.

[16]

Is she looking at you?

Kalli didn't answer as she did her best not to exist. The sound was growing louder, echoing through the hall. It came from everywhere and nowhere all at the same time.

The creature in the room didn't move. Glowing red eyes seemed to home in on Kalli. She shuddered and I felt it. *It's looking at me, Mel. What do I do?*

I stood.

I'm coming!

No, don't! her voice screamed in my ear. Kalli didn't move a muscle as she faced off with the silent figure. The sounds in the background became a shrill wailing that reminded me of something.

Kalli took a deep breath to steady herself. *I don't think it sees me. It knows something is off, but it can't detect me.*

What are those noises?

Kalli shuddered as the sounds continued in the background. *I don't know but it's creeping me out.*

It felt like an eternity before anything changed. Finally, the eyes turned away from Kalli, and a hoarse voice croaked, "Keep it down out there."

The wailing got louder like a spoiled child throwing a tantrum before stopping completely. Kalli and I looked around in hopes of seeing what was making the noise only to be greeted with nothing but shadows.

A few seconds later, she stepped into the room. From inside, I was able to get a better idea of what caught Kalli's attention. Flasks and vials lined one wall. Rows of vials and beakers that wouldn't have been out of place in a meth lab took up half of the room.

It was further apparent that the creature, an old crone as it turned out, didn't see us as she ignored the intruder in the room completely. I wanted to inspect her but was unable to do so through Kalli's eyes.

She tiptoed her way through the room over to the workstation with the table with the vials. *I don't know what I'm looking for. Also, if I try to pick anything up, she will notice.*

Look. There are some notes on the other end. Can you read what they say?

Kalli made her way down the table, closer to the crone. The old woman had retreated to the far end of the room where there was a cage with something inside. I squinted my eyes, wanting a better look, but Kalli was focused on notes.

Kalli, look over there. There's a cage. What is that?

Kalli looked up and gave a soundless shriek. It was a person.

That can't be!

It was Raverly, and it was moving. Kalli shook her head in disbelief. *That's impossible. He died. We saw his spirit. You took him back to Earth, right?*

That's right. What did you do with his body?

She covered her mouth. *It was buried. I'm positive.*

We watched in horror as the crone poked and prodded Rave's body. It uttered an inhuman groan and sat up, causing us both to scream. The crone crooned, "Good. Gather your strength. Soon enough, you will lead my army and finish the work that my useless child started. You will make a lovely pet, my puppet."

You need to get out of there, right now.

I wasn't sure what we were witnessing, but there had to be a better way to get an antidote. Kalli shook her head, reaching down to grab the notes. *If I can just get this without her noticing.*

I sat there on the throne in the middle of the forest and prayed for good luck. Kalli gently lifted the parchments and tipped them into her bag. The crone was still whispering something to Rave in the cage and didn't seem to notice.

Emboldened by her success, Kalli went after the vials next. She was on her fourth one when the crone reacted. "There! Intruder! Someone is in the keep. Come quick my pets, sniff them out!"

The wailing was back in full force as the darkness melted off the walls and took shape. With the shadows peeled from the walls, light that had previously been banished bled into the room. It suddenly made sense why it was as dark as it was in the basement. Wraiths materialized by the dozen and, suddenly, the room was filled with them.

While they still couldn't sense Kalli, there were so many wraiths that it was only a matter of time before one of them got lucky.

Screw this! I'm coming.

I was determined not to make the same mistake I made with Stephanie. Folding mana around me, I willed myself to Kalli's side. The toilet and I appeared in front of her.

She groaned despite herself. *Really, Melvin? You had to bring that thing?*

It was an accident. I had to come rescue you!

Kalli's outrage overpowered her fear. *I don't you to get rid of it!*

While they still couldn't see Kalli, the wraiths had no problem at all seeing me. All I could do was throw myself in front of her as they converged on us.

Then all hell broke loose. The number of shadows in the room doubled as more dark figures emerged to clash with the wraiths. A gravelly voice that sounded familiar said, "Pretenders shall be banished from the darkness. You shall not lay a single claw on our dark master."

On the other side of the sea of darkness, the hag pointed at me. "You! How dare you invade my sanctum! I will have you for my collection!"

I backed into Kalli as the hag stomped toward me.

Did you get everything you need? I think it's time for us to get the heck out of here.

Kalli nodded emphatically. ***Go, go, go, go!***

I folded mana over us, trying to leave the toilet behind this time. Just before we stepped into the void, I felt something grasp my tunic. Then we were standing in the vacant throne room of Celestea castle. Only we weren't alone. The crone came along for the ride.

In the light, she looked even older and more decrepit than she had in the dark. Hunched over almost in half, she wore a black cowl and had warts all over her face. She glared daggers at us as we backed away from here. "You must be confident to think that you can defeat me, even without my minions."

"Who are you?" I asked, not knowing what else to say.

"Hah!" the crone replied with a sneer. "You come to my home and claim to not know who I am?"

Then, I remembered that I wanted to inspect her.

Name: Altara Vestara
Class: Puppetmaster
Level: 93
Affection Level: Hostile

Vestara? Where had I heard that name before? I blinked at her. "You're related to Alariel! Are you Mardella's mother?"

Altara cackled. "Mother-in-law. What a disappointment she turned out to be. Defeated by a whelp. Tell me, how did you manage to best her?"

I, uh…" I stuttered, unsure how to answer the question. "She just escaped."

The latter part was true, except it hadn't been Mardella that fled. It was Malric. Altara pressed her advantage. "That woman wouldn't have needed to flee from you, child. What are you hiding?"

Kalli had her eyes closed as she concentrated her mana into the castle around us. I wasn't sure what she was doing, but I decided to keep talking to give her time. "She was scared of my potential as a manipulator. I almost deleted her."

"Child," she sighed, taking a step toward me, "do not play games with me. I know all about manipulators as well as that bloodline you possess. While it is true that you have great potential, you are still just a boy. If you want to live long enough to realize it, you had best respect your elders. Now, we are going to return to my keep and…"

Suddenly, a panel on the wall slid open behind the throne, revealing two suits of armor about twice the size of a normal human.

CLANG!

CLANG!

CLANG!

With every step they made, the throne room shook around us. Kalli opened an eye and said, "I've activated the castle's defenses. Do you think you can defeat ancient magic?"

Altara hesitated, watching the automatons as they lumbered toward her. Then she looked up at me. "Well played, manipulator. You may have saved yourself this time, but mark my words. You will be mine."

Then, in a flash of darkness, she was gone. Kalli heaved a sigh of relief and concentrated. The automatons turned and thundered back to their resting places. Just then, the doors to the throne room burst open, and Celestea entered, accompanied by a dozen guards. "Melvin! What is the meaning of this? Why are you in here by yourself? And how did you activate the royal protectors?"

"By myself?" I mumbled.

Then I remembered that Kalli was still ghosted. I quickly opened her menu to remedy the situation. Celestea gasped when she appeared out of nowhere.

Kalli glared at me before walking over to her mom. "Sorry, Mother. We were trying to find the antidote and accidentally brought an evil woman back with us. I had to call the guardians to make her leave."

"Did you have any luck?" Celestea asked, moving over to the throne to have a seat.

Kalli reached for her bag. "Right! I forgot about that. I did manage to get some things before we were attacked."

The first thing she produced was the notes I had seen. We looked them over together.

23-13-4452

+02:02:09

More progress has been made on the reanimation process. I will bring him back for certain this time. All that is needed is an emissary to reclaim his soul from the other side. Several vessels have been selected as potential hosts.

VK

23-27-4452

+01:09:27

The shadow nation is slowly expanding. Coverage of Celestea is roughly eighty percent. The child does well to hide our endeavors from the high house.

Plans for Luna may soon yield fruit.

VK

25-01-4452

+07:11:09

All is lost. The manipulator is beyond our grasp once again. Plans for expansion have been halted pending location of the child. The only hope is that one of the specimens may yet yield fruit. Only time will tell.

VK

I sighed heavily when I realized that none of the letters had anything to do with poison. Then Kalli pulled a handful of vials from her bag. She managed to grab four different liquids in all. *One of these might be the poison. Should we show them to Jorvais and see what he thinks?*

The problem was we forgot to invite Maya to the group to arrange for a ride back to the high house. I turned to Celestea and asked, "Does the queendom have any airships?"

Celestea looked at me like I had grown a second head. "Airships require high-level wind or gravity magic. It isn't something you can just buy with money. The captain usually provides the necessary magic for the ship to stay aloft."

I rubbed my chin as I thought about it. "I need to take a close look next time I see it."

Kalli smirked. *You want to make one. Don't you?*

Well, I can use wind magic after all? How hard can it be?

She shrugged. *I don't know. You had better be careful though. It would hurt if you crashed.*

Scrapping that idea, I decided to check in with Kiki and Alariel.

Hey, guys, we just made it back from the castle.

Alariel answered first, *Did you find an antidote? I forgot to mention, but the basement is probably a good place to look.*

Too late, Kalli explained. That was the first place I looked. *There were hundreds of those wraith things down there and a scary old lady.*

Then I remembered the most gruesome detail.

They had Raverly's body down there. How did they get their hands on his corpse? And why were they reanimating it?

What? Kiki asked, sounding on edge.

Alariel sounded slightly agitated as she asked, *Are you sure that's what you saw, and who is this old lady? I know all of the servants there and none of them are old.*

I'm just telling you what I saw. She teleported with us when we escaped, too. Then she teleported away when Kalli activated the castle. Her name is Altara Vestara.

Alariel shrieked, showing rare emotion. *That's impossible! Grandmother is dead. I saw her body at the funeral. She's been dead most of my life.*

Kalli replied, trying her best to soothe her. *I saw her in person as well as her menu. That is her name, and she is very old. I don't know what to tell you about the funeral. Do you think they faked it?*

Alariel sounded shaken when she replied, *I don't know. I need to go to the castle and see for myself.*

Kiki quickly added, *I'll go with you.*

No! Alariel gasped, taking a few quick breaths to calm herself. *If what Melvin says is true, it isn't safe for non-family.*

I am family! Kiki barked.

Alariel sighed. *Not like this. While you are family, there may still be some in my family that don't accept you. I can't run the risk of them doing something. I need to get to the bottom of this on my own.*

Kiki growled. *Do I need to remind you what my bloodline is and what it means? I may not have reached my full potential, but you aren't allowed to play the 'my family is more powerful than yours is' card because we both know that isn't true.*

Let's take this discussion private. Alariel said in a voice just above a whisper. *Melvin, I'm sorry we can't be of more assistance right now. As you can see, we now have some things to sort out.*

Kalli replied for me, *Don't worry about it. I hope you work everything out. Please, let us know that you are safe after you visit the castle.*

Alariel chuckled. *Don't worry. It's my home. I'll be fine.*

We'll be fine, Kiki corrected.

Then the chat was silent.

What now? Kalli asked in MateChat.

Let's ask Lavender about the poison. We didn't bring it up the last time we saw her.

[17]

"CAN I COME WITH YOU?" a tiny voice spoke as we headed into the bathroom. "You're going to Lavender's house, right?"

Kalli turned to look at Shiviria. "We're trying to find a cure for this poison. It's probably going to be boring."

"I don't mind," she replied, looking hopeful. "I just want to hang out with you guys."

Do you mind, Mel? Kalli asked privately.

It was hard to tell whether she wanted me to object or not. The last thing I wanted to do was stand in the way of two sisters bonding.

No, I don't mind at all.

There! The decision was left in Kalli's hands. Kalli motioned Shiv toward the portal door. "Come on."

Together, the three of us crossed between worlds. I looked back at the mystical door as we passed through the bathroom in Lavender's house. The idea that a door like that could exist so casually made me shudder.

Lavender must be very powerful. She even has a door that goes to Luna.

Kalli gaped at me. *She does? How do you know that?*

I sat on the bed and Kalli plopped down next to me waiting for an answer.

She sort of visited me up there.

I could tell she was getting mad. Why hadn't I told her about that? She then took a few breaths to calm herself. *Well, that's wonderful. If she has a door to Luna, then you can take me there, right?*

Shiv looked back and forth at us, watching our expressions change as we had our private discussion. "You two are talking in your minds again, huh? Talk to me, too."

Kalli smiled and patted the bed next to her. "Come here. We will talk out loud. Sorry, sis."

Shiv sat and smiled. "I like when you call me that. It's so nice having a sister."

"I agree," Kalli chirped, laughing with Shiv.

"I want a sister," I complained.

Kalli stuck her tongue out at me. "Did you forget? You have two of them."

I thought about Kiki and Maya. It felt different somehow. I rubbed my chin and amended, "I want a little sister."

Just then, the door burst open, and Lavender strode into the room followed by Sylvia and Eddie. Sylvia beamed at me and announced, "I'll be your sister!"

Running over to the bed, she tackled me. I pushed her off and yelled, "Don't touch me. I'm contagious, er, poisonous. It can spread through my mana."

Lavender waved me off. "It's fine. So long as you don't push your mana into them, they won't be infected. It's actually quite hard to spread what you have."

"You know about it?" I asked, wondering why I was surprised.

Lavender nodded and pulled up a chair. "Actually yes. I knew this was going to happen. I see glimpses of the future. Before you ask, I cannot get involved. Any direct action on my part changes things, and usually not for the better. The best I can do is offer you guidance and hope you make wise decisions."

"Why me?" I asked, wondering if Lavender played the role of mage whisperer for every awakened she came across.

She let out a long sigh and said, "I honestly shouldn't get involved. It is your destiny to save or destroy the world as we know it. Let me rephrase that. You have a big role to play. Both of you do."

Kalli shuddered next to me when Lavender mentioned her. "What do you mean? I'm not special. I'm just an orphan."

"Hmm," Lavender said, rubbing her chin. "I suppose the two of you don't see it. You have a profound effect on each other and the worlds around you. Kalliphae, you may have been raised in an orphanage but that does not define you any more than the ancient blood that flows through your veins. And Melvin, I am sure you are becoming aware that your bloodline is special, but that by itself has little meaning. There are a great deal of people with M blood. It's the two of you together who're causing ripples."

Kalli and I looked at each other and shrugged. "I get that I feel special when I'm with Kalli, but how does that affect the outside world?"

Lavender shook her head. "Try to observe the world around you and the impact you have on it. Again, I cannot tell you all I know of the future or it will change. That's my destiny as a fate. Contrary to popular belief, I cannot change the threads of destiny. All I can do is occasionally pluck the strands and hope they don't snap."

"The dark lands!" Kalli shouted. "We changed that. All those people, Mel. Together, we changed their lives."

A smile appeared on Lavender's face as she nodded. "Yes, dear child. That you did. You also had an impact on the Academy during your brief tenure there. Every time you awaken someone, you change their destiny. Take young Sylvia for example. She wouldn't exist without your intervention."

I jumped to my feet, shaking my head. "No! You can't say I'm changing the world just because I saved a life. People do that every day and the world doesn't change."

"It does for that person," Lavender argued. "You didn't just save one life. You saved thousands. Additionally, people notice when you do these things. Powerful people. It was inevitable that this was going to happen, which is why you must be trained."

"What about the poison?" Kalli asked. "Can you help us with that?"

Lavender shook her head. "I am not an alchemist. This is one of those things that you must work out for yourselves without my help. It may be frustrating not to be able to use your mana directly on people, but I assure you that you can heal them using the methods you worked out in Tierra. You can also be healed by Sylvia's hugs, so don't fear that. It would make her sad if you did."

Sylvia jumped up and wrapped herself around my hip to demonstrate. I immediately felt her mana washing over me. She smiled up at me and said, "Hugs are good, right?"

I nodded and patted her on the head. "Yep, they sure are."

"So, what are we going to do about the poison?" Kalli asked, frowning at me.

Since Lavender was out of the question, we were back to the drawing board. After thinking about it for a minute, I suggested, "I guess we need to have those vials identified."

Lavender winked at me and replied, "Yes. That would be a good idea. I know of a person. I can have her meet you at the guild in San Diego."

"How do you know about…" I began, realizing instantly that it was pointless to ask Lavender how she knew things. "I mean, thanks for the recommendation."

She smiled. "Another thing. Be careful how you interact with the gods while you are poisoned. As beings of pure mana, your particular infection can cause lasting damage to not only them but also to their believers who lend them mana."

"Wait a second," I began. "I summoned Byakko just the other day. Will that be a problem?"

Lavender shook her head. "No. You're fine there. He never placed his mark on you. The act of summoning is safe. Just warn them that you are corrupted when you do."

Kalli raised her hand and fidgeted beside me. Lavender smiled when she noticed. "Yes. I mean, yes, I can show you to the door. Also, you don't have to raise your hand."

"You know what I was going to ask?" Kalli asked nervously.

Lavender nodded. "Yes. You wish to visit your home world. Well, your long-lost ancestor's homeworld. Melvin has only seen a small part of it. I must warn you though. You may not like what you find."

When we both nodded, Lavender continued, "Very well. I will schedule an appointment with the guild tomorrow at noon for you. That should give you sufficient time to explore Luna and get a good night's sleep.

Shiviria tugged on Kalli's sleeve. "Can I come with you guys? I want to see Luna too."

Lavender smiled at her. "Actually, Shiviria, I have something I'd like to show you that I am sure you will enjoy. Eddie and Sylvia can come too."

Shiv looked back and forth between the enchanter and us, unsure of what to do. "But it's my homeworld, too!"

Kalli knelt in front of her. "I promise I'll take you with me next time for sure."

Lavender stood. "Then it's settled. The two of you try to come back early. You will want a full night's sleep for tomorrow."

She offered Shiv her hand, and it was apparent that the topic was not open for debate. As she got to the door, she turned. "It's the other door in the restroom by the way."

"The other door?" I started to ask, but she was gone.

Kalli and I made our way back into the restroom, once again speaking in MateChat.

I swear there was only one door in here.

When we arrived in the restroom, we noticed a new door on the far side of the room. It definitely was not there before.

———

Stepping through magical doors was the best way to travel between dimensions. There was no teleportation sickness, and we always arrived right where we meant to.

In our case, it was the throne room of Celestea Castle. The duplicate. Or was Gaian Celestea the dupe. Thinking about it made my head hurt. Kalli made her way over to the throne and ran her finger over it. *Are you sure this isn't Gaia?*

I nodded, looking around for the gods.

I'm pretty sure. It's not exactly the same. Did you notice there's a lot less furniture?

It was true. On Gaia, Celestea had furnished the throne room with several sitting areas so that people could be comfortable while they waited for their chance to have an audience. The throne room on Luna was barren, except for a pair of thrones and a regal red carpet.

Kalli sat gingerly on the throne, looking like she expected it to bite her or something. *Is this connected to the same magic as our castle?*

I shrugged.

I'm not sure. It did let you sit, so there's that.

She smiled at me and stood. *I want to see Luna. Can we go outside?*

Together, we made our way out of the throne room. Kalli gave me a suspicious look when we didn't head for the front door.

I want to see if we can get on the roof. The first time we came here I thought there might be a good view from up there.

She said nothing and let me guide her through the endless halls of Celestea castle. I tried to bypass the machine room, but Kalli tugged on my hand as she tried to enter. *I just want to see it. I won't touch anything.*

I walked into the room slowly, thinking about world magic while Kalli examined the console. She pointed at the red button. *What does that one do?*

Her comment made me remember that I had the same reaction the first time I saw it. I checked the status menu to see if anything changed.

Current Power Level: 57% [Low]
Connected Locations: 3 [20% Connected]
Error: Maintenance Required
Faults Found: 23 [Reset? Y/N]
Temperature: 250 Degrees [Within Limits]

Outside of being low on power, it seemed relatively stable. Kalli's finger hovered over the button as she tossed me a mischievous glance.

I don't know what it does, but you probably shouldn't press it.

She looked at the screen I was examining and asked, *What does it mean three locations? I know it connects the two castles but where is the third location?*

After staring at the screen for a few seconds, I was forced to admit that I had no clue.

I'm not sure. I wonder if there's a way to find out.

We scoured the room after that. Beyond the console was a large gray window that I thought was a mirror. As it turned out, it was just very dirty. The two of us spent twenty minutes polishing it enough so we could see through.

What was on the other side astonished us. I looked through the foggy glass at a vast room filled with tanks of some sort. The window was a good forty feet above the ground floor of the other room, though it had catwalks on multiple levels.

Each tank was about the size of a coffin if it stood upright, just the right size to house a human. About where the face would be was a round glass portal. From our vantage, they were too far away to see if they housed anything.

Kalli began searching the room. *We need to find a way to get down there!*

I nodded and made my way to the exit.

There might be a stairwell somewhere. I'll delete the window if we don't find anything.

Kalli nodded and followed me wordlessly. It took us forever to find it. The room was actually connected to the dungeon which was four levels below the control room.

The door to the chamber was locked but that was easy enough to **DELETE**. From the ground floor, the room looked even more impressive. I could see the control room window four floors up in a chamber that seemed to have eight levels. The tanks lined the outside of each floor, connected to each other by pipes that hummed with a mysterious energy.

I was still marveling over the sheer size of the place when Kalli screamed. Teleporting to her side, I pushed her out of the way. She glared at me. *I'm fine! But something moved in there!*

[18]

THE GLASS WINDOW on the tank was just as dirty as the window in the control room had been. Whatever was in there, it had been dormant for a very long time. I strained my eyes trying to see what Kalli had.

Suddenly, it happened. Deep red eyes peered at me from the darkness. I yelped and threw myself back, becoming entangled with Kalli and crashing onto the floor. She squealed and shoved me off her. "Ow! That hurt."

I knew she was upset. She was talking out loud. I whispered, "There's something alive in there."

She reached over and clung to me, reverting to MateChat. *Do you think we should leave it alone?*

I thought about it. While Lavender had told us not to use the machine, she never said anything about freeing people trapped inside of it.

I think we have to. Why else would Lavender not let us take Shiv? She knew we were going to do this. Maybe these are your long-lost relatives.

Kalli frowned, looking up at the portal. It looked lifeless again. *I don't know. I thought my ancestors were banned to Gaia. None of*

the stories my mother told me said anything about leaving people
behind, and definitely nothing about them being prisoners.

Of course, Luna wasn't abandoned. Thinking of the gods, I called out to them, "Lamentus. Jagriel. Are you guys there?"

Nothing happened. Kalli gave me a curious look. *Do we have to pray to them? Or maybe summon them like you did with Byakko and Lamentus.*

I never thought about properly summoning gods before. Since I needed to summon one, I decided to focus on the god I had the most experience with. I formed an image in my head of the massive green ape and activated my summoning skill.

Nothing happened once again, and I was beginning to worry that the poison was having an impact on my skills. Then the room began to rumble. Green mist rose from everywhere and nowhere all at once, and then the god was standing before me. He glared. "Why have you summoned me here? This place is forbidden, even to us."

"Why?" I asked, slightly out of breath. "What is this place?"

Lamentus backed into the center of the room, getting as far from the tanks as possible. "This is the sin that got your ancestors banished from Luna. The reason the gods congregate here. To ensure foolish mortals don't unleash hell on the cosmos."

"Hell?" I balked. "Give me a straight answer. What's in these tanks?"

He scratched his furry backside and sat on the floor. "I believe you would call them ancients, for they lived in a time long passed."

"Shouldn't we set them free?" Kalli asked, looking nervously at the tank.

"That is a question that has been debated for centuries, young one," Lamentus informed us. "They were entombed in this room many generations ago by the first of the Celesteans. There is a good chance that they are no longer sentient, just living husks lending their power to the infernal machine."

"What is the machine, anyway?" I asked quietly. "What does it do?"

Lamentus laughed. "You should know. Do you recall when you

invoked world magic on the human named Mardella? You activated the machine for the first time in millennia."

I was dumbfounded. "That spell was supposed to use mana from Luna itself. Not from prisoners."

He shook his head and explained, "While it is true that the mana you used originated on Luna, it cannot be pulled directly from the planet. It must be gathered slowly from a great area. A conduit is required. In this case, an empowered being to gather and process that mana."

"So, they are mana batteries?" I asked, feeling sick to my stomach.

"More or less," Lamentus agreed.

Kalli tugged the sleeve of my shirt. "We have to do something. We can't just leave them like that."

"I agree," I replied, moving toward the tank.

Lamentus held up a massive paw. "I would advise against that. The occupants of those tanks have been prisoners for thousands of years. You might just bring about the apocalypse if you release them."

Walking up to the tank, I placed a hand on the glass, wondering what it would take to release the occupants. I shuddered when a withered hand appeared on the other side and pressed against the glass.

I looked back at Kalli.

I think they are sentient.

A surge of raw emotion came through our connection. Kalli was just as passionate about it as I was. *What should we do?*

Do you want to find out what the red button does?

Kalli's smile told me everything I needed to know. I took her hand in mine, and we made our way back through the maze of the castle to the control room. Looking down at the red button somehow made what we were about to do feel real.

Kalli tossed me a sidelong glance. *Isn't this dangerous? I thought we weren't supposed to use the machine.*

I think we're shutting it down. Besides, Lavender did say that we're having an impact on the world. This must be one of those decisions.

I reached out to the red button, my finger lingering above it.

Lamentus, who had followed us, watched in silence from the back of the room. Kalli reached down and rested her hand just over mine. *If you think this is the right choice, then I support you.*

I couldn't be sure if I was making a good decision. On the one hand, I could be opening Pandora's Box. On the other, I might be saving an entire civilization from an eternity of torture.

Taking a deep breath, we pushed the button. A klaxon began blaring in the background and the entire castle began to tremble. For a moment, I worried that the building itself was going to collapse.

Then, flashes of light shone from the tank room, and we heard a strange hissing sound even through the glass. Kalli and I rushed over and pressed our faces to the window.

In the chamber beyond, we could see a strange vapor escaping from the tanks. Before heading back to the tank room, I cast a glance at the status panel.

Current Power Level: 13% [Critical]
Connected Locations: 3 [Disconnected]
Error: Emergency Stop Pressed
Faults Found: 666 [Reset? Y/N]
Temperature: 57 Degrees [Out of Bonds]

I stewed over the readings while I dragged Kalli through the castle once again. We got back to the chamber in time to watch the occupant of the first tank slump to the floor.

We raced over to his side. I wanted to cover Kalli's eyes because it was a naked man. It was strange because I expected him to be old or at least shriveled up from being trapped in a tank for thousands of years. In contrast, the man looked perfect. His well-groomed brown hair appeared to have been washed recently. From what I could see, he didn't have a single blemish on his skin.

My observations were cut short when he reached up and grasped my wrist with a surprisingly strong grip. "Who are you?"

Not knowing what else to say, I whispered, "I'm Murphy. Melvin Murphy."

I giggled to myself when I realized I sounded like a young nerdy James Bond. Kalli approached from behind and the man hissed. I thought he was going to complain about being naked in front of a girl, but he said, "Get her away from me. I recognize the foul stench of a Celestean anywhere. What they did is unforgivable!"

Kalli quaked and hid behind me. *Melvin, I think we made a huge mistake.*

There was little time to worry about it as more of the tanks began opening, depositing their contents on the catwalks all around us. Kalli gaped at the hundreds of people flopping about on the floor. *What do we do? There are too many of them.*

I didn't know what to do either. My usual brand of healing was off-limits because of the poison. Then, I thought about it. Lavender told me I could use the healing spells I'd worked on.

Focusing my mana into a beam of light, I practiced on the man in front of us. The man emitted a sigh of relief as a beam of invisible magic washed over him.

He looked up at me with renewed interest as he found the strength to sit up. "Thank you. I can't tell you what it means that you've freed us. However, I strongly advise you to get *her* out of here before the others recover."

The man was talking about Kalli. I held out my arms to shield her from him. "Hey! It was just as much her idea as it was mine to free you. You can't blame her for whatever you think the Celesteans did thousands of years ago."

"Heh!" The man snorted with laughter. "Bad blood cannot be forgotten so easily."

I was curious to find out more about the strange people from the Lunar machine.

Name: Not Available
Class: Not Available
Level: Not Available
Affection Level: Not Available

That was new. Finding no help from the System, I was forced to ask. "Who are you? Can you tell me more about your people and how you siphon mana from the planet?"

He raised an eyebrow. "Do you wish to use us as well? My name is Iolathar. I suppose you can call us the last of the ancients. The only survivors of our kind. We have been trapped here for an eternity."

"Who did this to you?" Kalli asked timidly from behind me.

"Do not speak to me!" Iolathar growled. "You're people lost that right when you used us as glorified fuel for your wicked spells."

"Hey!" I spat. "She is a big part of the reason you're free. I never would have pushed that button without her."

The expression on Iolathar's face softened. "Very well. I will at least hear her out. It has been a long time since I've spoken to one of her kind, after all. The others might not share my sympathy, though."

"Can we do anything for them?" Kalli asked, looking at the writhing figures around the room.

Everyone was naked. That was the least I could help them with.

Let's go find them some clothes.

Kalli looked around at all the naked bodies and blushed. ***Good idea.***

Between the two of us, we managed to make a care package for the ancients. I edited hundreds of robes while Kalli had Lamentus show her where the living quarters were. The layout of Lunar Celestea castle was similar to the Gaian version.

When we returned, the majority of the ancients stood gathered on the basement floor of the tank chamber. I noticed a pile of unmoving bodies stacked unceremoniously in the back of the room.

Iolathar approached when we returned with supplies. Many of the ancients behind him glowered at Kalli as we stacked the robes I created on a table.

He picked one up and slid it over his shoulders. "Thank you. It has been a long time since felt the comfort of clothing. I had forgotten what it feels like."

Kalli gathered her courage and announced, "I found rooms with bath chambers that you are welcome to use if you wish for some privacy."

"Do you speak for all Celesteans?" a woman asked. "Why are children the only ones here to greet us? Are we about to be ambushed by armed guards when we step from this chamber? I warn you, we will put up a fight. This construct of yours will not be sufficient to stop us?"

"Construct?" Kalli asked, looking confused.

I laughed. They were referring to Lamentus. "He's a god. Have you never seen one before?"

Iolathar gaped at him. "I do not believe I've met this god. Is he related to Polaris?"

"Never heard of that god," I replied.

Lamentus spoke for the first time since we turned off the machine. "If such a god did exist, he has been forgotten by the living. Such is the only way for a god to perish."

The woman spoke again. "That still doesn't answer my question. Why are only children here?"

I wanted to explain to her that I was sixteen, the age of majority. However, I bit my tongue and explained the situation. "As far as I know, you are the only ones on Luna. You and the gods. The Celesteans were banished to Gaia long ago."

"Good riddance!" Someone yelled from the back of the room.

Iolathar held up a hand for silence. "All feelings aside, these kids seem to have freed us. Whether a prank or not, we owe them civility at the very least. We accept your offer of hospitality."

[19]

IN THE END, we decided to return to my bedroom at Lavender's house to give the ancient's a chance to settle in. Iolathar was surprised when I explained to him that they were the only living beings on Luna.

I wasn't sure if Shiv returned to Gaia or decided to spend the night at Lavender's house. Kalli seemed perfectly content to have a sleep-over, which always made me happy.

I probed my core as we sat together in bed. Her presence beside me informed me that Kalli was along for the ride. *Do you think you can remove the poison somehow?*

The problem was, no matter how much I poked and prodded the particles, they just dissipated and reformed out of reach. There was nothing to target. Nothing to delete. It was like my mana was the poison. The only saving grace seemed to be that my core was too resilient for it to do any damage.

Kalli shared my immunity, but only because our cores were connected. I couldn't do that for the rest of the universe, so the poison was effectively cutting me off from using mana to heal or awaken anybody else.

That alone wouldn't have been bad. The problem was Orpheus and

Scuawk. We had to save them. Unfortunately, I couldn't think of anything and had to give up.

I can't figure this out.

Kalli rested a hand on my arm. *Do you want me to try what I did last time? What you taught me?*

I blinked at her.

What is that?

She twirled a finger through my hair. *You know, run my fire through your mana. It worked after you fought with Mrs. Shaw.*

I had repressed that memory. The moments after I was nearly killed by the vampire were still a jumbled fog in my head. Kalli wasted no time running her hands lovingly up and down my arms.

Then I felt burning mana pouring into me. The sensation was warm, and it tingled. My nose tickled as the spicy smell I associated with Kalli flooded my senses. Her mana pumped through my body in tune with her heartbeat.

I followed her progress and winced as she turned up the heat in an effort to eradicate the poison. She ended up pulling out of me completely when I yelped in pain. Wincing sympathetically, she touched my cheek. *I'm so sorry. Did I hurt you?*

I responded by leaning over and kissing her.

I love you. Did you know that?

She swooned in my arms. *Maybe a little. I love you, too.*

Congratulations. You have reached level 29

"I love leveling up!" I said, my whole body twitching from the experience.

Kalli rolled her eyes as we tumbled into the dream with the exquisite feelings of a level up. "You know. I can make you feel that way, too."

"Is that a promise?" I asked hopefully.

She climbed on top of me and smiled, pinning me down. "You know we can't do that in here. Lavender warned us. That doesn't mean we can't play though."

She kissed me softly and I sighed. "You know, if there's only one person I'm allowed to touch like this for the rest of my life, I'm happy that it's you."

Kalli smiled. "Me, too."

We spent the next several hours, or perhaps only a few minutes, making out. It's hard to tell in a dream. When Kalli climbed off me to catch her breath, I whispered, "I might have an idea about our poison."

"What?" she panted.

"Well, it's risky," I admitted. "We can ask Mardella. She poisoned us after all. There should be something she can tell us about it."

Kalli stared at me for a long time. "I don't like that woman. She nearly killed you. She's the reason you're poisoned in the first place."

I nodded while I listened. "Don't forget she's our prisoner. She can't hurt us in there."

Kalli raised an eyebrow at me. "Fine but I'm coming, too."

———

We tiptoed down the hall, not wanting to make our presence known to any of the other prisoners in the ring. Kalli and I looked at one another when we got to the end of the hall. *Should we knock?*

I shrugged. We had to let her know we were there somehow.

KNOCK, KNOCK, KNOCK!

A weak voice from the other side of the door grumbled, "Really? You knock on a cell door? What do you want?"

I swallowed before replying, "Tell us what poison you used."

Mardella laughed before erupting into a fit of coughing. She chose not to answer our questions when she spoke, "Did you know that the spirit body doesn't need food, drink, or toilet? The problem is the soul doesn't realize this. It's been torture. I'm starving and thirsty and I keep making messes in my cell. I don't have the ability like you to make food out of thin air. I'll tell you what, provide me with a meal and I'll try to answer your questions."

Kalli tugged my sleeve. *You can't go in there. It's a trap.*

I echoed her thoughts. "I can't go in there. You'll obviously try to escape."

"Without a body?" she asked in a sarcastic tone. "Not likely."

"You'll just steal one of our bodies," Kalli barked back.

A cackle escaped Mardella's lips. "Is that what happened to my body? Is some interloper off galivanting around in it? You promised you would do what you could for me, but you never returned."

Mardella sounded desperate. I repeated the question. "Can you help us with the poison?"

Her defiant voice replied, "Not until you do something for me. I believe it's basic etiquette to provide at least bread and water to prisoners."

I sighed, debating whether or not to risk going into the cell with Mardella. She hastily added, "Look, you don't have to come in. Just put it through the window."

It was true, there was a barred slit running along the top of the door. I stood on my tiptoes, attempting to peer into the darkness. What I saw made me feel sorry for the woman. Mardella was hunched in the corner on the far side of the tiny cell. There was no furniture of any kind. Just Mardella and a pile of what appeared to be excrement in the other corner. Mardella, who had been watching me, looked away in shame when my eyes traveled to the poo.

DELETE

When it was gone, Mardella apparently sensed it and cracked a small smile. "It's a good thing there are no flies in this place. That would have driven me crazy. Can't say as much about the smell. I never thought I could make myself sick, but that was before you locked me in this place."

Looking around the ground, it looked clean a little too clean to be a traditional prison. There were no rocks or pebbles anywhere. There wasn't even any dust.

I reached into the fanny pack and pulled out a handful of the pebbles that I kept for editing purposes. Dropping them through the slit, I waited patiently for Mardella to reply. She looked at the pebbles and muttered, "What are you doing?"

I replied, "Place those where you want me to put things. We can start with a meal, and I'll make you other things like a bed, and some kind of commode."

"It will still overflow," she grumbled. "Eventually…"

Sighing, I resigned myself to the inevitable. "I'll come back every week to empty it for you."

Mardella laughed. "Such an attentive warden. That poison must really be getting to you."

"Not us so much," I admitted. "Some other innocent people were infected. You don't want to kill innocent people, do you?"

She laughed again. It was a haughty laugh of contempt. "You know nothing about me. My people were slaughtered to the brink of extinction by your girlfriend's relatives."

My first thought was of Kalli. I took her hand in mine. While I could feel her shock at the accusation, she wasn't letting it get to her. I spoke with a calm I didn't know I was capable of, "What are you trying to say? If you are playing games with me, I will never come back, and you can drown in your own crap for all I care."

Mardella seemed to realize I was serious when she replied, "Have you ever heard the story of why the Celesteans were banished from Luna?"

I had to rack my brain to remember the reasons the gods gave me. "They were sent to Gaia for tampering with forbidden technology and draining the planet's mana."

Even as I said that I realized they were banished for imprisoning the ancients. But what did that have to do with Mardella? Was she…?

She snickered, looking up at me. "That's correct. In the distant past, her ancestors and mine lived in harmony in what was truly a paradise. All my life, I heard of the many crimes committed by the Celesteans. Unforgivable sins that were never truly repented for. The truth still lies on the green planet in the sky. You've been there. I know you've seen the evidence of what I say."

Kalli gasped and covered her mouth with her hand. *Melvin, she's an ancient. At least, she's one of their descendants.*

Suddenly, something Mardella had to say was more important than the antidote. I found myself growing excited as I said, "You need to tell us everything you know about the ancients."

It was Mardella's turn to be shocked. "Who told you that name?"

I decided to be honest. "Iolathar did."

Mardella frowned. "I don't know who that is. Okay, make yourself comfortable. I will tell you an old bedtime story. Long ago, the Celesteans and the ancients lived in peace on Luna. While life did exist on Gaia, they were mostly beast-men and half-breeds. We presided over them from the heavens and did what we could to make their primitive lives better. It was during that time that the Celesteans did the unthinkable. Over time, they became dissatisfied with our duality. We lived longer and were generally more powerful than they were. When the first of our kind disappeared, we turned to the Celesteans for help solving the mystery. It wasn't until the end that it became obvious that we were betrayed. The last of us escaped to Gaia and hid for millennia among the beast tribes. The Celesteans followed. We thought for many generations that they migrated to pursue us, but we eventually discovered that they could not return as well. It was only recently that we emerged from the ashes. Yet, I never wanted revenge. On the contrary, It was always my goal to return to the land of my ancestors. It is *my* birthright. Or at least it was before you stole my body."

I almost felt sorry for Mardella. Until I reminded myself that she poisoned me while trying to plunge her sword through my heart. That and Stefanie. I couldn't contain my emotions. "If you're so innocent, why did you kill Stefanie? Why did you kidnap Wendy? Why did you try to kill me? Don't even get me started on that accursed contract."

"All a means to an end," Mardella replied without a hint of remorse. "Everything I did was for my family. To get home. On Gaia, we are the darkness that lurks in the shadows. On Luna, we have a chance to change all of that. I doubt you will believe me, but I had nothing to do with your friend's death. As for your contract, I just needed your bloodline. As you have aptly demonstrated, you possess unique traits that allow you to come and go from Luna whenever you wish. Your blood could have solved all my problems. I'll also have you know that I treated Wendy like family during her stay in Dabia. She wasn't even kept under guard as you found out when you liberated her. Everything could have been handled peacefully. I was even willing to overlook the fact that you restored Celestea after I went to great lengths to destroy it. The final straw was when you corrupted my daughter. Thanks to you, I will never see a proper heir and our blood will die out."

I sighed, momentarily stunned at Mardella's twisted logic. What Kalli said next changed everything. "Mardella, the ancients still live. They were just prisoners. We freed them all."

For a moment, nothing happened. Then, a whimpering voice spoke, "Fine. I'll tell you about the poison. I'll do anything. Just, please tell me more."

[20]

"YOU GO FIRST!" I growled, still mad that she poisoned me.

Mardella let out an audible sigh and pleaded. "Can you at least let me have some water first?"

"Position the pebbles," I replied, waiting for her to make the first move.

She slowly dragged herself to her feet. It was strange watching a being made of pure mana slither around as though her non-existent body was crippled.

Mardella spread the rocks around the room. First, I made her a fluffy couch. I figured it would be comfortable as well as something she could sleep on. Then, I made a coffee table next to it.

After instructing her to place a few more pebbles on the table, I made her a fish plate at her request as well as a glass of red wine. It was odd for someone who was dehydrated to drink alcohol, but then I reminded myself that it was all just mana in the first place.

I made her some more furniture as well as a commode. It wasn't magical or anything as I didn't know how to make those. That was something I would have to learn.

"All right, I gave you what you wanted. Now, tell me more about the poison," I insisted.

Mardella made a show of slowly chewing the food before washing it down with a long sip of wine. "Very well. It's not poison. Though I can see why you would think it is. It's cursed mana. One of my familial skills is the ability to infuse our mana with emotions. If you paint your sword with a strong enough hate, it becomes potent enough to consume a person. I am not surprised that it had no effect on you."

"But you don't have a bloodline," I said, confused by the explanation.

She took another bite before explaining. "My kind existed before bloodlines. It's only natural that we were bypassed when they were handed out. The creator probably thought we would be too powerful. Either that or he thought we were extinct by that point. We were in hiding for many years because of what the Celesteans did to us."

"My mother would never hunt you down," Kalli screamed. "It was you who burned the castle to the ground and killed countless people."

Mardella sighed and took a few seconds to reply. "I agree, that was a mistake. There was no way for me to know that at the time. All I knew was that the Celestean existence was a threat to me. We fought and scraped to become powerful enough to end your line. I just needed one of you alive to take me back to Luna. I had no clue you had been banished."

"How do we cure the cursed mana?" I asked, trying to get the conversation back on track.

She stood and hobbled over to the door. "If you let me out of here, I could help you fix it."

"I don't know how to do that," I admitted. "Even if I did, we don't have a body for you."

Mardella sighed and ran her fingernails over the coarse wood of the door. "You said that two others were affected by the curse. Give me one of their bodies. They are dead anyway. They just don't know it yet. I will cure the other unintended victim as well as the two of you."

I looked to Kalli, running out of ideas. She shook her head. *Absolutely not! We can't sacrifice an innocent person just to cure ourselves.*

But what if they both die?

She grimaced. *At least we wouldn't be the ones to kill them.*
They wouldn't be dead. Whoever we choose would be in here.

Kalli gave me a piercing look. *That might just be a fate worse*
than death. You saw Mardella, she's in agony.

I heaved a heavy sigh.

You're right. You always are.

She cracked a smile, and I turned back to Mardella. "We can't do
that. We will have to find another way to get you out of here. Is there
anything we can do about the curse for now?"

Mardella cackled. "Why would I tell you that? Curing the curse
seems to be my only ticket out of here."

I pounded my fist on the door, eliciting a squeal of surprise from
Mardella. "Any help you give us today will be the only motivation I
have to help you get out of here. If we figure this out without you, you
can rot in here for all I care."

A booming voice from behind me made me jump, "If you wish to
purge your core, come to me boy. I am the master of all things
ethereal."

I left Mardella to negotiate with Kalli as I walked down the hall to
investigate. The voice had come from the first door. A shirtless man
with a long wispy beard stood at the door with both hands on the bars
in the narrow window.

Standing a good distance back, I asked, "How do you know what to
do? You don't even know what exactly the curse looks like."

He laughed. "It doesn't matter, boy. Purifying the soul is an ancient
art and a well-trained monk can void any manner of corruption."

"And you just intend to tell me how to do it?" I asked, trying to
inspect him.

Name: Longinus Rei
Class: ???
Level: ???
Affection Level: Unknown

I blinked at the menu, unsure why it was telling me what it was.

His gruff voice replied to my question. "Good question. I'm not sure. Perhaps I'm just bored. Maybe it's been too long since I've taken a disciple. Either way, you're the ring bearer for now so I might as well get in your good graces. As things stand, you're my only way out."

Kalli made her way down the hall to me. *She's useless. I don't* *think she will help unless we let her out. What's the deal with* *this guy?*

I shrugged.

I don't know. He says he wants to help us for free.

Finally, I made my decision. "How do we start?"

"Well, I suppose it's too early for you to trust me," he began. "So, getting you to touch my hand is out of the question. Tell me, have you begun refining your mana at all?"

I nodded, remembering my lessons with Chogu and the refinements I'd set up in my core. Then, I realized he probably couldn't see me well through the door and replied, "I started refining my mana back on Earth about a year ago."

"Well, that's a start," he said softly. "What about the girl?"

Kalli and I exchanged a glance, and she admitted, "I haven't…"

Longinus twirled his beard around his finger. "Hmm. I suppose a good place to start would be for you to show her how to do that. The other prisoner already admitted that your core is filled with hate. You are going to have to purge it from the inside. To do this, you are going to have to not only refine your mana to a greater extent, but you are also going to have to infuse it with qualities that counterbalance the hate. This is a very high-level technique. Outside of that woman in the other cell, I may be the only person in existence who can teach you properly. Now, if you'll just let me out…"

"I don't trust you," I said, not meaning for my voice to carry, but it did. "Thank you for the advice, but I am going to work this out for myself."

"Have it your way," Longinus muttered and I heard him walk away from the door. "Remember, I offered to help."

Without answering him, I took Kalli's hand and withdrew from the ring.

We both woke at the same time, drenched in sweat. Kalli wiggled in my arms. ***What will we do now? We can't trust either of them.***

I let her go and sat up.

Well, we still have options. There's no sense stepping into a trap unless we try everything else first.

A glance at the clock told me that it was eleven AM. We were running late. Kalli noticed as well and gasped, ***We have to be at the guild by noon.***

Don't worry, I have a plan.

The two of us darted into the bathroom, rushing to get cleaned up and ready to go. When she was satisfied, Kalli made her way over to me. ***Okay, so what's the plan?***

I took her hand and wrapped mana over both of us.

We're going home.

For some odd reason, my childhood home always felt like home no matter where I was staying. I thought I saw a glint in the cosmos was Quetzalcoatl's shame as I stepped into the void.

Then we were there. Back in that tiny apartment. Mrs. Garcia was the only one home cooking lunch in the kitchen. She screamed when we arrived, "I thought you said you weren't going to come back."

"Sorry," I replied. "We just needed a way to get to town quickly. That smells good by the way."

When we let ourselves out, I led Kalli over to a grass field next door to the apartment complex. I only stopped once I was sure we were out of sight. Kalli raised an eyebrow at me. ***What now? Why are we here?***

I think it's time we brought your old friend back.

Meanwhile, in Poland…

A young woman sat in a leather chair surrounded by screens. While she appeared to be a small child in stature, she was actually a full-grown woman. Disheveled cyan hair fell across her shoulders, entwined with over-ear headphones. Thick glasses rested on the bridge of her nose, and she wore a long white lab coat which wasn't entirely necessary while she was sitting at her command center. She just felt at home in it.

On one of the screens, a man she'd never seen before gave his report. "The sky was green. I was taken to a place with trolls, goblins, and ogres."

She cut him off. "How did you get back. I received data that the portal closed."

"Well, sir, that's difficult to explain," the man began. She was used to being called sir. The woman went to great lengths to mask her identity. That included the deep male voice of The Administrator. The man continued his report. "There was this boy. He used magic to move me from one place to another. Then they took me to a bedroom in a castle and took me to a door in the bathroom. Next thing I knew, we were back on Earth. Then this beautiful woman brought me to an American government facility, and I flew back on a giant winged bird."

That settled it. The High House of Earth was involved. While the woman had never interacted with HHOE, she had heard a lot about them. They were how her contact got her involved with IMP, the International Magical Prisons corporation.

She let out an involuntary sigh before she could mute her microphone. "You've done well, what was your name, Antoni? Thank you for returning with this report. I will see to it that you get a special bonus on your next paycheck."

She didn't wait for Antoni to reply and cut the connection. What was Natalia thinking, sending a fool through the portal? She was the next one to interview.

Pushing a red button, the woman spoke into her microphone, "Get me Natalia Boszczyk."

"Right away, Administrator," a voice confirmed.

The woman twirled in her chair while she waited, craving the dizzy sensation the motion brought. Then she took a moment to go over the readout from the portal generator.

Portal Projection Project:

Test 01: Failure
Test 02: Failure
Test 03: Failure
Test 04: Failure
Test 05: Failure
Test 06: Failure
Test 07: Failure
Test 08: Failure
Test 09: Failure
Test 10: Failure
Test 11: Failure
Test 12: Partial Failure

Note: Stable portal manifested on the 12th and final test. Test subject passed through the portal. Portal collapsed 7 minutes 23 seconds after creation.

Conclusion: Unsuitable for inter dimensional travel.

That wasn't good enough for Zofia. That was her name, though nobody knew about it. To everyone still in her life, she was merely The Administrator. Nothing more. Nothing less.

"Mr. Administrator, sir," the voice chirped over the speaker. "I have researcher Boszczyk on video feed three."

"Connect her," Zofia said flatly.

A disheveled woman appeared on the screen. Obviously, Zofia had woken her. "Can I be of service, sir?"

Zofia leaned closer to the screen. It wasn't that Mrs. Boszczyk could see her. She just wanted to see her face twitch when she chastised her. "Tell me something, Natalia. Why did you send a grunt through the portal? Do you consider yourself above doing field research? Please, tell me I was not mistaken when I assigned you to your post."

Mrs. Boszczyk's left eye began to twitch as she gathered herself to her full height. "No, sir! I am the right scout for the job. You see, the other researchers assumed the twelfth test would fail and didn't show up. I stayed behind to gather data while utilizing a worker to test the stability of the portal. Unfortunately, the portal closed of its own accord before I had the opportunity to follow."

"Is that so?" Zofia sneered into the microphone. "It appears to me that this mere worker showed you up. What do you intend to do to make up for it?"

"Anything." Mrs. Boszczyk replied.

A sinister grin appeared on Zofia's lips. "Excellent. Prepare another mana battery. I am sending a special scout to accompany you this time. She has my utmost confidence, and you are to obey her every command as though they were my own."

"Yes, sir." Mrs. Boszczyk answered. Zofia could sense reluctance in her voice.

[21]

KALLI SQUEALED when the phoenix answered my summons, "Oh, Suzaku! I missed you so much!"

The large fiery bird nuzzled Kalli affectionately.

I told you he was just waiting for you to come back.

Kalli beamed as she hugged the great red bird's neck. *I wish he could come to Gaia with me. Is there any way to make it happen?*

I shrugged. It wasn't like I didn't want to. The idea of Byakko meeting some of the Gaian gods made me chuckle.

I don't think it's possible. They wouldn't have any believers over there.

Kalli nodded mournfully. *I know. Suzy just explained it to me.*

Look on the bright side, maybe Lamentus will let you ride him.

Kalli's face twisted in mock disgust. *Ew! I don't want to mount a fat green grizzape.*

A what?

She gaped at me. *A grizzape. What do you call them?*

I don't know. Just ape, I guess.

She stuck her tongue out at me. *That's just silly.*

When we took to the sky, I regretted not having easier access to air travel on Gaia. Sure, there was the airship, but I had to send for it, and it wasn't always guaranteed that they would allow us to use it.

Do you think Mrs. Hodgins is working today?

Kalli shrugged, her hair caught in the breeze. *Probably. What day is it?*

Tuesday, I think.

We landed in the alley behind the strip mall containing the guild office. Kalli smiled as Suzaku shrunk and twisted into an elaborate design around her dress.

When we entered the guild, a bored-sounding receptionist greeted us. "Good afternoon. Please, present your guild cards."

It had been so long that I was worried I'd lost mine. Kalli and I scoured our bags but managed to produce the plastic cards.

Melvin Murphy
Summoner: Level 16
Status: Academy Student
Guild Rank: D
Restrictions: None
Guild Fame: 1062

Kalliphae Hellquist
Pyromancer: Level 12
Status: Academy Student
Guild Rank: D
Restrictions: Magical Contract (2)
Guild Fame: 845

She looked at our cards and back up at us, "Are these up to date?"

We shook our heads and I proudly announced, "I'm level thirty-six now."

"That's very nice," she said with a slight roll of her eyes. "Please, wait patiently while we update your files."

"But we're just here to…" I began to object.

She shushed me with a finger to her lips. "Shh, wait patiently while we prepare accurate guild cards for you. It won't take but a moment."

Out of nowhere a gray-haired blur emerged and tackled Kalli, wrapping the startled girl in a hug. "Kalliphae! How many times have I told you to call me when you come to Earth. I've missed you!"

Kalli blushed and struggled to breathe against the onslaught of the overbearing woman. Mrs. Hodgins looked over at me and smiled. "I'm glad you're well, too, Melvin."

I wondered when exactly it was that Kalli stole my best Earth friend. Well, before I met the gang at the Academy that was. Mrs. Hodgins finally let Kalli go and directed us back to the library. "Come this way, you two. Helga, we will be in my study. Have their cards brought there when they are ready."

"Yes, Mrs. Hodgins," Helga said, her tone much more professional.

Mrs. Hodgins led us through the library through a chained-off door that I thought led to the restricted section. It wasn't what I expected but in a way, it was so much more.

Grand offices that by themselves could have been full buildings lined a circular open-roofed courtyard. Mrs. Hodgins led us to an office that might as well have been another library. Three stories tall, her office consisted of a series of desks with comfy reading chairs, surrounded by multi-level bookshelves.

She grinned at us conspiratorially. "I have access to so many rare and exotic books now. It's all thanks to you, Melvin. Not only did you introduce me to this world but when you awakened me, I was able to grow and evolve at a much faster rate than I could have ever imagined possible. I'm level twenty-four now and I'm the head researcher at this branch. I'm also in charge of appraisals after the last one got fired for undervaluing items submitted by guild members."

Her comment brought back memories of haggling with the guild over artifacts we found under the ocean. At least Kalli kept hers. She walked around the room looking at the books that lined the walls. "Have you read all of these?"

Mrs. Hodgins smiled, running her fingers over a few of the books. "I've read a great deal of them. Some of the skills I picked up are the ability to speed read and read multiple books at once. Combine that with my ability to retain the majority of what I consume and my dream of truly understanding this world we live in is slowly becoming a reality.

GONG!

GONG!

GONG!

We all looked at a grandfather clock that rested in a corner of the room. It was noon! Kalli and I looked at one another in alarm and I started for the door. "We need to get back. We have an appointment with…"

Actually, Lavender didn't tell us who exactly we were supposed to meet. We probably should have said something to the receptionist about our appointment. Mrs. Hodgins shrugged us off. "Don't worry, kids. Lavender explained all about your dilemma and I've instructed Dr. Pemblescrap to meet us here."

"Dr. Who?" Kalli asked, sounding out the name in silence.

"Pemblescrap," she repeated. "She is the highest level alchemist in the western United States. If it's a potion or formula of any kind, she will be able to identify it."

Just then, a green-skinned woman wearing a witch's robe and a pointy hat poked her head in. "Hey everyone. Am I fashionably late?"

"Never!" Mrs. Hodgins chirped, making her way over to one of the tables with more than one chair. Every chair in her office looked comfy.

"Is it normal to have green humans on Earth?" Kalli asked, covering her mouth in embarrassment when we all looked at her.

I shook my head and Dr. Pemblescrap laughed. "No, dear child. This is an unfortunate side effect of my chosen profession. I've been poisoned more times than I can count. Eventually, my skin just didn't bounce back, and here I am, the wicked witch of the west."

"You're a witch?" Kalli gasped in amazement.

Everyone laughed, and I shook my head.

Another Earth movie. I'll tell you about it later.

Kalli nodded and smiled. *We're going to have to watch some of these movies together.*

It's a date!

"Oh, right," Dr. Pemblescrap muttered absentmindedly, digging in her pocket. "I got the new guild cards for you two."

Melvin Murphy

Summoner: Level 36

Status: Self-Proclaimed Emperor

Guild Rank: C

Restrictions: Self-Imposed Contract (1)

Guild Fame: 22,642

Kalliphae Hellquist

Pyromancer: Level 29

Status: Crown Royalty

Guild Rank: C

Restrictions: Self-Imposed Contract (1)

Guild Fame: 17,111

"Self-proclaimed?" the words escaped my mouth against my will.

The other three stared at me and Dr. Pemblescrap explained, "The guild declares your status based on a lot of things. Currently, that is what you identify as. When it comes to royalty, the System seems to frown on people who declare themselves to be royal as opposed to historical institutions."

"Sue me for being ambitious," I grumbled, wishing I could change my card.

Then, I remembered I could. A quick edit fixed my dilemma.

Melvin Murphy

Summoner: Level 36

Status: Emperor

Guild Rank: C

Restrictions: Self-Imposed Contract (1)

Guild Fame: 22,642

Item: Guild Identification Card (Edited)
Components: Plastic, Ink, Mana
Item Rank: D
Item Level: 1
Item Owner: Murphy

Upon taking a closer look, I noticed that while the edited tag did appear on the item itself, the inscription on the card looked normal and untainted. I was careful not to let any of the others see as I stuffed it back into the fanny pack.

Dr. Pemblescrap looked at the two of us expectantly. "So, which of you has treasure for me to examine? I have to tell you, I am more than a little excited."

Kalli reached into her bag and took out the vials she managed to steal from Altara's lab. Each one was very different from the next. Dr. Pemblescrap examined each in turn.

The first was a sinister-looking thick red liquid with bubbles trapped inside. The second was green and nearly opaque. It reminded me of what I expected poison to look like. The third was a clear liquid that could have just been water. Finally, the fourth vial contained a pure black fluid that looked like death itself.

"Very peculiar," Dr. Pemblescrap whispered, holding each vial up to the light. "Where did you get these?"

"A very evil person's house," Kalli replied, her voice ice cold. "We sort of stole them."

"Really?" the older woman replied, shaking the red one experimentally. "These are unlike anything I've ever seen before."

Was she the best alchemist in the western US?

Name: Geronima Pemblescrap
Class: Alchemist
Level: 83
Affection Level: Studious

"What do you mean?" Kalli asked, sensing my apprehension.

"This is not alchemy," she said, setting the vial down and picking up the black one. "I think this red one is congealed blood of some sort though I can't be sure. There seems to be some kind of impurity present that isn't chemical in nature. All of them have an odd aspect that I just can't put my finger on."

"Mana," I said absentmindedly.

"What do you mean?" Mrs. Hodgins asked, giving me a curious look.

Kalli and I exchanged a glance. *Should we tell them about Mardella?*

I shrugged.

I don't know. I think it's safe to tell them about the emotional mana. We should just leave Mardella out of it. Especially where she is right now.

She nodded, and I spoke out loud. "The foreign element is mana infused with raw emotion. We found out that our cores are corrupted with hate-filled mana."

Dr. Pemblescrap looked at the vial in her hand with renewed interest. "Are you saying you can infuse mana with an emotion? And infuse it into a concoction like this? Very peculiar."

"Well, we're not certain that that's what this is," I explained. "We just got information about what happened to us. How do you know what's in those vials? You just held it in your hand. Can you see something?"

She laughed swapping for the clear vial. "I have a special ability, Chemical Appraisal. It allows me to know what a potion consists of at a glance. Obviously, the level of the mixture matters, but I am sufficiently high level that most potions can't get by me. I'll admit, I was a little curious why these aren't spilling their secrets for me. Infused mana is a new one that I've never heard of. I think I'd like to meet this Altara."

"I doubt that," Kalli said with a grimace. "She'd probably kill you before you got to ask any questions."

Dr. Pemblescrap rubbed her chin as though she were weighing the pros and cons of information versus potential death. After a while, she reached into a rather large purse and began piecing together a complex chemistry set. Vials and beakers of various sizes interconnected by tubes and passing over open-flame heat sources filled the table we sat at.

Gas masks and goggles were handed out to everyone, and she advised us. "Please stand at the far side of the room. There is a very real chance that these might react in unpredictable ways."

We all stood back, crouching behind a sturdy oak desk as the alchemist began her experiment. She began with the red liquid. I watched closely as it bubbled up out of its vial, sucked into a tube that fed it into the contraption.

As it passed through the first round chamber, it heated and quickly began to boil. When it passed into the next tube, the bubbles were gone. From there is split in three directions, each one filling a different vial.

Mrs. Pemblescrap removed one of the new vials and held it up to the light. Frowning, she dug in her bag and pulled out a bottle with a clear liquid inside. Using a dropper, she applied a single drop to the vial.

"Ah," she let out a moan as the liquid frothed and overflowed. "I wasn't expecting that."

"What happened?" I asked, unable to contain my curiosity. Perhaps alchemy was a useful class.

Dr. Pemblescrap removed her gloves and reached into her bag for a fresh pair. "That was a failure. I hoped to separate the potion into its base components but, instead, it spoiled. Don't worry, though. We still have two more samples. I'll test those later. Pick a color, clear, black, or green?"

"Black!" I announced, deciding that was the most evil-looking one.

"Very well," she replied, replacing the empty vial the red potion had come in with the black one.

The process started innocently enough. We watched in silence as the black fluid invaded the tubes connecting it to the large, heated flask. Then…it exploded.

[22]

MY TOP PRIORITY was to protect Kalli at any cost. That was probably a mistake. I threw myself on top of her, placing myself between Kalli and the black fire. A blood-curdling scream informed me of my error.

"Mrs. Hodgins!" Kalli screamed, trying to push me off her.

I refused to budge until I felt the last of the black flame dissipate. An alarm sounded in the distance accompanied by the sounds of people running. I rolled off Kalli, still feeling a prickling sensation in my back.

Kalli leapt to her feet and rushed over to the desk Mrs. Hodgins had been standing behind. Her expression when she looked up was panicked. "Melvin! Come quick. She's hurt!"

With a groan, I pushed off the ground and rushed to Kalli's side. While Mrs. Hodgins had managed to turn, she didn't quite make it and half of her face was covered in the muck from the blast. Kalli whimpered out loud. "Do something, Mel."

I hesitated. I was poisoned, cursed. Wouldn't healing her do more harm than good? Where were the guild healers? I almost cried out for help when I remembered what Lavender said. It was possible to heal but only with light magic. No mana. Mana was bad.

Turning on my magic light beam, I focused the healing wave on

Mrs. Hodgins' face, saying a silent prayer as I let the spell wash over her. Whatever it was that got on her began to bubble and drip off. She groaned, letting me know she was at least alive.

At the center of the blast, Dr. Pemblescrap stood frozen with her hand outstretched, covered in black goo. The only thing saving her eyes from the muck was her thick glasses. I wasn't sure how she did it, but the explosion seemed to have not affected her at all other than stunning the green woman.

Heavy footsteps in the distance got my attention and soon the room was flooded with people covered with shiny plastic-looking robes that also covered their faces. I continued to do my best for Mrs. Hodgins as they swarmed into the room.

Kalli waved frantically and shouted, "Over here! Mrs. Hodgins needs help."

One of the shiny fire mages rushed over and removed her hood. "Move out of the way. How is she hurt? What exactly happened?"

"We were testing a poison," I began weakly. "It exploded."

The woman who removed the hood glanced up at me while applying a strange paste to the side of Mrs. Hodgins's face. "That's forbidden outside of the lab. Who authorized this?"

I didn't know what to say. As far as I knew, Mrs. Hodgins and Dr. Pemblescrap were high-ranking guild members. Noticing our worry, the women's expression softened. "Look, she's going to be fine. It looks like you managed to get whatever that was off her before it did any real damage. We won't know for sure until we run some tests, but it looks like she might get away with just a scar or two."

Kalli let out a long sigh, apparently having been holding her breath. She fell to her knees and took one of Mrs. Hodgins's hands in her own. "Don't worry, I'm here for you."

Wondering how the guild handled magical injuries, I asked, "Is there a hospital for the awakened?"

The woman nodded as she continued to treat Mrs. Hodgins. "Yes but that's only for serious injuries. The local hospital is more than adequate for injuries like this. Our medics will see to it that she has the proper ointment for her malady, and they will send us samples of her

THE ACCIDENTAL CORRUPTION

blood to make sure there are no surprises but other than that, she should be fine."

Heaving a sigh of relief, I climbed to my feet and made my way over to the wrecked table where the potion exploded. Dr. Pemblescrap was coming out of her stupor, looking around in mild surprise.

Another of the robed men pulled his hood off. "Geronima, what's the meaning of this? You know better than to conduct unauthorized experiments outside of quarantine."

She grinned sheepishly. "It was just a simple poison deconstruction. This boy never told me if contained anything volatile."

"I told you we didn't know what was in it," I argued, not wanting to be thrown under the bus.

"Who are you?" the man asked, redirecting his glare to me.

I wanted to know who he was, too.

Name: Dazon Wren
Class: Actuationist
Level: 73
Affection Level: Serious

Another new name and class I knew nothing about. It would help if the System could tell me what his role was with the guild.

Deciding not to be rude, I introduced myself. "My name is Melvin Murphy."

The glare turned into a raised eyebrow. "I see. The Melvin Murphy. What brings you here today?"

Did he know of me? Did Mrs. Hodgins tell him...or someone else? It was hard to be sure. Kalli explained for me, "We came to visit Mrs. Hodgins."

"And this magical experiment?" Dazon inquired, running a gloved finger through the ashes on the wrecked table. "Did either of you have a part in this mayhem?"

"We brought samples of something we thought was poison," I explained. "Dr. Pemblescrap wanted to run some tests on it. I didn't know there was a protocol."

"Indeed," Dazon muttered, returning his stink eye to Dr. Pemble-scrap. "Very well. This is coming out of your pay, Geronima."

It was when I turned to walk back to Kalli that he stopped me. "Wait, Mr. Murphy, you're contaminated."

I froze. Did he sense the poison? Was there some sort of skill that allowed him to analyze my mana? It all made sense when he said, "Can you not feel that? You have a sticky black substance on your back. Come over here and let one of my men take a look at you."

While the explosion did manage to burn me a bit, I knew exactly what he was talking about. "That's not from the blast. That's my armor. I own an artifact."

"Wait just a second." Dazon gasped, taking a renewed interest in my back. "I recognize this armor. It's from the museum. I was there the day you stole it. The powers that be told me to let it go but I've always wondered who was brazen enough to march into a secure facility and walk out with a top-class relic."

"Secure?" I spat the word. "Did you know Kalli was abducted from that place? Where were you when that happened? She could have been killed."

I was deflecting, but I had a point, and he knew it. Dazon cleared his throat and explained, "While we go to great lengths to safeguard the more valuable artifacts in the museum, we had little reason to believe that any patrons would be in danger. Those at risk typically come with their own protection. Still, I apologize. We were caught off guard. She was kidnapped by a vampire, right?"

That part wasn't clear. While Mrs. Shaw was ultimately behind the kidnapping, I always thought it was Eddie's dad that grabbed her in the first place. Either that or Mr. Bellview. Speaking of the man in red. "Hey, Mr. Wren, does Mr. Bellview still come here? As a bounty hunter, I mean."

He raised an eyebrow. "I'm sorry but we don't give out information like that. Why do you ask?"

"I was thinking about hiring him to help me find someone," I replied, realizing what I was worried about.

"Who?" Kalli and Dazon asked at the same time, though Kalli's question came through in my mind along with a wave of worry.

"My mom," I managed to choke out. Why was I getting emotional? "She's been missing for a while now."

Dazon looked at me with sympathy in his expression. "I'll see what I can do. Do you trust Mr. Bellview? Is that why you requested him?"

Well, that, and he owed me a favor. I grinned. "Yep! I trust him."

"Very well." He bowed. "If you'll excuse me."

Then he tore from the room. I was so grateful to get off the hook about the artifact that I didn't even notice the other woman poking and prodding my back. "It looks like this boy is going to need to go to the hospital too. His skin is red from the explosion. We need to be cautious since we don't know what contaminants were released."

———

I was dragged kicking and screaming to the hospital. Well, not really. I just didn't want to go. Kalli chose to ride with Mrs. Hodgins to the ambulance while I was brought in a car. She seemed to be fine, but I had no way of checking because of the corruption in my core. Dr. Pemblescrap offered to ride with me, but I turned her down flatly. It wasn't like I was a kid and, besides, I didn't even know the woman.

At the hospital, the doctors tried to cut my artifact off with scissors. It was funny watching their faces as the artifact reformed over and over.

Then someone gave me a black wristband. The nurses that had been fawning over me suddenly all couldn't get out of the room fast enough. The orderly who applied the wristband nodded and informed me, "As far as they are concerned you now have the plague. Don't worry, an expert will be by shortly to give you a once over. If he determines that you aren't a risk to yourself or the community, you'll be free to go."

"What about the others?" I asked, worried about Mrs. Hodgins.

"Others?" He looked at a clipboard. "Oh, right. It looks like minor injuries. She might have to stay overnight, but she should be fine as well."

———

Meanwhile, in Ukraine…

The man with the pointy beard walked slowly through a decimated street.

It was here that the boy removed a tank from existence.

His brother. Sibling. Relative. Someone he was related to. The man had a nose for these kinds of things. The person who invaded his war was indeed of his bloodline. The M bloodline.

The first question he needed to establish was what this person was doing in his territory. His war. Standing at the spot where the tank vanished yielded no clues. The tank simply wasn't there. Whatever magic this was, it had to be powerful. 's didn't know weak magic. That was a given.

He strode across the street to the spot he had seen the boy. The M in question was still a child. Perhaps just at the age of maturity, perhaps a little younger.

BANG!

BANG!

BANG!

Mosquitos! He looked up to see three bullets frozen in midair, trapped in his static distortion field. Just across the street, three masked rebels stared blankly at him, not believing what they were seeing.

He normally didn't stoop to swatting flies but, in this case, he could leave no witnesses. If the wrong people were alerted to his actions, the whole war would have been for naught.

Producing a wand with a flick of his wrist, he swished it back and forth, like a conductor directing a symphony. Black lines appeared in the air around the rebels moments before their bodies were torn apart.

He re-holstered his wand and dusted off his hands. He hated wasting mana on insignificant pawns. Such a waste. Then he remembered his mission and marched over to the spot where the boy vanished.

He could smell it. Magic in the air. Teleportation was powerful. A mage had to rip a hole in the fabric of time and space to do it. That kind of damage left its mark. Like a syringe plunging into the belly of a diabetic. It was small but it was still there.

A gloved hand reached out and stroked the air, caressing the gash left behind by the magic. All he had to do was peel the portal open again, and he could follow. A line in the void was drawn. A line that would lead him to the boy, and ultimately to their father.

Putting thoughts to action, he folded his mana into the gash and stepped into the void. The hunt was on!

[23]

THE TRIP to the hospital was a short one. I willed the artifact armor into a bracelet so the doctors wouldn't be suspicious when they examined my back.

When the nurse approached to draw blood, I hesitated. I didn't know the extent of the corruption in my body and didn't want to risk passing it to an innocent unawakened.

Mrs. Hodgins was admitted right away. They told me I wouldn't be able to visit her. Unfortunately for them, I had Kalli. A quick trip to the restroom and a short teleport through the hospital, and I was by her side.

Mrs. Hodgins sat up and gave me a reassuring smile. "What's with the frown? I'm fine. Something like this isn't going to keep me down. What's an old lady need with a perfect face?"

From the looks of things, she was going to have a pretty gnarly scar on the left side of her face. As far as the explosion went, she was right, it could have been a lot worse. I felt guilty even though it wasn't exactly my fault. We brought the potions, after all.

Kalli looked up at me with red eyes. "I think I'm going to stay with her. At least until the blood tests come back."

I nodded and sat on a couch in the corner of the room. It felt just like the good old times, like when I hung out with Mrs. Hodgins in the library. She told us about the guild and the various awakened that passed through.

While not an adventurer herself, she spent a lot of time talking to them as they visited the library doing research. As the head scholar in the biggest guild branch in San Diego, everyone who wanted restricted books had to pass through her.

Kalli told stories about Gaia and how we cured the plague and built an empire. Mrs. Hodgins smiled when we told her exactly how Kalli and I got out of the contract.

She snorted when we told her about the prophecy, grimacing in pain as she aggravated her wound. Tutting at Kalli she waggled her finger. "I think that prophecy is a good thing for the two of you. Nothing like a prophecy baby to make hanky-panky less appealing."

Kalli blushed. "There wasn't going to be any of that going on even without the prophecy, right, Melvin?"

I nodded, only partially in agreement. Damn that prophecy. Before I was forced to give an answer, Dazon Wren entered the hospital room. Behind him was a familiar face wearing his custom red suit and hat.

"Mr. Bellview!" Kalli cried out, beaming at the bounty hunter. "How is your wife?"

Mr. Bellview returned the smile, a weird look on his normally serious face. "She's great. In fact, she can beat me in a foot race now. When you awakened her and made it so she can walk, she ended up with a courier class that gives her bonuses to stamina and speed. It's not that we need services like that with email and all but she's enjoying it. She got a job delivering magical items."

The idea of Mrs. Bellview running with the wind made me chuckle. She was the person that started my life as a healer. It was a shame that I couldn't heal anyone else with my mana until I cured the poison.

Mr. Bellview surprised me by placing a hand on my shoulder. "So, what can I do for you? Director Wren says you have a request for me."

"Oh, right," I began, not quite sure how to phrase my request. "You see. My mom's missing. She said she had to go somewhere, but I have no way of getting in touch with her. Do you think you can help me find her?"

Mrs. Hodgins said, "Melvin. You read your mother's letter. She's fine. She told you not to go looking for her."

"I have a bad feeling about it," was all I could say.

Mr. Bellview settled into the couch next to me and asked, "Do you have the letter? May I see it?"

I shuffled around in my bag for a moment before presenting it. Kalli looked over Mr. Bellview's shoulder as he read the letter.

My Dearest Son,

First, I want to tell you not to worry about me. I didn't go off searching for you even though you forgot to check in with me when you left Earth. (I will talk to you about that later!)

There is something that I have to do. You might not hear from me for a while but, please, understand that I will miss you every single day. Don't worry about me.

I have left some money for you with the guild. Consider it your inheritance. I can't put a timetable on my return, so just keep living your best life until we see each other again.

Love always,
Mom

"Well, it sounds like she doesn't want you to go looking for her." Mr. Bellview said after reading it. "But, I'd be happy to look into it for you. I have some connections that can help. After what you did for us, I owe you one."

"Thanks," I replied. "I just want to know that she's okay."

"Let me see that," Dazon said, looking at the letter. "Did you know about this, Vanessa? The part about leaving money with the guild?"

Mrs. Hodgins smiled and nodded. "That's right. She said there's a vault for Melvin in the crypt. Said it's from his father."

"My father?" I asked, shocked at the revelation. "Did you meet him, Mrs. Hodgins?"

She shook her head. "No. Your mother only mentioned him. I believe she went to go see him about something."

I always assumed my dad abandoned us. Could Mom possibly have known how to get in touch with him all along and just never told me about it?

I felt a soft touch on my shoulder from Mr. Bellview. "Do you still want me to track her down?"

After thinking about it for a few seconds, I nodded. "I can't believe my mom knew where my dad was all along. I've wanted to meet him since before I can remember."

"I'll get right on it." Mr. Bellview promised. "Top priority."

"In the meantime," Dazon added, "you can come visit the crypt and see what she left for you."

The thought did intrigue me. Kalli smiled and urged me on. *Go, Mel. Mrs. Hodgins will be fine with me here. You can get me when you're done.*

In the end, curiosity won. "I'd like to see what my parents left me."

Dazon smiled. "Okay, kids. Are you ready to go?"

Kalli shook her head. "I'll wait here, thanks."

———

The vault wasn't in the guild building where I expected it to be. It was at a fully functional Jiffy Lube. Or beneath it in any case. Dazon led me into one of the oil change bays down a stairwell to the pit beneath the cars.

On the wall was a series of panels with various switches and levers. Dazon opened one of the panels revealing a tiny black button. When he pushed it, the floor started to descend.

Down and down we went until a thick metal door was revealed.

Green light flooded the chamber, and a female voice called out, "Please, state your names."

"Dazon Wren, Director of Guild office four four two seven," Dazon said. "Now, you. Say your name."

"Melvin Murphy," I croaked, reminded of the high house security system.

A series of clanking sounds echoed from the door, and it swung open. Dazon stepped into the hall beyond and motioned for me. "Come, your vault is in here."

He didn't have to tell me where. A green light lit the path to my assigned vault. It was deep in the crypt. We passed by rows of what looked like mailboxes and safety deposit boxes before coming to small doors that looked like closets.

After descending twice, Dazon whistled. "Wow, I didn't think it was going to be one of the big ones. The letter said money, right? Your mother must have left you a fortune."

That didn't make sense. Mom knew I needed money for Kalli's contract, didn't she? Did I actually forget to ask her when she told me she knew about magic? I could have saved so much trouble if I'd just asked my mom for money.

Then again, if Mom was so rich, why were we so poor? I was still mulling over it when we arrived. A garage door stood between me and my inheritance.

Dazon looked back and forth between the door and me. "So, um, I guess you'd like a little privacy, wouldn't you? Do you need my help getting back to the hospital?"

I shook my head. "No, I can get back to Kalli no matter where she goes."

With a final sad look, the guild director reluctantly shuffled off toward the exit. I waited patiently until he was well out of sight. Then, I realized I forgot to ask him how to get the vault open.

The moment I touched the door, the security system spoke again, "State your name."

"Melvin Murphy," I repeated.

The door slid up unceremoniously revealing a room filled with…

junk. I waded into what must have been a hoarder's dream. Furniture that looked unlike anything I'd ever seen on Earth filled the room. For all I knew, it was probably from another world.

Kalli commented, startling me, *That doesn't look like money.*

I sighed and began wading into the mess.

I noticed. Mom must have left something in here for me if she felt it was important enough to tell me about in the note. Also, there must be a reason she said it was money. I think it has something to do with the word inheritance.

What would Mom want me to find? I climbed over an old couch made out of a substance that felt like water with a solid surface. Everything was wedged together as if the person who packed it was playing furniture Tetris.

I considered deleting some in an effort to see if there was anything in the back. The problem was, if I did that, I might delete what I was looking for. That was probably how hoarders got started. Everything's important!

It took a while, but I managed to make a hole in the wall of furniture. On the other side was a single table. It wasn't a special table. Just an ordinary four-legged table.

On top of the table were two items. A black candle and a dollar bill. After turning the candle over in my hands, I looked at the dollar. There was a handwritten note.

Burn only in your darkest hour.

———

Meanwhile, very near Kalliville…

A trio stepped out of a portal. Two wore hazmat suits. The third was different. The scout wore no protective suit. She had on an oversized lab coat and glasses. In her hand was a stopwatch. She glanced at it expectantly as she waited.

"One minute," she said more to herself than to the other two.

"Two minutes." She marked off another minute, not really expecting anything to happen.

"Excuse me, miss," Natalia's muffled voice came from one of the hazmat suits. "Are you sure it was wise to come without any protective…"

The girl held up a hand, silencing her. "Three minutes. It's perfectly safe. Antoni demonstrated this fact. Do you not trust your own eyes?"

The worker, Antoni, took off his hood. He was braver than Natalia. Zofia made a note. "Four minutes."

The portal was stable. Well within her calculations. "Five minutes."

There was smoke coming from the west. A village or town perhaps? "Six minutes."

Was portal stability a constant or a variable? She would find out in a minute. "Seven minutes."

Now she would find out. Ten seconds. Still good. Fifteen. Did it just flicker? Twenty. It was unstable. Twenty-five seconds. It vanished. "Seven minutes, twenty-five seconds. Are you positive it was twenty-three seconds last time?"

Natalia fumbled with her hood before, finally, taking it off. Perhaps there was hope for her yet. "Yes, twenty-three. I am positive. The variance might be because you timed it from the destination rather than the origin."

That was a possibility. The portal may not vanish from both sides at the same time. She would have to compare notes with the technicians upon her return.

For now, it was time to explore.

[24]

ONE DOLLAR. One lousy stinking dollar. That actually felt more in line with what I'd expect from my family. We were poor after all. This wasn't Harry Potter where the young hero had a vault full of gold and gems waiting for him all his life.

The writing on the bill was clearly from Mom. Whatever it was for, she thought I needed the candle. I was still getting used to mom knowing about the awakened world. For her to not only possess a relic but also to know I was going to need one was mind-blowing.

Item: Candle of ?????????
Components: Wax, Wick, ??? ????
Item Rank: SS
Item Level: ???
Item Owner: M

Double S. That was new. I always thought the System was capped at S. It was strange that the System couldn't identify it, though. That usually meant the item predated the System. If that was the case, why did it know the rank?

Was there anything else in all that junk? Kalli wanted to know.

Of course, I couldn't leave any stone unturned, so I was forced to go back through the boxes I'd seen stacked among the furniture. It looked like things someone might put into storage when moving from one house to another. Only none of it looked like anything I'd ever seen on Earth before.

A quick probe into a strange-looking table sent shivers down my spine. There was mana in the furniture. It was all magic. The question was, for what purpose? What did it do?

Deciding that I couldn't infect furniture with corruption, I pushed mana into the table. It reminded me of Kalli's old wand and how it absorbed mana as it passed through. That didn't make any sense though. How did someone pass mana through a coffee table? And why?

Moving on, I started opening boxes. It reminded me of one time when my mother and I moved in the past. The boxes were packed by room or so it seemed. There were magical kitchen appliances, and I had no idea what they did.

None of the appliances had plugs of any sort. One had a round hole leading to a plastic bowl. When I applied mana to it a vicious-looking blue aura appeared in the hole and words glowed on the side of the device.

THE COBBER

At least it wasn't a sex toy. That would have been weird. For that reason, I skipped the box labeled Mom and Dad's room. One of the boxes at the back caught my eye. A faded label on the side said, **FAMILY**. I swallowed hard. It was Mom's handwriting. I knew because of the strange way she dotted her I with a little heart.

It was a little embarrassing to go through what could be my past with an audience. Kalli could feel my nervousness. *Do you want me to give you some privacy?*

While I was worried about what I might find in the box, Kalli was a part of me, and I wanted her there for it.

No. Let's do this together.

I felt her smile and that gave me the courage to open the box. At first, the contents of the box were a little disappointing if not downright embarrassing. Baby clothes, presumably mine, were neatly folded at the top of the box.

Something I discovered a little deeper caused my breath to catch in my throat. A leather-bound volume rested atop a taped-up box.

M&M Photo Album

Could it be? Was I finally about to see what my dad looked like? Why did mom keep this from me? So many questions swirled through my mind.

The first several pages were filled with pictures I recognized. Pictures of me when I was a baby. Pictures of me growing up. I rapidly flipped through the book, frustration mounting as I saw more of the same.

Until the last page that was. There was a single picture of my mother. It was a much younger version of her standing next to a man who looked familiar.

I knew him. I'd seen him before. We even spoke to each other. It was the man from my dream. The one resting on a throne surrounded by women.

What did he say to me? I was the last person he expected to see? Kalli breathed in my ear. ***Relax, Mel. It's going to be okay. Is that your father?***

Her voice grounded me and brought me back from the edge. I set the book aside and picked up the taped box. A quick shake confirmed it to be full of something. There was no label or anything on the outside to tell me what that might be. The System didn't even want to help.

Item: A Box
Components: Cardboard
Item Rank: F
Item Level: 1
Item Owner: M

That was strange. Shouldn't the owner be Murphy? Did the System somehow cut it off? Was this all dads? Or perhaps mine? I ruled out the last idea because my stuff always showed up as Murphy.

Deciding to just get it over with, I ripped off the tape and opened the box. Inside were hundreds of letters. I opened the first one.

Dearest Michael,

It's been a year since you left. Enclosed are more pictures of your son. I miss you. He misses you and he's never even met you. I want you to know I've named him Melvin. You know, after your other name. I know it's not the same, but I don't want him to get bullied too much. At least this way his friends can call him Mel.

I know you wanted me to go with you, but I have to follow my heart here. I don't want to share you. Please, understand. The time we had together was magical, and I don't regret a single moment of it. You showed me a world that I could never have imagined in a thousand dreams.

Melvin is my dream now, and I am going to raise him to live his best life. I hope you think of me from time to time. It's probably best that you not visit. At least not until you are ready to stay and be the father we both know Melvin deserves.

Love always,
Sam

PS: I've enclosed some pictures and a little something to remember me by.

Tears flowed down my cheek as I set the letter down. So, Dad was called Michael, huh? Also, what did Mom give him to remember her by? I probably didn't want to know. What was this about dad having another name? So many questions.

I flipped through the other letters. They all seemed to be her hand-writing. I grabbed the last one from the bottom.

Michael,

It happened. He's awakened. When it didn't happen at twelve, I was beginning to think it might never happen. He's been keeping the whole thing a secret from me. The jokes on him, though. I used some of the tools you left behind to keep tabs on him.

I think he has a girlfriend, though neither of them is willing to admit it. There was a bit of drama recently, and I think he got into trouble with a vampire. He seems to have worked it out. The two of them, he and his friend (girlfriend?) are heading to the Academy.

Did you want to train him yourself? I've kept my promise to not tell him about you. I guess I always hoped you could come back when it was time.

I hope you are getting these. It wouldn't kill you to send a reply every now and then.

Sam

I dug through the box and looked over some of the other letters but there didn't appear to be anything newer. Did she stop writing? Could it have been that Dad just kept the newer letters somewhere else?

It also made me wonder who left the message on the dollar bill. Was that Dad, too? That would mean this was his vault and not Mom's. But why would she leave the message telling me where to find it. The whole thing was leaving me with more questions than answers.

I looked through the rest of the vault and didn't find anything remotely as interesting as the family box. When I sat on the sofa and buried my head in my hands, Kalli whispered through MateChat in my ear, *Come back.*

A quick jump through the void, and I was back at her side. Kalli wasted no time wrapping me in a deep hug. Mrs. Hodgins sat up in bed. "Is everything all right?"

Kalli replied for me as my voice was lost for the moment. "It's fine. He just got news about his father. Everything will be okay."

I think she said that last line more to me than anybody else.

———

We stayed in the hospital for two more days before they allowed Mrs. Hodgins to go home. It wasn't so much the damage from the explosion. That healed quickly and the guild sent healers over to make sure she only had minimal scars. The real scare was not knowing what was in that potion and how it would affect the old Scholar.

They weren't as worried about me considering the damage all but vanished in the first hour. Mr. Bellview hadn't checked back in yet. That probably meant he hadn't found anything. I kicked myself for not thinking to take the album or letters out of the vault. Not that they would have been super useful. I also didn't know how I felt about having my dad's picture.

He abandoned me, or so it seemed. Mom conveniently wasn't around to dispute it. Was I mad at her, or was I just worried? I knew I missed her.

Kalli was my rock. She nuzzled me and asked, *What should we do now? Do you know any other alchemists we can try?*

I have a couple of ideas. While we're on Earth, I think we should talk to my old master. Chogu taught me the basics of mana refinement. Perhaps he knows a thing or two about purging.

While I technically could have teleported back to my old dorm, neither of us was sure if it would work since I hadn't been there in so long. It wasn't like home where I had a lasting bond.

We decided to take the phoenix and fly along the coast. Kalli flew low to the ground when we passed the beach. I smiled, remembering Kalli wearing a swimsuit while we shared lunch.

That's where we had our first date.

She looked down and blushed. *I still can't believe people do 'that' under the pier. That's so icky.*

I laughed, remembering the security guard chasing us away.

———

Farther north in Anaheim, Kalli squealed when we passed over Matterhorn Mountain at Disneyland. *You promised to take me back. Do you want to go now?*

While we were in a hurry to save our friends, the doctors at the high house were taking care of the two people who were poisoned. I decided to make an executive decision and clear my mind for a bit.

A few hours should be fine.

———

We both remembered what happened the last time and neither of us wanted to get kicked out again.

Rule 1: No fancy dresses
Rule 2: No calling Kalli a princess
Rule 3: Absolutely no signing autographs
**Rule 4: Have as much fun as possible before getting
kicked out**

It was easy when you knew the rules. Kalli and I went on a bunch of rides. We may have cheated and magicked our way through some lines. I'm not admitting to anything. There's no shame in minor misuses of magic. Disneyland is the most magical place on Earth after all.

Kalli's smile was infectious as she held my hand and tugged me toward yet another line. This time it was Mr. Toad's Wild Ride. *This place is amazing.*

You know, the last time we pretended you were a princess. It turned out you're actually royalty.

She stopped and thought about it for a while. *I don't feel any different than last time.*

The only thing I care about is you're actually my girlfriend this time.

Kalli beamed at me. *We are so much more than that. You're my soulmate.*

When she kissed me, I decided Disneyland really was the most magical place on Earth.

I used some of the cash I had to buy us churros and frozen bananas. Kalli made me jealous when she swooned over Captain Jack Sparrow on the Pirates of the Caribbean ride. Damn that Johnny Depp.

Hours turned into the entire day. We only realized how long we stayed when the sun started to set. Fortunately, there was a parade and fireworks, so we didn't feel too bad staying late.

As the show came to an end, Kalli looked over at me nervously. *Where are we going to sleep?*

My first call on the M-Phone was to Joe. "Hello?"

Hearing my friend's voice made my heart swell. "Joe! Kalli and I are back in L.A. Do you think we can stay at your place for the night?"

Joe's frustration was evident in his voice. "I'm sorry, man. Wendy and I are still in Japan. If you come back in a week or so, we should be back. You won't believe what I found out."

"Hm, Do you know anyone we can stay with?" I asked, too distracted by our current predicament to pay much attention to Joe's latest revelation.

He replied, "Did you ask Run? He lives over there. I'm sure he'll let you stay for a day."

"Oh, yeah." I smiled. "Thanks, Joe."

"No problem," he replied. "Let's get together and have lunch or something when we get back. Or you can always come to Japan. It's awesome here."

I thought about it. I really did. Unfortunately, we were on a mission, and we had wasted enough time.

[25]

"TRUST ME. You do not want to stay in my house." Rundell said with a smirk. "I have a large family. Tell you what though, why don't you two stay in the RV."

"RV?" Kalli asked, looking to me for an explanation.

I turned my head to see a forty-foot recreational vehicle sitting in the space along the side of the house. Eyeing it suspiciously, I made my way over.

Kalli poked me as she followed along. *This looks a lot like the mecharriage Joe made. Did he make this, too?*

I smiled back at her, taking her hand in mind.

No. This is what he modeled it after. That or a bus. People make big vehicles they can live in while they travel. The problem is most of the ones I've seen are pretty dirty on the inside.

What we found was not dirty at all. In fact, Rundell and his family were a bit OCD with how they kept the camper organized and clean. Run grinned at us and asked, "Will this do?"

We both nodded enthusiastically, and he added, "Look, please take the sheets off the bed and put them in the laundry when you're done. Also, come over to the house after you've settled in. We're going to have dinner in the back yard, and you're both invited."

We explored the RV once Run left us alone. Neither of us brought a change of clothes, so we resorted to Kalli's patented method of cleaning them.

"**Pvruzth.**"

Kalli and I were so used to our unique form of cleaning that neither of us so much batted an eye as we thoroughly cleaned each other. We agreed it was funner to do each other rather than ourselves.

Once she was satisfied she was clean, Kalli plopped down on the bed, frowning at me. "I think I'm spoiled. This bed's kind of stiff. I remember sleeping on a bed made of straw back at the monastery, and now this is uncomfortable."

I grinned, getting an idea. "I know! I have just the thing for that."

The Cradle: Apply this magical spray to any bed or other surface to get the best sleep you've ever had. The magic will make even the hardest surface as soft as you want. It will also conform to your body for perfect lumbar support. A single bottle contains 100 sprays that last over a year.

It took me a while to dig the can out of my fanny pack. Kalli looked up at me from the bed, recognizing the can. "Wait, let me get up first."

Grinning at her, I held out the can menacingly. "Do you think this will make you softer as well?"

"I'm soft enough, thank you very much!" she protested as she tried to climb off the bed before I could spray her.

In the end, a healthy coat of cradle made the bed much more comfortable. We lay next to each other for a few minutes before deciding to go see what was for dinner.

The family meal turned out to be a lot bigger than we could have imagined. Run's family was huge. Thirty people crammed into the tiny well-landscaped yard. Children played around on a jungle gym and a treehouse in the back while the adults, which somehow included us, sat around a fire pit. Run and his father prepared dinner while we introduced ourselves to everyone.

Strips of marinated meat and vegetables lay on platters next to the grill as Run waited for it to heat up. On top of the grill was a griddle which Run's dad sprayed down with cooking oil before placing strips of beef with a satisfying sizzling sound.

I watched in silence for a while as the succulent smells of marinated beef assaulted my nose. Another girl in a floral-patterned dress dragged Kalli away.

Run nodded and said, "That's my fiancé, Randalia. She'll take good care of Kalli. Don't worry."

"You're engaged?" I gasped, forgetting about the food but only for a second.

He chortled and had to back away from the grill for a moment. "Serious, bro? Out of everyone, I thought you'd understand. When you know, you know, right? I've known Ran since forever and we've been in love since high school. I'd have married her already if not for our adventure on Gaia. She's still a little upset that I didn't tell her we were going."

"Yeah, we should have planned better," I admitted reluctantly. "My mom was also mad that I didn't call. I was just so worried about Kalli at the time."

"I get it, bro." He sighed, flipping the meat and adding a row of vegetables to a rack situated on a raised grill. "I'd have done the same thing for Ran. Ultimately, I think that's why she forgave me. Speaking of which, you two should totally come to the wedding. Joe's the best man and all, but you can totally be one of the groomsmen. There's only like thirteen of them so far."

I laughed nervously, imagining myself at the end of a long line of Run's brothers and cousins. "That sounds like fun. We will try to be there. When is it happening?"

Run rubbed his chin. "Hmm, maybe in a year or two. A lot of family members have to make accommodations so they can attend. Maybe by that time you and Joe will be getting married too."

Marriage was one thing I hadn't thought about yet. The idea both excited and terrified me. Being mated, intertwined, and even bound by an oath seemed like nothing in comparison to marching down the aisle in front of...wait, I didn't have any family besides my mom.

While it was true there were plenty of friends we could invite and Kalli's family that could go, I didn't exactly have anyone in my corner anymore. Were Maya and Kiki family now? Would the whole empire turn up? For that matter, was our marriage going to be some kind of royal affair on Gaia like Meghan and Harry? The thought terrified me. I wondered how Kalli felt about the whole thing.

Hey, Kalli, what do you think about marriage?

She gasped in my head. *A-a-are you proposing to me?*

I felt the blood drain from my head as I realized what I'd asked. Did I want to propose to her? On the one hand, deep down, I knew that she was the only girl I would ever love. Why was it so hard to make that official?

Still, I stammered my thoughts.

D-d-do you w-w-want to?

Kalli was silent for a while. Being shy didn't do her any good because we were connected. She had the opposite reaction as me. All of the blood rose to her face, making her blush in the mirror where Randalia was currently applying her makeup. In my eyes, she couldn't get any more beautiful. That thought only made her blush even more.

She then made me feel like the king of the universe. *Yes. I'll marry you.*

We both stood there in stunned silence for a few minutes, each in different parts of the house but feeling like we were standing right next to each other, our souls bared completely. After considering the implications of what she just said, Kalli added, *Eventually! We don't have to do the actual ceremony right now. We're still young after all.*

Right! Eventually. I don't mind waiting.

———

Food never tasted so good. People were talking to me, and I think I even replied to some of them, but I couldn't take my eyes off Kalli. She was stunning. Randalia did her hair up in a bun and gave her a little eye shadow which made her look a whole lot more grown up.

That combined with the fact that we somehow got engaged and I was burning with a fire that a thousand cold showers couldn't put out. I had no clue how I was going to sleep next to Kalli without burning the whole RV down.

The rest of the meal flew by in a flash. Before we knew it, we were back in the squishy comfy bed. Neither of us was tired. Neither of us could sleep. We lay side by side, looking into each other's eyes.

Kalli whispered, "Did we really just do that? Am I your fiancé?"

I flashed her a wicked grin. "Do you want to be my fiancé?"

She beamed. "I already said yes, silly."

"Then it's settled." I started to laugh, but she quickly shut me up with a kiss.

Then another, and another, and another. After a while, I rolled over on top of her, and she stopped me. "Melvin, we can't. You remember the prophecy."

So, I rolled onto my back, staring at the ceiling and trying to catch my breath. Kalli climbed on top of me with a smile that matched mine. "That doesn't mean we can't fool around."

———

I'd like to say we dreamed or entered our private dream world but neither of us slept. We climbed out of bed when the sun rose and decided to head to Little Tokyo to see if we could find Chogu.

Before we left, we packed up the bedding into the laundry and took showers. I wanted to take one together considering our new engaged status, but the tiny RV shower only admitted one person at a time.

Even though Kalli used up all the hot water, the shower still invigorated me enough to feel ready for the day. It took us twenty minutes to get from Run's place to Little Tokyo. We landed just outside of the forge and were happy to hear clanking sounds coming from inside. The blacksmith was in the building.

When we approached, Chogu was just finishing a project. I raised my voice so he could hear me over the sound. "Master, I've returned."

He turned, surprise evident in his eyes. "Well, well, well. My wayward disciple has returned. Do you care to explain yourself?"

Kalli and I looked at each other in panic for a moment. I was way too tired to come up with excuses. Fortunately, Kalli bailed me out. "I was in another world and Melvin had to come help me out. We came back as soon as we could."

"I see," he said with a smile. "So, you've come to resume your training, then?"

"Um," I stammered, worried we'd backed ourselves into a corner. "Not exactly. Master, we need your help."

He set the hammer down and folded his arms. "Let me see if I understand this correctly. You disappear without notice. Mind you, this is an apprenticeship you begged me for so you could learn my trade. Now you return only to ask for more favors."

I got down on my knees, hoping to show that I was truly sorry. "I wouldn't ask if it wasn't important, Master. You see, due to corruption that found its way into my mana, a few innocent people got hurt. If we don't fix this, there's a very real chance they might die."

Chogu twirled his beard around his fingers and sat on a bench next to the forge. "I see. Corruption of the chakra isn't unheard of. There are stories of it happening in the past. If my memory serves correctly, you are going to have to purge your core completely. This is a dangerous process that I am not qualified to teach. To do so would mean draining yourself of all mana and, as you know, mana is needed to sustain life. In other words, you will cease to exist for those few moments after the purge while your core reforms with fresh mana. In return, you will come back anew, reborn and stronger than before."

Kalli's eyes widened as we both realized the repercussions of what Chogu was telling us. *That means I have to do it, too.*

Suddenly another problem dawned on me. "Hey, what about the

other two people who are corrupted? One of them is only newly awakened. She couldn't possibly purge her mana."

Chogu frowned. "Then she will likely die. I don't know what to tell you, kid. Corruption in the ki isn't something an amateur can typically deal with. Consider it nature's way of weeding out the weak. On the bright side, she will be reborn. This is the way of all things."

That doesn't work at all.

Kalli frowned, still trying to work out a solution. *It doesn't but we should still learn what Chogu knows. That way we can at least be one step closer to fixing this.*

I took a deep breath and asked, "How do we purge our cores?"

Chogu groaned and stood, placing a soot-covered hand on my shoulder. "Look, kid. I want to tell you it isn't easy, and that may be true, but the reality is I don't know enough myself to teach you. I just know that it's possible. You could go back east and maybe try to seek out some monks but the odds of you finding someone both skilled enough and willing to teach you is very slim. I hate to say this but saving them is probably a lost cause."

"No!" I shouted, looking around for something to slam my fist on. When I found nothing, I continued, "I refuse to acknowledge I've killed them. I'll find a way to do it whether you help me or not."

"Hold on just a second," Chogu said softly, holding his hands up to calm me. "Tell me how you killed someone. I take it that you exposed them to the same thing that corrupted you, right?"

"Well, no," I admitted reluctantly. "My mana got corrupted and when I pushed my mana inside of them, it corrupted theirs as well."

"How?" he stammered, gaping at me. "How are you able to exert dominance over another person's ki? Should not their very essence expel you from their body?"

"Only when I touch their core," I replied, getting into the explanation.

"Their c-c-c-core?" he stammered, eyes growing wide. "You mean to tell me you've touched the soul of another human being?"

I rubbed the back of my head sheepishly. "Well, I've awakened several hundred people as well as countless trolls, goblins, dwarves, elves, and other creatures."

Chogu froze as he took in what I had to say. Then he burst out into laughter. "Boy! You had me for a minute there. Were that true, you would have broken the laws of nature itself. Now, answer me honestly. How did you corrupt the others?"

I sighed. That didn't go as planned. "I'm not lying. I did exactly what I said I did."

————

Even though Chogu kicked us out, I wasn't too worried.

It's not like he really knew what to do. Also, there's someone else we haven't talked to.

Who? Kalli asked, turning to give me a curious look.

The ancients. They invented emotional mana in the first place so they should know how to fix it.

[26]

WE CAN'T GO JUST YET. I wouldn't forgive myself if I don't visit Madam Himiko while were here.

I couldn't argue. Also, free food! We walked hand in hand through the Little Tokyo Plaza on the way over to Suehiro Cafe.

The lady of the house was almost unrecognizable. She smiled when she saw us and said, "Welcome, esteemed guests. I am so glad to see you are back. Wendy told me all about your adventure in another world. Please, have a seat."

Remembering that I'd awakened her the last time I saw her, I decided to check on her progress.

Name: Saori Himiko
Class: Ramen Hero
Level: 25
Affection Level: Proud

I gaped at her. She was glowing. The last time I'd seen her, she was only level two. Somehow, she'd gained twenty-three levels. That was more than either Kalli or I had managed in the same time period. I gasped as I asked, "How did you level up so fast?"

She beamed at me. "I gain experience when I make ramen. Even more so when I experiment and create a new flavor. I also have magic that enhances them. Wendy enrolled me in culinary courses at the Academy, which gave me access to a personal tutor and the library. Did you know there are ancient recipes and techniques that you can't find anywhere else?"

"That's amazing," Kalli replied, licking her lips as waitresses brought us bowl after bowl of ramen. "I miss the Academy. We've been running around so long that I almost forgot what it felt like to relax and learn new magic."

I was dumbfounded as I stared at Kalli. "You want to go back to school?"

She sighed. "I don't know. I want to grow and that means learning new things, right? Look at Miss Himiko. She hasn't even been studying for a year and she's level twenty-five."

Madam Himiko stared at us. "How do you know all of that? I can't tell what level you are. Does it show on my face or something?"

"No," Kalli admitted. "Melvin has a skill that tells him and I can also see through our bond."

She smiled. "I suppose I always knew you guys were special. Come, try the food. We have many new flavors."

I looked down to find twelve bowls sitting on the table. "So, that's why you brought so much?"

Madam Himiko shook her head. "Actually, only half of them are for you. I'd like you both to infuse some for me. It's been a while since I tasted someone else's mana and I'd like to use some of your essences for flavoring."

Kalli and I looked at one another in panic. She shook her head sadly at the Ramen Hero. "Actually, we can't. You see, our mana got corrupted, and that's why we're here. We need a cure. If you eat either of our mana, there's a good chance it will kill you."

Madam Himiko gasped, "Oh, my. That's terrible. Are your lives in danger?"

We quickly shook our heads, and I tried my best to explain. "No, we're fine since we have traits that keep us healthy. Two people I touched are in the hospital though."

Everyone took a step back and I realized that was probably the wrong thing to say. Madam Himiko smiled and said, "Well, enjoy the food. I hope you like the new flavors. If you need me, I'll be in the back."

Kalli frowned when everyone walked away. *You probably should have told them we aren't contagious.*

I laughed, picking up a chopstick, and doing my best to grab some noodles. The memory of Wendy teaching me how to use them made Kalli give me the stink eye. It was time for some damage control.

Do you want to go to the make-out room after this?

Unfortunately, that reminded her of catching me there with Wendy.

Aw, come on! I chose you, remember.

Kalli stuck out her tongue at me with a mischievous twinkle in her eyes. *Just messing with you.*

It was my turn to groan. We took our time enjoying the new ramen flavors that Madam Himiko invented. I immediately tasted the mana on the first bite. She had a special ability to alter the flavor of her mana just enough to compliment several unique recipes.

Did I tell you that her mana looks like ramen broth?

Kalli snorted, causing broth to shoot out of her nose. *Don't make me laugh! It makes sense though. That woman lives for ramen. She was a master before you awakened her.*

We polished off so much ramen that we could barely move. I pointed at a bowl with a small amount of dark broth remaining.

I think I like that one the best. It reminds me of Kung Pao sauce.

Kalli nodded appreciatively but pointed at another bowl with a yellowish sauce. *This one reminds me of tucca seeds. We occasionally ground them up to flavor gruel at the monastery. It tastes like home.*

So, what do you want to do next? Should we visit the Academy while were here? Or do you want to go straight back to Luna to ask the ancients for the cure?

Kalli mulled it over, thinking about our friends and how only Run was likely to be there. The thought that went through my head was

Alex, the jerk who Kalli punched when he was rude to me. I desperately wanted to show off how great Kalli and I were together.

She sensed my thoughts and shook her head with a tiny frown on her face. *You can do that another time but today we have more important things to do. Oh, and if we go back, I think I'm going to take another class.*

Slowly pulling myself to my feet, I walked around the table to take Kalli's hand.

I guess it's decided then. Are you ready to go home?

She nodded, and we were off.

———

The quickest way to Luna, we concluded, was to return to Celestea and use the bathroom door to go back to Lavender's house where we could take another door back to Luna.

We arrived in the throne room to find it full of people. Celestea was seated next to the throne where Shiv was seated. In Kalli's absence, she was the only one who the castle allowed to sit.

Celestea cried out in alarm, and then a smile crept onto her face when she realized it was us. "You two! Perfect timing. We need to discuss a threat to the queendom. And your empire, Melvin so this concerns you as well."

That gave me pause. Normally, Celestea did her best not to acknowledge that we'd set up an empire in the middle of her domain. Kalli gave her mom a look of concern and asked, "What's going on, Mother. What threat?"

Satisfied that she had our attention, Celestea continued, "I don't know what the two of you have been up to but you seem to be having an unnatural effect on the border between our worlds. We have received no fewer than four visitors from Earth in the last week. I need you to sort this out as they are violating the sanctity of our nations with their comings and goings."

I stared at her, heaving a sigh. "You're talking about Antoni, right?

That was one guy wearing a HAZMAT suit. He's harmless and, besides, I already sent him home."

She shook her head. "Well, he's back. And he's brought friends. That's not the least of it either, they set up their own village right here in Celestea. Do you know how this looks when people are setting up camp in your girlfriend's queendom? I suggest we send in troops and invite them to go home."

"We will look into it," Kalli promised, placing a hand on her mother's arm to placate her. "We need to look into another lead about our mana first, though, and…"

"That's not all," the queen cut her off. "We also had an interloper appear right here in the castle. The same way the two of you just did. It was an old man. He asked where the two of you were and marched right out the front door. I have no clue where he went through, so I suppose we will have to wait for him to pop up before he can be dealt with."

"Did you say he spoke to you?" I asked, exchanging a nervous glance with Kalli.

"That's right." Celestea nodded, slightly less sure of herself. "What does that mean?"

I rubbed my chin thoughtfully. "It could mean a lot of things. He might just know the language. Do you have any proof he's from Earth? Did I mention they teach ancient Celestean on Earth? Or it could mean…"

Kalli and I exchanged another uncertain glance. Siblings from the M bloodline had access to every language. Could it be another long-lost brother or sister? If that were the case, why didn't they just say so?

"First things first," I announced. "We need to make a quick pitstop to Luna."

"I want to go!" Shiv shrieked, raising her hand and jumping up and down at the same time. "You promised."

Celestea stamped her foot. "Absolutely not. I'll not have you going off to strange new worlds. You're eight. That's far too young."

"But, Mother!" Shiv stamped her foot in return, mimicking her mother's outburst. "You never let me go anywhere my whole life. You owe me."

"I let you go to that witch's houseM" Celestea pointed out.

Shiv pouted. "That's only because she promised to not let me out of the house. You still won't let me see the world. Kalli, you tell her. You owe me one. This is all your fault after all."

Kalli looked uncomfortable, not wanting to get involved. I gave her a curious look.

Why does she say it's your fault?

Kalli sighed. *Mother kept her in that cabin all her life because someone told her to wait there. They never left and, because of that, Shiv never had any friends.*

My heart sank. While Kalli and I hadn't had the best childhoods, at least we weren't alone all our lives. I didn't mind spending the majority of my time with my mother growing up, but I would have gone crazy without being around other people.

That made me want to stick up for her. "You should let her go. It's safe up there. We will look out for…"

Celestea rounded on me, a smile forming on her lips. "Then, it's decided! If it's safe, we can all go. Guards! Prepare an honor guard for the princesses. Someone find Charles. Tell him we are going on an outing."

We stood there in shock as guards raced about preparing for the journey. Celestea folded her arms and gave me a triumphant look. "Where shall we gather for this journey?"

I took great personal pleasure in turning her smile into a frown. "Everyone meet at Kalli's privy."

————

Kalli scowled at me when we got to the queen's suite. *You didn't have to announce to the whole world that there's a magical portal to another dimension in my bathroom!*

Oh, come on! The look on her face was priceless.

Twenty people marched through the door into my bathroom, and I was proud to note that there was still plenty of room to spare. Lavender spared no expense or magic on her accommodations.

We looked at the door leading to Luna and I announced, "Before we go, there are a few things you should know. The most important is that we freed the ancients."

[27]

CELESTEA STARED AT ME. "What is an ancient? You said nobody lived up there except for the gods."

"Wait," I replied, staring at her in disbelief. "You don't know about them? Tell me, what do you know about Luna and the castle up there?"

She paused to consider my question. "Not much, to be honest. Luna was lost to us many generations before I was born. I was raised on stories of how our ancestors came from the green planet in the sky and that our power is tied to it. There are some old books in the castle, but I don't think any of them mention ancient ones."

Kalli stepped between us and took her mother's hand. "Look, Mother, we don't have time for a full history lesson right now. Just let us handle everything, and I'll answer all your questions later."

Celestea nodded quietly and gave her daughter's hand a squeeze. Shiv took her other hand and whispered, "I'm ready. Let's go to Luna."

Our group consisted of Kalli's entire family, eight guards, and…

I waved at the robed man in the back. "Hey, Crypian. Long time no see."

Kalli's eyes narrowed when she saw him tagging along. "No prophecies! I mean it. Every time you make one around me, something goes wrong."

Crypian held up his hands in defense. "Don't worry. I left my quill at home. I just want to see the green planet, too. I'm truly sorry for all the unpleasantness my prophecies caused in the past."

"Unpleasantness? All of your prophecies are about my se..." Kalli cleared her throat, her face turning a cherry red color as she glanced over at her mother. "Well, all of your prophecies make me very uncomfortable. I believe you should refrain from making anymore without royal decree. At least about me or my family in any case."

The old prophet heaved a sigh of relief. "You can count on me, your Majesty. No more prophecies. My prophesying days are done. I am simply a scholar in pursuit of knowledge. Thank you for allowing me to accompany you on this grand adventure.:

Celestea stepped toward the door. "Enough dilly-dallying. I don't have all day. My subjects...I mean your subjects will be wanting an audience in the afternoon, and since you've been predisposed lately, it has fallen to me to entertain them all."

Kalli and I knew that her mother secretly loved holding court. Years of being deprived of the right to play queen must have made her miss it.

Without another word, I opened the door.

———

And ran right smack into Lavender. She stood in front of the door with her arms crossed, tapping her foot. "Melvin Murphy. Are you bringing mortal enemies that haven't seen one another in hundreds of years together for a reunion? You may not realize this, but the ancients have very real reasons to be wary of the Celestean's."

When she noticed everyone hesitating in the doorway, she added, "Worry not. I've spoken with them, and they trust you mean no harm."

I expected the ancients to be gathered together in the throne room but, to my surprise, only Iolathar was present. While the magic prevented him from taking the throne, that didn't stop him from pacing relentlessly about the room.

He looked up when he heard us coming. "Ah, you've returned. We have much to discuss."

I nodded, anxious to ask him about my issue. "Kalli and I have been poisoned by corrupted mana. Mana corrupted by hate. Can you help us?"

Iolathar rubbed his chin, looking me up and down as one would a piece of art. "You've learned more about us, then? Well, it is true that we have the unique ability to infuse feelings into our life's blood as you would an element. However, corrupting that natural source of life is considered sacrilege. I would like to know who did this to you. If it was one of us, I must insist that they be judged under our laws. If an outsider has acquired our blood right, it's important that we know as well, albeit for different reasons."

"I think we were poisoned by one of the ancients," I began trying to explain. "She desperately wanted to get back to Luna, though I don't think she knew you guys were still alive. She's, um, no longer with us, but her daughter and mother still are."

"I see," he replied, giving me a strange look. "Tell me what happened."

Just when I was about to tell him, Celestea cleared her throat. "Ahem, is this going to take long? I'd like to go outside and look around."

Lavender gave Iolathar a knowing look and said, "Come, I'll give you a tour. Please, bear in mind that this is now home to the ancients. Try to be courteous during your visit."

Celestea muttered something about "This was our home, too..." But otherwise followed without much of a fuss.

Shiv tried to stay behind with Kalli and I, but Celestea grabbed her hand and said, "Come along, dear."

"Aww, Mother." Shiv pouted as she was forcibly dragged from the room.

Once the room was cleared, I noticed we were left with one person beside's Kalli and me. Crypian. He stood quietly in the shadows, listening to our conversation. I shrugged considering he had been there when we defeated Mardella. He knew the story. Didn't he?

"So, the person who poisoned us was defeated in battle and went away," I explained, trying to avoid having to explain about the ring. "We don't know where she physically went after that."

Iolathar looked skeptical but didn't question my description of the battle. "Why were you at odds with this person?"

I rubbed the back of my head sheepishly. "Well, you see, she wanted me to marry her daughter and give her access to Luna. I refused both requests."

He nodded, not giving me any feedback. "Why wouldn't you grant her access to Luna?"

"We didn't know about you guys at the time," Kalli explained. "She made it sound like she wanted access to the power source that was up here."

Iolathar frowned. "Are you absolutely certain? Could it be possible that she just wished to free us from our prison?"

I shrugged. "It's possible. She didn't really tell us much while she tried to force me to marry her daughter, killed my friend, and then tried to kill all of us. Peaceful conversation wasn't her strong suit."

The ancient stared at me for what felt like an eternity. "Very well. You mentioned she has relatives. A mother and a daughter. Where are they now? Can you take me to them?"

I sighed. "The daughter will be easy. She's married to my sister. The mother, on the other hand, also wants to kill me."

Iolathar gave an exasperated gasp. "A lot of people seem to want to kill you. Are you sure there is nothing you're leaving out? And what is this about two women being married? That is highly irregular."

"They love each other," I explained, shrugging. "What's irregular about love?"

He took a bit to digest that, but eventually decided that it probably wasn't a good idea to argue. "Very well. Tell me why the mother wishes to kill you. I believe I would like to speak with her."

Kalli shook her head. "As Melvin just explained, she wants to kill us so that can't be arranged. If you want to meet one of them, your only option is Alariel. Now, can you help us or not?"

Iolathar heaved a long, drawn-out sigh. "Very well. I owe the two of you at least that much for freeing us. Come, have a seat. Let me take a look at you."

We followed him over to a bench where he sat down and held out a hand to Kalli. Stepping in front of her, I took his hand. "No! Me first. No offense, but I don't one hundred percent trust you yet."

He nodded and took my hand, beckoning me to sit. "Understood. I need to test your mana, so I need you to let some out. Can you do that for me?"

"Won't that infect you?" I asked, recoiling slightly.

"No. We are quite adept in the manipulation of emotional mana," Iolathar explained. "This is the last kind of corruption that would work on us. Think of it like a child throwing a tantrum. While abrasive to the ears, it's nothing more than noise in the end."

I did as he asked and pushed my mana out and let it wash over his hand. Iolathar kneaded the mana as it passed through his hands. "Very nice. I see now why you don't appear sick. Your mana is strong enough to resist the corruption. Whoever corrupted your mana used wrath, a forbidden emotion. Whoever did this to you has forsaken our teachings."

"Wait," I took my hand back, narrowing my eyes. "Are you saying there's an acceptable way of poisoning someone? Say if she used love to kill people. Would that be allowed?"

Iolathar laughed. I felt anger rising in me as he struggled to compose himself. "I'm sorry. You see, the idea of using love to poison someone is preposterous. Allow me to explain. The corruption you find coursing through your system at the moment is inside with wrath, a corrosive element. Unchecked, it will consume a normal person. Love, on the other hand, is a nurturing element which would only make you stronger. People who are well loved tend to live longer."

I smiled at Kalli.

I guess we're going to live forever, then.

She beamed at me as Iolathar continued, "You, however, are not normal. I've never seen anything like your mana before. It's almost like your mana ignores any impurities altogether."

I shrugged again, not wanting to tell him about my bloodlines.

Then, getting an idea, I asked, "Can my mana corrupt you?"

He raised an eyebrow at me. "What are you suggesting? Any mana can be corrupted. However, the ancients have safeguards in place to prevent any lasting damage to our cores."

"I'd like to examine you with my mana," I pressed, hoping he would give me permission. "If you'll just allow me to push my mana into…"

Iolathar held up a hand to silence me. "I'm afraid that cannot be allowed, I'm sorry. The integrity of my core is sacred to me. Allowing you to fiddle with it would be tantamount to sacrilege. Worry not. I will teach you both the basics of essence forging. Just like we taught our children in the past, I will bestow upon you the basics. I just want your sworn oath that you will only pass it on to your offspring."

I nodded but Kalli stepped forward and objected. "What about Orpheus and Squawk? They are going to die if we don't figure something out. Orpheus might be able to learn the technique, but I doubt Squawk will. We can't just let them die."

"Give them to me," Iolathar replied. Then, seeing the looks on our faces, he hastily added, "I do not mean as slaves. I believe we can save them over time. It won't be a simple process and may take many years. They can stay on Luna as our guests until the process is completed. That's the best I can offer for your friends."

Kalli and I exchanged a glance and nodded to each other, and she accepted for the two of us. "Please, teach us the basics. And we will talk to the doctor and see if the two of them are safe to be moved. When we left, Squawk wasn't doing so well."

Iolathar rubbed his chin and said, "If they cannot be moved, then I will go to them."

———

Meanwhile, in a remote section of Meltopia/Celestea…

Zofia nodded appreciatively at the campsite. A large tent not unlike a circus had been erected in the middle of a large grassy field. Inside the tent, a certain manmade portal flickered to life every day like the Old Faithful geyser. It was a bit of a hassle recharging the machine, but she was convinced they were going to find a reliable source of mana on the backwater planet very soon.

"Ma'am, we apprehended some more of the locals," Natalia reported from beside her.

Zofia nodded but said nothing. She desperately wanted to explore, to see what the new world had to offer. She was methodical though. Important resources needed to pass through the portal before she could begin her mission in earnest. For starters, they needed a portal generator on this side of the portal. That was paramount.

"The little green men have been found to be insufficient for harvesting." Natalia continued, not seeming to care if she was paying attention or not. "The mana yield does not meet the minimum requirements for a standard healthy subject."

"Then cut them loose." Zofia waved her off. "There is no point in retaining waste."

"What about the weapons, ma'am?" Natalia asked, switching subjects without warning. "The men have prepared…"

"No weapons!" Zofia growled, spinning on the startled taller woman. "It is imperative that we appear peaceful to all locals. We do not want to wear out our welcome before we are fully prepared."

She glossed over the fact that her men were systematically abducting unfortunate trolls that were caught wandering the open plains. She also chose not to inform her underling of the many weapons she possessed on her person.

"I think we should consult The Administrator," Natalia pressed on. "If he were aware…"

"He is aware," Zofia spoke softly, though her words filled the air with malice. "I have been given absolute control over this region. My word is to be taken as his word. Do you understand?"

Natalia nodded reluctantly. "Yes, ma'am."

Zofia chuckled to herself. It was obvious that Natalia was going to report her to herself the first chance she got. If only she knew. It didn't matter, though. The mission was right on track.

[28]

"Luna is beautiful," Shiv announced when she returned. "The ancients are building houses everywhere."

Celestea made her way straight to Kali. "Did you get what you came for? Did they help you with the poison?"

"Almost," Kalli replied. "Iolathar knows a technique that should help. We just have to learn it."

She smiled and nodded at Iolathar. "Well, that settles it, then. Learn this skill and cure yourself so you can get back to work ruling our nation."

Kalli gave her mother a pointed look but decided not to argue. Iolathar ignored Celestea and took a step toward the inter-dimensional door. "Shall we go see these friends of yours?"

———

Kiki, are you there?

I held my breath, hoping they hadn't left the group. We had to go back to Gaia before we could tell if the chat worked. After a few minutes, she replied, *What's up, baby brother?*

I have someone here who said he's related to Alariel. Do you still have access to the airship?

Alariel replied, ignoring my question. *That's impossible. My only relatives are my mother and grandmother.*

I decided to just invite Iolathar to the group. It was easier than trying to explain who he was.

AN UNKNOWN PERSON HAS JOINED THE GROUP

Is that some kind of joke? Kiki asked, sounding bewildered.

"Ancients…" I grumbled out loud before speaking in group chat.

They sort of got locked up and not included in the System somehow. Or before it was created. I'm not sure. Either way, they aren't in the System. Iolathar knows things about mana that can help with the corruption, but he wants to meet Alariel.

Iolathar corrected me. *I want to meet the grandmother, not the daughter.*

Alariel made a wounded sound. *Hey!*

The ancient cleared his throat before amending. I wish to meet you as well, Miss Alariel. Forgive me. I seek answers from your elders. It has been a long time since we were imprisoned, and I wish to know where your line came from and how they escaped.

"One thing at a time," I said out loud, not wanting to discuss things in front of Alariel. "Let's take care of the mana corruption first, and then you and Alariel can make arrangements to see her grandmother. I don't want my friends to die."

He nodded. "Agreed. We must save your friends first. Is it not possible for the grandmother to meet us there?"

"She's dangerous," I replied, getting a nod from Kalli.

Iolathars expression was grim. "She's family."

Kiki's voice cut him off before he could elaborate. *You need us to send the airship again, don't you?*

Yes, please.

After a few minutes, Alariel replied. *We're on the way. You need to connect one of your kingdoms to the network. It will cost you but the ability to fast travel is well worth it.*

———

Connecting to the network wasn't so bad. At first, the thousand gold per month made me panic. Collecting that much for Kalli's contract hadn't been easy. However, when you run a whole queendom/empire, a lot of money comes in from many sources.

Celestea had Kalli levy a tax system. It was a small tax, but it added up. Especially when the tax extended to the many nonhuman citizens that now called Meltopia their home. They jumped at the opportunity to pay taxes when it meant full equality with their human neighbors.

Kalli and I boarded the airship with Iolathar, leaving her mother in front of the castle making plans with crafters to make an official Celestean airship port.

Once we were airborne, Iolathar sat us down. "The two of you are going to learn to cure yourselves. The first thing you need to learn is how emotions work. Emotions are flares of mana from your core as you react to events in your everyday lives. Most people exercise very little control over their emotions and choose to drink in the effects as if they are a powerful drug. That is where the ancients differ. Through the generations, we have evolved to become the masters of emotion, employing them to enhance our overall mana quality."

"So, you're basically Vulcans without the pointy ears," I pointed out with a laugh.

Iolathar gaped at me. "I have never heard of this Vulcan race you speak of, though I assure you, we are not elves."

"How do you control your emotions?" Kalli asked. "It's not like you can help how you feel about something, or can you?"

He laughed, folding his legs under himself in a yoga pose. "By taking a heartbeat and evaluating the situation before you respond to it. It's the body's natural response to want to react to every situation instantaneously. You need to control the process. While it's normal to defend yourself when attacked, social queues allow for a measured reaction. Take for example a situation where a person says or does something that upsets you."

Kalli looked at me and stuck her tongue out. "I'm imagining a few situations right now."

"Good," Iolathar replied. "Now, the initial reaction is anger or sadness. Your core also decides how much emotion to dole out. Minor offenses get a ten percent reaction while major events in your life may evoke as high as a fifty percent flare of emotion. A well-trained ancient can draw out one hundred percent of that mana. Emotionally charged mana."

"Is anger or fear a bad thing?" Kalli asked, pursing her lips.

Iolathar laughed. "As ancients, we learn to embrace all emotions. They are simply your core's way of reacting to outside stimuli. Hate and fear are only bad things if you choose to channel them improperly. As you've seen with the corruption in your mana, wrath can be a potent weapon when used properly."

I closed my eyes and focused on the mana within my core. Iolathar was right. Every time I had a strong emotion, that feeling I had in my gut was a spike of mana that erupted from my core like a solar flare. It was much bigger when I thought of Kalli.

She sensed what I was doing and turned a deep shade of red. *Hey! Don't use me to channel your emotions!*

It was my turn to stick out my tongue.

You should try it. My love for you is strong.

She closed her eyes and, soon enough, she had a mana flare to match mine. Iolathar smiled and continued the lesson. "Very good. Now that you're able to make it happen on command, let's move on to the next step. First, you need to learn how to not have an emotional response. You need to learn to still your core. This part is going to take a while as suppressing emotions is no simple task."

"How do we do that?" I asked, not quite sure where to begin.

"Meditation," Iolathar replied, closing his eyes to demonstrate. "Even when they are not powerful, emotions are always present just below the surface. I want you to focus within and smooth the surface of your core. Make it as smooth as the glassy surface of a tranquil sea. You will know you have succeeded when you feel at peace with the universe."

Kalli and I sat together and attempted to purge our cores of emotion. It was much harder because of our connection. Kalli growled at me as my mana surged over our bond, causing a ripple in her core.

Cut it out! I'm trying to be at peace over here.

I can't help it. Besides, you're doing it, too.

She giggled and slapped my arm playfully. Iolathar opened one eye and spoke in a solemn voice. "Focus children. If you need to separate yourselves to master this, I suggest you do so."

"But our cores are connected." Kalli sighed, trying to concentrate again.

Iolathar opened his eyes and stared at us. "I'm afraid the two of you might not be able to master this particular technique. It's hard enough to do with a single core. I believe it may be nigh impossible to accomplish with a pair of cores in tandem."

"We can do it!" I said with more conviction than I felt.

Kalli's voice echoed in my ear. *We can do it. With our bond, we can do anything.*

That was all it took. Together we closed our eyes and stilled our souls. I pictured the tether that bound our cores as a scale balances two pans. At first, there were ripples of mana coming from both sides. Slowly, the ripples calmed and faded until there was perfect harmony between the two of us.

When I shifted my attention to my core, the surface was smooth and clear, revealing a swirling inferno of mana just beneath the surface. I could feel Kalli finding the same result in her core.

I was startled by a tap on my shoulder. I looked up to see Iolathar with the airship captain. Stretching my stiff muscles, I asked, "What? Is something wrong?"

The captain laughed and said, "Nothing wrong. We're here, mate."

Kalli and I struggled to our feet, our legs stiff from the voyage. Iolathar offered a slight smile in recognition. "The two of you have done well. While not perfect, I see you made progress."

"How did we get here so fast?" Kalli asked, remembering the journey to the high house often took most of the day.

"Fast?" Kiki snickered from behind us. "You've been meditating for over a day. The airship stopped at the cabin to pick us up. Iolathar told us not to disturb you."

Kalli and I gaped at each other.

It's only been a few hours, right?

She shrugged, but I could tell she felt the same as I did. Iolathar beckoned for us to follow. "Come. Time is of the essence if we want to save your friends. The two of you synced nicely. There may be some hope for you yet. What you just did is a significant accomplishment."

A flash of blue hair told us we had a stowaway. Kalli saw it from my mind's eye, too. She scolded her sister with a giggle. "Come out, Shiv. We know you're there."

To both of our surprise, Shiv wasn't alone when she came out. The old prophet Crypian stood behind her. He raised his hands and pointed at Shiv. "She made me do it!"

"I did not," Shiv shrieked, hiding behind her sister. "I snuck aboard by myself. He followed me."

"Well, I could hardly let her wander into a dangerous situation by herself now, could I?" Crypian argued as though he was only looking out for Shiv's safety.

"Enough you two!" Kalli barked, hands on her hips. "I get it. You two are here. Now, behave yourselves and come with us."

———

During the walk to the volcano, Shiv elbowed her sister's side. "I'm hungry. Can we get something to eat?"

Kalli started to shake her head but her stomach betrayed her by growling loudly. "Look, we can get something to eat after Iolathar saves our friends."

Iolathar chuckled as he followed behind. "I ate during the voyage. You should have made yourself known to me, little one. I would have happily shared."

Shiv pouted in silence as we continued the trek to the glass tubes. Feeling sorry for the girls and more than a little hungry myself, I edited up some teriyaki kabobs and handed them out.

Iolathar accepted a kabob and said, "I had a chance to get to know Alariel during the voyage. She is indeed an ancient though she knows not of our ways. The only thing her family seems to have inherited over the years is a feeling of rage toward the Celesteans. I am going to begin her training in the same fashion I did with you."

"Do you still want to meet her grandmother?" I asked, between bites of my kabob.

"And her mother," Iolathar replied. "Alariel assures me she lived through your encounter with her. I see why you are wary of me meeting them. Your girlfriend is Celestean. Worry not, I assure you, ancients do not hold grudges."

I wondered if he would feel that way after meeting Alariel's grandmother. When we arrived at the tube, we were greeted by the usual disembodied voice.

"Greetings, travelers. Present yourselves for identification."

"Scanning."

"Bloodline confirmed."

"Welcome, Lord and Lady Murphy of the M bloodline. I see that you've brought guests today. Please, enjoy your visit."

Since Kalli and I were used to tube traveling, we ushered the others into the tubes before us. Shiv yelped as it whisked her away. Crypian and Iolathar followed, and then Kalli and I brought up the rear.

When we arrived at the reception kiosk, an unfamiliar human face greeted us. She looked me up and down with a disapproving stare and said, "Lord Murphy. Please state your business."

"That'll be enough of that," Maya said, stepping out of a room in the back. "Don't mind Primmy here. She heard what happened to

Squawk. She knows her place and won't let it affect her duty. Isn't that right, Primmy?"

"Yes, my Lady," Primmy replied, bowing her head to Maya. "It won't happen again."

"Good," Maya said. "I heard you found a healer for Squawk and your butler. That's excellent news. Come, to the infirmary."

[29]

"I SEE," Iolathar said for the umpteenth time as he knelt beside Squawk's bed.

I couldn't tell if he was referring to the fact that she had the head of an ostrich or if he was making some more profound discovering about the corruption to her mana.

Kalli and I sat on the floor meditating. The more control we got over our emotions, the easier it was to sense the world around us while we did it.

We also learned that balancing our emotions worked sort of like water. Mana laden with emotions that seeped out of our cores sent ripples through the connection. That was how we were always in tune with one another's feelings.

The group connection was similar but to a much lesser extent. Rather than getting the full wave of emotion, it felt more like observing waves roiling across a distant sea from the safety of shore.

I smiled when I thought about all the emotions I ever felt from Kalli. We really were bonded.

Do you think relief is an emotion or just a feeling?

Kalli opened one eye to peek at me. *I know what you're thinking, and eww! Now, send an emotion through our bond. I want to try something. And before you ask, not that one.*

There was only one choice, and I was pretty sure she knew it. My heart swelled with affection for Kalli, and I let it surge out. The wave rippled through our bond and was met in the middle by an identical wave of Kalli's making.

They collided in the space between our cores that was connected by a tether. We both watched in awe as the mana melded together in an exotic explosion. Then the surged ended. As one, we smoothed and calmed the emotion flowing through our bond so that it was contained within the connection just as we had done with our cores on the airship.

When we opened our eyes, we saw Iolathar smiling and nodding at the two of us. I gave a frantic look at Squawk and Orpheus who both appeared to be unconscious. "Shouldn't you be focused on healing them?"

Iolathar gave me a reassuring smile. "Worry not. It is done. For now. I've done all I can to stabilize them. True salvation will come with time and for that, they both must return to Luna with me. However, there is a problem."

"What's wrong?" Kalli said in a worried tone, staggering to her feet before realizing they had fallen asleep.

I tried my best to stabilize her but was also a little stiff from how we'd been sitting. Kalli fell over on top of me, and I struggled to catch her. We both looked up at Iolathar in a tangle of limbs. He just shook his head. "These two are fine. It's your sister who's the problem. I cannot cure her the same way I did your friends and I refuse to teach her the way."

"That's okay," I began. "We can show her..."

"No! I forbid it!" Iolathar barked. "Did you forget your oath to me? Only you two!"

Then I understood. "I'll do it. Once I learn how to purge this corruption, I'll heal her myself."

"That..." Iolathar paused, tasting his reply. "...works for me. Cleanse her with the knowledge I impart to you."

Maya didn't look pleased with the decision but held her tongue. Iolathar rose from his seat and walked over to Alariel. "I do believe it's time you introduced me to your grandmother."

Alariel and Kiki didn't answer right away and gave Kalli and I concerned looks. I shrugged and asked, "Do you think it's safe to go there alone with her?"

Alariel replied, "She's never been a threat to me. I'm family. I don't think she would do anything bad while I'm around."

"I still don't feel comfortable with this," Kalli said, climbing to her feet once again and offering me her hand to help me up. "You haven't seen what it's like down there in her basement. She's got Raverly's corpse in a cage for some reason."

"Aw, is baby brother worried about us." Kiki teased, walking over to me. She nuzzled my head with her knuckle and continued, "Don't worry. We'll be careful and not do anything to make her suspicious. Besides, I have experience with evil family members."

———

There wasn't much left to do after that except see them off. Maya was in a bad mood after not being cured or taught how to cure herself. Iolathar took us aside and left us with homework. "Now that you've learned to calm your emotions, you need to control them. There are two ways of dealing with the corruption. The first is to identify and isolate the specific wrath you were infected with. This is complicated because every person feels things in a unique way. That is why I am going to suggest you focus on the other method. You currently feel emotions as a reaction to your environment. This leaves your mana vulnerable to emotional attacks at all other times. I can see from your mana that you are light based and Kalliphae is fire-based. You must train your mana to have a natural affinity with a personal emotion as well. Doing so will leave no room for any foreign emotion to be present. Before you swoon over one another and decide on love, let me warn you. Your natural affinity to an emotion should have nothing to do with outside factors and everything to do with who you are at your core. What emotion defines you? Once you figure that out the rest should be natural. I know this knowledge won't help you with your sister. I'll teach you how to treat her once you've mastered this. With that said, I wish you both well until we meet again."

Once the airship departed, Kalli and I had to decide what to do next. Maya retreated to her house, obviously displeased with the decision not to cure her right away. I was fairly certain that it had something to do with her man servants.

It took some work to find Crypian and Shiv who had wandered off. When we found them, Kalli rushed over to Shiv and said, "I think I'm starting to know why Mother doesn't let you go out."

Shiv rolled her eyes and replied, "Not you, too!"

"We're about to head back," Kalli explained, reaching for her sister's hand.

"Do we have to?" Shiv whined, pulling away. "We just got here."

Kalli gave me a worried look.

We can always practice what Iolathar just showed us. We don't have to be home for that.

Kalli gritted her teeth and gave Shiv her best scowl. "Fine! We can stay another hour. You stay out of trouble and don't bother the nobles."

"Yipee," Shiv and Crypian cheered at the same time, getting a dirty look from a passing maid. Shiv cleared her throat and croaked. "We'll meet you back here in five hours."

"One hour," Kalli repeated.

"Three," Shiv argued.

"Two hours is fine," I said, patting her on the head.

That earned me a sour look from Kalli, but Shiv didn't press her luck and ran off toward one of the tubes.

When did she figure out how to use those?

Kalli smirked, watching them shoot off to areas unknown. *You should see her around the castle.*

A grinned, and we found a grassy area to settle down in. It was a bit odd that there was grass so close to an active volcano but, then again, nothing made sense about the high house.

What did they say the name of this island was, Solitair?

Kalli nodded, adjusting her posture to make herself more comfortable. *Yes. That's what it's called. Have you decided on an emotion to try first?*

If I was honest with myself, I haven't even thought of it yet.

No, you?

She shook her head and closed her eyes. *Not yet.*

I closed my eyes as well and tried to find an emotion. My identity. If I chose rage, would I become an indestructible green rage beast? Iolathar said not to choose love but there were other emotions like love. Passion, lust, and affection were all choices. Maybe not good ones, but they were still options.

But were they me? What was I? What emotion did I feel most of the time? What did I feel before Kalli? I liked to think I felt anger at the people who bullied me but that wasn't entirely true. The truth was, I felt a strange sense of indifference toward them, choosing to avoid rather than confront.

What was I then? There was only one word for it. I was bored. All my life it felt like a hole existed in my soul that was only filled when I met Kalli. No. It wasn't just that. Magic made me whole. It was a part of me, a birthright, that I was denied up to that point.

What am I now? I sat there for what felt like an eternity trying to figure that out. I needed to put my feelings for Kalli to the side and try to find out what was left. There was a short time when I had magic before I summoned Kalli. What was I? That's right. I was curious. I let the emotion flood through my body, opening up a burning desire in me to learn. To read more books. To understand. A swarm of emotion erupted from within me like molten lava from the heart of Solitair. I could barely contain myself and Kalli noticed. She opened her eyes and gasped. *Wow, Mel. What is that? What am I feeling right now?*

Curiosity. I want to learn everything. I can't believe I ever stopped. The universe is huge with so many things I still don't know. I want to see it all. Experience it all.

Is that all. She pouted and squeezed her eyes shut again, trying to come up with an emotion of her own.

Realizing she was struggling, I tried to help.

What have you tried so far?

She sighed. *I wanted to do brave, but I don't know if I'm confident enough for that. Confidence is right out the window too for the same reason. Is it possible to not feel confident enough to be confident?*

You are brave! You're the bravest person I know. You saved my life several times. You never back down when someone threatens those you care about.

Kalli opened her eyes, and a tear streamed down her cheek. *But I was scared every single time.*

I think bravery is doing things even though you are afraid. The fear makes the emotion more powerful.

She sat still while she digested what I said. *Is bravery the word for it? Is that an emotion?*

Confidence maybe?

Kalli closed her eyes again and I felt her trying on different emotions for size. She swelled with confidence and came to a conclusion. *I think I like this one.*

It suits you.

Together, we practiced honing our emotions. I felt like an actor in a play trying to feel sadness or anger on demand. It was a little easier when I channeled it by bringing up memories that invoked them.

Infusing mana with emotions had strange effects on the body. Some would deaden pain while others sharpened it and made everything more acute. Certain emotions gave me energy. The lovey dovey emotions gave me a certain kind of energy that I had no way of dealing with at the moment. I tried to avoid those. Curiosity filled me with a strong desire to learn. The more I felt it, the more I realized it was the feeling for me.

The problem was that I didn't know how to lock it in. It felt like every emotion wanted to burst out of me the instant I felt them. I knew the only way to purge myself of corruption was to embrace my chosen emotion, but Iolathar left that part out of his explanation. I had no clue when he was going to be back.

"Hey," a voice whispered in my ear while somebody poked me.

I jerked my eyes open and found Shiv leaning so close that I could smell her breath. She had eaten recently. "You know, you could have just agreed to let us explore for five hours if you wanted to play boyfriend and girlfriend with Kalli."

"No." I yawned, realizing I was getting tired. "We really do need to get back.

That was when I noticed Kalli leaning against me breathing softly. She was fast asleep. I wondered what she dreamed about when I wasn't with her.

Kalli. Wake up. It's time to go.

She jerked awake, slowly rubbing the sleep from her eyes. *I wasn't asleep. I just needed to rest my eyes for a minute. What time is it?*

Shiv gave her sister a conspiratorial grin before announcing, "It's been five hours. Five. You two slept out here for five hours. You could've just let us stay all day. As it was, we had to come back and check on you every hour."

"Sorry." Kalli sighed, yawning again. "I hope you had fun."

"Boy, did I?" she squealed, flapping her arms as she told us about her adventures exploring the strange new place. "I met some really neat people. They gave me snacks and everything."

Kalli stretched and stood up, looking out at the sun setting behind Luna. "I'm glad you had a good time, but you shouldn't accept food from strangers."

"They aren't strangers." Shiv pointed out. "They sell food to the workers out of something called a restaurant. Since Melvin is related to Maya, they said I get to eat for free. Crypian, too. He was there. He watched me."

"Did he now?" Kalli smiled, offering me her hand to help me up again. "That was nice of him."

Crypian rubbed the back of his head sheepishly. "Anything for the royal house, your Majesty. I'm just glad I can make up for my prophecies in some small way."

Kalli glowered at him, not happy to be reminded of Crypian's specific brand of prophecy. She turned to me and said, "Are you ready to go?"

"No time like the present." I grinned, already gathering mana for the teleport. "Everyone, gather together."

And just like that, we went back to Celestea.

[30]

"WHERE ON GAIA have you been, young lady!" Celestea shrieked when we appeared.

The throne room was dark, but I saw her sitting on a bench in the corner. It wasn't Kalli she was looking at. She stared Shiv down as only a mother could.

Shiv cowered behind her sister and whispered, "Help me, please."

Kalli glared at her but said, "Look, Mother. We decided to let her tag along. Don't worry, she was supervised the entire time."

Celestea jumped to her feet and strode across the room until she was right in Kalli's face. "You had no right. She's my daughter."

"So am I," Kalli reminded her. "And I'm sorry. I should have asked you first."

Celestea held her gaze for a long second before heaving a sigh. "Honestly, I can only pray that one day the two of you have children, and then you can see what it feels like to worry."

A tiny voice from behind us said, "Don't worry, your Majesty. They both will and Queen Kalliphae's will be twice as rambunctious."

We turned just in time to see Crypian slink around the corner. Kalli chased after him, shouting, "Get back here! You did not just do what I think you did! You promised no more prophecies."

Once she was out of earshot Celestea chuckled. She had a funny look in her eye so I asked, "What?"

Without missing a beat, she replied, "Oh, I just asked him to tell me about my future grandchildren."

———

I can't believe it. Kalli was livid. *The nerve of him! After promising not to make any more prophecies about me, too.*

Personally, I didn't mind prophecies about Kalli and I becoming a family. They always made me feel warm and toasty inside. We were a family.

You know your mom made him do it, right?

Righteous anger flared in her as she rounded on me. *Oh, she's going to hear all about it from me. She knew how I felt about his prophecies. I told her! I'm going to make him give her a prophecy just to see how she likes it.*

That's a terrible idea. What if he says something bad is going to happen to her?

Kalli gave me a scandalized look. *I know. It's not like I'm going to actually do it but that doesn't mean I don't want to.*

I gave her a hug to try and take her mind off things.

It's late. We should call it a night.

Kalli stretched her arms above her head and a yawn slipped from her lips. *You're right. You should sleep over.*

I didn't give her a chance to have second thoughts and jumped into bed.

Let's do this.

She stuck her tongue out. *Not like that. We just need to go deal with something tomorrow morning and it would be best if you were here.*

I was curious.

What are we doing tomorrow?

She gave me her most charming smile. *Do you remember when mother said there were some strange people from earth here on*

Gaia? Well, they went and set up camp. I told mother we would speak to them.

Congratulations. You have reached level 37
Congratulations. You have reached level 38
Congratulations. You have reached level 30
Congratulations. You have reached level 31

We collapsed into each other's arms as we entered the dream. "It's been a while since we leveled together."

Kalli grunted as she came down from the intense sensation. "Twice each. That was too much."

I remembered she fell asleep back in Solitair. "Why didn't you level up earlier when you fell asleep?"

She sighed, pushing herself away from me and stretching again. "I told you, I wasn't sleeping. I was resting my eyes. There's a difference."

"Do you ever sleep without me?" I asked, not remembering the last time I dreamed alone. "What do you dream about?"

Kalli scratched the back of her head as she thought about it. "Actually, I don't know. You're always in my dreams, so I doubt I'd know if it wasn't really you."

"Are you real now?" I asked, starting to have doubts.

She gave me a playful look and danced around me. "Ask me something dream me might lie about?"

"Wanna do it?" I grinned, knowing full well how real Kalli would respond."

"No! Ew!" she gasped, shaking her head vigorously. "Why would you ask that, you know I'm not ready for that. I don't want to be a mom yet."

I stood up and put my hands on my hips. "Well, I bet dream you would have said yes."

"No, she wouldn't!" Kalli insisted. "Dream me has more integrity than that."

I took a few steps forward and kissed her on the nose. "Are you sure?"

She kissed me back. "Quite sure!"

"So, what should we do tonight?" I asked, giving her a serious look.

She pushed me away again. "I think we should work on our emotions. You know what I mean, so don't even say what I know you're thinking."

I nodded, and we sat on the floor, closing our eyes to focus on our mana. We managed the first stage almost instantly. Our cores were glassy smooth as we contained our emotions within. Then we slowly let it out along our connection.

Once that was done, we focused on refining our individual emotions. Confidence for Kalli and Curiosity for me. Remembering that Iolathar mentioned that we never fully utilized our emotions in mana, I tried to focus my curiosity. To somehow make it stronger.

What even was a pure emotion? Was it feeling something so powerful that you became it? Did I have that much conviction? Well, maybe for Kalli.

For her, it was harder. I could feel her trying to be more confident. It was something that traditionally came from practice and experience. I sent her a little confidence of my own which only seemed to make her curious. Or was that her way of returning the favor?

We meditated for a couple minutes. Or was it an hour? I could have been days. Time seemed to work differently when I focused internally. We mediated for so long that we forgot to make out.

———

I yawned, somehow not feeling rested despite oversleeping. Kalli was in a similar state as she pulled a pillow over her head. *Ugh. Maybe we should start the day after lunch.*

Unfortunately, her mom was having none of it. She barged into the queen suite and scowled at us. "If the two of you are going to blatantly be irresponsible, I am going to have insist on a royal wedding in the near future.

Kalli threw the pillow at her. "Mother! I am only sixteen years old. I'm not ready for all that yet."

"Then, perhaps I suggest a more appropriate sleeping arrangement," Celestea countered, placing the pillow at the foot of the bed.

Kalli gave me a conspiratorial grin. *Yeah! At your place next time. Sounds good to me.*

Celestea glared at us, obviously aware of the fact that we could communicate in private. "You were so well behaved as a child. Whatever happened to you."

"I don't know, mom," Kalli muttered, using the informal variation of mother. "Someone abandoned me when I was little and I just turned out this way. At least Melvin takes me as I am."

"I didn't..." Celestea stammered, backpedaling while looking at me with a hurt look on her face. "I had to stay away for your safety. You couldn't possibly understand how much it hurt not to look for you."

"Mother, I..." Kalli began but Celestea had gone, the tapping of her shoes echoing down the hall as she ran.

Kalli turned to me, that same hurt look in her eyes that I had just seen in her mother. *Am I wrong? She can't keep treating me like a five year old. Even the castle acknowledges me. Why can't she?*

I had limited experience with parents. Just my own mother who was never very strict. Unless you counted forcing me to eat my vegetables. If Kalli needed advice on that, I was an expert.

I think arguing with mom is just a rite of passage that we all go through. Don't worry, she still loves you.

Kalli sighed and made her way over to a wardrobe to select some clothes for the day. Her nightgown already morphed into her traditional dress so all she needed was clothes to go along with it.

While I didn't like using the M armor as clothing, I did a sniff test on my clothes, and they seemed fine. No need to go back to my room for a fresh set. Kalli wrinkled her nose and pointed to the bathroom in disgust.

A short while later, and wearing a clean outfit, I emerged, and we made our way to the dining hall. The idea was to eat breakfast and go investigate the mysterious Earthlings. That was such a strange thing to say; Earthlings.

Gaia was suffering an alien invasion and I was being sent as the token alien to go sort them out. I felt kind of like superman. There was a part of me that wanted to edit in some flight, super strength, and heat vision to play the part.

Laughing to myself, I shrugged it off. Another time. To both of our surprise, we found Charles, Kalli's father, waiting for us in front of three heaping plates of food. He nodded solemnly to Kalli and pulled out a chair beside him. "Good morning, sweetheart. Have breakfast with your old man?"

Kalli gave me a look like a deer in the headlights. She was even more nervous than when we fought Mardella, but she took her seat next to him anyhow. Charles smiled and pushed a plate at her. "I don't know what you like anymore so I had the chef whip up some of everything. Come, Melvin, you, too. Sit down. Please."

I nodded and took a seat next to Kalli, careful to keep her between me and her father. We ate in silence for a few minutes before he started talking. "Look, honey, about your mother. She means well. It's been hard for us. No, wait. It's been even more difficult for you. I don't want to lessen what you've been through. We both know you struggled in that orphanage. Also, we respect Melvin for everything he's done for you and support your relationship with him. But, you see, you're mighty young, and, well, sometimes kids don't see clearly at your age. What you want today might not be the same thing you want tomorrow."

Kalli chewed her food in silence for much longer than she actually needed. I could tell she didn't want to swallow and be forced to answer. Finally, when she could delay no longer, she swallowed and replied, "I get it, Father. Father. It still feels so weird to say that. I thought I was an orphan. I know you guys went through a rough time. You need to understand that Melvin is family to me. He has me and I have him. We're a team. I don't know what the future holds, but I can't see my life without him in it. I love you both, and I want you to know that I listen to you. I've thought about what mother said earlier and she's right."

My heart sank for just a moment. Then, she continued, "I will marry Melvin."

Both Charles and I choked on our food at the same moment. That was the last thing I'd have imagined Kalli saying, and she was a part of me. The thought of marrying Kalli made me feel light as a feather.

"I'm in love with him and there's no point pretending I'm not," Kalli continued her speech. "Marriage is just a formality at this point. If doing it will appease mother, then that is what I'm going to do."

Charles wiped his bearded mouth with a napkin, clearing away food he's coughed up. Then he sat there for a moment, staring wide eyed at Kalli. When he was able to form words again, he said, "Look, honey. There is a protocol to these things. Especially among royalty. You see, first your suitor needs to ask for your hand in marriage. Then, if I agree that he is suitable, we sit down with his parents and negotiate. There are things like dowry that must be discussed. We know nothing about his family for starters."

"Well, my mom's what you call a peasant," I supplied helpfully, a lopsided grin on my face.

Kalli scowled at me. *Not helping!*

Charles ignored the exchange and asked, "What of your father? Do you know him?"

Kalli held up a finger and pointed out. "Melvin is a member of the prestigious M bloodline. His father is very important."

"I did hear something about that at the negotiations with Dabia," Charles replied, scratching his chin. "We will have to set up a meeting. Can you get your parents to visit Gaia or would it be best for us to come to Earth?"

I shook my head. "My mom's missing and I've never met my dad. I suppose I can introduce you to my sisters, Kiki and Maya."

"Maya Halifax is your sister?" Charles asked, his tone betraying his surprise. "That certainly helps matters. I'll send a letter of request to her."

"Request for what?" Kalli asked, raising her eyebrows.

Charles cleared his throat. "Well, for, uh, permission for Melvin to marry. These things are complicated, dear."

Kalli shook her head. "I don't need anybody's permission to choose Melvin. Right, Mel?"

I threw my hands up in defense. "No. You don't. Besides, I chose you first."

Kalli snickered at me. "That's debatable."

"I did summon you, didn't I?" I pointed out.

"Oh, now you're trying to say you did that on purpose?" Kalli said with a smirk. "I call dibs. I kissed you first."

I wasn't sure if this was a battle I wanted to win, but it sure was fun having it. Charles looked like he wanted to disappear. "Okay, okay, fine. No negotiations. Just, please, no eloping. If we're going to do this, we're going to do it properly. It will be a queendom-wide affair. First, you will need to select a ring and propose properly. I can help with that."

Kalli stood abruptly. Charles and I watched as she fished through her bag for a moment. Her hand emerged clutching the mana diamond we made together. "Melvin gave me this a while back and promised to make it into a ring for me. So that means you don't have to worry about it."

I grinned, and we both watched Charles appraise the ring.

And you said you wouldn't marry me for a long time. You didn't even last a year.

She stuck out her tongue. *Pfft, it's not like we aren't already pretty much married. We are both in this till death do us part. You gave me your last name. You even gave me the diamond and said it was for when you marry me. The only thing left to do it announce it to the world. I'm not ashamed of you. I don't mind being Mrs. Murphy. But just so you know, that part about the kids, you will be waiting a long time for that, married or not.*

Charles seemed satisfied with the diamond. "Would the two of you at least do me the honor of allowing me to have this made into a ring? I believe I know just the person to do it."

Kalli smiled and kissed him on the cheek. "Sure thing, Dad."

He touched his cheek where she'd kissed him. "Say that again."

She tilted her head in confusion. "Fine. You can make the ring. I'm sure I'm going to love it."

"No," he whispered. "You used to call me Daddy when you were younger."

Kalli blushed and glared at me. Then she turned back to Charles with a smile on her face. "Okay, Daddy it is. Thanks, Daddy."

[31]

THE EARTHLING CAMP, the name the Meltopian's gave it, was uncomfortably close to Kalliville. We decided to spy on them first. With guns and other long-range weapons from Earth, it was dangerous to not take precautions. Fortunately, I had a few tricks up my sleeve.

ENTERING WORLD EDITOR MODE

Since the camp was inside of Meltopia, it was easy to see what they were hiding. At the center of the camp was a giant tent. The System was even kind enough to label it for me.

PORTAL ROOM

It would have been simple enough to just delete it, but I still wanted more information about who this was, and it was pretty obvious that they would just build it again. Perhaps they came in peace?

The area was swarming with people but none of them seemed to be armed. Or awakened for that matter. They all had strange names;

Casimir, Melchior, and Ola to name a few. Then I saw him. Antoni was back, and he was speaking with a woman names Natalia and a child named Zofia.

I knew Antoni, so I was confident I could get some answers from the man. He was friendly enough. The thing that surprised me was why he would come back? Did they work out a way to go back and forth?

He was still level one. So was Natalia. Then I inspected Zofia.

Name: Zofia
Class: Technician
Level: 1 (23)
Affection Level: Eternally Curious

Kalli, look at that kid.
I waited for a moment as Kalli focused on Zofia. *That's strange. She must be a peasant. She has no surname. Also, what's up with her level?*

That's not true. Even people you'd call peasants get last names in my world. Well, I think they do. I don't know about her level. We need to talk to her. Do you think we can lure her out?

Kalli frowned. I could feel it even though I couldn't see her. *Isn't it considered creepy to lure children away from adults?*

I sighed. She had a point.

Do you think Antoni and Natalya are her parents?
Kalli followed my gaze. *No. They both have different surnames.*

No matter how I looked at things, the safest bet seemed to be to lure someone out and speak to them. Since Kalli wouldn't let me talk to Zofia, I decided to go with Antoni. We had history.

As we watched, we discovered the Earthlings were transforming their camp into a pseudo village. They erected walls and added more tents all around the main one. The smaller ones served as living quarters for men and women in oversized white lab coats.

The workers came and went, climbing through a large portal that seemed to come to life every few hours. It only stayed active for a couple minutes at a time, but the Earthlings were very efficient with that brief window. Shipments of cargo were slid through in large carts with teams on both sides expediting the process.

It appeared to be machine parts of some sort. I couldn't tell what they were building, but its location in the main tent gave me a couple of ideas.

I worried Antoni was going to leave through the portal but when the sun set, he tucked into one of the tents for the night. After a while, Zofia was the last one left outside.

Come on, Kalli. It would be so easy to just grab her right now. We can ask her a few questions about her level and have her back before anyone notices.

Kalli scowled at me. *No! No children. Wait for her to go to bed, and we can visit Antoni.*

After about an hour of carefully inspecting the machine, Zofia walked slowly back to her tent. Just before entering, she looked up at the sky. From my perspective in World Editor Mode, it felt like she was staring right at me. Of course, she was probably just looking at Luna. The green planet in the sky was definitely a different experience from the night sky on Earth.

We gave her a good hour after her lights went out to fall asleep. No sense scaring the kid when we abducted one of the workers. Even though I wanted to be the one to go in, Kalli wouldn't allow it. Several people volunteered to go in my stead.

I had to turn down Esha. She was, in effect, the general of our army and therefore indispensable. Boombrix also wanted to go, but I worried that her unique way of talking might startle the man. The last thing we needed was for him to panic.

In the end, we went with one of the humans, a member of the royal guard named Schneider. His mission was to infiltrate the camp, deliver a handwritten letter to Antoni, and compel him to come speak with us.

I didn't clarify if that meant bring him back at sword point, and I hoped it wouldn't come to that. Before allowing Schneider to enter the camp, I did a sweep through World Editor Mode.

Camer's had been set up overlooking all entrances to the main tent. Whoever was in charge seemed to be more concerned about someone smuggling contraband out than with any outside threats. I supposed it was probably because they met the locals and deemed them to be relatively safe.

Still, it's strange that there are no guards.

Kalli nodded and replied, *No weapons. No guards. No security. It's almost like they don't care if they are attacked. How do they deal with monsters?*

Now that I thought about it, we watched them all day and nothing entered the valley. Something peculiar was going on. Getting my mind back on track, I began editing the cameras to disable them. Because I didn't want them being turned back on by whoever was controlling them, I deleted the power cables.

I also located a large box labeled, "Security Control." Another quick **DELETE,** and that was gone.

Through guild chat, I instructed Schneider.

Go into Antoni's tent and hand him the letter. If he makes any noise or you run into any trouble, I want you to retreat immediately.

His gruff voice replied, **Your Majesty, rest assured, I am more the skilled enough to dispatch a dozen of these so-called scientists and a hundred laymen. I will be back with Antoni without fail.**

I don't want anyone dispatched. If anything goes wrong, we will send a delegation in the morning.

He didn't seem too happy with my order when he said, **As you wish.**

———

Meanwhile, in Zofia's tent...

234

The Administrator sat in her second favorite swivel chair and watched the event unfold on her tablet. Her tent was made of a special material that blocked out the light. To the untrained eye of an outsider, the lights in her tent appeared to be out.

She was first alerted to signs of a breech when the dummy cameras went offline. *Magic, kek.*

Then a red light lit up on her display informing her that the fake security control system was somehow disabled. She had to give the Gaians credit, there were no outward signs of intrusion. The system just went offline.

If she didn't know better, she might have assumed it to be a system failure or a flaw in the installation process. However, that was impossible. She had done the work herself.

Suddenly, a motion sensor went off. The invasion was coming. How they had lasted two whole weeks was beyond her. Zofia was about to activate the first line of defenses when her hidden camera caught sight of the intrusion. A single man clad in black tiptoed into the outer ring of tents.

She was curious. Would they try to abduct her. She was clearly in charge. She didn't hide the fact. They didn't go for her though. The man in black entered the tent of one of the workers. Antoni? Why?

Zofia shrugged. He was expendable. Mindless grunts were easy to come by. She launched a series of special purpose drones to scout the area around the camp. The enemy had to be close.

With bated breath, Zofia accessed the camera in Antoni's tent. She was surprised by what she found. Antoni sat on his bed in silence reading a letter while the man in black waited patiently.

Did the man bring the letter or was it something Antoni already had with him? She wanted to rewind the video, but it was imperative that she watch events as they unfolded. She didn't dare move the camera to get a better view of the letter just in case it alerted the invader.

After reading the letter, Antoni folded it and set it on the bed. Then he climbed to his feet and followed the man in black out of the tent and into the night. She waited a respectable amount of time before donning a dark purple hoodie that did the best job of concealing her long teal hair. It was a bit darker than she liked but stealth was important for this mission.

First, she snuck into Antoni's tent. She needed to read that letter. She wasn't sure if she was being watched, but curiosity won out over caution.

When she got into the tent, she threw back her hood and scooped up the letter.

Dear Antoni,

It has come to my attention that you're back. I see you brought friends. While I'm not saying you aren't welcome, I need to know what you're intentions are.

Please, come with Schneider who will guide you safely back to my camp. I am sure we can come to an arrangement that is beneficial to all of us.

Melvin

She now had a name to go with the leader of the locals. Also, the letter was written in English.

Zofia looked down at a bracer on her left arm and punched a few buttons on a screen embedded into it. A holographic map appeared with a red dot indicating the tracking beacon she installed in Antoni. The Administrator was thorough after all.

———

Kalli smiled and waved at Antoni as Schneider led him into the room. "Antoni, you came back. Welcome."

He gave me a weak smile and returned the wave. "Yes. I'm back. Sorry about this."

I motioned for him to take a seat when he got close and asked, "So, what's going on over there? It looks like you guys are moving in."

Antoni's eyes widened, and he sounded nervous when he replied, "Look, sir. I only work for the company. I'm a contractor, actually. They tell me when to load and when to unload. I got this assignment because I came through last time and survived. I could go get my manager, Natalia, if you want…"

"That's enough, Antoni," a female voice spoke from the darkness. She pulled back her hood, revealing…the kid. "You can go back now. Thank you for leading me here."

"But I didn't…" Antoni gasped, his expression changing to fear. "I didn't say a word. I came just like they asked me to."

"You're dismissed," the girl said firmly.

"Aren't you a little young to be issuing orders?" I asked, giving Zofia what I hoped was a stern look. "Antoni is our guest. He's welcome to stay as long as he likes."

"But he is my employee," Zofia replied with a scowl. "He will do as I say."

"Do you want to be welcome here?" Kalli asked, scowling at the kid. "If you send him back, you can go right along with him!"

Hey, wait Kalli. If you send them both back, we won't get any answers.

She winked at me. *Don't worry. She won't go. She came here because she also wants answers.*

Zofia sighed and sat next to me, huffing. "Fine! He can stay. So, do you want to tell me why you abducted him?"

"We didn't abduct him!" I hissed back at her. "Now, do you want to tell me why a little girl is out of bed so late?"

Antoni gasped, but I didn't care. Zofia gaped at me for a second before her lip curled up in a smirk. "I'll bet I'm older than you, little boy. You're from Earth, aren't you?"

"Heh," I puffed my chest out and proudly announced. "I'm sixteen. You can't be older than twelve."

She made a gagging sound, ignoring the fact that I ignored her question about me being from Earth. "I'm twenty-one, moron."

'There's no way," I groaned, embarrassed by be shown up in the age department.

Satisfied that she's won the age war, Zofia asked, "How is it, exactly, that you know Polish."

"It's magic." Kalli brushed her off. "Now, if the two of you are done one upping each other, we need to get to the bottom of something. What exactly are you doing here?"

[32]

ZOFIA FOLDED her hands in her lap and began her story. "We invented a portal generator. I can't say why it led us here. We just punched a hole in reality, and this was the destination."

Kalli waited for her to pause before asking, "It looks like you're setting up camp here. Is it your intention to stay permanently?"

The two of them locked eyes for a few seconds before Zofia answered, "I can't say for certain. The administrator makes the final decision. As it stands, we are here to collect data on your world and learn what we can about this portal. We need to understand whether the location is an anomaly or if it's possible to reach other destinations as well."

I took a deep breath and said, "Okay. If you intend to stay, you are going to have to register with the empire and submit to oversight. We can't allow you to set up and do as you like. We will send some guards to safeguard you from monsters as well as a representative from the empire to keep tabs on your operation. In return, you may choose a delegate to speak on your behalf."

Zofia looked over at Antoni for a moment before coming to a decision. "Understood. We will register with your empire but only so long as we conduct business here. Antoni, please inform Natalia. I shall stay behind as the delegate."

Antoni looked back and forth between me and Zofia. Clearly, he was being dismissed again. Kalli shook her head. "It's dangerous to be out alone at night. He can return in the morning with the guards."

For a split second, a look of rage washed over Zofia's face. Just as quickly, it was gone, leaving me to wonder if I'd seen it in the first place. She stood and said, "Understood. If that will be all, I'm sleepy and wish to retire for the evening. Do you have sleeping arrangements set up or shall I sleep on the ground somewhere?"

Kalli got up and walked over to her. "No, that won't be necessary. Melvin can make you any kind of bed you like. Right, Melvin?"

"Um, sure," I muttered, caught off guard by Kalli. "But first, there's one more thing I'd like to see. Do you have any identification on you that can confirm your age?"

The truth was, I didn't need it. The first thing I did after she told me she was twenty-one was to inspect her again. The System had a category for age, and that part at least she hadn't lied about. Unless she figured out a way to hack the System, that was.

She shrugged and fished around in her cloak, removing a plastic card.

Republic of Poland
Surname: [Redacted]
Given Name: Zofia
Document Number: ZZC108201
Expiry Date: 11.09.2031
Date of Birth: 07/11/2001
Sex: F

It only took a second to match up the birthdate on her ID with the age in her status. The redacted name was curious. How was that possible on a legal identification card. I knew that wouldn't fly in the US. I handed her the card and asked, "Is there anything you'd like to tell me about your last name?"

Zofia shook her head. 'My surname is a thing of my past and I'd prefer to leave it that way."

Kalli spoke before I could. "And that's fine. Now, what kind of bed would you like?"

There were so many more things I wanted to learn about Zofia and the people that came through the portal, but Kalli allowed her to go to bed. Antoni was good company, but he knew next to nothing about what they were up to.

When we were alone that night, I decided to discuss the day's events with Kalli.

Why did you invite them to the empire and not Celestea?

She smiled guiltily at me. *I don't want my mother to try and take over like she always does. This way we can keep an eye on Zofia without alarming mother.*

Does this have anything about her forcing you to marry me?

I only realized how I felt about that when the words were already out of my mouth. Kalli frowned. *Is that what you think this is? That my mother forced me to do it? Think about it. We both know it's going to happen. I just said it first. Maybe I should have proposed to you before announcing it, but it happened spur of the moment with everything going on this morning. Trust me, I would never marry anyone just because someone told me to. I want this.*

I should have proposed to you and asked your dad for your hand like he said.

Kalli kissed me on the cheek and explained, *I probably would have told you to wait. We should wait. We're too young. I expect father would have told you that if you'd asked him. I'm sorry for ruining this.*

I wiped away a tear that was forming in her eye.

The only way you could have ruined it is if you say you don't want to marry me. I'm with you. I can marry you today or wait under you're ready. It makes no difference to me so long as we are together.

Kalli replied by falling into my arms and kissing me. It felt like we needed to spend extra time making out after forgetting to the previous night. Then I had to go think out loud and ruin it all.

I think I'm going to add that camp to Meltopia in the World Editor.

Kalli pushed me away and gave me a confused look. *Why do you want to do that? They don't want to be part of the empire.*

They want to stay here and here is the empire. It's not like we can go to Poland and just set up a village of our own. If they want to stay, it should be by our rules. Otherwise, we can just delete the big tent and send them back to Earth.

Kalli sighed. *I don't like it. Can we do it peacefully?*

As usual, my resolve collapsed under Kalli's gaze.

Fine. We will ask them nicely.

Kalli kissed me again, and we went back to making out.

———

It was a good thing we got the kissing out of the way before going to sleep because we spent all night doing emotion training. I was getting better at it. One thing about Zofia that intrigued me was her affection level, eternally curious. Perhaps I had a kindred spirit.

I couldn't help thinking of her as a kid. She looked twelve. I had to remind myself that she was five years my senior, an old lady.

Congratulations. You have reached level 39

Kalli toppled over when I leveled. Once the overwhelming effects wore off, she glared at me. "A little warning would be nice! I lost control of my emotions because you surprised me."

"It surprised me, too," I whined, desperate to collect myself.

Congratulations. You have reached level 32

Not even ten minutes later, she did it back to me. Controlling my emotions was hard enough without experiencing a full body level up sensation on full blast through the connection. It didn't help that girls felt it so much more than guys did.

When I picked myself up, I saw Kalli dripping with sweat and trying to catch her breath. She gave me the stink eye and said, "Don't even say it!"

———

All too soon it was morning. Zofia was up before us, issuing instructions and handing some kind of datapad to Antoni. He waved goodbye to us as he accompanied the guards back to his camp.

Zofia followed us back to a large building that I'd set up as a mess hall. I made it a point to offer her some ruffalo sausage and green eggs. Her reaction didn't disappoint. She swallowed when she saw it and her complexion turned a light shade of green.

Then she surprised me by picking up a fork, and whispering, "Curious."

A smile parted her lips after taking the first bite. "Surprisingly tasty. My compliments to the chef."

Kalli, not having touched her food, just stared at me. *You did that on purpose. You could have just given her Earth food.*

I shrugged.

I wanted to see how she would react. She is eternally curious after all.

I talked to her while she ate. "I'm going to add your camp to the empire. It's a magic thing but as long as it exists in the empire, it's going to be a part of it. Are you okay with this or do you need to go back and ask permission?"

Zofia rubbed her chin and asked, "Will it startle anyone? I don't want to cause a panic."

"I might build a wall," I explained. "But I can build around your people. There should be no cause for alarm."

Zofia took out her datapad and punched something in. "Okay, they are prepared. Thank you for the warning."

I looked to Kalli, who nodded. *See. That wasn't so hard.*

Sticking my tongue out, I began.

ENTERING WORLD EDITOR MODE
UNNAMED VILLAGE DETECTED
WOULD YOU LIKE TO GIVE IT A NAME? Y/N?

I grinned.
Let's call it Antoni Junction.
Kalli's voice asked, *Why junction?*
Because it connects our worlds.
Feeling a subtle nod from Kalli, I input the name in the world editor.

WOULD YOU LIKE TO LINK ANTONI JUNCTION TO THE
EMPIRE?
Y/N?

Again, I chose **YES**. Mana poured out of us as usual. It felt different though, either we were getting used to it or our recent emotion training was making us stronger.

Then, I saw it.
Kalli, look at your mana pool.
She panicked for a moment before I directed her attention to her stats.

Name: Kalliphae Murphy (Edited)
Class: Pyromancer
Level: 32
Hit Points: 3,200
Mana: 32,000
Stamina: 3,200
Strength: 20
Dexterity: 30
Agility: 30
Constitution: 50

Intelligence: 60
Wisdom: 50
Charisma: 75
Luck: 5

She gasped. *How did I get so much mana?*
Then, her eyes widened when she saw mine.

Name: Melvin Murphy
Class: Manipulator (Unlocked)
Level: 39
Hit Points: 3,900
Mana: 129,000
Stamina: 3,900
Strength: 25
Dexterity: 25
Agility: 25
Constitution: 50
Intelligence: 85
Wisdom: 30
Charisma: 10
Luck: 20

It must be the training we've been doing? That somehow expanded our mana capacity. We will have to ask Iolathar when we see him.
Kalli nodded. *Do you think he's okay?*
Good question. I'll try them in group chat.
Kiki? Alariel? Are you guys there?
We waited several minutes for them to reply. Nothing. Kalli fidgeted. *I'm worried, Mel. What if something happened to them?*
Then we will rescue them. That's what.
There was no question. We always rescued our friends when they were in trouble. Then I remembered I was in the middle of a task. Going back to world editor mode, I erected some walls around the

camp. While the scientists seemed startled, they tried to go about their business while ignoring the walls growing around them.

Once Antoni Junction was fully integrated, I was able to get a lot more detail about the structures.

Item: Interdimensional Portal Generator
Components: Mana, Metal, Rubidium
Item Rank: B
Item Level: 1
Item Owner: TGB

The first thing that jumped out at me was mana. It incorporated magic. It only made sense. But why use so many unawakened if they were awakened? Also, what was Zofia?

That was when her tent caught my eye.

Item: Command Center
Components: Computers, Data, Data
Item Rank: B
Item Level: 1
Item Owner: [Redacted]

How did she do that? Did she have her name legally changed to Zofia [Redacted]? Was there a legal name eraser? I had a strong feeling I could erase my name from the System, but Zofia wasn't a manipulator. What was a technician, anyway?

I was about to snoop through the command center when Kalli pulled me back. *Don't.*

But don't you want answers?

Kalli whispered in my ear. *She's not our enemy.*

I whispered back.

Yet...

[33]

FINDING a place to house Zofia where Celestea wouldn't find her was a challenge. I didn't want to take her to one of the villages in case she was up to something. The castle or the City Under the Mountain were the only two options.

The problem with the City Under the Mountain was that if Kalli and I left the empire, the language barrier would be back. In the end, we came up with an idea.

"Do you intend to make me sleep in the bathtub?" Zofia asked, eyeing the swimming pool sized tub. "It is magnificent, but it's not exactly what I had in mind when you offered to accommodate me."

"Don't worry," I replied, walking to the portal door to Lavender's house. "You'll get a room."

Once open, the door looked like it led to just another room in the castle. I wondered if Zofia could tell she was back on Earth.

As usual, Lavender was there to greet us. She bowed slightly to Zofia. "Welcome, Zofia no last name, lady of many secrets. Your room has been prepared for you. Melvin and Kalli, I trust the two of you are making progress toward a cure. Sylvia has missed you two. Now that you're back, it's time to resume your training."

"Training?" I asked impatiently. "We don't have time for—"

"Nonsense." She waved me off ushering Zofia over to the door. "Your life hangs in the balance. Trust me, this training is very important. Give me half an hour to get Zofia settled in and meet me for a late breakfast."

I stared blankly at after them as they left.

Now what?

Kalli shrugged. *I don't know about you but I'm taking a shower.*

Want company?

She stuck her tongue out. *Nope!*

I plopped down on the bed and looked up at the ceiling.

I wonder why she's so insistent on training. Doesn't she know we need to sort this corruption out?

I felt the warm water against Kalli's skin as she closed her eyes to enjoy the sensation. *I don't know, but she always has a reason. She hasn't steered us wrong yet.*

Do you think Shiv and Eddie will join us again?

Kalli lathered up a luffa as she replied with a song-song voice in my ears. *Perhaps. One way or another we can use the training and leveling up never hurt. I'd like to practice some new spells. I can't rely on beginner spells forever.*

I yawned. My bed always felt the best. Whether it was in my old apartment with my mom or in the dorm over at the Academy. That, or any bed where Kalli was asleep beside me.

She was washing her hair when she sensed my train of thought had shifted to her. *You are such a boy! Mind always in the gutter. Now, get ready because I'm almost done in here.*

I wasn't sure what she meant by get ready. It was obvious though when she emerged and shoved me into the bathroom. *Now, go clean up. You smell.*

———

"Melvin! Kalli!" Sylvia cried when she caught sight of us.

We joined the group in a grand dining hall where Lavender had a feast prepared for breakfast. Sitting around the table were Lavender, Sylvia, Eddie, and Zofia.

Lavender, it seemed, had supplied Zofia with a teal dress to match her hair. She was not happy about it at all. She tugged at the ruffles that went up her neck and looked like she would rather be wearing anything else.

Noticing my gaze, Lavender chuckled and said, "I took the liberty of washing her field attire while she bathed. Don't worry, child, you can have your gadgets and weapons back when you return home."

Zofia replied with a wordless scowl. Kalli smiled at her and said, "I think you look very cute in that dress."

"Weapons?" I asked, slightly alarmed that I failed to check if she was armed.

"It's a personal defense system," she muttered. The way she picked at her eggs made me think she might actually be twelve.

Sylvia insisted on sitting between Kalli and I. "Tell me about all of your adventures. Lavender tells me you visited a house built into a volcano."

"Let them eat," Lavender said, giving Zofia a loaded look. "You can ask them to tell you stories later."

The meal was good, and I probably ate too much. I couldn't decide between the pancakes, ham, many different kinds of sausages, and more desserts than I could count.

Once we were finished, Lavender said, "Now, Melvin and Kalli are going to do some training. The rest of you have your lessons and I expect you to get to it. Zofia, if you would be a doll, please watch over Sylvia and Eddie while I'm gone."

She stood, and Kalli rose to follow. Then they both glared at me. I looked up with a mouth full of bread pudding. "One more bite."

———

"Why can't the others come?" Kalli asked as we marched through the door leading to Homestead.

Lavender flashed a smile over her shoulder that told me she was up to something. However, she didn't say what that was.

We walked in silence to the portal room, and Kalli gave me a nervous glance. *What do you think the training is going to be?*

I shrugged.

It must be big if she's this serious about it. Either that or she's playing with us.

Stepping through the portal, we found ourselves in The Shadowlands once again. Kalli and I stood side by side, scanning the dark forest for monsters. There were no sounds like there were the previous time.

"Okay, you two," Lavender said from behind us. "I'm going to let you have the first attack."

"Where's the monster?" Kalli asked, scanning the sky. "Is it invisible?"

I spun around to find Lavender leveling a staff at us. Kalli noticed the same moment I did and rounded on her as well. She flashed that same wicked smile and said, "Well? Have at thee."

"But..." Kalli began.

Lavender laughed. "Come now, child. We cannot harm one another in here. You can go all out without fear."

Kalli rolled up her sleeves and said, "Don't forget, you asked for it."

Lavender looked straight at me and said, "Melvin, this time your focus is offense. Show me some attacks."

Kalli beat me to it. Her body burst into flames, and she surged forward. A solid wave of flame crackled to life on her fingers and surged directly at Lavender.

Just when I thought the beam was going to hit her, she vanished only to reappear four feet to the left. Kalli flicked her wrist and the flame turned to follow.

I watched in awe as the two of them danced around for a while. Then Lavender stirred me from my trance, shouting, "Melvin, attack!"

My first plan of attack was to work my manipulation skill. I dug in my fanny pack and fished out a handful of pebbles. Throwing them at Lavender, I selected one to edit. Using the same trick I used in the past on a group of treants, I edited one.

Item: 100-ton boulder (Edited)
Components: Stone
Item Rank: B
Item Level: 1
Item Owner: Murphy

The boulder flashed into existence and slammed into the ground, raising a giant cloud of dust. Kalli snuffed her fire out, and we waited for the dust to clear. *Do you think she died?*

Lavender's voice answered from behind, "Nope. Still alive."

We spun around again to find Lavender standing there brandishing her staff. Kalli closed her eyes and held her palms out, producing brightly glowing balls of fire that proceeded to rotate around her.

Not wanting to resort to the artifact armor yet, I tried to come up with an offensive use for my healing laser. While I knew I could temporarily blind her, I had yet to come up with magical ways of attacking with the light.

I knew how to use Kalli's fire spells and the wind magic that I'd learned at the Academy. I'd never sought to weaponize my own innate mana.

Thinking lasers and phasers, I wondered how movies made laser guns so potent. The problem was, I knew they didn't work like that in real life. Still, this was magic!

Picturing a phaser from Star Trek, I fired a test shot at the new Lavender.

It went right through her. Kalli unleashed a few fireballs and the illusion finally vanished. Standing behind us again, Lavender said, "Haven't the two of you been learning new applications for your mana? Now try putting some oomph into it."

Kalli got it before I did. The flames around her roared as I felt the raw emotion she fed to her mana. The remaining fireballs tripled in size causing me to take a step back to avoid getting hit by them.

Curiosity wasn't going to cut it for what I had in mind. That was fine because it wasn't about finding my affinity. It was about explosive emotions. I channeled my inner Hulk and went with rage.

The mana that came out was much more potent but also a hundred times more difficult to control. It exploded out of me in all directions. The force of it knocked Kalli to the ground. I stopped immediately and rushed to her side, only to watch her fade away into nothing.

KALLIPHAE MURPHY HAS BEEN SLAIN BY MELVIN MURPHY!

"Time out." Lavender laughed. "Friendly fire. You just sent Kalliphae to respawn. Work on getting that under control while I go fetch her."

I'm sorry!

Kalli sent me a mixed bag of emotions. She was annoyed yet slightly amused. *You're going to pay for that later!*

So, rage was off the table. It was a powerful emotion but impossible to control. I tried curiosity, but it made the light want to shine more than burn. I needed another emotion that was me but aggressive.

Kalli had courage which seemed to lend itself perfectly to the fire that flowed through her veins. Thinking of light, things like divine might and righteousness came to mind. Was I any of those things?

Then it hit me. While Iolathar warned me not to use love, there was another emotion I felt for Kalli that could lend itself to my mana perfectly. Devotion.

Pouring the conviction of our bond into my mana, I let it swirl around me again. Something clicked and I was coated in what felt like liquid armor. It was somewhat like the artifact armor wrapped around my chest. Was emotional mana at play there, too? Did the great and mighty M already have that technique mastered?

Experimenting with my new mana, I extended it out in different directions. I could control it. First, I made a sword in my left hand then I tried shooting a beam like Kalli's fireball. It exploded against the boulder, shattering the massive rock.

Just when I was getting confident with my new spell, I heard an appreciative whistle behind me. Kalli flashed a smile and spoke out loud. "Impressive. I guess I'm going to have to step my game up."

I was wondering what she meant when the green fire sprang to life from the amulet and swirled around her in a perfect storm of what she dubbed Luna Fire.

She laughed and pointed the attack at me. "Try guarding against this."

I focused my newly found armor into the path of the blast but was still blown back several feet. Her flames tried to spread around my shield, causing me to expand it by feeding it more mana.

I felt her passion and her mana flared, threatening to overwhelm me. Did she also tap into her feelings for me to make her mana more potent? No fair!

She stuck her tongue out. *Two can play at that game. You killed me once. Now, it's my turn.*

I saw Lavender out of the corner of my eye. She stood watching us with her arms crossed. However, she made no move to stop us. Was she enjoying this?

I tried to wrap my mana around the flame and snuff it out. The more I stretched it, the weaker it became. Kalli sensed that through our bond and focused her mana on a weak point in my shield.

The first sign it was failing was a series of green spiderweb cracks in my otherwise invisible shield. Suddenly, her flame burst through.

At that point, I had no choice but to rely on my artifact. The black armor surged and covered my entire body in an instant, moments before Kalli's Luna Fire hit me.

Even through the armor protected me from the blast, I still felt the intense heat. Pain wasn't a thing in the game, but pressure and temperature certainly were. Kalli's fire was hot. It was nothing like the times she used her fire to clean or tickle me.

"Enough!" Lavender barked.

We both froze, our respective attacks fizzling out as we turned to face the enchanter. She clapped and said, "The two of you have developed some nice mana. However, you're pulling your punches with each other. Now, it's my turn to attack."

[34]

Lavender's movements were different than before. Rather than dodging our attacks of flickering and vanishing, she held her staff out and blocked them. The staff began to glow under the combined force of our spells.

Then she held it out to us and whispered an incantation. A blinding green light shot out of the staff and straight at me. I tried to dive out of the way, but it turned to follow.

I squeezed my eyes shut and braced for the impact as I focused both shields into place. Kalli shuffled around me and I sensed her place herself between myself and the blast. When I tried to push her out of the way, she brimmed with courage. ***Don't worry. I'm fire… Oomph.***

**KALLIPHAE MURPHY HAS BEEN SLAIN BY LAVENDER
???!**

There was a brief pause and a thud as the spell slammed into her. Then she was gone. I felt her presence in another part of the world as she continued her sentence. *…proof. **Ugh, she killed me again.***

I opened my eyes and saw Lavender strutting away. She flicked her hair over her shoulder and said, "Sit tight. I'll be back in a moment with your girlfriend. Try to work out how to not let that happen again. It's important."

Then she was gone, and I was all alone. The only fact that remained was that I froze and got my girlfriend killed.

Sorry, Kalli.

She wasn't upset. *Don't worry. We'll get em next time.*

The thing that Lavender said made me think. How was I supposed to not let it happen? Get stronger? Be ready to push Kalli out of the way? Perhaps a shield that covered us both?

I dusted myself off and climbed to my feet. The attack Lavender used on us was eerily familiar.

I think she reflected our magic back at us.

Kalli sighed, sitting at a cafe table sipping a bowl of soup at she waited for Lavender. *I know she did. That was my green fire she used on me. What I didn't realize was that she mixed it with your light magic. I guess I need to build up immunity to you.*

I'd never felt Kalli's Luna Flame before. I wondered if that would instantly kill me, too, if Lavender used it on me. We both had no clue what her actual magic was like. For all we know, she was well out of our league.

I decided to practice by working on my shield. The artifact armor had a few too many unknowns and it felt like it would consume me if I used it too much.

It began with a tiny bubble. I pushed mana into a barrier around myself. Devotion seemed like a good emotion to make a shield stronger. It meant I wanted to protect someone I loved after all.

From there, I worked on projecting the bubble away from myself. It wanted to cling to me but, slowly, I was able to push it a few feet away from myself.

Could I use it to protect another person? I quickly edited up a test.

Item: Kalliphae Shared Mannequin (Edited)
Components: Cloth, Leather, Thread, Cotton
Item Rank: D
Item Level: 1

Item Owner: Murphy

Making it look like Kalli helped me want to protect it. I focused my attention on it and slid the bubble into place. Once I was satisfied, I just needed something or someone to attack it.

A flash of light got my attention. I looked over just in time to see Lavender's attack strike my shield, destroying it and the mannequin. She covered her mouth with her hand and laughed. "I hope I didn't burst your bubble."

Kalli flashed me a look of annoyance. *Was that thing supposed to be me?*

My face burned and I suddenly felt ashamed of my handiwork.

Well, I tried to edit something so I could feel like I was protecting you.

She stood over me with her hands on her hips and a scowl on her lips. *Well, it looked nothing like me.*

While she was a little annoyed, she wasn't mad at me. Not really. Lavender gave us a few minutes to perfect the bubble and come up with a strategy. It didn't help.

Lavender was on offense once again as soon as the fighting started. Before we had a chance to attack, she leveled the staff at us. A series of small metallic disks shot out of the end and flew straight at Kalli. I closed my eyes and projected the shield bubble at her. I saw from inside the shimmering bubble that Kalli also put up a shield of her own. Green flames swirled around her inside of the bubble, obscuring her from view.

At the last second, my courage in the shield failed and I shoved Kalli out of the way. I barely had a chance to get my shield up when the discs struck me. The last thing I heard was Lavender say, "Nope. Bad idea."

YOU HAVE BEEN SLAIN BY LAVENDER ???!

Kalli was upset at me again. *Why did you do that? We had a plan.*

After a moment in the dark, I appeared at a table in a diner. The innkeeper, Phylis, set a bowl of soup in front of me with a smile. "You have about five minutes to eat that while Lavender comes to collect you. I'd hurry if I were you."

I sampled a bite of soup to delay answering Kalli. We both knew that a mouth full of food didn't prevent MateChat, but she was patient anyway.

I'm sorry. I didn't want to watch you die again.

She heaved a sigh. *You need to have faith in yourself, Mel. I do.*

"Um, excuse me," a man seated at a nearby table said. "Are you Melvin Murphy?"

I stopped and turned to inspect the man. He was older than me and had a full beard. Also, he looked vaguely familiar.

Name: Huge Yak Man
Class: Fighter
Level: 1
Affection Level: Comatose

Such a strange name. "Is that really your name?"

He blinked at me. "I didn't tell you my name."

"Don't worry about that," I replied. "I can see your name. Why do you know mine, and what do you want?"

Kalli was echoing my question in my head, more than a little curious why an NPC knew my name. He seemed to shrug off my questions and said, "I need you to come with me. There is someone who wants to meet you."

"That doesn't sound dangerous at all," I said, slurping my soup. "I don't think I will."

He stood so suddenly that I thought he might attack me. "Look man, I'm begging you. I need to get back to my family and getting you to this woman is the only way to make that happen."

"That will be enough of that," Lavender announced as she strode into the room. "What did the vampire say to you?"

"Vampire?" Huge asked, with a shocked look on her face. "She promised to help me wake up if I just set up a meeting with this boy, Melvin Murphy."

The conversation was confusing. I only knew one vampire, and she was dead. Then there was the other question. "What do you mean, help you wake up? You're awake right now."

Lavender answered for him, "He's in a coma. For Huge here, this is the only place he can be awake. Out in our world, he's laying in a bed somewhere in a coma."

A part of me wanted to reach out to him, to touch his core. But there was that pesky corruption, making me a death sentence to everyone I touched. If the vampire really was Carmilla, could meeting with her for a couple of minutes mean saving the guy?

I looked to Lavender to see what she thought. After locking eyes with me for a few seconds, she nodded. "Very well. Give me a minute to collect Kalliphae, and we will also go."

A few moments after she was out of earshot, Huge gave me a pleading look and said, "She said she will only help me if you come alone."

Kalli whispered in my ear. *Don't you dare!*

I sighed. We were in a video game. What could possibly go wrong?

Look. I'll teleport straight to you at the first sign of danger. Also, you'll know where we go through the connection. I want to help this guy if possible.

That seemed to placate her. *Okay, fine, but the first sign of danger you had better teleport.*

———

The houses on the top of the hill looked like some kind of Club Med resort. A series of houses overlooked the beach with a big three-story mansion right in the middle.

"I think I'm going to call you Big Yak," I informed the man. "It sounds better than calling you Huge."

He laughed. "Don't you get the name. Try saying the whole thing out loud."

"Huge Yak Man." I did as instructed. "I get it. The actor. Still, Big Yak it is!"

Big Yak motioned to the mansion. "She's in there. She's been waiting to meet you for days. Ever since you first set foot in Homestead."

Kalli was back in Homestead. *We're almost there, Mel.*

I steeled myself for my second encounter with Carmilla. "Well, Big Yak, if you want me to meet her by myself, now is your chance."

He swallowed hard and stepped up to the double doors. They swung open. Without hesitating, he stepped inside.

"This is a very bad idea," I muttered to myself as I followed him in.

We walked up a strange staircase and down a hall on the second floor. Big Yak bypassed most of the closed doors until we came to a slightly ajar one at the end. He called out before entering. "Ma'am, I've brought the boy you requested. You just wanted to speak with him, right?"

A familiar voice replied, "Yes. Talking is about all I can do anymore. Anything else and that pesky AI will put me in timeout."

"What do you want, Carmilla," I said, backing away from the door. "If you want revenge, it probably won't work. If you kill me, I'll just respawn in that diner."

"What did you take from me?" she asked in a low raspy voice.

I tried to remember if I took anything from Shara or from her house. "Nothing, I think. I was only there for a little while. When we left, I didn't take anything."

"No, you fool," the voice spat the words. "I felt your touch on my soul. You discovered something that night. I want to know, did you steal my legacy."

"Oh, you mean your bloodline," I blurted the words out before I thought about their meaning.

"So, you did take it," Carmilla said with a hint of menace in her voice. "That is the birthright of my daughter. You will bestow it on her!"

The door creaked as it opened fully and there she was, Carmilla Shaw was standing in front of me once again. I took a few more steps back. I wasn't the same kid I was the first time we met. "Wasn't she born with it? I can't exactly give someone a bloodline."

"That's not entirely true," Lavender said from behind me. "Though you cannot assist Lady Shaw in your current condition."

Carmilla surged forward, stopping a few steps short of me. "What do you mean? I was told that his bloodline would be sufficient if not his class."

"Why do you need my help in the first place?" I asked again. "Shara has the bloodline."

Carmilla shook her head. "She doesn't have all of it. Not the important part."

"The boy doesn't have the curse," Lavender said with a smirk. "He deleted it."

Carmilla wasn't buying it. "If he can delete then he can also add. It's basic logic."

Lavender argued back, completely ignoring the fact that Kalli and I were there. "It's not that simple. Melvin cannot bestow curses. If your daughter wishes to embrace your legacy, she might make the pact of her own free will."

"I must speak with her," Carmilla said, a hint of desperation in her voice. "She will listen to her mother."

"What about me?" Big Yak asked in a tiny voice. "You promised to help me if I brought Melvin."

Carmilla laughed. "You have two options. Wait for the boy to free himself of his affliction or convince the fate here to summon my daughter."

[35]

WE WALKED AWAY from the mansion on the hill even more confused than when we had gone in.

Do you think I should help her?

Kalli, who had been quiet since we got there, gave me a worried look. *I don't like her. She tried to kill you. However, Shara was always nice to us. If she needs help, we should at least think about it.*

I had thought about it, and that was the problem.

Don't you think she might want revenge for her mom's death?

Kalli shrugged. *Maybe. We should definitely be careful if we meet her.*

Lavender and Big Yak walked a few paces behind us, speaking quietly. I slowed to catch part of the conversation. "Listen, Mr. Huge. While I cannot intervene in your medical situation at the moment, I can put you in touch with your family."

"You can?" Big Yak asked, his eyes widening in shock. "I'd really like to contact them. I'm told I've been in a coma for five years. They need me. I need them."

Lavender nodded. "Yes, I can. You need to be prepared for the worst though. It isn't easy to explain how you are able to communicate even though you are comatose. Remember, they know nothing about the program."

"Oh, right," Huge replied. "How am I going to do that?"

Lavender smiled. It was a sympathetic smile I didn't know she was capable of. "You'll find a way. Love finds a way. Just be yourself and explain it to her."

I thought we were headed back to the battlefield, but Lavender seemed to have thought we had enough for one day. She herded us all into Phylis's diner and summoned an old rotary phone for Big Yak. She set it up in a corner for him and asked, "Do you know how to use one of these?"

Big Yak picked up the receiver, holding it to his ear. His eyes widened when he heard a dial tone. "How does this work without being plugged in? Oh, um, yes. I know how to use it."

"Did you just remember you were in a simulation?" Lavender asked with a chuckle. "You'll be muted to this world while you communicate with the outside one. That way you can have privacy."

Lavender motioned to Phylis to bring out some food and turned her attention to us. "The two of you did well today. However, you need to have faith in each other. I want you to work on that. You are far stronger as a team than you are by yourselves. That makes you special, even more so than you both already are."

While I did like the things she was saying about us, my attention was focused on the mouth-watering food coming out of the kitchen. "Um, Lavender, why is the food so good here and at your house? I've never tasted anything like it."

Kalli elbowed me hard in the ribs. *Melvin! Focus. Lavender is trying to talk to us.*

I frowned, trying to replay what Lavender just said. It didn't matter, she was laughing along with half the restaurant. "Of course, the food here is better. It's S-ranked. Let's just call it a System hack. Only chefs with the most experience and training can achieve high-ranked signature dishes in the outside world. Using the System both in Homestead and at my house, I can easily designate the S rank to meals, giving them the highest possibly flavor."

"Tell us more about teamwork," Kalli said, mentally urging me to put my fork down. "We are paying attention. At least I am."

Lavender smiled. "It's fine. No more lectures for today. The two of you have choices to make. Three paths lay before you. The dearly departed vampire requested help with her wayward daughter. A not-so-young lady lies in wait back home, plotting her empire on Gaia. Last, the ever-looming shadow of corruption threatens to alter your future. I have placed new doors in your room to assist with the journey."

Kalli and I looked at one another in confusion as Lavender strode from the room.

Why does she keep doing that?

Kalli giggled, taking another bite of food. *She is a prophet type. Maybe it's her job to be mysterious like that.*

We finished up and returned to Lavender's house. Back in our room, we noticed three new doors.

V. World

TGB HQ

Solitair

"Are you planning to leave me here?" an annoyed voice asked from behind me.

I turned to find Zofia, still dressed in the ruffled dress, scowling at me. "Do you want to be taken back to your camp? Or perhaps wherever you come from on Earth."

She shook her head. "No. I demand you return my clothes and take me with you when you leave. My mission is to observe you and negotiate for the company. I can't do that if you leave me behind. Besides, I am not comfortable wearing this…this…thing."

While I knew Kalli loved her dresses, nobody liked to be forced to wear something. She gave Zofia a sympathetic look. "Didn't Lavender say you brought weapons in that other outfit of yours? How can we be sure you won't attack us if we return them to you."

"Isn't it true that you can kill me with a thought?" Zofia countered. "It's only prudent that I protect myself. None of the gadgets in my arsenal are designed for preemptive attacks. They are, how should I word this, for self-defense."

Kalli returned her attention to the doors. *We could drop her off at home. I assume that's where the second door leads. We can also get a look at where she comes from.*

Lavender had highlighted our choices, implying how they had an impact on the future. Then she conveniently laid the paths out like a Choose Your Own Adventure novel.

On the one hand, Zofia was right there and needed to be dealt with. Then there was the corruption. We were well on the path to dealing with that and there was no reason to return to Solitair just yet. That could wait.

The last option was also the riskiest. Shara had every reason to hate me and want me dead for what I did to her mother. Of course, there was the fact that she seemed to be at odds with her mother. I couldn't decide.

Which door should we take?

Kalli gave the doors some real consideration. She heard my thoughts through our bond and hers were fairly similar. The difference came down to her wanting to handle Zofia before sparing any mental energy on Shara.

We both looked back at the kid and, finally, Kalli spoke, "Will you show us the gadgets if we return them to you? We want to trust you, but it would be reassuring to know what we're dealing with."

"Will you show me your magic?" Zofia shot back with a smirk.

"Uh oh," was all I managed before Kalli jumped into action.

A sinister smile that I thought was reserved only for me appeared on Kalli's face as she replied, "Certainly. It would be my pleasure."

"Pvruzth."

Fire erupted from Kalli's outstretched hands and quickly engulfed Zofia. She shrieked and tried to back out of the door, but it was no use. Kalli's fire was relentless. The ruffled dress billowed as the flame caressed it as a summer breeze would. Her teal hair fanned out behind her as the fire flowed through it, smoothing out any knots and tangles.

Zofia stopped screaming by the time Kalli was finished. She closed her fists and the flame retracted into her hands. It felt like an out-of-body experience watching Kalli do it to someone else.

Sounds of running footsteps echoed through the hall before Eddie and Sylvia burst into the room. Sylvia blew Kalli and I quick kisses before asking, "What's wrong? We heard a scream. Is everyone okay?"

Zofia's face burned crimson red as she collected herself and smoothed the ruffled dress before climbing to her feet. "No! Everything is not okay. Can I have my stuff back now? I'll show you my defenses. Just don't do that again."

After changing in the bathroom, Zofia emerged looking much more comfortable. She pulled a button on her lab coat and a blue barrier shimmered around her. Then she held out what looked like a smartwatch and pressed a button. A bright red laser beam flashed out and burned a hole in the wall. She turned a tiny dial on the watch and the beam turned blue. The hole in the wall began to freeze.

Zofia shrugged and explained, "It's a matter of acceleration versus deceleration. Make particles move faster, and they burn. Make them slow down, and they freeze. The shield around me destabilizes matter. We haven't performed sufficient tests against magic, so I'm not one hundred percent sure what would happen if someone cast a spell at me."

It felt like she was leaving a lot out, but I decided to let it go. After having confronted her, I made an executive decision to get the meeting with Shara out of the way. "We're going to make a pitstop before taking you home. Just wait here with the other kids, and we will be back shortly."

"I. Am. Not. A. Child," Zofia said, enunciating every word. "I'd appreciate it if you stop treating me like one and take me with you."

"But it's going to be dangerous," Kalli said, realizing where I intended to go.

Zofia twisted a knob on her watch and a small metallic device that looked like some kind of drone rose from the back of her lab coat. A red marker appeared on my chest for a moment before the drone returned to its pocket. She winked at Kalli and said, "I can be dangerous, too. Don't worry, I'll keep you children safe."

"Fine," I muttered, not happy at being called a child by an unawakened, who looked like she was twelve. "It's your funeral."

Then I walked over to the door marked **V. World** and stepped through. The first thing I noticed was the red sky. It was evening on another planet and a blood moon flooded the world with crimson light.

Kalli gasped as she stepped through the door behind me. Behind her, Zofia stepped through the door, commenting, "Another world, eh?"

Directly in front of us stood a dark mansion. It looked like something out of a horror movie, or at least a haunted house. Either way, it stopped just short of having a sign out front that said, "A Vampire Lives Here."

SLAM!

Before we could take another step, we heard the sound of the door slamming shut behind us. I spun around just in time to see it fade and disappear. Eddie scowled at Sylvia. "Why did you do that? Now, we're stuck here."

Sylvia shrugged and gave the boy a reassuring hug. "Don't worry. It'll be fine. I had a vision."

"Why are the two of you here?" Kalli asked. "It's dangerous."

Eddie peeled Sylvia off him and scowled at her for good measure. "It's her fault. She wanted to see what was behind the door. I didn't know she was going to close it."

Sylvia ran over to me and clung to my shirt. "It'll be fine. Right, Mel? Tell them."

"Um, I don't know." I hesitated, looking to Kalli for advice. "I don't think you should have come. We don't know what we're walking into."

"I do." Sylvia chirped. "Shara missed you both. She will be more happy than mad. Trust me. I had a vision."

"When did you start having visions?" I asked, kneeling so I was face-to-face with her.

"Since you awakened me," she confessed. "Part of my training with Lavender is learning how to translate the future."

Kalli knelt beside us. "What do you mean translate?"

Sylvia giggled. "That's what Lavender calls making sense of what we see. When I have a vision, that's only one possible future. Anything I say or do can have drastic consequences."

"Dummy." Eddie barked at the girl. "Telling us about the vision changes the future. That means telling us it's safe makes it unsafe."

"Nuh-uh!" she whined. "I told you all that it's safe in my vision. If I saw myself saying it, then I can say it in real life, and it won't change anything. That's how it works?"

"That's just silly—" Eddie began.

He was cut off by a head pat from Kalli. "Shh. It's already done. Let's just get this over with."

Sylvia beamed at Kalli. "Right, she knows we're here. Let's not keep her waiting. It's rude."

[36]

THE MANSION in the woods was far creepier than the Shaw estate on Earth. I wondered if it was the red light or the sinister design of the building. The mansion was the deepest black I'd ever seen, looking almost like a shadow rising up from the ground. The red light of the atmosphere gave the building and surrounding forest a grim aura.

We slowly crept to the house, as if any noise on our part would inform a scary monster that dinner had arrived. Even though Sylvia claimed to have seen the future, she still clung to me.

Even Kalli was nervous, giving me directions in my head, *Be ready to teleport us out of here, Mel.*

Eddie and Zofia brought up the rear. Zofia seemed to be the only one not intimidated by the whole ordeal. Or maybe she was too traumatized by her dress experience to care if death crept up on the spooky red planet.

I only stopped thinking about it when the door of the mansion creaked open. Two stone gargoyles peeled the doors back revealing a very old man in a wheelchair. He looked at us with a tired smile on his face. "Ah, it's you. I never expected to see you again. Certainly not of your own free accord. Tell me, did my wife send you?"

"Rick Shaw?" I gasped, both chuckling at his name and wondering how it could be the same person.

Only two years had passed, and he looked at least twenty years older. His wife had recently died. That might explain it. "She did send us. Lady Shaw is worried about Shara and asked us to come talk to her."

Mr. Shaw looked back upstairs before replying, "While I appreciate you coming all this way, I think it would be best if you not see her. While I do love my wife, I believe she is mistaken in sending you. The last thing Shara needs is—"

"I'll think for myself, Daddy," a familiar yet different voice came from the shadows. "With that said, you can all turn around and go home. Nothing you have to say will change my mind."

A gothic-looking woman stood at the top of the stairs. Her jet-black hair and facial features looked remarkably similar to Shara's. She wore gothic makeup that sort of made her match the decor in the house.

My mouth fell open when I inspected her.

Name: Shara Shaw
Class: Hemamancer
Level: 73
Affection Level: Moody

I wasn't sure if I was more impressed with her level or class, but I was shocked to find out that the woman in front of me was Shara. "What? How? Why are you so old?"

She rolled her eyes and descended the stairs. "Time passes differently on The Blood Moon. It's been twelve years since the last time I saw you the day you killed my mother."

"I'm sorry about that. I—" She cut me off with a raised hand.

"Look, I don't blame you," she said with a sad smile. "Mother had her issues. I won't let anyone speak ill of her, but I know what she was capable of. Even Daddy knows you were only defending yourself."

Shara paused and exchanged a loaded look with her father. In the end, he backed down with a tiny nod. "As I said, it isn't your fault.

However, if you've come to try to convince me to take up her legacy, you can tell her that it's never going to happen. I don't care if I can live forever by doing it. I refuse. It's disgusting."

"But, honey pie," Mr. Shaw said in a hoarse voice.

Kalli took a step toward Shara. "The last thing we want to do is change you or force you to do something. We only came to make sure you are okay."

"Hah!" Shara squealed, sounding more like her younger self. "You're about ten years too late for that. The time that I needed a friend was when we were mourning my mother. Where were you then?"

Sylvia chose that moment to step out from behind me. "Hi. My name is Sylvia. I just wanted to say he was scared back then. Your mom just died, and he was afraid the other vampires were going to eat him."

Shara stared at the kid for a second before throwing her head back in laughter. The childish way Sylvia explained things took away the tension that was in the room.

I said, "I'm sorry, Shara. I should have tried to send a message to you. At least to apologize."

She sighed and shook her head. "It's fine. It's been years. I'm over it. I still don't want to be a vampire, though."

"Have you told your mother that?" Kalli asked. The only person yet to say anything was Eddie. I knew the two of them had history.

"She's stubborn," Shara replied, tossing her long hair over her shoulder. "I can't tell her. She won't listen."

Kalli walked toward Shara who glared at her but didn't back away. "I know what it's like to disagree with your mother. I just found out I have one after growing up as an orphan. Now she wants to make up for the lost time by making me a queen like she was. I don't mind being the queen. I love the people of Celestea, but I don't want to be like my mother. I want to do things my way."

"Me, too!" Shara roared, stomping her foot for emphasis. "Why can't parents just understand and let us be what we want?"

Kalli hugged Shara, who was shaking. "Have you at least tried telling her that? She thinks something is wrong."

"I can't." Shara sobbed into Kalli's shoulder. "You don't know my mother. There's no reasoning with her."

Kalli patted her on the back. "What if we go with you? We will stand by you when you tell her how you feel."

"I don't know." Shara hedged. It was obvious that she was intimidated by her mother. "It's not that I don't love her. I just don't want to do the things that are necessary to be a vampire."

"But, honey." Mr. Shaw began. "You're the only heir. Surely, you want to continue the family bloodline."

Did Shara lose her bloodline somehow? I had to check.

Skills: Controlling Voice, Splatter, Purification
Traits: Bloodline: Shaw, Specialty: Blood, Blood Regeneration, Control, Longevity

"She has the bloodline," I said in confusion. "Won't she pass it on to her children?"

Mr. Shaw shook his head. "You don't understand. My love was the queen of the damned. The original vampire. If Shara doesn't pick up the mantle, the title and control of this planet will pass to another family."

Shara sagged against Kalli, shaking slightly. Kalli replied before I could. "I don't get it. What's so important for her to be a vampire? She has a blood class and the Shaw bloodline. Isn't that enough? Can't you tell you're hurting her?"

"She won't be immortal if she doesn't accept the thirst." Mr. Shaw said, hanging his head in shame at his own words. "The other families will use that fact alone to exterminate us."

"Why not go back to Earth?" I offered, still a little creeped out by the red moon. "You lived on Earth before."

Mr. Shaw shook his head, shifting the wheelchair so he could look at me. "I'm afraid that just isn't possible. Blood Moon is the last safe haven for our kind. Only the strongest are able to thrive away from this place. The Shaw family has ruled for so long that the other families won't rest until the blood is eradicated. This house is all that stands between us and extinction."

"And that's why he's kept me prisoner in this house for the last decade," Shara said, scowling at her father. "Yet you all have the nerve to ask me why I'm not jumping for joy at the opportunity to fill mother's shoes."

"You can live on Gaia," Kalli suggested, offering Shara a weak smile. "Nobody will hunt you in Meltopia. Also, Melvin has your bloodline too. Your mother passed it to him when she bit him."

Mr. Shaw's ears perked up. He tried to stand but staggered a bit until Shara rushed over to help. "Give it to me! Give me the bloodline, and I'll protect the family."

"But I—" I began, weighing the potential of bestowing a bloodline to someone other than Kalli. The only way I knew how to do it was through our bond. Or perhaps by passing it on to my children. Neither of those options were available to Mr. Shaw. "I can't. I don't know how to do that. I can't even touch you without killing you right now. Kalli and I have a sickness we have to sort out."

Shara's ears perked up as she helped her father back into the wheelchair. "You're sick? Maybe I can help. I specialize in blood or chi-born illness. I can purify even the worst sicknesses from your blood."

Kalli and I looked at one another. I shook my head. "No. It's too dangerous. An ancient mage corrupted our cores with wrath. If our mana touches you, it might corrupt you, too."

Shara paced around as she deliberated. "How about this. You each give me a sample of your blood. I should be able to analyze it and get a better idea of what's wrong with you. That should be safe. I can take precautions to keep from being infected myself. Trust me, I have years of practice with this."

"But our corruption is in our mana," Kalli explained.

Shara grinned, rubbing her hands together as she explained, "Your blood is just an extension of your chi. While it's true that it exists to ferry what you need around your body, that also includes mana. While not as pure as the mana in your core, it will tell me everything I need to know about what's going on inside you."

"Absolutely not." Mr. Shaw said. "I forbid it. It's too dangerous."

Shara winked at us before whispering in Mr. Shaw's ear. "Think about it, Daddy. If we cure them, perhaps they can give you the blood-line and solve all our problems."

"Well, I—" he stammered before resigning himself to her plan. "I suppose. As long as you take every precaution."

Immediately, Shara's demeanor perked up. "Come with me. I want to show you guys my lab. Don't save dinner for me, Daddy. I'll be in the cave."

We followed her up the winding stairs to the second floor. Sylvia clung to me, and Zofia lagged behind, trying to look in every room as we passed. Kalli smiled at Sylvia as she walked beside us, and Eddie raced ahead of us, trying to get Shara's opinion. "Hey, Shara, do you remember me?"

She smirked at the now younger boy. "Sure do, squirt. It looks like I'm older than you now. Is Lavender treating you well?"

He shrugged. "She's all right. You got old. I can't believe you don't want to be a vampire. Then you'd be powerful and live forever."

"That's right," Shara chuckled. "You decided to be a warlock so you could be stronger than me. How is that working out for you?"

"I'm loads stronger than you now," he bragged. "Ask, Kalli. I can shoot a void beam now."

"Level twelve, huh?" Shara said with a sarcastic whistle. "I bet you're up to slaying gophers and hedgehogs now, eh?"

"Am not!" Eddie scowled. "Just the other day, I killed a giant monster. Right, Melvin!"

I just nodded, not wanting to get involved. It probably wasn't a good idea to tell Eddie about Shara's level. She always was an over-achiever.

Shara stopped at a large door and pressed her hand to a panel on the wall. Moments later, I heard the sounds of gears turning and a lock clicking into place. Then the door slid into the wall.

Inside was a very large and messy room. Clothes of all kinds littered the floor, including several pairs of underwear. Shara blushed and ran back and forth scooping them up and sliding the whole mess into a closet before returning to guide us through the room. "My lab is back here. Are you ready to see blood magic in action?"

[37]

SHARA'S LAB reminded me of a marriage between Altara Vestara's dark lab and Geronima Pemblescrap's portal chemistry set from the guild. All that was missing was Raverly's body in a cage. She had multiple blood samples in jars along the wall and various tubes on long tables.

When she saw me eying the blood, she explained, "Don't worry. This blood was all given willingly. We sponsor hospitals on several different planets."

"What are you going to do?" Kalli asked, looking at the blood nervously.

Shara laughed, revealing several sinister-looking fangs. "Don't worry. I don't plan on biting you or anything. That's way too gross for my taste. I don't know how my mother did it. As far as blood collection goes, I employ a few methods. We can go with the Earth method and use needles, or you can let me use my magic on you. There's some discomfort involved either way. The human body wasn't designed to bleed on command. It likes to keep its source of life inside of the body."

I frowned. "Why do you mean by life source? Are you saying you plan to take a piece of my core?"

Shara ran a finger along a vein on her wrist. We all watched as it pulsed and twitched just beneath the surface of her skin. A dot of blood appeared on her skin, and she pulled her finger back, tugging a red thread from her vein along with it. The thread pooled into a ball that floated in midair as she siphoned more blood from the vein. When she was satisfied, she severed the connection and picked up a vial with the other hand.

After depositing the blood securely, she licked the wound. Noticing we were still watching, she blushed. "Oops. Sorry, it's a bad habit. Don't worry, I won't lick you when I'm finished. You can apply pressure to stop the bleeding when I'm through."

Zofia, who watched the whole process closely, asked, "What do you do with all that blood?"

Shara looked over her shoulder at her collection. "Well, for the most part, I run experiments. Using my magic, I've learned how to purify most forms of bloodborne illness and toxins. The same concept can be applied to weaponizing blood with both disease and poison. It was a hard-won lesson that Melvin taught though my mother that it's unwise to take any foreign fluid into your body."

"So, you don't plan on drinking their blood?" Eddie asked, earning him a look of disgust from Sylvia.

Shara made a gagging noise. "The ignorance of people is astounding. What use would even vampires have drinking blood? They would just digest it if they did that. The way it works is that vampires absorb the essence from the blood through special mana ducts located in the mouth and throat. Surely, you knew this, Melvin. You did it instinctually when you bit my mother."

Everyone turned to stare at me. I threw my hands up in defense. "No, wait just a second. I had no clue what I was doing. I just copied your mother. Now that I think about it, it had to have been her mana for me to absorb her traits. I doubt I'd be able to do it again."

Shara nodded. "Vampires and hemamancers have an abnormally large amount of mana in our blood. It's how we control it as well as we do. Once I collect your blood, I am going to cast a spell on it to identify the impurity. With any luck, I'll be able to use my magic to purify it."

Kalli held out her wrist. "Go ahead and do it to me."

Shara fished around in a drawer and pulled out a butterfly needle with some tubing attached to it. "How would you like to do it? Magic of melee?"

Kalli shuddered and looked away. "I think I'll go with magic."

Shara put the needle down and walked over to Kalli with a fresh vial in her other hand. "You might feel a little pinch when I do this."

I wanted to protect Kalli. "A little pinch," was hospital slang for: "This is going to hurt like hell." In Kalli's case, she only yelped when the thin line of blood emerged from her wrist. I felt the sting through the connection and offered Kalli my hand. She knew what I was offering and squeezed it while Shara completed the blood draw.

When she had enough, she released the connection and Kalli took her hand back to press a thumb to the wound. Because of our shared regeneration, the tiny hole didn't bleed before the wound repaired itself.

Shara took the vial over to a window and was looking at it through the red light of the outside sky. "Very interesting. Your blood is rich with mana. Possibly even more so than mine."

"Can you do anything for her?" I asked hopefully, trying to see what Shara could in Kalli's blood.

She frowned and shook her head. "No. Your blood is too potent. It would likely overwhelm me if I tried to do anything directly do it. Are you a higher level than me? I don't know how that's possible, but there is more mana in your blood than I thought possible. I thought my blood was pure mana, but I don't even have a fraction of what you do."

Kalli shook her head. "I'm only level thirty-two. You're seventy-three, right?"

Shara nodded. "Peculiar. Anyhow, If your friends aren't as powerful as you, I should be able to cure them with no problem. Maybe I can get a better idea of what's going on with you when I help them."

"Are you willing to come to Gaia?" Kalli asked hopefully.

Shara hesitated, looking back at the wall of blood. "You're going to have to give me a little time to clear this out. Some of my experiments won't keep if I leave them. Bear in mind that time is accelerated under the blood moon. Much time will pass while I'm gone. Also, we will have to drop Daddy off with Mother. I refuse to leave him alone in this house. Even with the guards, we might still be attacked."

Wondering if I could repay the favor, I asked, "Who's attacking you? Maybe we can help."

She shook her head, looking off into the distance through the window. "It's not your war to fight. My mom was the original vampire. All others owe their blood to her because she created them. By not assuming the throne, I've created a succession issue. There are differing views on what should be allowed, and the darker sorts are trying to impose their views. The only thing stopping the bloody apocalypse is my control of the blood moon. If the Shaw Bloodline falls into the wrong hands, it could spell the end for a dozen worlds."

Kalli looked over at me nervously. *That's why Lady Shaw was so interested in you. You might also have control over this blood moon thing.*

Shara nodded, reading our body language. "That's right. I've heard you may have taken more than just blood from my mother. If you absorbed Shaw blood, you're probably a target, too."

"So, let's get your dad to Homestead!" I announced, wanting to hurry to save Squawk and Orpheus.

———

It took Shara most of the day to pack up her experiments. We were each shown to guest rooms while we waited. It turned out that there were a lot more servants in the large house than I thought possible. They were all retainers loyal to the Shaw household.

Kalli and I shared a room and tried to work on our emotional training, but it wasn't easy babysitting a bunch of rambunctious kids. Sadly, that included Zofia. While Eddie and Sylvia fought like siblings, Zofia decided to explore every restricted area in the house. We never managed to get any meaningful training done before another knock at the door revealed a maid or butler dragging one of the children in to tell us they had broken something or been caught somewhere they shouldn't be.

Shara insisted that only a couple of hours went by in the outside universe while she took her time packing her void bags. When she was finally ready, she admitted that while they had portals to Earth, they lacked access to Lavender's house or the video game that housed Homestead. That was why Mr. Shaw needed our help getting to his wife.

With that in mind, we decided the easiest way would be to teleport back to Celestea using Kalli's home point. We all held hands and I focused on Kalli's home, hoping this wouldn't be the time we gave Celestea a heart attack.

After I folded mana around all of us, we vanished.

———

"There she is!" a familiar voice shouted, pointing a shaky hand at Zofia. "Make her answer for what she's done."

I had to stand in front of Zofia as several villagers dressed in tattered clothes tried to get at her. Kalli rushed over to a familiar woman nursing a gash on her arm. "Beatrice! What happened?"

The woman looked up at Kalli with tears in her eyes. "Kalliville. It's gone. They destroyed everything. Killed everyone. There's nothing left. They are headed to the other villages, too. You need to stop them."

"Who did this?" I asked, my heart sinking.

I realized the man I was holding back was the chief of Kalliville, Otto. He pointed a shaky finger at Zofia. "Her people did it! The Earthlings are attacking. We are being invaded by aliens."

Zofia shook her head. "The TGB would never—"

Otto cut her off. "I witnessed it firsthand. They marched in with Earth weapons and technology. Their leader demanded our leader and said he intends to destroy all of Meltopia if you don't meet with him."

Kalli gave me a worried look, but I shook my head. "Where is he?"

"He said the next stop is Mount Wendy," Beatrice replied, wincing as Kalli helped her with a bandage. "He said he will destroy one town per week and all you have to do is meet with him, and he will stop."

Kalli and I locked eyes. *Don't you dare, Melvin! It's a trap.*

Zofia peaked her head around me, staring straight at Otto. "What's his name? I can tell you right now if this person works for the TGB. If he does, I will stop him myself. We do not condone wanton violence!"

Otto glared at her. "I will never forget his name. It's Grigori. Grigori Rasputin."

The name sounded strangely familiar. I turned and asked, "Wait a second. How did you speak to him?"

Otto paused and shrugged. "I don't know. He spoke our language."

I saw Celestea in the corner sitting on a bench. She had moved out of the way the moment we got back, content to let us handle things. I normally wouldn't mind, but I needed her to answer a few questions. "Celestia. Can you tell me if the humans from Earth found a way to speak our language? I mean when Kalli and I aren't here."

She shook her head but said nothing. Zofia held a data pad and confirmed. "I've contacted our camp. Not only can they not communicate with your envoy, but nobody has left the camp. It wasn't us."

"Liar!" Otto bellowed. "Your people with their weapons and metal carriages blasted down our walls and burned our buildings. You killed women and children. You savage!"

"It wasn't us," Zofia repeated, standing her ground. "The TGB exists for knowledge. We experiment to learn things. Never destroy. Destruction without purpose is meaningless. Lives are commodities that should never be wasted."

Otta gaped at her speechlessly. I tried to placate him. "We are going to get to the bottom of this. I'll meet with this guy and one way or another, we will make him go away."

"We should rally the army." Otto bellowed, giving me a fierce look I didn't know he possessed. "They killed my family. We should kill theirs."

"Where's Esha? "I asked, considering what a war with Earth would look like.

"The City Under the Mountain," Celestea replied. "She's been informed. We also have a small army here in Celestea and the castle has magic defenses for the city, but the villages are too far away. I recommend evacuating everyone and having them come here."

"Good idea, Mother," Kalli said, walking over to me. "We know where they will attack next. Let's evacuate Mount Wendy and bring everyone here. We can focus on the other villages after that."

The shock of another invader was starting to wear off. I didn't want to make the same mistake I made last time. This time, I would be prepared. "Don't worry. I've got a plan."

[38]

THE NEW DOORS in my bedroom were too convenient to have been placed there by accident. Lavender knew what was going on. She had to have. That was all the proof I needed to put my plan into action.

We returned to her house to drop off Eddie, Sylvia, Shiv, and Shara's father. The kids wanted to accompany us, but we decided it was too risky.

"It isn't fair that you get to go on adventures and I don't," Shiv complained to her sister. "You're not that much older than me. If adults are going to handle it then you should stay home too."

Kalli gave her sister a sympathetic look. "I wish that were the case. We have to do this because the majority of the empire is still low level. Don't worry, though. We're not going empty-handed."

"Can we at least go with Shara to cure Squawk and Uncle Orpheus?" Shiv asked hopefully. "There's no danger on Luna."

Kalli looked back at Shara. "How about this? Mr. Shaw is going to visit his wife in Homestead. Why don't the four of you go have an adventure in that world and do some more training? I'm sure Lavender—"

"Wait just a second there." Zofia stomped her way over to Kalli. "Please, tell me you aren't lumping me in with the children again."

Kalli took a step back. "No, of course not. I just figured you wouldn't want to get involved—"

Zofia pressed on, folding her arms. "Let me get this straight. First, you accuse my organization of attacking your people, and then you turn around and tell me it's too dangerous for me to be there? Absolutely not. I want to see this threat from Earth with my own eyes. And if that name isn't some kind of sick joke, then I am curious to see what kind of person this Grigori Rasputin is."

I turned to look at her. "That's right. I know that name. I've heard it somewhere before."

Zofia sighed and rolled her eyes, making her look very twelve years old. "Leave it to an American to not know world history. Rasputin was an infamous holy man for the Russian Orthodox Church. He died in 1916 at the age of forty-seven. At least, that's what the history books say. If this is to be believed, he somehow lived on and would currently be one-hundred-fifty-three years old."

I stopped. That's where I'd seen him. "Isn't he the old undead guy from the movie Anastasia? Are you telling me that was a true story? I knew cartoons were real."

Even though I was joking, I started to wonder if I could edit a cartoon and make it real. It was going to require some testing. Kalli elbowed me. *Focus, Melvin. We have real issues to deal with.*

So much for recreating Lord of the Rings.

Sorry!

I cleared my throat, trying to get back on track. "Fine. Zofia, you can come with us but you need to understand it's going to be dangerous. We don't know what this guy is capable of other than the fact that he's destroyed a village."

She nodded. "I can take care of myself."

"It sound's like it's settled then," Lavender said, entering the room behind us. "I'll take the children for an outing in Tierra and the rest of you can go deal with this Rasputin. I have full confidence in all of you. Remember this. Fate brought you all together for a reason."

We all looked at each other. It was an odd group to say the least. We had a vampire who looked older than we remembered, a strange woman from an Earth corporation who looked younger than she was, and the two of us, a couple of kids who probably had no business defending our planet from a boomer villain from a bygone era.

With one final glance at Kalli for support, I decided to toss them all a group invite, wondering if the technically unawakened Zofia could even see an invite let alone join one.

Kalliphae Murphy has joined the group.
Shara Shaw has joined the group.
Zofia [Redacted] has joined the group.

She managed to accept the invitation with no issues. I chuckled at Zofia's name and finally asked the question. "How exactly did you get your last name redacted? It's even on your ID card."

Zofia looked down at her datapad for a moment before coming to a decision. "I guess it's no big secret. I had my name legally changed to [Redacted]. There's no law in my country preventing it and I prefer my privacy. Surnames only exist for those who wish to be looked up. The government can use this name for their records and to ensure I pay my taxes. That is all they require."

Kalli giggled. *She did the same thing you did to my surname.*

She had a point. I idly wondered if there was some legal form I was supposed to fill out when I did that. Then I remembered our guild cards. The guild already knew about it. It must be connected to the System.

"Are we doing this?" Shara asked impatiently. "I can't be away from Blood Moon for too long."

I nodded and the four of us stepped through the door into the high house, Solitair.

———

To say Lavender had a sense of humor was an understatement. We came out in a bigger bath chamber than even the one in the Queen Suite back at Castle Celestea. Fortunately, it was unoccupied.

It was quickly obvious that we entered Maya's estate. Several male servants jumped in surprise when we entered a lavish bedroom. A heart-shaped bed that looked big enough for ten stood in the center of the room.

One of the servants recognized me. "Lord Melvin. To what do we owe this honor? Master Maya will not be pleased that you've seen her bedroom."

"Is she home?" Kalli asked hopefully, it's important that we see her right away."

The servant shook his head, staying on his hands and knees beside the bed. "No, my Lady. She meets with the council today."

"How do we get there?" I asked, eager to speak with my half-sister.

The servant pointed toward the door. "The elevator, my Lord. You can go anywhere on the island through the tubes."

"Can one of you please guide us?" Kalli asked in a syrupy sweet voice.

"Of course," the servant replied, climbing to his feet.

I was surprised by how big Maya's house was. The servant walked us down long halls, covered with dark blue carpets. Paintings of Maya lined the walls, each done by a different artist.

When we finally made it outside, I was surprised to see rows of servants on their knees. I turned to the first and asked, "Do you always wait out here for her like this? I thought it was only when you knew she was coming."

He gave a knowing smile and replied, "We are all well taken care of for our services. Not a single one of us is here against our will. It's just a shame that—"

"What is it?" Kalli asked, her concern flaring between our bond. "If there's something I can help with, I'd like to try."

The man blushed. "Um, well. You see—"

"I doubt you'd want to help them even if you could." The man's face lit up at the sound of his master. Maya popped out of a tube and landed right in the middle of her lined-up servants, eliciting gasps from all of them. "You see, it's all your fault that I can't have sex with them in the first place."

It was Kalli's turn to gasp. Blushing, she couldn't meet the servant's eyes when she said, "I'm sorry, but I can't help you with that."

"Please, tell me you come with good news," Maya pressed on, disregarding the awkward atmosphere.

I shook my head. "We haven't cured ourselves yet, though we're well on the way. The reason we came is that we need your help."

"My help?" Maya asked with a puzzled look on her face. "What do you need this time? Oh, and how did you get into my house?"

———

Maya insisted on seeing the portal door in her bathroom. The first thing she did when she saw it was to open it and step into my bath chamber.

She had a smile on her face when she returned. "At least turn-around is fair play. It's a bit awkward having a door to my brother's room in the bath chamber, but it seems to be the normal spot for such rooms. Tell me something, does this witch who makes them always place them in such compromising places?"

I had to think about it for a bit. "Well, the one connecting Kalli's room and mine is also in the bathroom but the portal on Luna is in the throne room. Then there's the portal to Blood Moon, which is outside."

Maya was astounded. "So many portals. And all of these connect to your room? Tell me, something brother. What exactly is your arrangement with this Lavender?"

I shrugged. "I couldn't tell you."

She winked at me, and Kalli scowled at her. It was fairly obvious how Maya thought favor was supposed to be earned. We spent the next several minutes bringing Maya up to date about our efforts to cure the corruption and the invaders from Earth, both TGB and Rasputin.

Zofia chimed in when I mentioned her organization. "Just in case you think all non-magic organizations are evil, the TGB is not the vilest company in Poland. That would be the ZUS."

"But you are admittedly vile," Maya said with an approving nod.

"Tell me more about this ZUS. Do you think this Rasputin works for them?"

Zofia scoffed and shook her head. "Does nobody on this planet read about Earth's history? Rasputin was a self-proclaimed holy man that they say enchanted the empress and single-handedly brought on the Bolshevik Revolution and ended the empire. Oh, and also the ZUS is called the Social Insurance Institution. You might as well call them the Socialist's Office of Thieves if you ask me. Very corrupt."

"Neither of those have the acronym ZUS," I pointed out, laughing.

Maya gave me a consoling look and explained, "That would be the auto-translate trait kicking in. She isn't speaking your language, and the System changed it. You and I are hearing different things from her as well. She would have to enunciate the words slowly and separately to bypass it."

Zofia tried again, enunciating the foreign-sounding words. "*Zakład. Ubezpieczeń. Społecznych.*"

"Wow." Kalli swooned. "I love your accent."

Zofia blushed and covered her mouth, mumbling, "I don't have an accent."

The auto-translate kicked back in, and the accent was gone. Maya walked past us and opened the door to her room. The servants were still kneeling next to the bed. She motioned to the hall and said, "I don't normally invite guests into my room. Let's go to the conference room, and we can discuss what you need."

———

"Okay, what exactly do you want from me, brother," she said with more than a bit of sarcasm, making it obvious that she felt I was using our relationship to get her to help. "Why should the high house get involved in what is essentially an unawakened matter."

"Because your world is being invaded," I explained, grasping at straws but desperate for help. "Don't you guys have rules about who you allow into your world?"

She shook her head. "We charge people a tax if they require our

288

assistance to bridge the two dimensions. It's a deal we brokered with the high houses of dozens of worlds. Interdimensional travelers pay both coming and going. As you should be well aware, those with sufficient magic to make the journey on their own are free to do as they please. Otherwise, you'd be public offender number one."

She had a point. I made the commute almost daily. "But what about the fact that he's destroying villages in my empire? Surely you have a problem with that."

Maya laughed. "Is he not also destroying villages back on Earth? Why don't you go back there and ask your own embassy what they are doing to stop him? You'll find that once a mage reaches a certain level of power, the governing body ceases to have any jurisdiction."

"Then how do you deal with them when they go on killing sprees?" Kalli asked, horrified.

Maya's expression hardened as she answered the question. "We don't. Once an awakened reaches a certain level of power, there is only one way to stop them. War."

[39]

THE MEETING with Maya wasn't a complete bust. She agreed to convene the council and send a delegation to our meeting with Rasputin. That way the high house could get an idea of what they were up against and react accordingly.

She was also eager to meet Shara on the off chance the vampire could do anything for her condition. I explained that since Shara already considered Kalli to be too potent to cure directly, she likely would be as well.

"So, what am I going to do?" Maya asked, pouting as we walked past one of her servants. "If I don't pay these guys soon I'm going to have a mutiny on my hands."

"Why don't you pay them?" I asked, wondering if she expected to be serviced before she coughed up any gold.

"I can't," she moaned. "I pay them with affection. I can hardly do that while I'm a walking MTD."

I started to feel sorry for the servants. They served Maya for a reward she couldn't currently give them. She might never be able to give it to them again.

Since the agreed-upon time was in three days, we teleported back,

THE ACCIDENTAL CORRUPTION

and Maya was to join us by airship with some representatives from Solitair.

We arrived in an empty throne room. It was odd by itself that Celestea wasn't there but not a single person occupied the room. Kalli and I exchanged a nervous look.

Do you think something happened?

She ran toward the door, Zofia and I hot on her heels. We sprinted through the maze of corridors until I was completely lost. Kalli knew where she was going, getting much more accustomed to the place than I was.

She didn't bother knocking when we arrived at a large oak door. Once inside, she calls out. "Mother? Father? Are you here?"

Not getting an answer, she ran through the room, leaving Zofia and me at the door. There were several rooms connected to the chamber we came in through which only had a couple of fancy chairs and a low coffee table. When Kalli returned, she was frowning. *They aren't here. I wonder where they could be.*

I could tell she was worried Rasputin got to them. He was likely the same old man that appeared in the throne room. We followed Kalli as she ran off again, desperately trying to find answers. That was until we ran into one of the butlers. Kalli skidded to a halt and asked, "Excuse me, have you seen Celestea?"

The butler bowed deeply. "Your Majesty. Lady Celestea has departed for Mount Wendy with Lord Charles to personally oversee the evacuation."

Kalli gasped, clutching my arm. *We need to go there!*

I felt how desperate she was for her parents to be safe. Not really thinking about it, I extended a hand to Zofia. She looked at it suspiciously before taking it. Then I folded mana around us, and we were off again.

———

"Kalliphae!" her mother gasped, clutching her heart. "You need to stop doing that. It's going to be the end of me."

291

"You scared me when you weren't in the castle," Kalli cried, running to her mother.

"Oh, sweetheart," Celestea replied soothingly, embracing her daughter. "This is how we feel as your parents every time you step out that door. Both you and your sister."

The scene in front of me sent a jolt of pain through my heart. Here I was, my own mother missing, and I hadn't done a whole lot to look for her. Not that I could. She didn't exactly leave any clues. Kalli noticed my distress and looked up at me. I shook my head. It was not the time to worry about that. We had villagers to save.

From the looks of things, Celestea and Charles had things well in hand. Most of the village was packed up into ruffalo-drawn wagons and only a handful of villagers remained. I felt a pang of sadness at the sight of the buildings Joe and I created. Was it all going to be destroyed? What did this Rasputin want with me? Three days couldn't go by fast enough.

Once the last of the wagons were packed, I stopped Celestea and Charles from boarding the last one. "Let me take you back to the castle. It will be quicker, and Kalli won't worry."

Celestea shook her head. "Even though these villages are part of your empire, this is my queendom and I will not be afraid to travel with my people. How do you think they will feel if their queen abandons them at the first sign of danger?"

"We want to come with you," Kalli said, starting for the carriage.

Celestea shook her head, barring her daughter's entry. "Only one of us needs to be here and that is my responsibility. You and Melvin go make a plan to deal with this threat. As it stands, I have to let you do that. Give me this one small thing. Besides, I've got your father here to protect me."

I didn't have to have a bond with Charles to know he remembered the last time he faced magic. It was written all over his face and the look he gave Kalli. While Celestea was a somewhat skilled pyromancer, she probably wouldn't last long if Rasputin chose to attack them on the road. I took solace in the fact that he didn't kill them in the castle when he first arrived.

After some convincing, Kalli, Zofia, and I stayed until the last wagon was safely on the road. Then something hit me.

I want to see Kalliville. You know, what's left of it.

Kalli nodded wordlessly and accepted my hand. The question was, what to do with Zofia? Turning to her, I explained, "We're going to check out the village that was destroyed. Do you want us to drop you off at the castle or back in your camp?"

Zofia looked thoughtful for a moment and said, "I'd like to see the damage caused by this Rasputin, but it might be best if we make a pitstop at my tent. I can pick up some more defenses just in case."

Kalli offered Zofia her hand and said, "Fine but you're giving us a tour while we're there. I think it's about time you show us firsthand that you had nothing to do with this. A little trust will go a long way."

Zofia huffed but took Kalli's hand. "That's fine. There's not much to show. We are currently spending all our resources to stabilize the portal."

Then we were off again. The next time we appeared, men and women in white lab coats dove for cover while others in overalls ran in every direction. Zofia pressed a few buttons on a watch I hadn't noticed on her wrist and made an announcement. "Attention workers. This is Zofia, representative of The Administrator. What you just witnessed is just a standard inspection by the local government. Please go about your daily tasks and stay out of their way. Natalia, please report to the command tent."

We waited patiently while the workers collected themselves and went about their duties. Once she was satisfied, Zofia began walking and motioned for us to follow. I wanted to see what was in the big tent firsthand, but Zofia had other ideas, leading us to one of the small ones. "So far, we haven't brought any weapons through the portal, so all we have here are defenses to ward off the local wildlife and allow us time to escape should you have attacked us. However, we do have guns and other primitive weapons on the Earth side of the portal. Anything fancy would have to come from headquarters."

Natalia was waiting for us in the tent with her arms crossed.

"You're back! Is there any news of the treaty? I haven't been able to get ahold of The Administrator."

Zofia took a seat and crossed her legs, looking like a kid that was playing at being an adult. "As I've told you before, I am the lead for this project and have been given full authority by The Administrator to handle all communications. With that said, you will address any concerns to me and only me."

"But we tried, Miss Zofia," Natalia pleaded, refusing to sit and pacing back and forth. "You stopped responding and your locator went off the grid. We feared the worst for a while. I felt it only prudent to inform the-."

Zofia laughed. "It's only been a few days. Diplomacy takes time and there were extenuating circumstances beyond my control where electronic communication just wasn't possible."

"Understood." Natalia stiffened at the rebuke. Picking up a clipboard, she proceeded to read off a report. "Progress on the portal is-."

Zofia cut her off again, waving her datapad for emphasis. "I'm well aware of your lack of progress. Tell me, why are you having so much trouble with the mana batteries."

Natalia flashed us a nervous glance as she flipped several pages of her report. Not finding what she was looking for, she set the clipboard on the table. "As I am sure you're well aware, our current batteries take nearly a month to fully charge. We simply cannot keep up with the demand."

"And what of your efforts to stabilize the portal?" Zofia asked with a yawn. Clearly, she wasn't pleased with her subordinate's reply. "If you do the math, it should be possible to trick the... Well, it should be possible to make a permanent portal between worlds."

"But we haven't—" Natalia began to say something before being cut off by a loud scoff from Zofia.

"Very well, I will do it myself." Zofia stood, glaring at us as if it were somehow our fault. "Come, the supplies I told you about are in another tent."

She didn't say anything else as we followed her through the camp.

None of the other scientists even so much as looked at us, scurrying around like they were on a mission. For all I knew, they were.

Do you think she wanted us to see that conversation?

Kalli shrugged, suppressing a giggle. *I think she was just showing off that she's in charge around here. Whether that's to the people here or to us, I don't know.*

We made it into another tent a few seconds behind Zofia. She rummaged through a crate and withdrew a few wristbands. "Here, put these on. They are called kinetic dampeners. They activate if anything approaches you going faster than a certain velocity. While it won't save you if you're hit by a car, they do a number on bullets. Since this Rasputin seems to be from Earth, it's probably a good idea to assume they have guns."

"These stop bullets?" I asked, sliding the bracelet on my wrist.

Item: Kinetic Dampener
Components: Geode, Platinum, Focusing Crystal, Grade
E Mana
Rank: C
Item Level: 1
Item Owner: [Redacted]

I chuckled when I saw her name. Anyone else seeing the item would think the owner had their name encrypted. However, it was just Zofia's last name.

Zofia adjusted a similar bracelet on her wrist and tossed the two of us bulky sweaters. "In theory, the dampener will prevent bullets from dealing life-threatening damage. You have to keep in mind that not all bullets are the same. While smaller shells may not do damage at all, a high-caliber round will go right through the shield. Our testing finds that it works best when paired with a bulletproof vest. If you have magic means of protecting yourself, that might work even better."

I looked down at the tiny device, scared to probe it with my mana. The corruption was capable of anything, and I didn't want to risk it.

Zofia rummaged through several other crates. I noticed items disappearing into her lab coat, but she offered none of it to us. When she was satisfied, she walked over to us and offered her hand. "I'm done. We can go to Kalliville now."

I shook my head. "Let's take a peek in the big tent before we go."

[40]

THE PORTAL GENERATOR took up most of the space in the big tent. Something that looked like a radar dish pointed at a large area on the far side of the tent that was mysteriously clear of crates. Zofia questioned me as I examined the strange machine. "You're from Earth, correct? Do you have any education in physics or molecular science?"

While I had taken a physics class in high school, it was obvious that the machine in front of us was several levels above anything taught in a public high school. Zofia smirked at the frown on my face. "I figured. You're still young. There's plenty of time to indulge your curiosity. "

"You are a very curious person aren't you?" I asked, remembering Zofia's affection level was eternally curious. "Would it bother you if I accidentally broke this?"

She frowned, watching me carefully. "Well, we have backup modules for every part in that generator as well as a replica on the Earth side. Call it quadruple redundancy. You couldn't shut down the portal without virtually destroying the TGB if that's what you're thinking of doing."

I shook my head beginning to probe the generator. "Actually, I wanted to try something but, since my mana is corrupt at the moment, it might have an unintended consequence."

Zofia smirked, taking the data pad out of an oversized pocket in her lab coat. After swiping at it a few times, she gave me the thumbs up. "Go ahead. I've cleared the area just in case you make something explode."

The thought of making it explode worried me a bit.

Perhaps you might want to wait outside.

Kalli crinkled her nose, stepping closer to me. *Not if you don't.*

Realizing I couldn't make her go, I traced my fingers along the generator to the spot where I'd felt something. Mana leaked from behind a locked panel. It wasn't artificial mana inside of the power source. The mana came from a person. "Zofia, where do you get the mana to power this?"

She answered without looking up from the data pad. "We have an arrangement with a local prison back on Earth. Inmates spend time in a special capsule to earn time off their sentences. Our machine traps and contains mana that naturally emanates from them. Obviously, it's only effective on the awakened. I tried doing it to myself once, and the results were negligible."

There was so much about the awakened world on Earth that I didn't know about. Prisons for the awakened existed. A real-life Azkaban. I wondered if Earth had supervillains like the current occupants of my ring.

Pushing mana into another object for the first time in forever, I probed the mana battery. A small trace of mana leaked from the device. It was what I sensed in the first place. Further investigation showed the mana in the battery was provided by different people. The mana in each cell battled with one another which was causing a leak.

I reported my findings as I continued my investigation. "Using mana from more than one person is inefficient. The mana rejects mana of another type, kind of like blood cells do. That's why you have a leak."

Zofia grunted acknowledgment that she'd heard me as I continued to prod the battery. It was easy and easy problem to fix by removing the mana and replacing it with my own.

Much more efficient.

Kalli giggled, feeling what I was doing through our bond. *Do you think the corruption will make it malfunction?*

I guess there's only one way to find out.

Zofia's curiosity was rubbing off on me. "How do you activate the portal?"

She frowned, putting the data pad away. "Do you need something from Earth, or do you just want to see my operation on the other side?"

"It's nothing like that. I want to see if my mana corrupted the portal," I explained. "Worst case scenario it transports us someplace else. That might be bad for your people. If it happens to me, I can just return to Kalli."

Kalli shook her head, speaking out loud so Zofia could hear as well. "That won't work since I'm coming with you. If we run into trouble, we can teleport back to the castle."

I nodded and Zofia huffed but complied by punching a few commands on the data pad. The generator hummed to life and began to shake and the two of us took a few steps back just in case. Zofia's eyes widened, and she looked up at me. "What did you feed it? It says it's operating at one thousand percent capacity but that's not normally possible."

I shrugged at her, a feeling of pride welling up inside me. "What can I say? My mana's pretty potent."

Zofia chuckled in spite of herself. "This might yet be a mutually beneficial partnership. Are you ready to see where we go?"

We nodded, and she punched a button on the data pad. The dish began to glow before shooting what looked like a laser toward the far end of the tent. Only, it never got there. The mana I'd pumped into the machine attacked the spot at the far end of the tent and ripped a hole in the world. The space itself appeared to have torn whatever wall existed between Gaia and the void. Rather than seeing the path between worlds that I normally saw whenever I kept my eyes open while teleporting, what we saw looked like a mirror of the tent room.

Zofia peaked through the rip and spoke in a sad voice, "That's Earth. Your experiment failed."

We stared at her. Had she wanted something to go wrong? I shrugged off the idea and offered Kalli my hand. Together we crossed the distance to the portal I poked it. The experience was somewhat different than normal teleportation. The portal itself felt like the surface of water. Cool to the touch, the portal rippled when my fingers passed through. Gathering courage, I pressed my face into the portal and was surprised by what I experienced. Everything was different on the other side, from the air pressure to the composition of the air. The ambient light didn't have that green tint that I was accustomed to on Gaia.

Zofia popped out of the portal beside me and whispered, "I wouldn't linger in the portal if I were you. I'd hate to imagine what would happen if it closed while you were only half in."

Kalli heard that and shoved me through. I flopped onto the floor only to be flattened as she came flying through right after me. Zofia cleared her throat, looking away and pretending to busy herself on the data pad.

When we gathered ourselves, Zofia waved her arms, startling workers on the other side of the tent. "Tada, this is Earth. Seen enough? Ready to go back?"

"Where are we?" I asked, making my way to the entrance of the tent.

While I had gone to Ukraine once, I hadn't had much time to appreciate my first trip outside of the United States. Zofia followed us and replied, "This is Poland. Do you need to know exactly where it is? I'd prefer certain organizations not come prying if you know what I mean."

"The government?" I asked, raising an eyebrow. The area surrounding the tent had been fenced off with some kind of temporary material. Outside of the camp was a forest as far as I could see. I heard water rumbling somewhere in the distance.

Kalli doubled down on Zofia's earlier statement. "Are you breaking the law?"

Zofia's eyes narrowed. She looked annoyed. However, her smug demeanor quickly returned when she answered. "Law's don't exist for half of what we do. We just prefer to stay below the radar. Unlike you magic folks, we can't just wave a wand and make the powers that be fall in line."

Seeing the blue sky was the final confirmation that we had crossed back to Earth. I wanted to explore, but Kalli tugged my sleeve. *We need to get back. Don't forget about Kalliville and Rasputin.*

I desperately wanted to forget about it. Since our fight with Mardella, it seemed we were running nonstop from one place to the next. First to deal with the corruption and save our friends, then dealing with multiple invasions from Earth. I glanced back at Zofia. It was her company that caused all of it. It just couldn't be a coincidence that Rasputin showed up right when she did.

We headed back through the portal since it was easier than wasting mana on an extra teleport. Zofia ran ahead and flagged down a group of people in lab coats, whispering something.

When she was satisfied, she returned to us. "Okay, I'm ready to go."

"What was all of that about?" I asked, thinking she was up to something.

Zofia nodded toward the portal generator. "I told them to monitor the battery you charged and to report any changes to the portal immediately. Don't hold me accountable if it blows up and destroys your world."

"Can it do that?" Kalli asked, a surge of worry coming from her.

Zofia threw her hands up, waving off the danger. "Anytime you conduct experiments of this caliber, you have to be prepared for side effects on a monumental level. The knowledge we gain usually compensates the loss but don't worry, this device is really just a powerful magic-based computer."

Zofia was turning out to be very difficult to understand. I couldn't tell whether she was joking or not. "Are you suggesting that blowing up Gaia is an acceptable loss so long as you learn something from it?"

"It depends what we gain," Zofia countered. "There is always a tipping point. Consider nuclear fission for example. Countless lives were lost because of that invention. Was it wrong of scientists to come up with it?"

I didn't know how I felt. "I prefer to avoid anything that leads to death when I can help it."

Zofia gave Kalli a pleading look. "Please, tell me he isn't going to try to defeat this Rasputin with the power of love. I might have to reconsider my stay here if this place gets invaded."

Kalli squeezed my hand reassuringly. "I agree with Melvin. Killing should only be a last resort. We need to find a way to make this man go away peacefully."

"Even after he killed your people?" Zofia challenged, crossing her arms. "I don't think I could dismiss my people so easily as you do yours."

It was true. He had murdered people. Would it be too harsh to imprison him in the ring? If I did that, Longinus could be released. He promised to help us get rid of the corruption if we let him out.

Kalli and I exchanged a glance. *Let's deal with that when the time comes. We don't even know what he's going to say.*

That's true. Let's go see what happened at Kalliville.

We motioned for Zofia to join us, and I folded mana over us once more.

The magic of the empire still recognized Kalliville as a village and allowed me to teleport there without much active thought. The debris that was left couldn't be classified as anything but ruins. The walls I'd placed around my first village were splinters in what could only be described as a series of craters.

"Magic didn't do this?" Zofia commented, peering into one of the craters. "Some kind of artillery was used here."

The carnage left behind in the buildings that were destroyed made me want to be sick. Almost every collapsed building had battered remains of villagers. The survivors had been forced to leave their fallen loved ones behind in their haste to flee.

We need to bury all of them.

Kalli nodded, gingerly removing part of a wall from a child's body. There were tears in her eyes. *I take it back, Melvin. Rasputin needs to pay for this. How dare he murder innocent people just to have a word with you. That's inexcusable.*

I still wasn't sure if I was up to the task of defeating the man much less murdering him. However, I felt the same way Kalli did.

We will make him pay for this.

It took us several hours to extract the dead from the rubble, and that was with me **DELETING** everything in our way. Zofia gawked at me as I worked my magic. I'd never dealt with burial rites on Gaia before. Kalli assured me that cremation was something that was socially acceptable. With local plagues and lack of land, it was often practical for small villages to send their loved ones off in a funeral pyre.

I quickly returned to Celestea Castle to pick up the survivors. Otto gathered them all together, and I brought them back to the ruined village. While I was gone, Zofia and Kalli somehow managed to put together a wooden pyre and laid out the bodies as best as they could on it.

Otto broke down in tears when he saw them. "Thank you so much for honoring us, my Lord."

I shook my head sadly. "I only wish I could have done something to save them."

"Just avenge them," he growled under his breath. "That is all I ask."

When the time came to light the fire, Kalli held me back. *Let me do this. I think they will see the Luna Fire as something special.*

I stood back and watched with the survivors as Kalli approached the pyre and clapped her pendant. It glowed and sucked up the fire she offered, purifying as it emerged a rich green color similar to the light coming from Luna. Everybody gasped as the flames blanketed their bodies. Unlike regular fire that took a long time to consume, the Luna Fire made quick work of both body and pyre. In almost no time, nothing was left but green flames dancing on the ground. Kalli held out the pendant which sucked all of the flames up.

Zofia pointed out deep tracks in the ground just outside of where Kalliville used to be. "Whoever this Rasputin is, he's brought tanks.

That means you need to be prepared for guns and other things. Can you fight against that?"

I looked down at the kinetic dampener on my wrist. The truth was, I'd never really been shot at. Just that one time in Ukraine. Deleting that tank had been easy enough. But what if I didn't see it coming or they shot at Kalli? Could I protect her? She felt my worry and sent reassurance. *It's going to be okay. Maya is coming with a delegation from the high house. I'm sure they will sort it out if things get out of hand.*

Just as she said that, a humming sound echoed across the open plain. After a while, I spotted the source of the noise. An airship in the distance was heading toward Celestea.

I guess we should get back to the castle and tell Maya what we found.

[41]

WE ARRIVED BACK at the castle about an hour before the airship arrived. It was impressive how fast they traveled. The same journey took half a day by mecharriage. Kalli fidgeted and couldn't stop pacing. I knew what was wrong. She was worried about her patents.

Do you want to go find them? I can make us a car, and we can be there in no time.

She shook her head. *Mother is right. I have to trust her to do things like this. I just can't shake a feeling that...*

Kalli didn't need to finish the thought. There was a madman on the loose, and he was killing villagers to get to me. The only solace we had was that he told Otto he would patiently wait to meet me in three days at Mount Wendy. I decided to distract her.

Wanna make out?

She spluttered, stopping mid-stride to stare at me in shock. *Really? Is that all boys ever think about?*

I shrugged and was surprised to be rewarded with a kiss. She wrapped her arms around my neck and stared into my eyes. *Thanks.*

I smiled.

Anytime.

———

Maya arrived with three other women. They looked more like a middle-aged book club than the accomplished mages I needed to scare off Rasputin.

My older sister began with a round of introductions. "Ladies, this is my half-brother, Melvin Murphy, and his girlfriend Kalliphae. Melvin, I'd like to introduce you to a few members of the Gaian high council. Meet Ladies Marisa, Chala, and Henrietta. They have agreed to audit this threat. As I told you before, we do not regulate the high-born when it comes to their interactions with peasants. All we can do is ask that he communicate his intentions to the high house. I'm sorry I can't do more. A war between worlds would be catastrophic on an unprecedented level. This really is for the best."

The first thing I did was inspect the newcomers to see how useful they would be.

Name: Marisa Merryweather
Class: Astromancer
Level: ???
Affection Level: Snooty

Name: Chala Chole
Class: Vulmancer
Class: ???
Affection Level: Gabby

Name: Henrietta Webb
Class: Paper Mage
Level: ???
Affection Level: Proud

A glance at their levels filled me with relief. Maya brought in high-level mages to help us. Even Rasputin would think twice before going up against four level one hundred plus mages.

After exchanging greetings, Maya cut to the chase about the reason for her visit. "Where is the vampire? I'd like to get this corruption taken care of before we go into a hostile environment."

I looked up at Luna in the darkening sky. Maya followed my gaze with a hopeful look on her face. Shaking my head, I announced, "I'll go get her. Wait here."

They weren't happy about my decision to deny access to the green planet. That much was obvious. Kalli stayed behind to play host while I made my way to the portal door to fetch Shara. Arriving on Luna, I discovered the throne room bustling with activity. Children I hadn't noticed on prior visits swarmed me as I stepped through the door. It was strange to consider any of the ancients as children considering they had all been kept prisoner since before I was born. The machines beneath the castle must have done something to preserve their bodies.

A blue-haired girl looked up at me with wide blue eyes that matched her hair. "Excuse me. Who are you? Are you friends with Lavender? Did you bring snacks? She promised to bring more snacks."

I shook my head, backing away slowly. It was Kalli's job to handle the littles, and she was back on Gaia. Still, in typical Kalli fashion, she attempted to help through our bond. *Tell them I'll bring treats next time.*

I tried, "Um, we will... Maybe, tomorrow? I don't know how to cook. Wait, I can edit you something. What do you like to eat?"

My promise to make food was met by loud cheering. It attracted the attention of somebody outside, and several adults stormed into the room. "What's all the noise? Oh, who are...? Wait, you're Melvin, aren't you? I remember you. Welcome, sir."

I waved them off, editing up a platter of cupcakes for the children. Hopefully, they weren't allergic. "Thank you. Have you seen Shara Shaw? The, um, woman who came to cure the two Gaian patients?"

The woman waded through the throng of happily snacking children to make room for me to follow her. Together we exited the castle and proceeded down the path. Like Shiv said when they visited, new buildings had popped up all over the place. Even in the distance, I saw smoke rising from chimneys all along the lake outside the castle.

"Right this way," the woman said, motioning to one of the first buildings we came across. "We cleared this home to house your sick friends. The one you seek is with them now."

Shara looked up from a series of vials she had resting over an open flame when I walked in. "Melvin, I didn't expect you so soon. Is everything okay?"

I sat next to her, curious about what she was working on. Orpheus and Squawk were nowhere to be seen, but I assumed they were both resting behind one of the closed doors. Realizing Shara was waiting for an answer, I replied, "Someone back on Gaia wants to meet you when you get a chance. How are Squawk and Orpheus?"

She smiled and motioned toward the closed doors. "They are going to be just fine. They are resting now. I've begun their treatments but curing them will be complicated. At least for me."

"Aren't the ancients helping?" I asked, wondering whether Iolathar returned. "Why is it complicated?"

Shara tipped the contents of one of the vials into the other, causing a white foam to rise. "I'm not sure. They are waiting for someone to return from the moon. The problem with me curing them is that without someone to help with their core, the only way I can remove the corruption is by turning them."

"What do you mean?" I asked, dreading the answer.

She sighed, looking up at the foam through the light. "I mean I will have to give them the curse. That alone will replace all of the mana in their core. I'm ninety-nine percent sure it will cure them."

"Are you going to make them into vampires?" I asked, taken aback. "I thought you rejected the curse from your mother."

"I did," she replied, blinking away her frustration. "That doesn't mean her blood doesn't flow through these veins. I am a carrier whether I wish to embrace it or not."

"How will that cure them?" I asked, still not following what she was suggesting.

Shara put the vial down and steeled herself for a lengthy explanation. "So, normally, I can cleanse tainted blood. You can say it's a natural byproduct of my bloodline. The problem is that while their cores are corrupted, they will just continue to create more bad blood every time I cleanse them. The only method I have of affecting their core is to turn them. The curse effectively makes them undead which alters their core on a fundamental level. That should eradicate the corruption. However, I can't be one hundred percent certain without testing it."

A sinking feeling developed in my gut as Shara explained her plan. I doubted Squawk or Orpheus wanted to have an undying thirst for blood or an aversion to light for that matter but what could I do? Then again, there were perks weren't there?

Shara laughed at my confusion. "Don't worry. It's just a last resort. In the meantime, I've been purifying their blood while we wait for the head ancient to return. That relieves most of the symptoms."

"Where is he?" I wondered out loud, realizing Shara didn't know by the blank look on her face. "Don't worry, I'll go see if anybody has heard anything. In the meantime, can you spare a few minutes to come look at my sister back on Gaia?"

She glanced at the door again. "Well, these two aren't going to die anytime soon. The ancients also have a method of alleviating their symptoms. They refuse to actually treat them until their leader returns, but it should be okay if I leave for a few hours."

"I'll check on Iolathar when we get back to Gaia," I replied. "He should be with my other half-sister."

Shara had a sad look on her face but laughed to cover it up. "You have a lot of sisters. I'm an only child. I think I'd like to meet your sisters. Let's go."

I waited while she once again gathered up her belongings. "Are you ready?"

She nodded, heading for the door. "Okay. Come on."

Grabbing her hand before as she walked past me, I folded mana over the two of us, and she yelped as we were suddenly whisked to Kalli's side. Shara glared at me, gasping for breath. "Don't. Do. That. Without. Warning. Ugh. Mother was notorious for doing that."

Kalli smacked me in the back of the head, speaking out loud while giggling. "Bad Melvin!"

I quickly straightened and stood at attention after receiving judgmental looks from Maya and the council members. Shara appraised the four women in turn. Finally, she extended a hand to Maya. "You're the infamous sister of this brat I take it?"

Maya raised an eyebrow, gently taking Shara's hand with a gloved hand of her own. "Charmed. You're the vampire I've heard so much about?"

Shara tossed me a quick glare, recovering almost immediately. "I see the rumor mill is hard at work on this planet. For your information, I've renounced the curse. I'm just as human as you are. Probably more so considering your core is corrupted."

Maya smacked her lips, withdrawing her hand. "Touché. My brother tells me you have a cure. Will it work on me?"

"Probably," Shara replied, a sinister smile forming on her face that reminded me of her mother. "It involves turning you. Are you game?"

Maya gasped at her words. "Into a vampire? Will I develop an aversion to light and a thirst for blood?"

Shara cocked her head back in laughter. "That's right, as well as a dislike for garlic, all things holy, and above all else, you'll hate having a stake driven through your heart. Seriously, you mortals and rumors are beyond me. The only thing I can assure you is that you'll require mana through blood. Your core will stop generating any."

My sister looked torn. On the one side, she was being offered a way to touch her servants without killing them. On the other, she might be tempted to bite them. She eventually sighed. "Why not? Vampirism is but another path to immortality. I can see myself playing the role."

"Oh, gods, another romantic," Shara replied, rolling her eyes. "Shall we retire to someplace private? The process is somewhat intimate."

"What, uh, what exactly are you going to do to me?" Maya asked, looking nervous.

Shara winked, tossing that sinister smile over her should at us. "It's not what I'm going to do to you. The turning can have some interesting results. I've never done it myself, but my mother told me stories. Baby vampires can be quite insatiable."

Maya looked like a deer in the headlights. I could tell she wanted to do it, but she also looked scared for the first time since I met her. She tossed a helpless look back at the councilors. "Do you mind waiting here, ladies? I have a curse to be rid of."

Shara grinned, accepting Maya's hand as she offered it. "Mother is going to be tickled pink when she meets you."

———

We didn't see either of them again that night. Kalli and I found rooms for Zofia and the councilors before retiring for the night.

I couldn't help but laugh when Kalli's dress transformed into a nightgown. She glared at me. *What?*

I'm sorry. You only have that one pair of clothes, don't you?

Kalli pushed the door to a changing room, revealing hundreds of colorful dresses. *Can you believe there isn't a single dress in there without a ruffle or laces? This is the only thing I own that I can just be myself in. You can't talk. You always wear that ratty T-shirt.*

I tried to defend myself.

I don't own many clothes. We should go shopping back on Earth once we cure ourselves and save Gaia... Again.

Kalli giggled, pointing an accusatory finger at me. *You're a lousy manipulator, do you know that? Why don't you just edit up some clothes? If I had your skill, the first thing I'd do is make the perfect outfit.*

I froze. Why hadn't I thought about making more clothes with my skill? Or other things for that matter. We had been so distracted with everything going on that I neglected to use my most basic skill for practically anything.

Fine! What kind of clothes would you like?

She shook her head, still pointing at me. *Nope! You first. Give me a show. You can't stop till I like what I see.*

My plan had been to do some emotional training, but it had been a while since I just relaxed and enjoyed spending time with Kalli, so I started editing my outfit.

[42]

"What is this madness?" Shiv asked with her eyebrows raised as she walked into our room.

Both Kalli and I lay sprawled on the floor surrounded by piles of discarded clothing. That wasn't to say we were naked or anything. In fact, we were probably overdressed. The two of us stayed up late trying out various outfits, each one gaudier than the last.

I ended up in a two-piece suit that was red on one side and blue on the other. It matched my eyes in that it was red on the opposite side of my red eye and blue on the other. Kalli yawned and sat up, wearing a suit of her own in place of the dress she normally wore. Hers was Luna green, as she liked to call it, and made her look like Christmas morning to me.

We both yawned and turned as Shiv and Sylvia picked up some of the various outfits we had tried on overnight. Kalli looked around. "Where's Eddie?"

Shiv rolled her eyes. "We put him in time out. He's insufferable."

Sylvia giggled, holding up one of the dresses to her chest. "She's just saying that because she likes him, and he accidentally got us killed in the game."

"I do not!" Shiv cried out, glaring at her friend. "Kalli, don't believe her. He's just annoying."

Kalli smirked at her little sister. "You say that now but you'll see boys in a different light someday. They grow on you."

Sylvia made a face and I couldn't help but smile.

Thanks, babe!

That earned me a trademark eye roll. *You know, I still find you annoying at times.*

———

I spent the next hour making outfits for the two younger girls to go along with mine and Kalli's. Shiv insisted that hers match her sister's though she didn't look half as good in green as Kalli did. When I tried to recommend any other color, she shook her head and said, "No! Make it the same."

After that, we made our way to the throne room to see if Maya had finished whatever she decided to do with Shara. However, when we got there, we were met with another problem. Kalli rushed over to an attendant standing by the throne. "Where is my mother?"

The attendant had a panicked look on his face. "I'm afraid I don't know, your Majesty. Your mother and father never returned."

Kalli grabbed my hand as she swept past me. *We need to go find them, now!*

I was barely able to nod as she dragged me out of the castle. We practically sprinted down paved streets that reminded me of Dabia as Kalli chose the shortest path to the castle gates. *You said you can make something that will let us go fast, right?*

Oh, right. Yeah, a car. I can make one.

The problem was, I'd never driven one. That was Joe's department. I also felt nervous not having Maya and her high-level friends. I was lucky that Shiv and Sylvia hadn't been able to keep up. It would have been a nightmare to try and protect them along with Kalli should we run into trouble. As it was, I was prepared to teleport away at the first sign of an ancient mage, or a tank for that matter. While I was somewhat confident I could delete a tank if needed, I didn't want to risk Kalli's life on a gamble.

The town of Celestea was a lot bigger than it seemed. I'd visited parts that were close to the castle, but there was a lot more to it than I'd seen. Humans and non-humans mingled in the streets as they went about their daily business at open-faced markets. If not for the threats coming from Earth, my empire might have finally been able to enjoy peace.

———

Item: Mustang (Edited)
Components: Metal, Leather, Oil, Fuel
Item Rank: C
Item Level: 1
Item Owner: Murphy

I took one look at it and...
DELETE

Item: Automatic Mustang (Edited)
Components: Metal, Leather, Oil, Fuel
Item Rank: C
Item Level: 1
Item Owner: Murphy

Kalli blinked at my second creation. *It looks exactly the same as the first one.*

I felt the heat rise to my face as I imagined Kalli laughing if she knew the difference was just that I couldn't drive stick.

Trust me, they are two completely different vehicles!

The only reason we didn't die in a fiery wreck was that the road ahead of us just so happened to be smooth and straight. After about ten miles, I started to get the hang of things. We were thrown into our seatbelts a few times as I tried the brakes. Kalli frowned and rubbed her chest where the belt cut into it. *Ow! Is it supposed to do that?*

I shook my head.

Sorry, that pedal is sensitive. I'll do it better next time.

She gasped, *Don't press that pedal ever again.*

I laughed, considering the alternative.

I can't make any promises, but I'll try not to.

We saw the smoke coming over a hilltop before we got there. Kalli cried out when we saw the caravan in the middle of the road. What was left of the wagons looked like they had been attacked by a dragon. Or a tank. All of the ruffalo were dead, and several wagons had blown up entirely.

A small group of survivors huddled near the front of the caravan. They started to flee when they saw us coming. Our only salvation was that we were faster than they were on foot. Kalli leaned out of the window and called out as we got close. "Don't worry. It's us. You're safe now."

I gently applied the brakes that time, and we slowly rolled to a stop. Once I applied the parking brake and turned the car off, as I'd seen my mom do thousands of times, we climbed out and approached the survivors.

A woman threw herself to her knees in front of Kalli. "Oh, it was horrible, your Majesty. We were set upon by fire-breathing dragons. A vile wicked man took your mother and father. He gave us a message for Lord Melvin."

"What was it?" I asked, feeling both fear and rage as Kalli's grief washed over me.

The woman took a deep breath. "He says, don't even think about running away or he'll kill them both."

Kalli fell to her knees and wailed, *Oh, no! Melvin, what are we going to do?*

I dropped next to Kalli and wrapped my arms around her shoulders.

Don't worry. He used it as a threat, so that means he plans to keep them alive. All I have to do is show up and I'm sure he will return them.

Kalli shuddered. *What if he kills you?*

I forced a grin onto my face, sending out confidence I didn't feel.

I'm not easy to kill, remember? Worst case scenario, I'll use the ring.

It took a few minutes, but Kalli eventually composed herself. I gathered the survivors of Mount Wendy, about thirty-five of them, and said, "Leave your things behind. We are teleporting back to Celestea. You'll be safe. Kalli and I will get her mother and father back tomorrow when we meet with the person who's done this. Representatives from the high house, Solitair, are at the castle as we speak to protect us."

Halfhearted nods came from the survivors, but they gathered together anyway. I droned off the pre-teleportation instructions as I began to wrap mana around the group. "Take a deep breath and hold it."

We appeared suddenly in a crowded throne room. Shiv cried out the moment we arrived. "Where are Mommy and Daddy? Kalli? What happened?"

I saw Maya and her group sitting in the back of the room along with Shara and Zofia. They paid little attention to the drama as we appeared with the villagers.

Kalli took Shiv's hand and walked her out of the room to a small private chamber behind the throne. Even though I wasn't with her, I heard the conversation and saw Shiv break down in her sister's arms as Kalli explained what happened to their parents.

I decided to make my way over to Maya. She looked pale but otherwise the same arrogant mage that I had come to know. When she saw me, she flashed a grin that included a pair of shiny new fangs. "Hi there, little brother. Notice anything different about me?"

I laughed, pretending not to notice the chompers. "Oh, I don't know. Do you mean the fact that you're looking at me like a piece of meat?"

She laughed and shook her head vigorously. "Oh, heck no! I just got rid of that infernal corruption. The last thing I'm going to do is consume more of your mana and go through that all over again. Shara tells me that if I break this core, there are no refunds."

Shara nodded her agreement, and I wondered how she made Maya a vampire in the first place. "How did you not get infected when you bit Maya? Shouldn't the corruption have gotten you too?"

She shook her head, opening her mouth to show she had no fangs. "That's another myth. You don't make vampires by biting them. If that were the cast, Earth would have a lot more vampires because that's how most of them choose to feed. Also, I told you, I'm not a vampire. I turned her by killing her core and replacing it. There are various ways of doing this, but the quickest way is to stop her heart. There's a brief window where a person can be saved when their core is completely devoid of mana. I did it by forcing my mana through the shallow channels located in her fingers. As you know, Shaw mana contains the blueprint for an undead core, which essentially makes you a vampire. When we are alive, we have the choice of whether or not to consume our lust for blood and become cursed. For your sister, she chose the path before I initiated her. While I advised against it, she is well aware of the pros and cons and chose to do it anyway."

Maya gave me a weak smile. "I feel wonderful. I think I like this even better than, well, you know."

I gaped at her. "You know we could have found a better way, right?"

She shrugged, hopping to her feet. "It's fine. I've grown more powerful this way. Ironically, the change means I'll probably live thousands of years longer than I would have otherwise. Shara assures me I can still reward my servants, so I don't see the downside."

"You say that now," Shara muttered. "I've seen firsthand what the thirst can do to a person. At least you already have what my mother was seeking."

"What was that?" I asked, my curiosity getting the better of me.

Shara laughed and glared at me for a second before composing herself. "Your blood. Mother's demise was her greed to have the most potent blood of all. M blood."

———

It was a rough night for all of us. Kalli stayed with Shiv as the younger sister didn't want to be alone. I felt for them. My mom was missing, but at least I was relatively certain she was safe. At least I hoped she was. We all knew Celestea and Charles were in mortal peril.

Maya and Shara left for Homestead, likely meeting with Camilla to go over instructions on how to be a better vampire. If anyone knew how to do it, that woman did. It would also have the added benefit of getting the old vampire off my back. Hopefully.

I found myself lying in bed, unable to sleep. Rasputin wanted something from me, and I had no idea if it was something I would be able to give him. The one thing I did know was that I wanted Kalli to be safe. I debated asking her to stay behind or locking her in the dungeon.

She must have heard me because her voice echoed in my ears, *Don't even think about it.*

It was going to be a long night, and I doubted I was going to get any sleep.

[43]

Focusing my emotions while Kalli was distracted added a whole new level of difficulty to balancing my core. Under normal circumstances, the two of us balanced the ebb and flow of mana between ourselves.

With Kalli focused on her sister, I was forced to focus on my own without the support of my other half. Infusing emotion into my core gave me the ability to better understand the wrath put there by Mardella's tainted blade.

I concentrated on my sense of curiosity and how it redefined my essence as I entwined it with my life force. It felt similar to the way Kalli had become a part of me. She noticed I was thinking about her, but her faculties were focused on her sister, and she blocked me out. Focusing on only myself was both less complicated and more difficult at the same time.

It was the first time since I'd met Kalli that I closed off the connection we shared. Even before we became intertwined, mated, or even grouped, I'd still felt connected to her. Thinking back, I'd felt a spark the moment I heard her voice in my bedroom the night I summoned her.

I shook my head to clear my mind. Focus was what I needed to control my emotions. My feelings for Kalli were so strong that it bled from my core in waves that rippled through my body and made me tingle. It was the opposite of what I needed, tranquility.

Now that I knew what it meant to infuse emotions and control them, I had a better understanding of how it worked. The revelation also granted me a basic understanding of Mardella's wrath. It was no longer just little black specks tainting my mana. I could embrace it and feel the rage as though it were my own. With understanding came control. Almost immediately, I found I could lessen the anger boiling within me. It wasn't a pure emotion as it didn't make me angry or moody. The feeling was more of a burning within my soul that demanded near constant attention. I wondered what it felt like for people who didn't have a bloodline to shield their cores.

Rather than scrubbing the taint from my body like id assumed id have to do, I found myself embracing the foreign emotion. From what I knew of Mardella, she represented one of the few surviving ancients. At least that was the case before Kalli and I released her ancestors from their prison in the machine. I understood why she was mad even if I didn't agree with her methods.

The problem was, mana didn't know Mardella's past. The wrath in me found purchase in my own frustration. Anger at Tim for bullying me. A feeling of betrayal from my mother for disappearing. Righteous fury at Raverly for killing Stephanie. I kept those feelings bottled up inside of me and the poison provided the fuel that allowed my feelings to burn like an inferno.

Understanding the source of my rage helped ease the pain and, by concentrating, I saw the dark noise begin to dissipate. Then I started to feel funny. My body tingled all over, and my concentration started to lapse.

———

I was being tickled. My eyes shot open, and I saw three giggling girls on top of me. Kalli pinned me while Shiv and Sylvia tickled me relentlessly. I struggled to get up while also hiding my armpits from the assault. "Stop... No... Ugh... Let me get up!"

The girls were all out of breath from laughing by the time I managed to squirm my way free. I took my time getting revenge on all three of them. Their alliance quickly shattered when I went for Shiv. Sylvia teamed up with me while Kalli tried to save her sister.

When we finally wore ourselves out, I sat up to catch my breath.

I thought you were going to sleep with Shiv.

Kalli gave me a strange look. *It's morning. We have to head to Mount Wendy in a few hours. We came to wake you up.*

The horror of what we were about to face suddenly came flooding back into my mind. Not only did the fate of the empire rest on what was about to happen, but Rasputin also had Kalli's parents. Hopefully, Maya and her friends were up to the task of helping me deal with the threat.

Kalli read my mind because she tugged me out the door. *You can get ready in a bit. We both need to eat something before we go.*

Breakfast was a somber affair. Kalli had to have a long talk with Shiv about not coming with us to the meeting. Shiv stomped her foot and refused to eat anything, practically screaming, "They are my parents too. I should be there."

Kalli set down her fork, giving her sister a sympathetic look. "Someone from the family needs to stay behind. If anything happens to me, you'll be queen."

"I don't want to be queen," Shiv whined in a shrill voice. "I want to be with my family. If you die, I'll be all alone."

There it was, they both thought their parents were already dead. I tried to say something sympathetic. "We don't that they're…"

Kalli pressed a finger to my lips. "Shhh, we agreed not to talk about that."

We finished the meal in silence. Maya and her group arrived toward the end of breakfast along with Shara and Zofia. Shara walked over to me and whispered, "I'm not going with you today. It's not my battle, and I should check in on the patients on Luna. Come see me when it's over to let me know you're both okay."

"We will," Kalli acknowledged, giving Shara a nod and a smile before turning to Shiv to add. "Everything is going to be just fine."

————

We only ended up placating the girls when Shara offered to let them accompany her to Luna for the afternoon. Shiv refused to let go of her sister and was crying when they disappeared around the corner.

Are you okay?

Kalli held out her hand toward where her sister just was. She turned and gave me a weak smile. *Why does it feel like the world is crashing down around us?*

We were in over our heads, and I knew it. It wasn't the first time either. I'd always found a way to survive against high-level people. Even evil dragon gods couldn't bring me down. I held onto that hope and reached out to hug Kalli.

Don't worry. Everything's going to be fine.

We had Maya and her friends. They looked confident. Well, arrogant for sure, but they looked like they could handle themselves in a fight. With any luck, I could sit back and let the adults handle things.

I was brought back to reality when Kalli pushed me away. Everyone had gathered around us. Several guards from the castle as well as Esha and one of the goblins. I scratched my head trying to remember her name. Boombrix. How could I forget such a unique name? Then I spotted Zofia at the back of the group.

"Are you sure you want to do this?" I asked, giving her a nod. "It could be dangerous."

Zofia nodded back, patting something in her pocket. "I can take care of myself. Besides, I want to see this threat with my own eyes. Whoever this is, is likely responsible for events taking place on Earth. Don't expect me to get involved though."

Maya took my hand in hers. "We're ready. Take us to Mount Wendy."

Taking a deep breath, I folded mana over us, and we were off. Off to save Kalli's parents. Off to see Rasputin. Off to meet my doom once more. How did I get myself into these things?

————

"What time did he say he would be arriving?" the lady known as Henrietta Webb asked for the third time. "Some of us have pressing matters and cannot meander around all day long."

"I told you I don't—" I started to repeat my answer, but Kalli cut me off.

"What he means to say is that Rasputin didn't give a set time. All we know is he wanted to speak to Melvin here at Mount Wendy in three days or he would destroy the village."

Henrietta folded her arms and harrumphed, making me wonder if the high house was filled with stuck-up nobles with too much self-importance.

BOOM!

Everyone dove out of the way as the ground erupted nearly twenty yards from us. I blinked a few times, the afterimage of the blast nearly blinding me. Whatever fired the shot was nowhere to be seen.

"What was that?" Maya asked, crawling to my side.

I shrugged and pointed down the path leading toward the village. "If I had to guess, I'd say it's a tank. That's a machine from Earth with a large cannon."

Maya shook her head and sighed. "I know what a tank is. I've been to Earth once or twice."

Before I could reply, an old man appeared, stepping out of the void. I wasn't surprised but I'd only ever witnessed a few people teleport before. He scanned our group, taking each member in. "Is the boy with, ah, there you are. I'll give you credit. I half-expected you to flee."

I climbed to my feet and took a step forward. Kalli was quick to come to my side, leveling her wand at the man. I really needed to remember to use mine more often.

The man that stood before me was not as old looking as I expected him to look. While he did have that ancient quality about him, he looked more wild than anything. A mop of disheveled brown hair stuck out in every direction on top of its head and was only matched by an equally disheveled beard that hung down to his navel. He had piercing red eyes that seemed to want to bore into my core. Yet, he was smiling at me.

Name: Grigori Rasputin
Class: Soulmancer
Level: ???
Affection Level: Impatient

He waited impatiently for me to speak. Might as well try diplomacy first. "I'm here. What do you want with me and why are you killing innocent people?"

Rasputin sniggered, looking over my shoulder at the abandoned Mount Wendy. "Are you talking about the pawns? Why do you care about them? They exist to die at our bidding. Have you not come to embrace your destiny? We are gods after all."

It took a moment for that to sink in, and I took a closer look at the man.

Skills: Death Touch, Tamper Soul, Force Leech, Essence Shift
Traits: Bloodline M (14), Enhanced Regeneration, Enhanced Mana, Absorption, Mastery: Soul Magic

I blinked for a few seconds, taking in the bloodline. Rasputin was my…brother? I felt like Luke Skywalker when he discovered his father was Darth Vader. Maya gasped as well. "Melvin, stay away from this man. He's a slayer."

"A what?" I asked, backing away slowly.

Rasputin laughed, licking his lips as he turned his attention to Maya. "Oh, what a glorious day it's turning out to be. Not only did you show yourself, but you brought me a delicious snack as well."

Rage flooded from my core when I realized he was referring to Kalli as well. Maya stepped in front of me and raised a hand toward Rasputin, palm held out. "You will leave this planet at once. We have an accord here and M classes are forbidden from quarreling. If you attack one of us, it's the same as attacking all of us. I suggest you go back to Earth and…"

He was on her before I could blink. Rasputin vanished and reappeared next to Maya, grabbing her outstretched arm with a bony hand. He sneered at her, revealing a mouth full of blackened teeth. "Excellent! Inform them that I will be coming for them. I prefer my prey cower in fear before I devour them."

Maya glared at him, and her arm glowed red. Rasputin howled and let go as his hand began to smoke. She rounded on him and held out her other hand. The haze I remembered from our training appeared around Rasputin and icicles formed on his robe.

He shook them off and lunged at her, trying to grab her again. It was Maya's turn to teleport, and she appeared ten feet away, already launching another spell. The battle continued with the two of them teleporting around, neither able to catch the other off guard.

The guards we brought from the castle were useless. They gave chase but could never keep up with the battle that was moving steadily farther away from us. Boombrix held a bomb in her hand, but she hesitated to throw it with Maya in the area.

I took a look over my shoulder at the three women Maya had brought with her. They huddled together watching the battle unfold, but not one moved to help. I ran over to them, shaking Marisa Merryweather. "Aren't you going to help your friend? That's why you came, isn't it?"

She shoved me off her and replied in a haughty tone. "No, boy. We are here to record your demise. As a rule, the high-born don't get involved in the affairs of lessers. Or the M born for that matter. Your sibling rivalries are too dangerous even for us."

"Worthless," I spat the word, rushing back to Kalli. "We have to help her."

Kalli was a few steps ahead of me.

"Pvruzth."

Flame shot from her wand which quickly turned green when she channeled it through her amulet. It danced back and forth, trying desperately to follow Rasputin as he blinked in and out of reality. Maya seemed to have the upper hand. Her magic created a fog in the air, burning or freezing Rasputin every time it touched him.

I tried my best to help my sister. Deleting the ground under Rasputin a few times. The problem was that he seemed to be floating and wasn't affected by the terrain at all. I tried to shoot him with rays of light. The laser beams seemed more effective than Kalli's flames at first.. Unlike Kalli's attack, the beam shot out instantly, so I was able to land some hits. The problem was, other than possibly giving the man a sunburn, I wasn't doing much damage with my attack.

Suddenly, Maya dropped to her knees. Rasputin appeared next to her, wiping his brow. "Finally. That took longer than expected. You've been under the effect of my touch before you even thought to resist. Your soul is slowly bleeding out of you along with your mana. When it runs out, you will cease to exist. I suggest you give in and allow me to…"

Kalli's flame engulfed the man, picking him up off the ground. He writhed in midair, screaming in agony as the ancient magic of the artifact consumed him. Then it was gone, pushed away from the old man in a burst of light.

Rasputin began to cackle uncontrollably. "Foolish child. Do you think I am so weak as to succumb to such a weak attack? Even if you managed to acclimate yourself to an artifact, your pathetic mana level can't…oof."

ZAP!

He gasped as a solid beam of teal light went right through his newly formed barrier and struck him in the stomach. A look of terror crossed his face as his body began to morph and transform into something impossible.

He glared at Zofia who stood behind the three stunned high-born ladies holding what looked like a futuristic laser gun. "How…? No magic can pass through my barrier. It is invincible."

"That was not magic," Zofia stated with a calmness that I wished I felt. "It is science!"

Rasputin staggered away from Maya clutching his chest. He was

THE ACCIDENTAL CORRUPTION

turning into a...a cartoon? It was impossible and I wouldn't have believed it if I didn't see it with my own eyes.

His attention was solely focused on Zofia. "You will pay for that, girl! Mark my words. I will make you pay."

His magic still worked, and he folded mana over himself and vanished.

[44]

EVERYONE FROZE the moment Rasputin vanished. Only Maya made any noise as she gasped for breath on the ground where Rasputin dropped her.

I raced over to see if I could help. "Maya, are you okay?"

She whimpered, grasping her chest. "I'm...dying..."

"What?" I asked, speaking louder as I turned to look for her friends. "Come quick. Maya needs you."

Only, they weren't there. Zofia stood where the other mages from the high house had been, trying desperately to stow a device of some sort that was too big to fit in her lab coat. "Where did they...?"

Maya clutched my sleeve feebly and whispered in a raspy voice. "Don't worry about that. They were cowards. Please, take care of Rumierre."

"Who?" I asked, stroking her hair softly in an attempt to comfort her. "Besides, you aren't going to die!"

She shook her head, struggling to keep her eyes open. "I feel it in my core. I'm fading away."

Throwing caution to the wind, I placed my hand over her chest like I was going to give her CPR. Then I flooded her body with mana, attempting to heal the damage inflicted by Rasputin's soul magic.

"No! You mustn't," she groaned weakly, trying to push me away. "Whatever he did can affect you, too."

I didn't care at the moment. There was no way I was going to let my sister die if I could help it. At first, I didn't see anything out of the ordinary. Mana flowed through her channels that I'd awakened the last time I connected with her. Then I saw it. Blackened mana pulsed through her system that felt like sludge, devouring her life force faster than she could create it. The damage it was doing was catastrophic.

I flooded her core with mana, hoping that if I pushed enough in, it would expel the toxic mana. Rasputin's mana was unlike anything I'd ever seen. Working like the plague I'd cured when I first arrived on Gaia, it ate away at her core. While Maya's soul was putting up a serious fight, it was slowly being overwhelmed by the curse.

Sweat poured down my face as I dumped more and more mana into the effort to save my sister. No matter what I did, the rot continued to consume Maya's core. Realization set in that I was having no effect on the dark pulsing mana, and I removed my hand from her chest.

"It's no use," I gasped, trying my best to hold back tears of frustration. "I can't stop it."

Tears dripped onto Maya's cheek, and she feebly reached up to wipe my face. "Don't blame yourself, dear brother. I understand. Please... Don't forget... Rumierre."

It took me a moment to grasp what she was saying. Blame myself? Was it my fault she was there? Probably. Was it my fault I couldn't save her? Maybe. I should have trained more. Who was Rumierre? Wait, she said something about him. She wanted me to look after someone. I could do that, so I replied, "I promise."

She gave my hand a gentle squeeze. Then I felt it. The ring. "Um, sis, how much do you care about your body?"

Her eyes widened, and she stopped gasping for a moment. It was almost like she forgot she was dying as she asked, "My... Body?"

I nodded, nervous about what I planned to do but also desperate to save her at the same time. "What if I told you I have the ability to trap your soul in an artifact? You might be stuck in there while we figure out how to get you out but I'll do everything I can to make you comfortable."

She looked at me, her hand in mine, for what felt like an eternity. Then, with a look of determination, she squeezed her eyes shut and whispered, "Do it."

Taking a deep breath to steady myself, I took my hand from hers and pressed the ring to her chest. As I had done with Mardella, I pushed mana through the ring. The effect was significantly more pronounced when I wasn't half dead. Maya's entire body began to glow and panic surged through me as I saw the light dim from her eyes. Then it was back, only it was different.

She blinked at me and a grin appeared on her face. "Ah! I didn't expect you to take me up on my offer, boy. At least not this soon. Wait a second. What's this madness? Did you place me in a dying body? Are you trying to kill me?"

She ran her hands all over her body, frowning. "Oh, I see what happened. You didn't intend to free me. You did this to save someone who was dying. Worry not, a simple affliction of the soul is nothing to a grandmaster."

Maya stood, ignoring the fact that she had just been dying, and hunched over with a look of concentration on her face as though she were constipated. Light began to leak from every pore in her body which was quickly followed by an explosion of the blackened mana I'd seen earlier.

I was blown back by the force of it. Kalli rushed over to me. *Did you just...?*

My mind was a blur, and all I could do was nod. We both knew what I did and what happened. In the heat of the moment, I'd forgotten that the ring worked as an exchange, releasing one prisoner for every new one it accepted.

I slowly climbed to my feet and looked at Maya. She looked smug. "Longinus?"

She nodded, flexing her newly acquired scrawny arms. "You remembered me. I'm touched. However, didn't I tell you to get me a male body? Oh, well, I suppose it couldn't be helped. Come over here, and let me help you with that curse."

Kalli grabbed my arm defensively. ***Don't you dare! We can't trust this man.***

She looked at us and a smirk appeared on her face. "Ah, well, I wouldn't trust me either. However, you still did me a favor and I always repay my debts. If you wish to take me up on my offer, you will find me at Wuru Peak. There is an old monk I'd like to exchange a few words with, if he's still alive, that is."

I wanted to continue the conversation, but Maya punched the air and a portal similar to the one I'd seen in Zofia's big tent appeared. She winked at us and stepped through. Then it was gone.

———

Everything quieted down quite a bit after Maya left. We huddled with Zofia and the guards to come up with a plan. Esha scanned the tree line nervously. "It isn't safe here. Whatever caused that explosion earlier is still out there."

I nodded my agreement and replied, "You're right, there's nothing more we can do here. He didn't want to talk. He wants to hunt me. Let's go back to the castle."

Wrapping mana over the group, we returned home, minus one very important person. I could care less about the other three women from Solitair. They were worthless.

When we got back to Celestea, I immediately wanted to visit Maya in the ring. However, there was something important to discuss first. "Um, Zofia, that thing you shot Rasputin with, what is it?"

Zofia fidgeted, hiding her hands in her pockets. "That's classified."

Kalli offered the woman a warm smile. "Whatever it was, you probably saved us all. Is there any chance we can work out a deal to get more of those to use against Rasputin? It worked when magic didn't."

The girl, for that's truly what she looked like, rubbed her chin theatrically. "Well, I could make a deal. The question is, are you prepared to make a fair offer for what we have to offer?"

"What do you want?" Kalli asked, raising an eyebrow suspiciously.

"Isn't it obvious?" Zofia replied, rolling her eyes and looking even more like a kid. "I want power. Erm, I mean, the company needs mana. To power our designs. It's the only power source of its kind, and we don't have a steady supply. I'll supply you with enough tech to arm one hundred soldiers for, say, ten thousand mana batteries."

"Ten thousand?" I asked incredulously, throwing my hands in the air. "Where did you get that number? For that, you'd need to give us at least a million of those guns."

Zofia scoffed in outrage and stomped her foot. We both turned to look at Kalli when she started laughing. I couldn't fathom how she could be so lighthearted so soon after losing Maya. Or her parents for that matter.

What's so funny?

Kalli turned that charming smile on me, and I found myself unable to think. It melted my resolve every time. *You're both acting like little kids. Couldn't you tell she was exaggerating?*

She was?

She winked before turning back to Zofia. "I'm sure we can come to a satisfactory arrangement. Get us a list of what you're willing to provide and what you would like in return. Then, we can come to an arrangement."

Zofia gaped at Kalli, obviously wanting to continue our outrageous haggling. She sighed and nodded. "I'll get you a list. If you see Rasputin before I do, you need to tell me if he exhibits any after-effects at all. Please, write down any details. It's very important for my research."

Kalli nodded and turned that smile on Zofia. "We certainly will."

She frowned, obviously immune to the effect. "Very well. If that will be all, I think I'll retire to my room and work on that inventory list. You might want to start working on those mana batteries now. Our services don't come cheap."

I tossed Kalli a sidelong glance as Zofia marched off. *Do you even know how to make a mana battery?* She shrugged. *How hard can it be?*

I sighed, looking at my hand. Mana battery creation was the last thing on my mind. There was a difficult conversation I needed to have before I did anything else. Kalli sensed what I was thinking and placed her hand over mine. *Don't worry, I'll go with you.*

Again, I said nothing. Sometimes words just weren't necessary. She took me by the hand and guided me behind the throne to one of the hidden rooms in the back. The castle had many hidden rooms like that, quiet places where royals and nobles could go to host private conversations.

Kalli pulled a red velvet curtain closed when we entered one of the chambers. Together we sat on soft cushions around a small round table. *The castle's magic will ensure our privacy while that curtain is drawn. It can only be opened with my permission.*

I couldn't help myself and let out a small laugh.

Are you saying I'm your prisoner?

Kalli smiled, a feeling of relief coming from her. *It's good to see you smile again. Let's go see your sister.*

———

Together, we entered the ring. Howls of laughter echoed through the hall as we walked toward the solid oak door where Longinus used to be. "Maya? Are you in there?"

A weak voice answered from the darkness. "What have you done to me, Melvin? Was this whole thing a trap?"

I shook my head, trying to open the sturdy door. "No! You were dying. I couldn't think of anything else to do."

"What is this place?" Maya's voice asked. "Why is Mardella in here? You said she fled."

The door responded to my intentions, and something clicked inside. Realizing it was no longer locked, I pushed it open and stepped into the room. "I didn't tell you when I first figured out what it did because I'd just met you. Mardella tried to kill me, and this was the only thing I could do to survive."

Maya sat hunched in the darkness, shaking uncontrollably. "Is this a prison? Am I trapped in here for all eternity?"

I hadn't thought of that. In my haste to save my sister, had I condemned her to an eternity of suffering? I'd visited the afterlife. Maybe it was better? Stephanie seemed to like it in any case.

"I don't know what this is other than the fact that it's an artifact like the ones in your house." I tried my best to explain. "There are others in here who seem to be prisoners. You aren't a prisoner, though. I won't lock the door and I'll do everything I can to make you comfortable until we figure out a way to get you out."

She slowly climbed to her feet, walking through the open door. "Mardella?"

The laughing at the end of the hall grew louder. It sounded like the woman went insane. A dry female voice from the next cell over answered instead. "Don't worry. They all lose their sanity temporarily. It usually only lasts a few years. She's actually taking it quite well."

"Who's that?" Maya asked, walking over to the tiny window in the door to peek inside.

"My name is Vana, Nir Vana," she chirped, sounding a bit more cheerful to be introducing herself. "Before you ask, the only way out is if the master of the ring finds you a body and releases you. I'm next in line, though you might break that order considering you're the first to be released from the cell. At least by the current warden."

I stood on my tiptoes and took a peek into the dark room. A woman in a brown jumpsuit with short brown hair stood in the center of the room, staring back at me.

Name: Nir Vana
Class: ???
Level: ???
Affection Level: Undecided

At least she was who she said she was. Her eyes flashed when she saw me. "Boy, are you the current lord of the ring? Do you intend to grant our freedom?"

[45]

NIR VANA LOOKED young at a glance but there was something deeper on closer inspection. There was an agelessness in her eyes that gave me a feeling she'd been around for quite some time.

Not getting an immediate response, she continued, "What are your plans for us? If you release me, I promise to make it worth your while. Step into my cell and I will show you exactly how far I'm willing to go."

Maya grabbed my shoulder and dragged me away from the door. "That'll be quite enough of that, vile temptress."

I smiled at Maya. Here she was, a soul without a body, and she still protected me. "I'll get you out of here. I promise...somehow..."

I trailed off again, overwhelmed at the gravity of everything. Maya gave a weak chuckle and wrapped her arm around my shoulder. "Welcome to the wonderful world of being an M. Someone is always out to get you. Don't worry, you're strong. You'll find a way."

Taking courage from her words, I took a step toward the cell door again. "Tell me something, Mrs. Vana, why are you in prison? What did you do to get thrown into this place?"

Nir let out a laugh before composing herself by clearing her throat. "Ah hah, ahem. Well, I somehow doubt you'll believe a word I say, but why not? Let me tell you my story. I know not how long has passed in the outside world, but I was once mortal. I was born on Origin before time as you know it, I spent many lives molding the imperfection that was my soul."

"I know about Origin," Kalli announced, startling me and causing Nir to pause. "They taught us about it at the Academy."

"What do you know of Origin?" Nir asked with an air of haughtiness.

"Well," Kalli stammered, trying to recall what it was Mr. McDuck-enStein taught us, "it's a forbidden planet, right? They stopped sending adventurers there because nobody ever returns alive."

Nir chuckled. "That would make sense. Those people wouldn't want their secrets getting out. I'm afraid that's all going to change now. You let Malric out."

"Who exactly is Malric?" I asked, deciding I probably should have asked that question from the start. "He's just one man, right? What could he possibly do?"

Nir shared my sentiment. 'That's a question you should have asked before opening Pandora's Box. Now, he's out. Malric's been around long before I was born. There are legends about him. The most important thing you need to remember is that he is his own special brand of evil."

"Are you evil?" I asked, having a bad feeling about the prisoners in the ring. "What about Longinus and the others in here?"

A shrill voice came from Nir that I interpreted as some sort of a scoff. "I am an absolute saint compared to that man. However, I get the feeling that's not what want to know. In this place, knowledge is power. It's the only bargaining chip we have. If you want to know more, you need to tell me what your intentions are."

"What do you want?" Kalli asked. "We aren't going to kill you if that's what you mean. I mean, we won't make you more dead than you already are."

There was a brief pause before Nir replied in a low voice. "Freedom is what I want. I'd like to see the sky again. It's been several lifetimes since my soul's been trapped in this place. I suppose I'll settle for some modern comforts as well as your promise to at least consider freeing me."

Kalli and I exchanged a glance. *You can't free her, Melvin. We don't even know what she's done.*

I know. We need information, though. What's the harm of promising to think about it?

"How do we do this?" I asked. "I somehow doubt you intend to take my word."

Maya leaned close and whispered so only Kalli and I could hear. "She will likely require an oath. If you choose to make an accord with her, be careful what you say. It can be binding."

The sounds of footsteps echoed from beyond the door, and then a pair of beady yellow eyes appeared in the barred window slit. "As the woman says, words hold power. I know you have me at a disadvantage so I will do whatever possible to ingratiate myself to you. I have nothing to lose."

I nodded, keeping my distance from the door. "If you really mean that, tell me something for free. I don't think I can trust you if you don't tell me what you did to deserve being put in here. Don't try to tell me you're innocent because I won't believe you."

She smiled and thin fingers gripped the bars. "I told you that I've lived many lives through reincarnation. What I failed to tell you is that at some point I began seeking the perfect host. Normally, if you choose the path of reincarnation, your soul goes into a pool when you die to inhabit a newly created body. Your deeds in your past lives determine where you are placed. It is far less than ideal. There is nothing you can do to prevent being reincarnated into the body of an animal or an insect. Trust me, being reborn as a cricket can be very trying. I discovered voodoo, a new method of reincarnation where I choose the host and perform the rite while I am still alive. At first, I did it because I just wanted to stay human. Eventually, I grew addicted to finding better hosts. Awakened bodies enhance my soul when I take them over. Needless to say, one day I encountered a man of immeasurable power. I seduced him with the intent of taking his body for myself. Alas, I failed, and he imprisoned me in here."

Both Kalli and Maya looked mortified. The woman in the cell was a body snatcher. I raised an eyebrow and asked, "What happens to the other soul when you take someone's body? Do you evict it or do you have to share with the other core?"

Nir's eyes narrowed. "I would have thought that's obvious. When I reincarnate with another person, we swap bodies. In normal reincarnation, the unborn child or animal that I inhabit has no soul, so there is nothing to worry about. However, that method comes with some caveats. For one thing, most of my memories of my previous life are sealed. The only recollections that are possible come in the form of dreams or déjà vu. When I swap into a live body, I retain everything. I was so close to pure bliss when I made the mistake of going after that man."

"Who was it?" Kalli asked, curious despite herself.

Nir sighed. "He called himself Merlin."

I gasped, thinking about the books I'd read about the fabled wizard as a child. "You knew Merlin? The one from the stories? He was real?"

She laughed, shaking her head. "I'm sorry, boy. I can't answer that question. When I knew him there was no mention of his name in any books, but that was thousands of years ago. Perhaps he is more renowned now. Besides, this all happened on Origin."

"It must be a different Merlin then," I concluded. "My Merlin was from Earth from a place called…"

"Camelot?" she finished the sentence for me. "How did I know that, you ask? That was the name of the city where I met him."

"Camelot is on Origin?" I asked, completely stumped. "No wonder they can't find it."

I had to push questions about swords in stones and a thousand other fairy tales out of my head to get back on track. "Never mind about Merlin. Let's say I agree to consider your request. Are you willing to do everything in your power to help us?"

"Whoa there, tiger." Nir chuckled. "I'm happy that you know how to haggle, but I am not going to just give up everything all at once. How about we begin with your original request? I'll tell you about Malric and Longinus and you agree to make my life better in here and put me on your to-do list for a possible pardon. Let's face it, you let the other two go for much less and Malric at the very least makes me look like a saint."

"Tell me about them," I replied.

"Deal first," she spat back taking her head. "Give me some furniture in here as you did for the other prisoner. I'd also like some food. Do they still have curry in your world?"

"Sure they do," I replied, realizing I'd have to give her a show of good faith. "Move away from the door, and I'll take care of your room. As for letting you out, I'll be honest with you. You sound dangerous. Still, I'll consider it if you're willing to make an oath with my sister."

"I'll make the oath right now," she replied with a sweet smile. "She is the one you just made my new neighbor, correct?"

"My other sister," I corrected, moving up to the window. "My other sister is a contract specialist. She will make sure you don't cause any damage if we let you out. I'm afraid that's the only way I'll feel comfortable setting you free. Move back, you're still too close to the door."

"At least I'll be able to properly die on the outside." She sighed, walking to the far end of the room. There was no furniture at all in her cell. Whoever designed the ring didn't give much thought to comfort. Then again, I had a strange feeling that the ring was designed as a torture device.

"Are you saying we can't die in here?" Maya asked with a look of horror on her face.

Nir began to chuckle. "There is no release from his prison without the warden's say so. You have no body in here and while your soul is eternal, it has no way of passing on while trapped in the Ring of Souls. Are either of you familiar with the fable of Pandora?"

"Yes," Maya and I replied at the same time.

"Good," Nir said. "That will save me some time. The box in that legend is no myth. It was brought to the mortal plane by Apophis, the God of Chaos, and gifted to Zeus who legend says used it to unleash calamity upon Origin. However, none of that is the truth. The box was a soul trap, designed to imprison even the gods. A small bit of it was used to craft the Ring of Souls and is capable of confining up to seven cores at once."

While Nir told the story, I worked on making her cell like a hotel room. I made her a comfy bed, a bath, a couch, and a table, one of which I laid out a small feast including curry.

"Okay, so about Malric," she began between bites of curry. "He calls himself the Magnificent, but he was really a tyrant. I never knew him outside of the ring but there are legends of his ruthlessness on Origin. He subjugated the planet and had great monuments made in his name. He enslaved all of humanity and used the awakened as a private army to conquer world after world in every known dimension. Some say his conquest was complete, and he disappeared to rest, but I know by the fact that he was in here that someone managed to defeat him."

"What about Longinus?" I asked, looking back at Maya's cell where the old monk used to reside.

Nir shrugged, not looking up from her plate. "I'm not entirely sure. He was just some monk. There are quite a few of those. They seek enlightenment similar to me, but their methods are different. The only thing I know for certain is that he picked a fight with the wrong person and lost. That is how he wound up in here."

"What of the others?" I asked, counting four other occupied cells.

She laughed, looking over at me for the first time since she started eating. "You have two legs. Go over and ask them yourself. I don't know much about them other than they arrived recently."

[46]

THERE WERE four other prisoners in all. At a glance, they all seemed much different from the other three I'd met in the ring. They sat hunched in the corner and refused to meet my gaze when I peeked in the window slit. Still, I wanted to get to know who they were, so I started with the cell closest to Nir's.

Name: Pythia
> Class: Oracle
> Level: 92
> Affection Level: Hopeless

While she didn't have a last name, at least she had stats. Draped in a flowing white dress, Pythia huddled in the corner, bathed in darkness. I flicked a pebble into the room and edited it into a couch, causing her to jump. "It might be more comfortable to sit on that. Do you mind telling me why you're in here?"

She finally looked up, seeming to notice me for the first time. That's when I realized that Pythia was beautiful. It wasn't that I was attracted to her. Nobody could take Kalli's place. Pythia looked almost like a porcelain doll with perfectly straight brown hair that flowed down her back like a waterfall. It seemed a tragedy to deny the world her beauty.

She reached out to touch the couch, almost as though she didn't believe it was real. Then she rose to her feet, careful to make sure the dress didn't shift and reveal anything and took a seat on the couch. She folded one leg over the other in a very ladylike manner "I was locked in this cell because I refused to give my body to a man willingly."

"What man?" I asked, vaguely remembering the man in the dream where I got the ring.

Pythia shuddered, seeming to recoil at the mention of her captor. "I dare not speak his name. This is his prison. He may return at any moment. I warn you, he is not what he seems. He has become twisted on his quest."

"Did you commit some kind of a crime?" I asked, not sure who to trust.

She shook her head. "I was a holy oracle. My only oath was to the fates. I cannot give myself to any man lest I lose my gift."

"You have a gift?" Kalli asked in a low voice. "Are you an oracle that sees the future? Can you tell us what ours are? We can really use your help."

Pythia gave a little squeak, her voice cracking as she replied, "How did you know that? Unfortunately, I'm afraid my gift is blocked by the curse of this place. I can't even tell if you're here to hurt me or not."

"We aren't here to hurt you," Kalli confirmed, offering a weak smile I wasn't sure Pythia would buy even if she could see it.

"Unfortunately, we haven't quite found a way to let you out," I added, flicking more pebbles into the cell to make her a table and food.

The other three prisoners had similar stories. Each of them swore they were falsely imprisoned. One thing they all had in common was their beauty. It seemed as though the ruler of the ring had gone out of his way to find the most attractive women and imprison them. Not counting Malric, Longinus, and Nir of course.

Name: Helen
Class: Seductress
Level: 58
Affection Level: Intrigued

Name: Joan
Class: Paladin
Level: 113
Affection Level: Defiant

Name: Cleopatra
Class: Assassin
Level: 69
Affection Level: Coy

I peeked at Helen as she devoured a turkey leg off a freshly edited feast I'd given her. "You weren't from Troy by any chance, were you?"

She looked up, taking a moment to wipe her face with a napkin before replying, "I was there once a long time ago."

I tried to remember when in history the battle of Troy was. Thousands of years ago? I pulled out the M-Phone to see if I could look it up on Magi-Google, Moogle? No wait, that was a Japanese teddy bear. There was no service in the enchanted ring, not that I was surprised.

I turned back to Maya and ticked names off on my fingers, "So, we have Helen of Troy, Cleopatra, and Joan of Arc in here. Sorry, Pythia, I don't remember reading about you."

"It's okay," I heard her reply from the other cell. "I wasn't very memorable."

I made a mental note to look her up when I got out. "I presume you are all historical figures from Earth. The thing is, I don't remember anything in the history books saying you disappeared."

"They wouldn't have," Nir replied from her cell, having been eavesdropping on the conversation. "Every time the ring takes a prisoner, it releases one. The previous master of the ring knew what he was doing. Those four cells were revolving doors. You can rest assured the people you've read about in books were likely imposters."

"There is someone out there in my body?" Pythia gasped, startling me. "I need to get a message to Delphi. An imposter can do great harm in my skin."

"Relax moron," Nir spoke louder so she could be heard clearly. "You've been in here for hundreds of years. If your body was going to do any damage then it's already done."

"I thought you said they just got here," Kalli said, giving the woman a skeptical stare.

Nir replied with a snort. "One hundred years is next to nothing when you've been trapped in this wretched place for thousands of years. You lose track after the first millennia. As far as I am concerned, these four are babies."

Wait til she finds out how old we are.

Kalli giggled. *Don't you dare tell her. Then she will never take us seriously.*

I was happy to hear Kalli's laugh. With everything that happened, I was worried she would never smile again. She put on a strong face for her sister but, deep down, I knew she was hurting. I could feel it. With that in mind, I made a decision. It was time to swallow my pride.

I turned to Maya and hugged her. She was taken aback but eventually rested her head on my shoulder and sobbed. I held her for a while until she calmed down. Then I whispered in her ear, "We are going to go see a powerful enchanter. She might know something about the ring that can help you."

She blinked away a tear. "Do you think she will know how to get me out?"

"I'm not sure," I admitted.

Maya sighed and let me go. "Then don't forget about your promise. Take care of Rumierre. The other servants as well but mainly him. I will die if anything bad happened to him."

"I promise," I replied, withdrawing my mana from the ring.

Back in the tiny room behind the throne, I stretched as I stood up.

Kalli climbed to her feet as well. *Are you actually going to tell Lavender that you did exactly what she told you not to?*

It was true that I'd ignored her advice and done exactly what she told me not to. I took Kalli's hand in mine after she undid the privacy veil.

If anyone is going to know how to fix this, it will be her.

———

Once again, Lavender was waiting for us when we popped through the portal. "Well, well, well, children. Look what the cabbit dragged in."

"Lavender!" I balked, staring at the woman sitting on my bed. "How did you know we... Well, never mind. We need your help."

"Indeed," she replied with a frown. "Is there something you'd like to tell me?"

I let out a heavy sigh. "Yes. I used the ring after you told me not to."

"How many times?" she asked, tapping her foot on the ground.

"You already knew, didn't you?" I asked, not answering her question.

She nodded and patted the bed next to her. I sat, and she said, "I was aware of the likelihood of you both entering and using the cursed artifact. More than that is hidden in fog. I need you to tell me exactly what you did, and more importantly, who you let out."

I gaped at her. "You don't want to know who I put into the ring?"

Lavender shook her head. She had a sad look on her face. "I am aware of the fact that you imprisoned the dark one that hunted you on Gaia and one more. It is far more important that you tell me who you let out. It can have an impact on the universe as we know it."

"Malric and Longinus got out," Kalli supplied, glaring at me for waffling over the details. "We know Malric is dangerous. However, we have bigger problems right now with Rasputin…"

"It was as I feared," Lavender said, cutting Kalli off. "That man and his son are the reason I can no longer see clearly. His existence threatens the fate of this universe. Possibly all of them."

"Is there anything we can do to fix it?" I asked, feeling panic start to rise in my chest.

Lavender smiled, giving me a boost of confidence. "Perhaps there will be. One thing is certain, this is part of your destiny. Whether good or evil triumphs, I believe you have something to do with it."

"There is a prophecy about him?" Kalli asked incredulously.

Her question caused Lavender to chuckle. "Of course there is. Dozens actually. However, that doesn't mean anything. It's a little-known fact that there are prophecies about virtually everyone and knowing the contents of them makes people do foolish things. In the end, knowing your destiny usually end up making the future worse."

Lavender reached down and placed a hand over mine, obscuring the ring. When her hand came off, it was done. She shook her head when she saw me panic. "Don't worry. I didn't take it away from you. I couldn't if I wanted to. As its owner, the only way you can be forced to surrender it is if someone kills you. The only two dangerous people who seem to know you have it are Malric and Longinus. I think it's safe to assume that neither of them will try anything so long as the creator lives. You two are also the only ones who know what either of them looks like. Don't be surprised if they come to you looking for a new body at some point. I've taken the liberty of placing an enchantment on the ring so that nobody else can detect it. The only way you will be able to interact with the ring now is by touching it with your mana. My enchantment will keep it hidden from all prying eyes. Even the creator has yet to break my enchantments."

"You know God?" I asked, mystified.

She laughed again. "No, silly boy. The creator of the System. He has sought me for a long time. Thus far, none have discovered my home unless I willed for it to happen."

I wasn't sure, but it felt like it was slightly impressive that Lavender knew the creator of the System. What kind of a man was he? I wanted to ask a thousand questions, but it was more important to save Maya and Kalli's parents first. "Do you think you can get my sister out of the ring?"

Lavender nodded. "I need you to trust what I am about to say. It might be better to keep your sister inside. At least for now. Inform her that I am working on a solution. You are going to need her in the future, and the only way you will have access is because she's in that ring."

I sighed. One thing Lavender could always be counted on was to give me a cryptic answer. It probably had something to do with knowing my prophecy. Kalli tapped Lavender on the shoulder. "What about my parents?"

Her expression darkened as she turned to Kalli. "I am afraid your parents are in grave peril. The two of you are going to be forced to confront Rasputin."

"How are we supposed to beat him?" I asked, a feeling of dread in my stomach. "He is too powerful. Can you come fight him with us?"

She sighed and shook her head. "There is a battle that I will fight with you but now is not the time. You have all the pieces to this puzzle. You need to believe in yourself and, most importantly, remember that you're a team."

[47]

A TEAM, *huh?*

I sighed when Lavender finally left. Why was it that adults left kids to fight seemingly impossible battles? The way I saw it, Lavender was more powerful than Rasputin, yet she told us to just deal with it. Any responsible adult would have directed us to the nearest authorities. The sad thing was that I had met the authorities on Gaia. While they talked a good game, they all shied away from conflict. Unless it directly involved them. Only Maya proved to have any backbone, and that had practically gotten her killed.

Kalli shook her head with a smile on her face. She had more reason to worry than I did, yet she chose to show a kind of courage that made me admire her. *We know how to beat him. Zofia showed us. His shields are worthless against non-magical attacks. Well, perhaps just from that special gun but if we outfit our troops with them, we should be able to find a way to win.*

Not just weapons. There was another way. A way I'd been hesitant to explore.

We have another weapon. Mardella may have accidentally shown us a new attack with her corrupted mana poison.

I could feel Kalli's doubt as she worked out what I had in mind. *But he's an M. He will be immune to it the same way we are.*

I pushed emotionally charged mana through the connection toward Kalli and felt her send a wave over her own to counter it. We were more powerful than Mardella ever was. That's why her poison was ineffective against us.

We have the ability to make it more potent than Mardella ever could. She poisoned a blade with mana. I'll inject mine directly into Rasputin's twisted core.

Kalli's eyes widened as she saw the flaw in my plan. *But, to do that, you would have to touch him. He already demonstrated that he can kill with only a second of contact. You'd need longer than that to infect him. Also, think about it, you can't save yourself the way you did Maya. What would happen if you tried to trap your core in the ring?*

It was an interesting question. I'd never thought of imprisoning myself. Could I do that if I was dying? The thought of being in there with no access to Kalli made me shudder. Then again, if she were the ring's master and came to visit me, it wouldn't be so bad. She read my thought and shoved me. *Don't you dare even think about it.*

It was only when we settled into bed that night that the shock fully hit us. Maya was essentially dead, and Rasputin still had Kalli's parents. So far, nothing we did had any impact on the guy. We didn't know where he was or where he was going to attack next. The only thing I knew with any certainty was that he wanted to add me to his collection. When I thought about it, why was he attacking me and not the Ms all grouped together in Solitair? Was he afraid for some reason?

Kalli had a thought that startled me. *He probably doesn't know where they are. He followed you from Earth and was surprised when he heard about the other Ms.*

The thought both relieved and terrified me. On one hand, he didn't know a whole lot about Gaia. On the other, he now had a new planet to conquer. How did the Ms on Earth deal with him? Were there other Ms? That was a puzzle I was going to have to solve. Who would know? I was positive Lavender did, but would she give me a straight answer if I asked? She was so secretive. Would other Ms help, or would they be like Rasputin and try to take my soul to add to their own powers?

Kalli nodded emphatically at the last thought. *It's too risky to get anyone we don't know involved. We have to fight with people we trust. Look what happened with Maya's friends. They betrayed her and left her to die.*

I hated feeling that we were on our own. We did have friends, of course. Joe and Run would fight if I asked them. Then I remembered the last time I'd asked them for help. Stephanie died trying to help solve my problems.

Never again!

Kalli was startled at the intensity of my thought, but she closed her eyes and nodded. *You're right. I hate that you're right, but we can't involve anyone else.*

I wish I didn't have to involve you.

She grabbed my shirt and pulled me close. *There is no way you're leaving me behind. We are a team.*

The thought of Kalli dying hurt too much to think about. Stephanie's lifeless eyes still haunted me. I imagined Kalli lying in that coffin and shuddered in Kalli's arms. We held each other for what felt like an eternity before eventually drifting off to sleep.

––––––

Congratulations. You have reached level 40
Congratulations. You have reached level 33

"I'm not going to lie. I needed that," Kalli whispered in my ear as wave after wave of euphoria washed over us.

We clutched at each other in the dream as we rode out the experience of double leveling by grinding against each other. When the sensation finally tapered off, I kissed Kalli on the nose. "When are we going to do that for real?"

Kalli pecked me on the cheek and giggled. "When are you going to propose? I know we told father we are going to get married but you still have to properly ask the question. A girl's gotta have some standards, you know."

She looked at me expectantly, waiting for a response. "The first thing I'm going to do after we get your parents back is make our engagement official. We will get them back, Kalli, I promise."

Kalli sniffed, wiping away tears that welled in her eyes. "I know we will. We are going to stop him and be done with this threat once and for all. Then we are going to get stronger so we never have to worry about threats like this again."

"Agreed!" I exclaimed, clasping her hands in mine. "For now, let's perfect this emotional attack. I think I made a breakthrough this morning. Try focusing on your emotions without the bond. Balancing it between the two of us is actually the opposite of what we need to counterbalance the cursed mana."

Kalli nodded, and we sat back-to-back, each shutting the other out to focus on our cores. The turmoil of everything going on around me faded into darkness as I both refined my mana and infused it with a sense of purpose I hoped would override Marcella's wrath. While her anger was potent, it paled in comparison to the destiny I had to live up to. Everywhere the light touched, the dark particles scattered before my mind's eye. Imagining my mana was a broom and I was sweeping a dirty floor, I pushed the cursed mana into a ball and forced it from my core. From there, it traveled through my channels like a tumor made out of mana. I corralled it like a sheepdog, keeping it intact as I moved it closer and closer to an area where it could be disposed of. Fortunately, the human body came fully equipped with a waste disposal chute, or I'd have been forced to try to expel it through the pores in my skin or, heaven forbid, my mouth.

———

Ew, Melvin! What's that smell? Kalli grunted weakly as I woke both of us up by having the mother of all accidents.

I naturally did the only thing I could think of to deal with the mess.

DELETE

Kalli blushed as I deleted my underwear along with the toxic mana that had stained them. I gave her a weak smile that betrayed my exhaustion.

At least I did it.

She gasped, covering her eyes with her hand. *Did you cure yourself?*

I shook my head, chucking at the fact that she was peeking through her fingers.

No, I purged it. The trick was to push it out with stronger emotion and more conviction. I think I can do it for you...

She shook her head. I could tell she wanted to do it herself. I knew that's what I would want if I were in her shoes.

———

It took us forever to fall back asleep, especially since I was bottomless. Eventually, we managed to nod off and I entered the dream world to another surprise.

Congratulations. You have reached level 41
Congratulations. You have reached level 42
Congratulations. You have reached level 43

"Wow, I guess curing yourself of emotional trauma gives a lot of experience points," I said, giving myself a pat on the back.

Kalli dragged me to the floor, getting back into a meditative pose. "Hurry up. Morning is almost here, and I want to be rid of this curse. Tell me more about how you did it."

I nodded, sitting with my back to hers. "I think it was determination. We have to win this fight. There's no other option. Everyone is counting on us to do it since the adults of Solitair all seem to only care about themselves. I don't think this is going to be the last person to invade our world, so the two of us are going to have to become strong enough to rid our world of all evil. How can I do that if some petty corruption manages to get the best of me?"

Kalli giggled. "Isn't that rather simple-minded? Are you sure it worked?"

I grinned triumphantly. "Sure, I'm sure. If you don't believe me, try corrupting me with your mana. I'll kick it out again."

"Um, ew, no thank you. The last time smelled back enough," she groaned, remembering I was currently half naked in the real world. "I also don't want you getting that stuff all over me."

I laughed, pointing out, "You know, if you succeed, you're going to stink, too."

Kalli shuddered at the thought. Then she closed her eyes, and I felt her focus on her core. I guided her as she tried one type of emotion, and then another. "Yes, that could work. Wait, you need a lot more emotion than that. Remember, it has to be stronger than Mardella's. That's it. Now try pushing the corruption out. Focus on the black particles and explode them out of your core. No, condense your mana until it explodes like a bomb. Let the explosion force the corruption from your soul."

Kalli elbowed me in the ribs, letting out a deep breath she'd been holding. "Stop distracting me! It's hard to focus with you rambling on like that. I'm not a mana master like you yet."

"Then let me help you," I argued.

"No!" she screamed, shaking with frustration. "This is something I have to do for myself. Something tells me I won't always be able to rely on you for everything. You've shared this incredible power with me, and I need to be able to control it. Lavender said the key to victory is that we work as a team. What good is teamwork if you wind up doing most of the work? I nearly died inside when you saved me with that armor and Mardella ended up stabbing you."

I zipped my lips and tried my best not to distract Kalli while she concentrated. I could feel her head throbbing from her intense concentration. A pressure was building within her, but I wasn't sure it was the good kind.

The emotion she chose to go with in her core was fundamentally different than what I'd used. Rather than conviction or determination, she went with righteous indignation at all of the roadblocks she'd experienced in her life and a fierce desire for independence. It was the same emotion I'd sensed in her when I first met her, back when she planned to earn a thousand gold and take control of her destiny.

Just when I was about to offer my help again, it happened. Her core flashed like a supernova, and Mardella's mana burst out in every direction. She panted heavily and slumped against me. She was too exhausted to speak out loud, but I heard her thoughts through Mate-Chat. *Okay, you can help me now. Let's get this crud out of my body.*

I'm on it!

Having already done it to myself, it was a simple matter of following Kalli's digestive tract with the magical waste. She shuddered against me as I forced it from her body.

————

DELETE

No wait, don't you dare! Kalli stammered just a second too late. *Ugh, I could have just cleaned it up with fire. Hey! Stop peeking.*

I laughed, covering my face but peeking through my fingers as she had.

Hey! You peeked first.

I yowled in pain when Kalli poked me in the eye, but it was worth it. We were cured. Now, all we had to do was deal with Rasputin…and any other baddies out there that wanted to take what was ours.

[48]

Congratulations. You have reached level 34
Congratulations. You have reached level 35
Congratulations. You have reached level 36
Congratulations. You have reached level 37

KALLI INSISTED on going back to sleep so she could benefit from the fruits of her labor. The benefits turned out to be four levels. We wrestled with each other for the second time that night as Kalli's levels hit both of us like a freight train.

When the feeling tapered off, we lay together looking into each other's eyes. Kalli smiled and pointed out, "We're both clean again."

"I don't know about you, but I'm probably a sweaty mess in the real world," I replied. "That was intense."

"Not like that." She giggled. "I mean our cores are pure. No more of Mardella's corruption. I'm sad for Maya. You could have cured her now."

Thinking about it made my heart ache. She had come along to help, and I'd gone and got her killed. Kalli shook her head at the thought. "No, you didn't get her killed. Rasputin murdered her. That's all the more reason we need to stop him for good. If you get the chance, you should imprison him in the ring."

"Wouldn't that mean Maya gets his body?" I asked, cringing at the thought. "I don't think she would like that."

Kalli paused, letting the thought sink in. "I don't suppose she would. Still, it might be a good way to trap him."

I considered the option but, somewhere deep down, I wanted to kill him. People who hurt my friends and family didn't deserve to live trapped in a ring. And if they did, why did I have to be responsible for them?

In the end, I conceded. "I'll do it if I get the chance."

I tried to keep it to myself, but my goal was to kill him with corruption if I get my hands on him. If Kalli knew how I felt, she never said anything.

———

We woke to find that we had slept all morning. Despite my best efforts to delete the mess we made, the two of us still decided that the best option was to **DELETE** the bed entirely. Fortunately, I didn't have to re-edit a new one. Lavender's house somehow knew what I'd done, and a new bed magically appeared in its place. I couldn't tell if it was part of the enchanter's illusion, but it certainly felt real.

The first stop we made for the day was Luna. Even though Shara and the ancients were taking good care of Orpheus and Scuawk, I wanted to cure them once and for all. Kalli and I split up for the task. She started on Orpheus while I worked on Scuawk. While I was a little nervous about anyone else curing people, I decided I had to trust Kalli. She'd proven her skill on the most important person in the world to me, herself.

The first thing I noticed when I probed Scuawk was that it was easier to cure somebody else than it was myself. Small rivulets of mana flowed through her mana channels. Her awakening had been stunted by the corruption, so only a trickle of mana escaped her core.

I paused when I got to her core. While I'd touched a lot of cores during my adventures, the only core I'd ever actually entered was Kalli's. It felt like a betrayal to enter the core of another. A person's core contained their life force. It was Scuawk's soul. That made the whole thing much more serious.

It had to be done, so I fortified Scuawk's core with mana and pushed my way in. The corruption was much worse than it had been with me. Her poor core just couldn't generate enough mana to keep the taint away. There was a third type of mana floating around that I didn't recognize. A little deduction led me to the conclusion that it could only have come from Shara. That or the ancients, but she told me that they refused to do anything without Iolathar. He was still missing ever since he accompanied Kiki and Alariel to her grandmother's house.

Focus, Melvin!

I felt Kalli's ears perk up as I chastised myself. She didn't say anything though which allowed me to get back to work. Because of the size of her core, the corruption was thankfully less of a challenge to purge. Her anatomy was a different matter though. While I was very familiar with the human body, the avian innards of an ostrich lady had me flummoxed. I knew birds pooped, so the endpoint was going to be fairly similar to a human body, but the path to get there was different. While it seemed to be streamlined at first, there were a number of organs that didn't look familiar that led to roadblocks.

Pushing around a ball of corrupting didn't leave me any time to pause what I was doing to take out my phone and look up avian anatomy. Kalli was also busy with her own task so I couldn't ask her to look it up. Fortunately, the path through Scuawk turned out to be fairly straightforward, perhaps even a little shorter than that of a human.

She squawked feebly when I finally managed to expel the corruption and whimpered. "I'm sorry, I think I had an accident."

After making sure I got all of it, I withdrew my essence from her and smiled down at my patient. "Don't worry. That was me. You are corruption free now. I'm sorry it took so long, but welcome to being awakened."

When I looked up to see how Kalli was doing, I was surprised to find her standing next to Orpheus with her arms folded and a smirk on her face. "I beat ya."

I groaned, drooping my head in defeat. "It's not a competition, you know."

It totally was, and she totally won. The problem for me was that we both knew it so there was no point in complaining.

"Did you get all of it?" Shara's voice asked, startling me.

I rounded on her and found her sitting in an armchair in the corner half hidden under a thick wool blanket. Judging by the look of her, she had been sleeping when we arrived, and I hadn't noticed she was there. I triple-checked Scuawk and proudly announced, "Yep, no more corruption."

"Same goes for Orpheus," Kalli said, sounding quite proud of herself.

"I'm not cleaning up that mess," Shara replied, standing up to stretch for a moment before stepping through the door that led outside.

Between Kalli and I, we had become pros at dealing with filthy messes. I deleted the soiled undergarments and Kalli cleaned both patients with her Pvruzth flame. Once that was done, I edited up some hospital gowns for the two of them so they could have some modesty.

"What will you do with me now?" Scuawk asked, looking a little nervous.

"Would you like to come work at the castle?" Kalli asked, using the voice she usually reserved for the children. Even I felt reassured.

Scuawk nodded vigorously, only stopping when her eyes started to lose focus. "I'd like that very must, Master."

"Just Kalli is fine," Kalli assured her. "I don't like to use titles. Not with friends."

Scuawk beamed. "I am honored to be considered a friend of the Queen and Empress. I will serve you with my life."

"Speaking of which," I replied, "I'd like the two of you to stay here on Luna until we deal with a situation back home. It isn't safe down there right now."

While Scuawk liked the idea, Orpheus objected. "If it's all the same to you, my Lord, I'd like to return forthwith. I've been away far too long and would like to resume my duty to the throne. If there is danger, I can be of use. I am a royal bodyguard after all."

I shook my head, but Kalli knelt next to Orpheus and whispered, "When you can prove to me that you are back at one hundred percent, I'll gladly accept you at my side. Until then, I'm commanding you to stay here."

To my surprise, Orpheus placed his hand on his chest and said, "Yes, my Queen."

———

When we stepped outside of the infirmary and found Shara waiting. "I am going to return to Blood Moon. I worry about my father even though I know he is safe at the moment with mother. If I am gone too long, I am afraid the magic will wane and something bad will happen."

"Thank you for coming to help," Kalli said as we walked toward the portal. "You've done more than enough. Both Scuawk and Orpheus would likely be dead without you."

Shara shook her head. "They would have been fine. Despite what they say, the ancients were doing a good job of caring for them."

We stepped through the portal, and Shara made a beeline for the door, heading for Homestead where her parents were.

When we returned to the castle, it felt eerily quiet without Kalli's parents around. It was probably the sinking feeling in Kalli's stomach that made me feel that way.

Zofia was waiting for us when we got to the throne room. "It took you guys long enough. Are you ready to make me some batteries? I've already got my people transporting weapons through the portal for you."

I shrugged. "You're going to have to let me see the battery from the generator again. I've never made one before."

"I can do that," she replied, making her way over to us. "I need to go back to the base anyway. There's only so much I can do electronically."

"How are you getting reception out here?" I asked, eyeing her data pad suspiciously. "Is it magic like my phone?"

Zofia raised an eyebrow, holding out her tablet so I could see it. "You are going to have to get me one of those magic phones as part of our deal."

The tablet in her hand was just a regular model from Max-Tech. I nodded and said, "I'm sure we can work something out next time I'm on Earth."

She held out her hand expectantly when she got to us. I took it and wrapped the three of us in mana. After a quick step through the void, we were standing in front of the large tent. Zofia held open the flap, motioning for us to enter. "I need to make a quick pitstop in my tent, and then I'll join you. I've had my team shut the generator down so you inspect it."

Several men and women in white lab coats stood around the generator. One of them held a camera, while another spoke quietly into a microphone. I chuckled to myself at the thought of them trying to figure out how I duplicated their technology.

I approached one that didn't look too busy and said, "Hey, you. Yeah, you. Can you do me a favor and take the power source out of the generator? I need to look at it."

It took the man a few seconds to react. At first, he shook his head, then he turned to the woman with the camera. She nodded toward the generator and gave him a "just do it already," look.

He slowly made his way to the generator and began to wrestle with a screw holding a panel in place. After a while, several other scientists came to assist him and, between the three of them, they managed to remove the battery. For the first time, I was able to take a close look at it.

Item: 4-Cell Mana Conversion Device (Rechargeable)
Components: Polarized Steel, Manganese Dioxide, Static Dampening, Fabric, Zinc, Potassium Hydroxide, Brass, Mana Sponge
Item Rank: D

Item Level: 1
Item Owner: [Redacted]

The first thing I noticed about the power unit was its low quality. A B- or an A-ranked battery would likely be much more effective. The thought of introducing Joe to Zofia would probably result in a vastly superior product. Either that or they would end the world together.

I looked over my shoulder at the three techs who were trying to hide in a corner and called out to them. "I need rocks. Pebbles will do. Get me a bunch of them."

There was no point using my dwindling supply of pebbles when Zofia had a team perfectly capable of getting more for me. Kalli had other ideas though. *Melvin Murphy. Be nice to the poor workers.*

I groaned, giving Kalli a tiny nod. "Never mind, I'll get some."

Together, Kalli and I gathered up a handful of rocks under the watchful eyes of at least a dozen workers. Some of them even helped out. By the time we finished, there was a small mountain of loose stones sitting in front of the portal generator. It was time to start editing.

[49]

"You know you have to fill them with mana, right?" Zofia muttered as she examined the first few batteries. "We have plenty of batteries. We designed them after all. What we lack is the mana to charge them."

I groaned, picking up one of the batteries. "You could have told me that earlier."

Zofia laughed. "I should have thought it obvious but we don't require help making our own inventions."

Each battery took an average of two minutes to charge. I realized I was probably ensuring that the TGB would have the ability to maintain their portal for a long time but our needs for technology outweighed the need to keep them off the planet.

Kalli sat next to me and copied what I was doing. She was a bit slower as she had less experience than I did, but she picked it up fast. After charging a few batteries, she started a conversation with Zofia. "You know, this can be the start of something. What do you think about your organization becoming a citizen of Celestea?"

"I don't know," Zofia replied, currently occupied with her nose buried in her tablet. "The TGB doesn't play well with others. What benefit would there be to registering with your nation? You just want us to pay taxes, don't you?"

Kalli shook her head. "No, not at all. I was thinking it might be a good idea to introduce some of the technology from Earth here on Gaia. For one thing, none of the villages have a sustainable privy system. It would be nice to…"

"We aren't plumbers." Zofia shook her head. "However, I'll see what I can do. Be warned though. Any deal you make with us is going to cost you. We can't just do favors all the time."

"What do you want?" I asked, a little intimidated by the woman.

She tapped a few more buttons on the tablet. "For starters, you will stop treating us like uninvited guests. If you want our help, we are going to establish a branch of the TGB here on your land. We expect privacy. That means no more inspections without consent. There will be no taxes. Our contributions to your primitive world will be enough to cover any taxes for all company employees. Finally, I want access to a magician or a wizard. In exchange, I will provide you with a group of scientists to bring you out of the dark ages."

"Do you plan to make this your base of operations?" Kalli asked, placing another battery in the finished pile.

Zofia stopped tapping on the tablet and glanced at Kalli. "No. Earth will always be our home. It doesn't hurt to be multidimensional though. Besides, that way we won't have to transport supplies back and forth."

"Do you need buildings?" I offered. "I can make buildings."

Zofia looked at the tent over her head. "I'd like to design my own headquarters. No offense to your building skills but my designs are unique."

Several of the scientists cast glances back at Zofia, but she shrugged them off. Kalli nodded her agreement. "I think we can meet most of your demands. Your assistance with building better villages will make life better for everyone in the empire. The problem is that we don't have any high-level mages or wizards to lend you. Mel and I are sort of it. However, I think Mel can offer you something even better. If you want it that is."

"We need access to a live wizard," Zofia replied, crossing her arms over her chest. "Our arrangement with the magic community on Earth gives us limited access to people with magic. Unfortunately, that resulted in many lies and simplifications. I need direct access to someone so I can make sure they tell the truth."

"Are you saying you want to torture someone?" I asked, raising an eyebrow.

"Not exactly," Zofia muttered, not backing down from the challenge.

Kalli stood suddenly. "Enough you two. I have an idea you both should like. We can give you direct access to magic and I guarantee no torturing of innocent people will take place."

"Again with the prisoners?" Zofia muttered, going back to her tablet.

Kalli laughed and pointed directly at Zofia. "No, I am offering to have Melvin awaken you. Then you can level up and figure it all out for yourself. It will probably make better sense to you as well because that way you'll feel it as you learn."

Kalli, we can't just...

She cut me off with a finger to my lips. *Don't worry. I already thought about that. You can impose a contract when you awaken her. Don't worry, it can just be something simple like she loses access to her magic if she does something like attack us.*

Kalli was a genius. The more I thought about it, the more I liked it. Not only would Zofia turn into something interesting when she awakened, but I could also impose a contract when awakening her to prevent her from doing anything evil.

Zofia tapped her foot impatiently. "Are the two of you done with your private conversation yet? I heard you can't touch me magically without killing me. Did something change? Are you cured of your sickness now?"

Kalli nodded. "We rid ourselves of the corruption last night. Mel can awaken you. If you agree to a few stipulations, that is."

"Like what?" Zofia asked, sounding suspicious. "I refuse to give up my freedom, so if you had something like that in mind, you can just forget about it."

"How about you agree to do no evil," I suggested, giving her a hard look.

Zofia sucked in a deep breath, not looking away. "Who gets to decide what is evil?"

That was the tricky part. I knew next to nothing about contract magic. I decided to see if I could get Kiki's attention in guild chat.

Kiki, are you there?

Several people replied, including Otto and Esha, but only to inform me that nobody had heard from Kiki or Alariel in weeks. I sighed. It was yet another mystery I was going to have to solve. Unfortunately, I didn't have time to think about it as Zofia continued to tap her foot impatiently. Probing the contract I made with myself to strengthen my bond with Kalli told me what I needed to do. "You decide if what you're doing is evil. I'm going to place a magic contract on you. If you break the condition, you will lose what I am about to grant you. At least, I'm pretty sure that's what will happen."

"You sound like you don't know," Zofia said after a moment's silence. "Are you sure I won't be penalized if I don't think what I'm doing is evil?"

"Why does it sound like you're already trying to find a loophole?" I asked, having second thoughts.

Zofia smirked, only making me more apprehensive. "The truth is, I never had any intentions of attacking you or your people. We are simple scientists with only one objective. That is the pursuit of knowledge. However, that doesn't mean we won't defend ourselves if provoked. I don't care if the rest of the universe labels me as evil, I will continue to walk this path."

I opened my mouth to say something, but Kalli cut me off again, "That works for me. Do we have a deal?"

"I'll think about it," Zofia muttered as she sat on the ground with her legs crossed and her nose buried in the data pad. She didn't say anything for a long time, leaving Kalli and I to infuse more batteries.

Kalli glanced at me as she added another fully charged battery to the finished stack we were making. ***Do you think she'll go for it?***

I looked over my shoulder at Zofia. She had her tongue sticking out of the side of her mouth in concentration as she looked intently at the tablet, completely ignoring us.

I think she wants to, but she's worried it's a trap. Normally, I'd love to awaken her, but I don't trust her. What if she becomes another Rasputin?

Kalli sighed. *Anyone you awaken has the potential to become evil. It doesn't mean it would be your fault, just like Rasputin isn't your fault. If she turns evil and the contract doesn't stop her, we will just have to do it.*

I felt the burden of the universe on my shoulders. Surely, somewhere in the cosmos was a government organization that was paid to handle threats of a magical nature. They couldn't all be like Gaia, could they?

Before I could say anything, Zofia set the tablet down and spoke in a firm voice. "I'll do it. Make me magical."

I wanted to give her Mickey Mouse ears as a joke, but she looked uneasy about the whole thing and I didn't want to make it anywise. Zofia and I left for her tent while Kalli continued to charge the batteries. She sat on her cot and looked up at me. "How do we do this?"

I pulled up a chair so I was close enough to hold her hands. "This is a bit different for me, too. How do you want to make the oath? You can either write it out or just make it verbal. Either way, I will bind your words to your core."

Zofia held her tablet out so I could see the screen. "This is what I promise."

I hereby promise not to use the powers you are about to bestow upon me for evil. I reserve the right to use any means necessary to protect myself and or the administration. Anyone that tries to impede our autonomy will be resisted to the best of my ability, both scientific and magical.

She looked at me expectantly, and I gave her a curt nod. "It's a good start. You need to add a clause that you agree to follow the laws of the land as well."

Zofia tilted her head to the side. "Do you have a list of these laws? I don't want to agree to anything without reading it."

The truth was, I didn't know the laws, so we ended up compromising.

I agree to follow all laws of the land that are both ethical and fair to all whom it governs.

"I agree with you," I said as we read over the clause. "If the law doesn't meet those rules we need to change it anyway."

Zofia cracked a weak smile. She was shaking and could tell she was excited, and maybe a little nervous. "Okay, what next?"

I took her hands in mine, leaning forward to look into her eyes. "You are making an oath that you intend to abide by this agreement to the best of your ability. Failure to do so will result in your core closing up and blocking any magic ability from being available to you. All you have to do to avoid this is do no evil and follow the law. Do you swear it?"

I was proud of myself. That sounded official. Zofia took a deep breath to calm herself and whispered, "I swear it."

Taking a final look at Zofia's status, I began the process.

Name: Zofia
Class: Technician
Level: 1 (23)
Affection Level: Eternally Curious

I passed mana through the tablet, focusing on the words. They began to glow as mana seeped from the device and into Zofia's hands. Inside her, she was different from any non-awakened I'd dealt with. While her passages were unopened, they were developed. It gave me the impression that she'd used them in the past.

Making my way to her core, I was amazed at what I saw. A constellation that reminded me of a galaxy swirled in the darkness. Upon closer inspection, the specks that I thought were stars were snippets of code. Only it wasn't modern programming. Ones and zeros orbited a central shining ball that I could only assume was the source of her mana.

I reached out to connect to the light, but the code interfered, pushing me back. It was almost like…

I don't think her body wants to be awakened.

Kalli gasped, seeing through my mind's eye. *What do you mean?*

I don't know. It's like her body is fighting back.

I managed to speak, "Are you sure you want to be awakened?"

Zofia sounded winded but managed to reply. "Yes. I am sure."

As though it was listening to her words, the code surrounding her inner core stopped swirling and an opening appeared. I took the opportunity to push forward, connecting my mana to her core. I suddenly felt a jolt when we connected and was flung from her depths. The next thing I knew the chair I was on got flung back and crashed through the flap in her tent. I rolled on the ground several times before coming to a stop in front of a startled worker.

Kalli started running toward me. *Melvin, are you okay?*

I sat up, and the world stopped spinning.

NEW TRAIT ACQUIRED: [Praevaricator Universum]

[50]

I MADE my way back into the tent to find Zofia sitting on the bed examining her tablet with great interest. "Um, are you okay?"

She looked up, a grin forming on her face. "This is interesting. I can feel it pulsing."

"Your mana?" I asked, not seeing any signs of mana leaking from her.

She shook her head, holding up the tablet. "No, the data. I can feel it. Actually, I can feel everything. Just from holding this, I can tell you every component that makes it, whether it's functioning properly, and how much power it's using. That's not what I'm talking about, though. I can feel the code as it passes from the hard drive to the processor, and then to the screen. It's mesmerizing."

I gaped at her as she set the tablet down and rummaged through her desk, scooping up another device I didn't recognize.

Item: Mana Omission Detector (MOD)
Components: Litmus, Plastinium, Battery, Screen, MBX Chip
Item Rank: C
Item Level: 1
Item Owner: [Redacted]

"What does that do?" I asked, watching her intently.

Zofia looked up as if she had been in a daze. "Oh, this? It detects mana. I usually use it to see if there are any magic users in the area but it's also useful to detect high levels of mana around an area or object."

"Can you take it apart with your mind?" I asked, thinking of Joe's ability as a technomancer. "Or perhaps build a duplicate out of nothing."

She frowned at the MOD, screwing up her face in concentration before giving up. "No, I can't do any of that. Like I said before, I can feel it thinking and talking in code. I think I can tell it what to do."

"Can't you already do that?" I asked, thinking I had a general idea of what she was saying. "Are you saying you can turn it off and on with your mind?"

Zofia shook her head, the frown slowly becoming a smile. "No. It's a lot better than that. I can reprogram it with my mind. Actually, I get the feeling that I can do that for anything with a processor."

She took out the gun she used on Rasputin. I took the opportunity to inspect it.

Item: Probably Improbably Nano Gun (PING)
Components: Mana Battery, Black Box, Aura Scanner,
Plastinium
Item Rank: C
Item Level: 1
Item Owner: [Redacted]

"Yes!" Zofia squealed, her voice rising to a shrill level as she pointed the gun at me. "You wouldn't believe what I can make this do now."

I dove out of the way, worried she'd gone crazy and decided to demonstrate on me. When I looked up, I found her staring at me with a puzzled look on her face. "What are you doing? Get up."

Debating whether or not to **DELETE** the PING, I slowly pushed myself to my feet. "Don't point that at me again."

"Sheesh," she sighed. "It's not like I was going to use it on you.

Well, not unless you want me to. I was just excited because I think I can make the PING do something it wasn't able to do before."

"What all can it do?" I asked, unsure if getting shot by it was a good thing or not.

Zofia laughed and replied, "It's almost better to ask what it doesn't do. To put it simply, it breaks rules. As you witnessed with Rasputin, it transformed him into something that shouldn't be possible. We devised a similar technique to break the wall between dimensions. The laws that govern the universe are not perfect. We found a way to circumvent many of those rules."

I could tell through our bond that Kalli wanted me to come back and help with the batteries. *She seems nicer than before.*

While I wanted to help, the PING was too interesting, so I stayed to see what Zofia would do next.

She seems happy.

Zofia nodded to the PING and pulled the trigger. A multicolored ray shot out and hit her bed. Suddenly, the bed began to float a few feet off the ground and spun upside down. It lingered for a moment before continuing the revolution and turning right side up again. Then it gently settled on the floor as if nothing happened.

I looked at it in shock for a moment before asking Zofia, "What did you just do?"

She was too busy snorting to answer, so I had to ask again. When she finally composed herself, she replied, "I just told it to do a barrel-roll. I know it's kind of pointless, but you have to admit, that's hilarious."

"Is that one of the settings?" I asked, curious about why she was so pleased with herself.

She shook her head, looking down at the PING like she'd just unwrapped the best Christmas present ever. "No, why would I include such a silly function? I just told it to do that, and it obeyed. I controlled it with my mind. No, wait, I reprogrammed it telepathically. Coding feels like a spoken language to me now."

"Well, your core is made out of code," I replied with a grin. "I guess that means you're a programmer."

"That's an oversimplification," she grumbled, setting the PING down and rummaging through the desk. "Coding is just a means to an end. It's like calling yourself a linguist because you speak the language. While I assure you I'm quite good at many programming languages, my true calling is that of a scientist. I wish to uncover the mysteries of the universe. By force if necessary."

"You're a lot more talkative than you used to be," I said, waving her off when she frowned at me. "It's not that I mind. I'm just curious. What changed?"

Zofia beamed. "You've given me the greatest gift ever. Do you know what it feels like to know magic is out there and have the superior intellect to make the most of it yet be denied any chance to ever experience it for yourself? I now understand why they call it an awakening."

That reminded me. "Why are you already so good at it? I've awakened many people and none of them jumped right in as you have."

Zofia looked at her hands, running a finger over a laptop she found in a drawer. "I've dreamed of this my entire life. Most people grow out of their imagination when they become adults but for me, it only grew stronger. I can do this because I know I can."

"So, it wasn't just your body that didn't grow up?" I asked with a small laugh.

Kalli slapped her forehead and groaned while Zofia scooped the PING up off the desk. "You know, I think I can make this thing shrink you. Then you wouldn't be able to call me small."

"Whoa, hey!" I cried, holding up a pillow that was lying beside me. "Don't do anything evil. Don't forget the vow you made. If you shoot me with that thing, your magic will be locked away."

"Will it?" she asked, not backing down. "Something tells me I'd be doing you a favor to make your body match your maturity level. Besides, you made the mistake of telling me I get to decide what's evil."

Fortunately for me, she set the PING down and went back to work on the laptop. My curiosity grew, and I walked up beside her. "What are you working on?"

She closed her eyes in concentration. "I'm trying to find a way to connect to the network back on Earth. That way I can get internet access here on Gaia."

"Maybe you can connect on wifi when the portal is open," I replied, feeling Kalli charge another mana battery.

Zofia opened her eyes suddenly. "Yes! The generator. That's a great idea. Perhaps there's hope for you yet."

"Thanks...I think," I replied as Zofia sprinted from the tent.

I followed her back to the main tent where Kalli hastily clambered to her feet as Zofia stood before the massive portal generator. We watched in silence as she considered the machine. I took the pause as an opportunity to inspect her again.

Name: Zofia
Class: Technician
Level: 23
Affection Level: Eternally Curious

Ah! She's actually level twenty-three.
Kalli smiled in approval. *So, she is.*

Still, something felt off about her. I'd seen a backward version of that when Eddie was ghosted. I decided to ask her about it. "Um, Zofia, are you aware you're level twenty-three?"

"Levels?" she asked, popping one eye open. "Like in a video game?"

"Yes," I replied, wondering how she leveled so much without knowing about the leveling system. "Usually, when I awaken someone, they start at level one."

"Oh, that." She shrugged, placing a hand on the generator. "I may have experimented on my body. It could be part of the reason why my growth was stunted. I figured there had to be a way to jumpstart myself, but I was never able to pinpoint where magic came from."

I debated telling her exactly where it came from but before I could say anything, something happened with the generator. It hummed to life and the portal manifested. Almost immediately, it rumbled and groaned before shuddering to a stop. Then Zofia wobbled and fell to the ground, panting heavily for a moment before retching and puking on the floor.

Kalli's eyes widened, and she rushed to her. "What happened? Are you okay?"

One glance at the still open battery slot told me what she'd done. *She activated the machine without a battery. It fed on her mana until it was gone. The same thing happened to me when I first summoned you.*

Kalli looked up at the battery slot in horror. *Oh, I never realized it was that painful.*

The memory of that fateful day and the discomfort replayed in my mind. I smiled when I realized that I wouldn't change it for the world. Kalli blushed, having seen my thought. *I love you, you know.*

Me, too.

We shared a moment as Kalli held Zofia's hair back while she emptied the contents of her stomach on the floor. The other scientists made no move to assist her, fingers stabbing their tablets as they feverishly raced to record the latest anomaly.

My curiosity got the best of me, and I decided to test Zofia's changes to the generator. I touched the battery slot and connected a stream of mana to it. Once again, it rumbled to life and a portal formed.

Zofia looked up, still shaking. "How are you doing that? That thing nearly killed me."

"I have more mana than you," I replied, yawning to give her an idea of exactly how much.

While the generator required a constant stream of mana, it only demanded a couple hundred per second after the initial burst to generate the portal. Zofia pouted as she watched from the floor. "That's not fair. How do I get more mana."

"Level up," Kalli explained, steadying Zofia as she climbed to her feet.

"What happens if I feed it more mana?" I asked, wondering what Zofia saw when she used her skill on the generator. All I saw was a huge chunk of mana-hungry machinery.

"I don't know," Zofia admitted. "But I wouldn't suggest…"

She was too late. Showing off my immense mana pool, I increased the flow of mana tenfold, flooding the circuitry with more mana than it asked for. It groaned under the stress of trying to accommodate the sudden influx. Zofia shrieked and ran over to the generator, placing her hand on the cool metal.

Something shifted inside of the machine, and I felt it draw even more power out of me. It wasn't more than I could handle, but it still shocked me that Zofia was able to modify the device that quickly. The portal that appeared was easily three times the size of the previous one we'd walked through. It filled the side of the tent and was now big enough to drive a truck through. Not wanting to be shown up by Zofia, I changed the composition of my mana by infusing it with intense curiosity.

It took a few minutes for the new mana to show any effect but, suddenly, the portal faded and was replaced by a new one. This was significantly smaller than the previous one, but it was red. The world beyond the portal appeared to be on fire and hundreds of creatures looked up at us with beady red eyes.

Kalli screamed and pulled my arm away from the generator. Even cut off from my mana, the machine continued to hum, and the portal didn't close. Zofia looked at me with a curiosity of her own burning in her eyes. "I dare you to go through and check it out."

Kalli shook her head. *Absolutely not! You need to close that thing before any of those monsters end up on Gaia. It's bad enough that we already have one madman running around wreaking havoc.*

Instinctually knowing what to do, I touched the generator again. This time, I siphoned the mana back into myself. Just as when Kalli recalled her flame after cleansing me, I felt my mana obediently abandon the hungry machine and return to my body.

With nothing to feed it, the generator shuddered to a halt and the portal died just as one of the monsters tried to pass through. A red muscular arm flopped to the floor, twitching momentarily before coming to a stop.

Zofia walked slowly to where it lay and prodded it with a gloved finger. "Well, that was interesting. How did you get the generator to change locations? I thought that was fixed by where you ripped the fabric of the universe. Now I have to rethink everything."

"I just changed my mana," I replied, satisfied that I'd won the mini-competition.

She inspected the machine for a few minutes before smiling. "Good. You didn't break it."

"What did you do to it?" I asked. "How did you get it to accept so much mana?"

Zofia grinned and patted the machine lovingly. "I just reprogrammed it. Rather than storing your mana, I allowed it to pass through and generate the portal directly. I see now that I'm going to have to reprogram everything I ever created. I never knew how inefficient all my designs were."

"Be careful your code doesn't come to life," I warned. "The last thing we need is some AI overlord trying to take over the world."

Zofia just shrugged. "Wouldn't it be entertaining, though?"

[51]

T AKING delivery of the PINGs was tricky. If they fell into the wrong hands, we could lose the war before it even began. Rasputin was aware of their power considering their effect on him. The question was, would the gun work twice?

I turned a PING over in my hands and examined it. "Do you think he might build an immunity to the effect?"

Zofia flipped a few settings on the PING in her hands and said, "That depends. The setting I used is something I like to call animacation. It interferes with the way light interacts with your body. We got the idea from the art used in cartoons. Another way of putting it is we found a way to simplify reality. Hmm, perhaps a better name would be the simplification ray. Either way, none of that matters. It simplifies the textures of whatever it strikes. In other words, you become a cartoon. I don't know how it affects magic. Would you like me to test it on you?"

"How long does it last?" Kalli asked. "If he's stuck that way, Rasputin may agree to surrender if we fix him."

Zofia held up a data pad with her free hand. "Well, he might still be affected. I hit him with the highest setting and, depending on how whether he can resist the effect, it can last anywhere from an hour to up to a week."

I considered Zofia's offer of being turned into a toon. It would be interesting to try my magic and see how it worked. More importantly, I wanted to see what Kalli looked like as a cartoon. Without asking Kalli what she thought, I gave Zofia a thumbs up. "Hit us with it...but only for an hour.

Kalli threw her hands in the air defensively. "Hey, wait! I didn't agree to..."

It was too late. Zofia, having been waiting for a chance to test the ray again, adjusted the settings and fired. The blast hit me in the chest and...tickled?

I looked down as the ray digitized my body. As Zofia said, the colors washed out of my skin and clothes and a thick black line marked the end of me and the beginning of reality. I held my hand up, admiring my hand, which looked like a sketch. All details of my knuckle were simplified. Even my fingerprints were gone, replaced by a swirl of what looked like ink.

Kalli slowly backed away from Zofia, who pointed the PING at her like it was a stick-up. "If you even think about firing that thing, you're getting a fire bath."

Zofia pouted, looking frustrated that Kalli stood between her and science. I decided to see what was different and pulled up my skills menu.

Skills: World Editor, Manipulation, Controlling Voice, Buff (Edited), Summon (Edited), Command Attention, Formulate, Cloud Judgement, Assimilate Technology, Dark Proclamation

Traits: Bloodline: M, Bloodline: Shaw, Bloodline Ramsey, Bloodline Celestea, Enhanced Regeneration, Enhanced Mana, Absorption, Control, Shimmer, God Eye (Edited), Perfect Pitch, Mantis Style, Track Scent, Magical Plague Immunity (Edited), Matechat [Kalliphae Murphy](Edited), Inseparable [Kalliphae Murphy], Intertwined [Kalliphae Murphy], Till Death Do You Part[Kalliphae Murphy], Praevericator Universum, Illusion [Animated]

Another purge was long overdue. I had way too many. There it was at the bottom. The effect of the PING was an illusion. It was similar to the de-buff that blocked magic from my eyes before I awakened and the illusion that Mr. Ramsey used to make a clone. Kalli and I had even disguised ourselves as trolls the first time we met Esha.

DELETE

The instant it vanished I was back to normal. Zofia stared at me in disbelief. Kalli, on the other hand, knew exactly what I'd done. She'd watched my actions through our bond, still glaring in my direction. *Why did you tell her to zap me, too?*

I sighed, a little disappointed but also feeling bad that I didn't ask her permission.

I'm sorry. I wanted to see how you'd look with it and if you can do magic while in that form.

I could tell she was still mad, but she surprised me by turning to Zofia. "Fine. Shoot me with it, too. We need to test this out on each of us."

"For science!" Zofia chanted as she pulled the trigger.

It was interesting being able to watch someone else get zapped. Rasputin's transformation had been so quick that I hadn't been able to appreciate it properly. Kalli's color brightened as the transformation took effect. Her hair turned crimson and her freckles even more pronounced against her pale skin. The dress appeared to shrink and adhere to her form, showing off her figure as though the clothes were painted on. Had I been a cartoon at that moment, I was sure my eyes would have popped out of my head.

I only noticed Kalli was looking at me when she held her hands out and cast a spell.

"Pvruzth."

The spell defied reality. A wall of crimson enveloped me obscuring my vision and making me see red. It felt the same as usual when she masterfully let her magic wash over me. She took special care to run her fire over every inch of me, even stopping to pinch my butt with it as she passed. Since when was she able to do that? Then again, I shouldn't have been surprised. Her control over the magic was so good that she eradicated all sweat and grime without harming a single hair on my body.

When she retracted the flame, she looked at her hands in confusion as the red ball of fiery ink vanished. Feeling extra clean, I made my move on Kalli, wrapping my arms around her and leaning in for a kiss. "You're hot when you're a cartoon!"

Zofia laughed. "The gun shouldn't affect body temperature. Did you need me to... Uh, never mind, I get it."

Kalli giggled and pushed me away. *Easy, tiger. That was revenge for telling her to shoot me, not an invitation to see if I taste different. Now, delete this and change me back.*

I still wanted to kiss her as a cartoon.

I will in a minute.

She kissed me, and I concluded that she tasted the same as usual. *We are getting PINGs of our own. We can do this later. For now, we have other settings to test.*

DELETE

I sighed, giving in to reason. While I wanted to play, there was no telling when Rasputin would be back, and we needed to be as prepared as possible. "What's next...um, wait! What are you doing?"

We both stared at Zofia in awe as she zapped herself. She became even shorter and looked more childlike than she already did. The lab coat became snow-white with only pockets and buttons for details, hanging down to her feet and looking more oversized than it usually was.

"What? I'm magic too now. I had to try it out," she explained, pursing her lips as she spoke into a tablet that looked more like an Etch-A-Sketch when in cartoon form. "Subject finds that she retains full cognitive magical abilities. Any electronics held in the target's hands are also affected by the ray. The functionality of the tablet appears to be nominal. I will test the PING on an inanimate object to be sure it sustained no adverse effects."

Zofia turned bright red when she realized we were staring at her. It was a rather exaggerated color for a blush. Now wanting to embarrass her more than she was, I decided to get on with the demonstration. "What else does it do?"

She walked past me to a crate with more PINGs and selected another, non-cartoon one. "Okay, just to be clear, these are limited models that have their functions restricted to features I think will be useful against Rasputin. I didn't want to overwhelm your army by giving them a multi-tool with over a hundred different settings."

"That's kind of you," Kalli replied, nodding in agreement.

All I could say was, "I want one of the deluxe models."

Zofia chuckled, looking back at her now cartoon PING. "We can negotiate later. For now, let me teach you how this gun can save your life."

We both nodded in silence, and she hoisted the PING from the crate and aimed it at the far wall of the tent. "This is something I like to call the 'Airbag.' It works as it sounds."

She didn't appear to change any settings and pulled the trigger. Something emerged from the tip of the gun and expanded explosively, creating a clap of thunder that temporarily deafened me. When the dust settled and I opened my eyes, what looked like a half-melted snowman stood in front of Zofia.

She appraised it for a second before saying, "One of you cast a spell at it."

Kalli and I looked at each other, and she stepped forward, leveling a hand at the foam.

"Pvruzth."

Her flame wrapped around the foam and began to eat away at it. While I'd expected it to go up in smoke, the foam didn't so much as smolder. Zofia nodded and tapped the screen of her tablet a few times.

Kalli gritted her teeth and clenched the pendant around her neck. Just as her flame started to turn green, I decided to cheat.

DELETE

The foam vanished instantly. Kalli scowled and I announced, "Non-magic items are weak to manipulation it seems."

Kalli's green flame sailed past where the airbag had been and lit Zofia's cot on fire. Eating through the thing material almost instantly, it jumped to the tent, which was soon engulfed in green flames as well. I did the only thing I could think of to prevent the entire camp from burning down.

DELETE

We found ourselves sitting outside next to a desk and a stack of crates. Passing scientists stopped to stare at the cartoon Zofia before shrugging and moving on.

For her part, Zofia took the destruction of her tent rather well. After punching a few notes into her datapad, she held out the PING again and said, "This next setting might be considered slightly unethical, but I decided to include it because a lucky shot may be the key to winning the battle. I call it turn-based but what it really does is make the target susceptible to suggestion. I've tested this on normal people but again, I lack test subjects who are magically inclined. Would either of you like to volunteer?"

Kalli swallowed hard and turned to look at me. *If I do this, you had better not make me do anything weird or I'll nev*er forgive you. Also, make sure you remove it after one test.

I could tell she was serious, so I answered her solemnly.

I promise.

Turning to Zofia, Kalli said, "Get it over with and zap me. Melvin gives the command though."

Zofia looked and offered the PING to me. "It's keyed to work for the person who fires it. She should only answer to you while under the effect of turn-based. We built this in so nobody else can hijack the command."

I accepted the PING and pointed it at Kalli. It was difficult to pull the trigger as the last thing I'd ever want to do was hurt her. "Are you sure you chose the right setting? Can you make sure?"

Zofia raised an eyebrow. "Do you think I'd make an error with technology? Besides, I triple-checked it telepathically. You're good. Zap away!"

Kalli scoffed at Zofia, and then I felt her clench her butt cheeks as she prepared to be zapped. I grinned as she blushed and stuck out her tongue. *Just get it over with already!*

Fine.

When I pulled the trigger, a golden ray shot from the PING and bathed Kalli in sparkles. She appeared dazed as she looked into my eyes but otherwise didn't move. I smiled and said, "Kiss me."

[52]

KALLI HAD a vacant look in her eyes when she leaned in to kiss me. The absence of a smile on her face made the whole thing feel wrong somehow. I stopped her with a finger to the lips and quickly examined her to find the source of the effect.

Mind Break

There it was!

DELETE

She blinked a few times before snapping out of it. Without warning, she smacked me across my cheek. *Don't ever force me to kiss you. I mean, you can always ask for one, but I don't think I'll ever want to be forced to do that. Don't feel bad. I know you were just testing the magic, but I felt helpless when you commanded me to kiss you and it still makes me feel sick even now.*

I backed away, horrified that I'd made her feel that way.

I...I'm sorry...

Kalli stroked my cheek where she'd smacked me, sending shivers down my spine. She then cupped my face in her hands and kissed me, the smile that made my legs turn to jelly back on her face. *See, it's so much better when it's by choice. Anyhow, I don't think I ever want to be shot with that again, it felt like I was suffocating.*

Wanting to see what it felt like, as well as discover whether I could break the effect, Kalli shot me with the turn-based ray. The moment it hit me I saw stars, and my head felt like it had been dunked in a bucket of ice water. As hard as I tried to concentrate, Kalli had me marching circles around her in no time. Even after she was satisfied with how it worked, she couldn't think of a way to break the effect. She ended up commanding me to sit before trying to talk me back to consciousness. My thoughts swam for what felt like an eternity as I fought to regain control of my free will. It may have been five minutes or an hour but, eventually, I regained enough of myself to pull up a menu. My vision blurred as I scanned the traits until I found the one I was looking for.

Mind Break

The words blurred as my eyes tried to focus. It took every ounce of willpower that I had to squeeze my eyes shut. Once I got them closed, the menu appeared much sharper in the darkness. Normally, seeing menus when my eyes were closed was annoying. The bright light in the darkness made them water. However, under the effect of the turn-based ray, removing distractions from the outside world helped me focus.

DELETE

When I opened my eyes, I was myself again. Kalli beamed at me and immediately threw her arms over my shoulders. *Good job! I know you could beat it.*

How long was I under?

She frowned, looking at the sky. *Not long. Less than an hour for sure.*

I frowned, realizing Kalli didn't have a watch and probably wasn't as good at telling time as people were on Earth. Our conversation got Zofia's attention, and she muttered at me while tapping more results into the datapad. "Did you break free by yourself or did the effect wear off?"

"I broke it," I replied, proud of myself.

"Subject managed to break out of turn-based in one-hundred-thirty-seven minutes," Zofia continued her report, before turning to me and asking. "Do you think you can do it faster if she shoots you again?"

I shrugged, thinking about the process I went through before turning back to Kalli.

Actually, do you mind if I use it on you one more time?

Kalli frowned. *I don't mind but why?*

I'm going to command you to break the effect in MateChat.

Moments later, Kalli looked at me with the same lifeless eyes as the previous time.

I command you to free yourself from the effect.

She didn't do anything.

Free yourself from Mind Break.

Still nothing.

Can you hear me?

Kalli nodded. That was a good sign at least.

Can you use the DELETE command?

She shook her head and I groaned.

I guess that doesn't work.

DELETE

Kalli let out a deep breath I didn't know she'd been holding. *Okay, that gets worse every time I go through it. I heard everything you said but nothing I did worked.*

I sighed, sagging slightly in frustration.

I know, and I'm sorry for putting you through that.

Kalli gave me a weak smile. *It's fine. At least we know, right?*

I handed her the PING.

Okay, shoot me again.

She frowned. *Are you sure?*

Yeah. This time I want you to tell me to remove the effect.

Kalli leveled the PING as me and once again I saw stars. The world faded once again but this time Kalli was there with me in my head. *Melvin, I want you to break out of this. Come back to me.*

Part of me wanted to go to her, to hold her in my arms. That wasn't right. What good would it do? There was something I needed to do first. Something important. I fought the fog in my brain as I tried to remember what it was. Then Kalli continued. *You need to delete the effect I put on you with the PING.*

That was it! I remember what I needed to do and how I needed to do it.

DELETE

Zofia looked up from her datapad when Kalli gave me a kiss as a reward. "Did he break it already or are you just having your way with him?"

"I would never!" Kalli protested, turning bright red. "Melvin woke himself all on his own."

I kissed her back.

You had something to do with it. I just followed your voice.

She smiled. *No. That was all you.*

I lulled my head to the side with a sloppy grin on my face, "Kalli is my master and has ordered me to kiss her?"

Kalli gasped and slapped me. Fortunately, she didn't use half the force she had the first time and it hardly hurt. "Stop playing around!"

I chuckled at my joke and turned to Zofia. "How long was I under that time?"

"Five minutes," she answered.

Put me under again.

Kalli took a step back and frowned. *What? Why? Haven't you figured it out?*

Now, I want to see how long it takes without your help. Just tell me to sit down, and I'll do the rest.

While she didn't like the idea, she agreed to do it. The second solo attempt took longer than the first. When I finally gasped for breath, Zofia yawned and said, "Two hours, twenty-nine minutes."

"Again!" I yelled out loud.

It wasn't until the eighth try that I finally got the hang of it. Even through the fog, I knew what I had to do. Actually, it was a series of things I had to do.

Close my eyes.

Close my mind.

See the System.

DELETE

Zofia whistled when I opened them and stood up. "Wow, a minute and a half. Impressive."

"Really?" I replied, not believing her words. "That felt like forever."

She raised an eyebrow as she typed my response into the datapad. "What did it feel like when you took two hours to get out of it?"

"Well, forever," I admitted sheepishly. "That was different, though. The other times I had to figure out what to do. This time, I knew, and it still took forever to close my eyes and my mind. I was concentrating so hard I thought I might pass out."

"A minute is very good," Kalli complimented me with a smile.

I shook my head. "If we were in a fight, I'd be dead if I took that long to break out of it. Especially if someone was giving me a command. Like to kill you, for example."

Kalli shuddered at the thought. While I was a little curious about what one of us would do if issued a command like that, I didn't want to test it. Something terrible might happen. Kalli read my thought and asked a question in MateChat, *Are you sure this is a good idea? Maybe we should ask Zofia to remove that one.*

She was right of course, but...

Think about it. Just one hit and the fight with Rasputin will be over before it starts.

In the end, we decided to keep the effect on our PINGs and have Zofia remove them from the ones we provided the army. It was just too dangerous to hand out to just anyone. Zofia walked down the line of crates running her hand over the sealed containers as she went. When she got back to us, she announced, "There, it's done."

"You took that part out of every one of them?" Kalli asked. "There must be thousands of them."

Zofia shrugged, looking smug. "There's seven hundred ninety-five. I just disabled the setting. Nobody will be able to make them use the ray except me. Well, unless you find another magically awakened technician, but then they wouldn't need my PING. They could just make their own."

The next setting Zofia showed off was called BANG (Big Angry

Negative-Resistance Gun). She took us outside the camp and pointed her PING at a nearby rock. The PING buzzed as it seemed to charge up before emitting what looked like a bolt of lightning. The attack was rather lackluster when it hit, fizzing out against the stone with little more than a burn mark as evidence of a hit.

Zofia smiled and said, "That attack uses a lot of mana, so you need to make sure any PINGs assigned to use it don't miss."

"But it didn't do anything," Kalli pointed out wearily.

Zofia smirked. "That, my friends, is because the rock didn't have any electronics inside of it. If you hit a tank or a computer with that setting, you can pretty much make it stop working. The BANG works by reducing the charge in any device to effectively nothing. I originally came up with it as a self-destruct method for a certain computer of mine, but I later found out that it's rather effective against any electronic. And trust me when I say, practically everything from Earth has it now."

To test the BANG, I edited the same rock Zofia shot into a fully functioning computer. To turn it on I had to also create a power bank. Zofia smirked at me when she saw it and asked, "Why did you make it Linux?"

I shrugged. "I didn't. I just called it **Cheap PC (Edited)**, and that's what came out. I guess the System knows what it's doing."

She leveled the PING and fired again. This time we were greeted by a shower of sparks and a clearly non-functional computer. I even tried rebooting to be sure. Both the PC and the power bank didn't work. Satisfied with the results, I **DELETED** both of them.

The final setting was some kind of plasma projectile. Zofia giggled like a schoolgirl when explaining how it worked. "Have you ever set your phasers to stun? While this isn't a continuous beam, it will stun any biological life form, awakened or not. It works by interacting with your nervous system and temporarily stops your body from responding to your brain. I've shot more than a few obnoxious mages with this."

To demonstrate, Zofia wanted to shoot me with it, but I didn't know how I felt about that. In the end, I turned to Kalli. "You do it."

Kalli frowned. She was doing that a lot lately. "Do I have to?"

THE ACCIDENTAL CORRUPTION

"You're the only one I trust to shoot me," I replied, trying to sound brave.

"How adorable," Zofia replied, rolling her eyes.

"All right," Kalli said, leveling the PING at me once again. "Here goes nothing. Don't blame me if this hurts."

An angry red bolt shot out of the PING and reminded me of a blaster from Star Wars. Instead of my head being doused in ice water, my body was instead. I dropped to the ground and started to twitch as Zofia said, "Oh, I probably should have told you to sit down for this. Now, just focus on breathing until you get through it."

I wanted to laugh at her comment but, unfortunately, I couldn't breathe. Whatever the PING did, my body wasn't responding at all. It was like being punched in the solar plexus while underwater. Just when I thought I was going to black out, my body started to react, and I gasped for breath. The rest of me took a bit longer to come around.

Once I finally managed to regain control of my extremities, I stood up. Zofia nodded and tapped her screen. "About forty-five seconds. You appear to have responded just a little faster than anybody else."

"Ugh," I groaned, taking deep breaths that still weren't enough. "I spaced and forgot to see what the effect was."

Kalli saved the day by whispering in my head through MateChat. *I saw it. It's called "stunned."*

Once I was back to myself, Kalli insisted on taking a shot of the stunner herself. I advised against it, but she scrunched up her face and said, *I have to get used to it, too. While I sort of felt it through the connection, I need to be ready for it if one hits me in battle.*

But nobody is going to shoot at you.

She shoved her PING in my hands. *What if Rasputin or one of his cronies get their hands on one?*

In the end, I shot my girlfriend…again. It was agony watching her writhe on the ground from the pain I'd inflicted. I knew what she was going through because I could feel it. In the end, she got up just a little faster than me. Zofia smiled at her and showed her the timer on the datapad. "One minute eleven seconds."

Kalli cheered before turning to me. "Now, there's just one thing left to do."

"What's that?" I asked, dreading the answer.

Kalli had a grave look on her face when she answered. No sign of the former elation was left on her face. "We have to find Rasputin and kick that son of a kronkey off our planet."

"And rescue your parents," I added.

Kalli nodded, a smile starting to tug at her lips. "Yes! And save my parents."

[53]

I DON'T LIKE THIS. Zofia's agitated voice was even more high-pitched in group chat. *It feels like a violation of my mind.*

Well, don't think naughty thoughts.

Kalli giggled at that particular piece of advice. *Like you're one to talk.*

The plan was to split up and place lookouts in all of the villages. We left Zofia at the TGB camp just in case Rasputin happened to target his fellow Earthlings. There was no point in sacrificing our visitors.

With both Kalliville and Mount Wendy out of commission, there were just eight settlements left in Meltopia counting Celestea. Of those, I felt reasonably certain that New Wrotor and the City Under the Mountain were safe since they were both underground. The city of Celestea could be protected by magic but only if someone from the royal family was there to activate it. While Shiv technically could do it, Kalli and I both agreed to have her stay with Lavender until it was safe to return.

That forced Kalli to stay behind and guard the castle, and she was not happy about it. That left me and the newly trained warriors of the empire to keep our eyes open for signs of an attack. We divided up the PINGs and handed them out to volunteers in each of the four remaining villages. We had no way of knowing whether Rasputin would attack Run Dale, Joefield, Stefania, or Melvin Heights.

Since I was the only one that could teleport, I rotated between the four villages, entering World Editor mode so I could observe the surrounding area from a bird's eye view. Unfortunately, Rasputin and his army were nowhere to be found.

We felt Zofia's nervousness through the group connection. She was so new to group chat that she broadcast everything. After pacing for a while, she thought more to herself than to anyone else, *This is pointless. For all we know, he fled back to Earth after I shot him.*

I knew how she felt. We all did. Waiting for an enemy that might never show up was mind-numbing.

I get it. If you have any better ideas, I'm all ears.

Zofia huffed, holding up a PING and cycling through hundreds of different settings. Her thoughts betrayed her as she revealed many more uses for the gun than she'd shown us. *I have a great idea. Why don't we hunt him down? Waiting for him to attack seems foolish.*

The problem once again was the fact that we had no clue where he was. Suddenly, Esha's voice chimed in, *My Lord, I need to see you in the City Under the Mountain. There has been a development.*

———

"What's wrong?" I asked immediately after exiting the portal.

Esha stood in front of a makeshift throne in the heart of her new city. She was not alone. "My lord, we have urgent news from Dabia. It appears Rasputin has killed the king. He established himself as the new emperor of Dabia and moves to declare war on Meltopia."

I nodded to acknowledge the revelation as I had a silent conversation with Kalli.

So, that's where he went!

Kalli sat on the throne in Celestea. *That's horrible. He's murdered King Thomas.*

But we know where he is. We can go after him now.

Kalli fidgeted with her hair as memories of our fight with Mardella fluttered through her mind. *We can't do this alone. We need help.*

I sighed, realizing how true that was but still rattled after the loss of Maya.

Solitair is no help. Go tell Lavender what's happened and see if she has any advice.

Kalli was on her feet and sprinting immediately. *I'm on it! What are you going to do?*

That was a good question. We were desperately short on allies.

I'll gather any humans I can to sneak into Dabia and see if Orpheus is healthy enough to help out.

Kalli smiled at the mention of Orpheus. Had they bonded since his return to the castle? *Just make sure he's fully recovered before you tell him what's going on.*

When Kalli stepped through the portal, I turned my attention to Esha. "Gather some men. We need humans for this. We're going to sneak into Dabia and deal with Rasputin."

The man who'd been standing beside Esha bowed deeply. "My Lord, save us, and we'll swear fealty to you. The continent will be united under your rule. The people of Dabia stand behind you. Anything you need to get into the castle will be yours. You need but ask. That includes the army if you think it will help. We will fight for you."

I remembered the mage army that Wendy distracted with a storm. "Whatever happened to that company of mages that was with you when I confronted Mardella?"

"My lord?" the man asked, looking at Esha for support. "The trainees under Mardella returned to the high house at the conclusion of the battle where you defeated her. I'm afraid the most we have to offer is the adventurers guild, and even they are giving Rasputin a wide berth."

"I don't blame them," I replied. "Perhaps they will feel differently if I speak to them."

"Are you high level, my Lord?" the man asked, looking hopeful.

I gave him a knowing smile. "Not particularly. However, I am an M, if you know what that means."

His expression softened at the revelation that I was at least a named awakened. "Anything you need, my Lord. Just ask and it will be yours."

I returned his nod. "How about we start with your name? Mine is Melvin Murphy."

He had that blank look on his face that someone gets when they have no clue who you are. "Ahem, I am Sir Harvey Francis, my Lord. Knight of Dabia, defender of the king. Ahem, I was I suppose."

Name: Harvey Francis
Class: Paladin
Level: 38
Affection Level: Loyal

I huffed my comment to Kalli since I didn't want to be rude.
Some job he did of protecting the king.
Kalli chastised me for the poorly timed comment. ***Be nice!***

————

My next stop was the high house, Solitair. I stepped through the door in Maya's bathroom and emerged into her bedroom where two servants knelt by the bed. The scene reminded me of a book I read where a dog never left his master's side after he died suddenly.

Both men looked up when I entered the room, a look of hopefulness passing over their faces before quickly falling when they recognized me. One of the men, the one who'd guided Kalli and me through the house, stood and approached me. "It's you. Do you have news of Lady Maya?"

Looking down at the second servant with his head bowed and eyes squeezed shut, I saw a tear stream down his cheek. The man in front of me waited patiently for an answer, but all I could say was, "You truly love her, don't you?"

He nodded. "Of course. Just as you love the red-haired girl who's always with you, I will be loyal to Maya until the day I die. Please tell me what happened to her. I need to know."

I nodded, inspecting the man to see if my assumption was correct.

Name: Rumierre Beaumont
Class: Paige
Level: 3
Affection Level: Defeated

"I do know where she is," I replied quietly, trying not to arouse the attention of the other man. his head shot up and the next thing I knew, both men stood in front of me at rapt attention. "Perhaps it would be best to just take you to her."

Rumierre perked up. "Do you mean to tell us that she's alive and you know where she is?"

I nodded emphatically. He took my hand in his and said, "I don't care what the cost or if it means my life. You must take me to her!"

"Very well," I replied. "Does your friend want to go?"

The other man also nodded. "Yes. I too would give my life for her."

With nothing left to say, I instructed them to hold onto me. While Rumierre took my hand, the other man grabbed me from behind and held on for dear life as I struggled to push our essences into the ring. The three of us appeared in the ring in front of the hall leading to the cells.

"Melvin, Is that you?" Maya called from the darkness.

"Master!" Rumierre cried, practically throwing himself into the cell with the other man hot on his heels.

An echoed grunt came from the room as one of the men threw himself at my sister. I decided to give them a minute and walked over to the second cell to check on Nir Vana. "Good afternoon, Nir. How are you today?"

"What do you care?" she replied in a dull voice. "I get the feeling you did not return to free me. While I still hold out hope that you will make another mistake at some point, something tells me I am the last of the prisoners you ever intend to release intentionally. That is with the exception of the one in the last cell who you incarcerated personally."

"I'm thinking about it," I admitted. "The problem is, you're dangerous."

She pressed her face against the tiny opening in her cell door. "What must I do to convince you that I'm not a threat? I'd be willing to do almost anything to get out of here. Even suffer reincarnation the normal way."

While I wanted to help, I didn't really know how I was going to pull it off in the first place. Bodies didn't just grow on trees. Unless... "Are you willing to submit to a contract on your core where you'll die instantly if you use your magic on a sentient person?"

A whispered reply slipped from her lips. "As I said, anything, even my death is acceptable if it means freedom from this place."

"Are you sure you don't mind dying? You won't hold it against me?" I asked the second question, feeling like a monster for what I had in mind.

"Death would be a release," she hissed.

"Give me a second," I whispered, walking slowly toward Maya's cell, hoping I wasn't about to walk in on something awkward.

While the trio was hugging and at least one of them was openly sobbing, they all had their clothes on so that was good. I cleared my throat to get their attention. "I might have an idea or two."

Maya raised an eyebrow, pushing the two men off her so she could make her way over to me. "What do you have in mind?"

"Well, it's two ideas really," I said, steeling myself for judgment and happy Kalli couldn't hear while I was in the ring. "The first one involves me creating a body. The second is a bit creepier, but I think I can use the ring on an animal. I'd let you choose what you want to be, but we could capture something, and I'll trap its soul in here and release you into its body."

"There is no way I'm letting you turn Maya into a Ruffalo." Rumierre scoffed, placing himself between me and Maya. "That is just barbaric!"

THE ACCIDENTAL CORRUPTION

"Now, now, lover," Maya soothed, brushing the man aside. "This is my brother you're speaking to. Besides, if there is any hope of me holding onto life, it will come from him."

"Do you mean to entertain this heresy?" the man sitting on the bed asked. "I don't know that I could love a raquirrel."

"Come now, my pets," Maya said with a playful smile. "Those aren't the only animals on Gaia. Perhaps a lovely ottercock, or a porcusaurus."

"Don't joke, my Lady," the man on the bed begged. "I believe your brother is seriously considering this."

"I assure you he is," Maya countered, shooting him a savage look. "I would be disappointed if he wasn't thinking of ways to get me out of here."

"Take my body," Rumierre said quietly, causing Maya to gasp. "I am nothing without you. If my flesh can please you one final time, I will gladly spend eternity in this prison."

Maya took his hands in hers. "I could never ask you to do such a thing."

Rumierre shook his head. "And you will never have to. I am offering myself, both my body and soul."

I stepped outside again as the two of them started to make out. Having made up my mind, I returned to Nir. "Are you sure you want to try this? I'm sure you overheard what I have in mind. You'll be the test subject to see if it works. I can't promise you won't die."

Nir's laugh was both melodic and terrifying at the same time. "I remember not when last I was free. Releasing my soul will grant me the freedom I've been longing. In other words, I am giving you my consent to do what is necessary."

"Give me a few minutes," I replied, returning to Maya's cell. "I am going to lock the three of you in here to test something."

Seeing the three of them entwined on the tiny bed made me add a cold shower to the list of things I needed to do when I got home. With a click that echoed down the hall, I sealed Maya and her servants in her cell and left the ring.

[54]

THE TWO MEN stood frozen in front of me as though they were statues. I vaguely wondered how long they would stay like that before the magic released them.

I fished a pebble out of my bag and tossed it on the bed.

Well, here goes.

Kalli, alerted to the fact that I was back, jumped into my head with questions. *Here goes what? Where did you go? What's happening?*

I visited Maya in the soul ring. I'm going to try to make her a body.

Apprehension flooded the connection telling me Kalli didn't like that idea at all. *Are you sure about this? Isn't that dangerously close to necromancy?*

It beats the alternative. I'd rather not steal a body if I can help it. Even if I think they deserve it, I don't want to bring my sister back in Rasputin's body.

She tried to talk to me while engaged in conversation with Lavender and someone else I didn't recognize. It was fairly obvious that her attention was mostly directed elsewhere. *Okay, I trust you, Mel. Just try not to do anything too evil.*

Looking back at the frozen bodies of Maya's manservants, I had a good point of reference for what a lifeless body should look like. The question was, what to call it in the System?

I tried something basic. Lifeless Body (Edited). The result was completely random. The husk of an animal I didn't recognize appeared on the floor in front of me. Trying again, I was a bit more specific. Lifeless Human Body (Edited). The first thing I noticed was that the body had an unwanted appendage. Also, it wasn't wearing clothes. The clothing thing I wasn't too worried about since I was sure Maya had outfits handy nearby. The next attempt was Lifeless Female Human Body (Edited). The third body was technically correct, but it was hideous and very old. While it was Nir I was making the body for, I was forbidding her from using her forced reincarnation skill, so it wouldn't be very nice to deprive her of a long life. Lifeless Decent-Looking Young Female Human Body (Edited). The result cracked me up, and I decided to go with it. There was just one final thing to do before attempting to free Nir Vana.

———

Back in the ring, I nervously approached her cell. "Hey, Nir. I might have a solution, but we need to talk first."

"What's it to be? Did you find a snake to put me into?" Her voice dripped with venom as she joked about her fate.

"Not exactly," I replied, rethinking things. "The body is human. I made it myself."

"Reeally…" She drew out the word, and I heard her footsteps as she returned to the window slit. "So, what did you wish to speak to me about?"

"We need to impose a contract so you won't abuse what I am about to do for you," I replied. "But I need some kind of assurance that you won't attack me the moment I open this door."

She heaved a sigh, her hands clutching the bars that lined the slit. "You truly know nothing about this place, do you? So long as you wear the ring, you are the master of this domain and everyone trapped in it. None can harm you and you control our every movement. Should you wish to torture me, you'd only have to envision it in your mind. Go ahead, try it. I can take it. Hey, where are you going..."

Her cries went unanswered as I had already made my way back to Maya's cell. I knocked, but there was no answer. Then I made the mistake of poking my head in the door to get her attention. "Maya, I need you... Whoa, sorry, I thought you were done. Never mind that. I mean, really, both of them at once? Gah, I really need that cold shower."

Maya emerged five minutes later by herself. Both of her servants were either too spent to get up or she told them to stay in bed. She tugged a robe over her shoulder and sighed contentedly. "Ah, I needed that. It's been so long and the stress from being trapped here was stifling. You know how it is. Do you think it's possible to get knocked up without a body?"

"I hope not," I replied, trying not to unsee what I'd already seen. "Anyhow, forget about that. I need to try something on you."

"Oh, my," she said, clutching her hands to her chest. "We mustn't. You're my brother. I mean, sort of."

I groaned, feeling the heat rise to my face. "That's not what I meant, and you know it. I need to try subduing you. Do you mind?"

Maya swooned even more, clearly enjoying my discomfort. "Brother! I didn't know you had it in you. You can tie me up or do whatever you like to me. Seriously, though, you just did me a huge favor. You can test whatever magic you need to even if it hurts."

Trying not to think about the naughty things Maya was implying, I started with a simple command. I spoke the words out loud as well, just in case the dungeon couldn't hear mental commands. "Get back in your cell!"

As if dragged by an invisible chain, Maya was dragged back to her cell. I continued, "Lock the door."

CLICK!

I let her out again and said, "Now, attack me."

"Do you want me to try and hit you?" she asked, raising her fists experimentally.

"No, use magic," I replied, bracing myself in case the magic failed. "Try to hurt me."

"Can I use magic in here?" she asked, seeming to direct the question at herself more so than to me. When her hand began to shimmer, she added, "Oh, wow, I swear I tried to do magic when I first got here, and it didn't work. Do you think it does now because you said I can?"

I nodded. "Now, try to hurt me."

While she still looked unsure, Maya pointed her hand at me, palm out. While the hand began to shimmer, the mist that came out of it stopped dead a couple of feet in front of me and fizzled out. She closed her palms and smiled. "It looks like there's a barrier around you. My magic isn't working."

"Are you sure?" I asked, still not convinced. Nir was likely much stronger than Maya. "I'm about to let Nir Vana out of her cell, and I'm going to have to touch her to put a contract on her. She says she can't hurt me, but I'm not sure I trust her yet."

I jumped when Maya placed a hand on my chest. "Brace yourself."

Then her hand began to shimmer. Suddenly, her whole body shuddered as the spell seemed to feed back on itself and reverberate within her body. She choked and spluttered as she fell back and landed on her backside. I rushed to her side only to find her laughing. "Well, I guess that answers that. I can't even hurt you with a sneak attack. My spell just backfired, and it never does that."

"Are you okay?" I asked, worried she'd caused damage to her core. "I can try to heal you if you'd…"

She held up a hand and laughed. "I'll be fine. If anything, I'll just have Rumierre massage it out for me."

"Good," I replied, helping Maya up and frogmarching her back to her cell. "Because I'm going to lock you up in here while I deal with Nir. Even though she can't hurt me, that doesn't mean you're immune to her magic. I'd feel better if you're in your cell where she can't hold you hostage."

Once the lock clicked shut, I returned to Nir Vana one more. Her beady eyes followed me as I approached the door. "Are you finally prepared to meet me, warden?"

Ignoring the obvious snark, I nodded and said, "Even though what you say seems to be true, I'm still concerned that you're going to try to pull a fast one. However, there's no way around it, if I want to do this, I'm going to have to deal with you directly. So, I guess what I'm saying is, come on out."

CLICK!

I waited patiently while she slowly pushed the door open and stepped into the hall. She seemed much smaller than she had in the cell. She wasn't short or anything, just very fragile like a porcelain vase. "You must believe me when I say I only wish for my freedom. I am willing to pay any price to get out of this place. Even at the expense of becoming mortal for a while."

"For a while?" I asked, wondering if she was already up to something.

Nir tried to hide her laugh. "Even you cannot live forever, young Lord of the Ring. Eventually, you'll pass on or be reincarnated and our deal with be concluded. Additionally, I won't remember our pact after I die. Such is the way of being reborn."

"I need to place a contract on your core," I began, thinking of the deal I made with Zofia. "You will need to swear to do no evil and to never use your unique skill on a sentient being. Also, I'd like you to—"

"There's more?" she asked, raising an eyebrow. "While I'm willing to do almost anything for this, you do plan on being reasonable, right?"

"Well, you see, there's this man who is threatening the world I'm on at the moment and you're very powerful…" I trailed off, choosing my words carefully. "I would like you to help in the battle I'm about to have with him."

She frowned, shaking her head. "My dear boy, I am no fighter. My techniques are largely experimental and very self-serving. Outside of various techniques to prolong my life and enrich my core, I never had much use for fighting. I've always found the best way to deal with foes is to appear weak and attack my enemies when their guard is down."

"Can you teach me any tricks?" I asked, growing exasperated. "Anything I can use to stay alive when I fight Rasputin?"

Nir stopped to ponder my request for a moment before replying,

"The good news is I've never heard of that name. That means he can't be too powerful because he's still a baby. Can you tell me anything about his class or the techniques he used against you?"

"He did something to Maya's core," I replied, trying to remember exactly how soulmancers worked their magic. "He touched her and her core began to disintegrate."

"Well, that's not good," She said, rubbing her chin thoughtfully. "You're core is what defines who you are. If you take that out, no amount of healing done to the body will save you. If the core is damaged too greatly, there is a strong possibility that reincarnation might not even be possible. Is it possible to run away? Perhaps that is the wiser choice in this situation."

Every fiber in my being wanted to run away. The problem with bullies was that running away from them only seemed to embolden them. "No, if we don't do something, he will take over all of Gaia."

"Has it ever occurred to you that if Gaia can't stand without the help of a child, then perhaps it should perish?" Nir asked.

It was a good question. Why was I risking my life, and more importantly Kalli's, just to save a bunch of people I didn't know well? We could flee back to Earth, and if we hid at Lavender's, there was little chance of him finding us. Even if he did, Lavender would be forced to deal with him before he got to us. The problem was, Kalli would never go for a plan like that.

Sensing my turmoil, Nir placed a hand on my shoulder. "How about this? I'll teach you a nifty trick to guard against invasive magic. Would that satisfy you enough to free me?"

———

A few hours later, I was finally ready to perform the editing. Or was it a ritual? A strongly worded contract bound Nir's core, and we practiced magic for the better part of an hour. All that was left was for me to plant her in a body. A fake body.

I took a deep breath and placed my hand on the body I'd created and organized my mana. Rather than pulling mana from my target into the ring, I focused my attention on the inhabitants of the ring that I was starting to feel. I then commanded the ring, "Produce Nir Vana's soul for this body."

The ring obeyed. A powerful essence passed from the ring into the vessel I'd prepared. The body beside me lurched and sucked in a large breath. Red eyes opened and blinked a few times. She took a few moments to examine herself before glaring at me, "What is the meaning of this?"

[55]

"WHAT'S THE MEANING OF THIS?" Nir Vana barked in a comically high-pitched voice. "Has the world changed so much that nobody bats an eye when a child wanders the land?"

I shrugged. "You said you wanted a body. You didn't specify…"

"This is practically a baby!" she growled, sounding cuter than ever.

I patted her on the head playfully, earning a glare for my efforts. "You are clearly not a baby. If I had to guess, I'd say you're about five years old. At least you're potty trained, right?"

"Potty training is a mental thing," she informed me. "Even if I was a toddler I could make sure to control my faculties until I could be placed on a proper commode."

"Well, you're not a toddler," I continued to debate. "And I can assure you, you're only going to get older. Now, let's stop arguing about age and tell me how the body feels."

Nir stopped in her tracks and looked down to examine herself. I looked away as she was still naked. While I was positive Maya had clothing, she probably didn't have anything that would fit a child. I marched over to the bed and ripped the blanket off, tossing it at her.

She cried out as the blanket hit her in the face. "Does this body make you uncomfortable? Well, good. I'm not exactly thrilled about it either. But, as you said, I suppose I'll get used to it as I age into it. At least you managed a female one. I've been male before, and I prefer female."

Once she managed to cover up, I asked, "Does everything feel normal? Will it work, or do you need me to put you back in the ring?"

Nir waved her arms around for a few minutes before giving me a nod and a thumbs up. "This will do. I would have preferred a fully mature body. The gods know I don't want to go through puberty again but, as I said, anything beats being trapped in that infernal ring. Do you happen to know where they keep the food around here? This body requires sustenance."

"Right, food," I nodded absentmindedly. "Give me a few minutes to free Maya, and she can help you get something to eat. Clothes too probably."

Nir jumped up on the bed and curled up in the blanket. Rather than sleeping, she propped herself up, resting on her elbows and staring intently at me. "That is going to be amusing, watching you make a body."

Trying my best to ignore the audience, I got to work.

Maya's Body (Edited)

The first try had caramel skin and curly black hair. She was younger than Maya had been and not as well-endowed. Nir perked up when she saw it. "If your sister doesn't want that one, I'll take it."

"What happened to being grateful I let you out?" I asked, pretending to be annoyed.

"I am," she confessed. "But isn't that proof that you could have made me a better body?"

I shrugged and got back to work without replying.

Middle-aged Platinum-Blonde Well-Endowed Woman (Edited)

Once again, it worked, but she was ugly. Perhaps not to everyone, but she clearly wasn't as good-looking as my sister had been. I decided to scrap it and try again.

Unbelievably Hot Middle-Aged Platinum-Blonde Well-Endowed Woman (Edited)

I was only satisfied when I started to realize that if I made her any better looking, I might have to worry about being attracted to my sister. Casting one last glance at Nir, I said, "Here goes nothing."

Nir stared at the newly created body. "Why didn't you make me one like that?"

I shrugged and placed my hand on its chest, careful not to touch anything inappropriate. Nir snickered as she watched me work. I steeled myself and spoke in a firm voice while I entrusted mana to the ring, "Produce my sister, Maya. I command you to release her."

Just as before, the body below me lurched as it drew its first breath. Maya sat up with a start and looked around the bedroom, and then down at herself. "Uh, why am I naked?"

I shrugged. "Sorry, the bodies don't come with clothes, apparently. I guess I could have created some, but getting you mildly hot enough was hard."

Maya gasped, looking down at her exposed breasts again. "My little brother is a deviant. I never would have guessed."

Before I could answer, she hopped to her feet and skipped off to a room in the corner that had been obscured by a vanity screen. Nir climbed off the bed and followed Maya over to the door. "Do you have anything fit for a child in there?"

"A child?" Maya asked, sounding confused. Then Nir disappeared into the closet after her. "Oh, I see. Well, aren't you just adorable?"

"That's the last thing this body is," Nir grumbled from just out of sight. "I want to hide in a cave and get older in peace. I absolutely despise children."

"Oh, don't worry about it," Maya chided the girl. "You're alive, and you should be grateful. I'll get you some clothes soon. You can stay here in the high house. We have an excellent…"

"You had better not say school," Nir roared, her voice filled with indignation. "The last thing I need is some pompous teacher who is centuries younger than me telling me how the universe works. Though I must admit, I could use a history lesson for the last millennia or so."

"Fine, no school," Maya conceded, stepping out of the closet wearing a dress that was several times too tight. "It would appear, dear brother, that you've made me a bit more top-heavy than I am accustomed to. I see you had some fun creating this body. I'm certainly going to enjoy breaking it in tonight."

Suddenly, her eyes widened. Maya ran back behind the vanity curtain and gasped. "Wow, that's something I haven't seen in quite some time. It would appear you've returned my innocence. I suppose I will just have to have Rumierre break this body in... Oh, wait, when are you going to release them? They must be worried."

"Oh, right," I said, having completely forgotten about the men who were currently serving as statues in the middle of the room. I focused on their souls trapped in the ring and said, "The two of you can return to your bodies now."

Suddenly the men gasped and lurched as though someone had pressed play on a paused video. A look of panic crossed Rumierre's face when he noticed the two strange women in the room. "Is that you, mistress? Please let that be you."

Maya gave a contented sigh as Nir pouted in the corner. "Yes, it's me, my pet. I am going to do things differently this time. For starters, I think I am ready to start a family."

"Get a room," Nir groaned, looking nauseated at the display of affection when Maya fell into Rumierre's arms.

"This is my room," Maya informed her. "Speaking of which, we are going to have to arrange accommodations for you. That cave you requested can be made available to you. There are many fine ones here on Gaia. Alternatively, I'd be happy to host you here in my home or elsewhere in Solitair. I am also sure Melvin can also find a place for you in Celestea. Melvin, do you have an opinion?"

"Not really," I replied, shaking my head. "So long as you abide by our agreement, you are free to live where you want. I'd be more than happy to put you up in the castle if that's what you'd like."

Nir cast another disgusted look at her body and shook her head. "Unfortunately, what I want isn't an option. This body is too young for independence. Even with my power, I would still be at a disadvantage on my own."

"Is it the age thing?" I asked, second-guessing myself. "I suppose I can fix that if it's really that much of a problem."

Nir sat on the floor to think for a moment. Maya and the two servants waited in silence while she deliberated. She came to a decision and crossed her arms over her chest. "I think I'd rather be an adult. Living an extra fifteen years is hardly worth the horror of going through puberty again. Besides, there are things I'd like to do, and none of them are suitable for children."

"All right," I replied, cracking my knuckles. "I have to warn you, though. I've never done this before, so I'm not sure what's going to happen."

Nir braced her hands on her knees and scrunched up her face in concentration. "Okay. I think I'm ready. Go for it."

It took a while to find the menu I was looking for.

Vital Statistics
Gender: Female
Identity: Neutral
Age: 6
Weight: 47 lbs
Height: 45 inches

I wondered if I was going to have to change all of the categories, or if aging her up would change her weight and height. Having no clue what was about to happen, I edited her age up to ten. The girl screamed as her body began to stretch like taffy. The problem was that it wasn't designed to grow so quickly. Stretch marks appeared on her arms and legs and bruises popped up everywhere as her body took damage from what appeared to be ruptured blood vessels and other internal damage.

She bit her lip and looked at me through watering eyes. "Stop! No more. I can't take it."

I thought about putting her age back where it started but ultimately decided that a shrinking body might be more dangerous than a growing one. There only appeared to be one other option. "Let me put you back in the ring while I make you a new body."

Nir was still doubled over in pain as she raised one eyebrow. "Do you mean it? Please, don't leave me in there."

"You have my word," I promised, walking over to free her from the failed body.

Once she was safely back in the ring, I looked at my wrecked creation. "It's a good thing I didn't try this on anyone's real body."

DELETE

Maya gaped at me as her two servants cowered behind her. "That class of yours is terrifying. Why don't you do that to Rasputin?"

"It only works on people lower level than me, and…" I trailed off as I remembered Nir Vana was higher level than me. Having a thought, I inspected Maya.

Name: Maya Xander Halifax
Class: Shimmer Mage
Level: 1 (152)
Affection Level: Sisterly Affection

"Hey!" I exclaimed. "I can see your level now. It used to be hidden. I think that's because you're over a hundred levels above me. Now you're level one."

Maya frowned, looking down at her body with renewed interest. "I don't feel any different."

"Try using magic," I offered. "Tell me how it feels."

Maya held out a hand and a look of concentration passed over her face. Her little finger appeared to shimmer for a brief second. When I looked up, I noticed Maya was sweating profusely and already out of breath. After trying to work her magic for a few more seconds, she let her hand fall and sighed. "Yep, definitely level one. I guess I'm going to have to level up again. Oh, well, it beats being dead or trapped in that ring. Don't worry about it, Melvin."

Her expression changed when she saw the worry on my face. Trying to hide my anxiety, I returned my focus to making a new body for Nir. I resumed the editing process, hoping to make something the old reincarnation expert would be happy to live in for a while.

Young-Adult mid-height full-figured moderately-good-looking woman with curly-brown hair (Edited)

While I did want her to be happy, I didn't want her to look better than my sister. I was choosing favorites after all. Part of me was thankful I didn't have to do this for Kalli. There was no way I'd ever be able to make her a body more perfect than the original. I wondered if Rumierre felt that way about Maya.

Once the body was done, all that was left was to bring Nir back. She only gasped a little when she inhabited the body, a reaction I was becoming accustomed to. Rising to her feet, she marched over to Maya and accepted the robe my sister offered. Then, after doing a full inspection of her new body, she smiled. "This will do nicely. Thank you, Melvin. I am forever in your debt."

[56]

WHILE MY GRAND plan to release Maya and Nir to help in the fight with Rasputin may have been in vain, the two of them were able to help me prepare for the upcoming battle. Nir taught me several techniques to evade touch-based magic.

"Got your soul," she chirped, running a finger up my spine as she slipped behind me. "It can happen that quick. For those of us who require physical contact, a simple touch is all it takes. I don't even need to make contact with your skin. My magic can go through clothes, and even some armor."

"What about artifact armor?" I asked, feeding the artifact that was currently encircled around my arm. As if awakening from a deep sleep, the armor liquified and flowed over my body until I was once again encased in a pitch-black metallic shell.

Nir walked up to me and rested her hand against the coarse artifact. Her face scrunched up in concentration for a moment and her hand started to smoke. Yelping, she quickly pulled it away, revealing angry red skin where she'd made contact. "Okay, that hurt. I can't speak for every mage but your armor effectively blocks my magic. You'll need to cover all exposed skin with it for it to be effective."

Maya had kicked us out of her bed chamber to a sitting room

before Nir started to teach me. Even with the door closed, it was pretty obvious that she was breaking in her new body with her two servants. Her hair was disheveled when she finally emerged. "Wow, I'd forgotten how sore things can get. It's going to take me a while to get the hang of this body."

Nir smirked at her. "You're up. Do you have anything to teach the boy?"

Maya frowned. "I wish I could go with you. Unfortunately, I'll hardly be of any use at my current level. I have no stamina and even less health."

I tried to remember what I knew about level editing. "I think I can raise your level up to half of mine. It won't be what it used to be but at least it will be something, right?"

Half of my level turned out to be level twenty-one. Both Maya and Nir flexed and shimmered as they acclimated to the influx of power that the additional twenty levels provided. Maya reported her findings first. "It feels superficial, but there's definitely an improvement over being level one."

"I was told doing it this way is cheating," I admitted reluctantly. "I used to modify my wand that way to make it more powerful."

"I've never seen you use a wand before," Maya replied, laughing.

I shrugged and fished around in my bag for Kalli's old wand. "The truth is, I always forget to use it. I'm still new to this whole magic thing. Kalli is better about using hers, but ever since I taught her how to do it without the wand, she's been using it less. She has been using that pendant artifact a lot lately, though. That's how she makes green fire."

Maya said, "I vaguely recall her using green fire. However, I was a little distracted on account of the fact that I was dying and all at the time."

"Never mind that for now," I said, trying to get back on track. "I need all the help I can get against Rasputin. Do you have any ideas?"

Maya looked thoughtful for a moment before replying, "Well, it's become rather clear that my so-called friends aren't going to be of any use. We could try asking around, but I am sure you'll just get more of the same. Gaia is a peaceful world, with Mardella being the exception. I don't suppose you can get her mother to help you out?"

The thought of Mardella reminded me that she was still in the ring. "Mardella was quiet today. Did something happen to her recently?"

Nir laughed. "The same thing that happens to all of us. The futility of being stuck in the ring got to her mind. Worry not. She should come out of it in a few centuries or so. I recommend against releasing her in this state. She will likely be insane for the foreseeable future."

Maya placed a hand on my shoulder. "Forget about her for now. Even if you release her, she will just be level one like us. I have an idea. I want you to touch my core. Do it as many times as it takes to collect my bloodlines. If I'm not mistaken, Rasputin is stacking M bloodlines to make himself more powerful. You're going to need all the help you can get if you are to face him."

"You said something about that before you died," I recalled. "You called him a slayer or something. You also said the other Ms here in Solitair would team up to defeat him. Is that an option? I'd love to meet some more of my brothers and sisters. Can we ask them?"

Maya frowned as she looked out a nearby window that showed a clear view of the sea thrashing about below. "I did promise to report back to them about the threat. Of course, it's probably a safe bet that one of the others already did so. They were no help personally, but Marisa, at the very least, is a huge gossip. The problem is going to be convincing them that I am still the same person in a new body."

"Can none of them identify you?" I asked since I'd figured all Ms had at least that ability.

Maya nodded with a smile. "That is very true. However, I am going to have to explain how this new body comes with a substantially lowered and edited level. At the very least, they aren't going to take me as seriously as they used to. You, too, for that matter. This is a problem you will likely continue to have until you reach at least level one hundred."

Leaving Nir and the servants behind, the two of us set out for a quick trip around the volcano in one of the tubes. It was fortunate that the magic recognized Maya's core because she had access to certain areas of the high house that I didn't. After a short hop through the tubes, we arrived at an amphitheater suspended above the cone of the volcano. The vast arena was populated with only a scattering of people. Maya's expression fell as she took in the scene. Approaching a nearby seated man, she asked, "Rubigeld, where is everyone?"

The man jumped when he saw Maya. "W-who are you?"

Maya muttered a curse and replied, "It's me, Maya. I got a new body. It's a long story. Never mind about that right now. I need to know where everyone went, particularly the Ms."

"They fled, m'lady," the man replied, clearly shaken. "Everyone who could secure transport off world left. News of your death started a panic."

"Cowards," Maya spat, turning her attention to me. "Did I mention I'm surrounded by worthless cowards who treat this planet like a vacation resort?"

"Why would they run?" I asked. "Surely, twenty Ms could deal with Rasputin, no problem."

"It's not that simple," Maya explained. "Even if they had overwhelming force, and I'm not sure they did, there was no guarantee that none of them would die. Especially considering Rasputin seems to have brought an army from Earth. What if he has awakened of his own that we haven't seen yet? No, the glorious high house of Gaia lives by the motto of running away and living to fight another day. I'm afraid these people are going to be of no use to you."

"That's fine," I sighed, already used to the adults in my world being useless when it came to dealing with problems. "Didn't you say something about your bloodlines?"

Maya nodded, tugging me away from Rubigeld, only talking when she was sure we were alone. "It's never a good idea to show off your abilities. The fewer people who know about us, the better. Even though Rubi might be harmless, there's no telling who he might tell if you let something slip. Let's go back to my house, and you can probe my core to your heart's content. It's the least I can do since you brought me back to life in such a lovely body."

We traveled most of the way to the house in silence with Maya only occasionally grumbling about the others being cowards for running away. When we arrived, she spent a long time talking to the servants lined up in front of her house. Apparently, Rumierre called them and informed them that the master was back. She had tears in her eyes when we made it into the house.

"Do you need a moment?" I asked as she settled onto a comfortable-looking couch.

Maya patted the spot next to her and shook her head. "No, it's fine. You're going to be doing all of the work anyway. Sorry you had to see that back there. I know it's weird, but I truly love all of them. My servants are my family."

"You should probably make preparations to evacuate," I said softly. "Just in case I don't defeat Rasputin. He will come for you next if I die."

"You aren't going to die," she said, giving me a fierce look. "There's something special about you that even the other Ms don't have. Besides, you saw his trump card when he defeated me. Men like that are usually one trick kronkeys."

"What is a kronkey?" I asked, chuckling at the strange-sounding name.

"Well it's a..." she began laughing as she spoke. "Well, you'd have to see one to understand. Don't worry about that. Focus on beating Rasputin. Come on, absorb my bloodlines."

"Where did you acquire them?" I asked, taking her hand in mine and beginning the process.

Maya stiffened at the question. I could feel it even though my mind was focused inside of her at the moment. "I was more than a little promiscuous in my youth. When I found out I had the ability to gain skills and traits through coupling with men, I went after some rather prominent ones. You wouldn't believe the pompous aristocrats I had to bed to manage two bloodlines. The Xander line I picked up from my first husband, but the Brent line was a stroke of luck from a one-night stand."

"Do you know what they do?" I asked, thinking about what I knew about my bloodlines. While it was fairly obvious what the Shaw bloodline did, I didn't know much about Ramsey and next to nothing about Celestea. When I touched her core, I didn't manage to get a bloodline, so I **DELETED** the skill and started again.

Maya grinned and replied, "Of course, dear brother. That's the benefit of being intimate with people you snag abilities from. Pillow talk! It also helps that I've had them for a while."

"What do they do?" I asked, eager to learn about them.

Maya laughed. "Geez! Have a little patience, why don't you? I obtained the Brent bloodline first when I was about your age. The boy I got it from was somewhat of a hooligan. The Brent family are known thieves and rogues. He used to sneak into the girls' dorms all the time, and nobody could figure out how he did it. We wouldn't have even known he was there if he didn't brag about it."

"So, it makes him sneaky?" I asked, **DELETING** another useless trait.

She pulled away from me, breaking the physical link between us. "You'll have to see it to believe it."

Then Maya vanished. I reached out to touch her again, but she was gone. "Maya? Are you still there?"

Distant laughter echoed throughout the room, followed by Maya's voice coming from everywhere and nowhere all at once. "It's a little bit sneaky, a little bit invisible, and a whole lot of magic. It's not infallible, but it's great when you need to sneak around or mess with someone's mind. The problem is, certain people can see through it, and then you're in trouble because you won't know until it's too late."

"But I can't see you," I replied. "And I thought the M bloodline was one of the best."

"That it is," she replied. "However, our family is not infallible. As you can see with this bloodline, there are certain things that are beyond us."

"What about Xander?" I asked.

"Ah, yes," she continued the explanation, appearing in front of me. "I married that man for a reason. The Xander line gives the power of persuasion. While it may not work against Rasputin, you should find it useful against his army. Men like him tend to manipulate the unawakened to do their bidding. Sometimes, a simple speech is all it takes to turn the tides of battle."

"I don't know," I muttered. "I'm not sure I can talk my way out of this one."

Maya grabbed me by the collar and looked me in the eyes. "You won't know that until you try. Have a little confidence!"

And just like that, I felt a surge of confidence.

[57]

CATCH ME IF YOU CAN.

I couldn't help but laugh out loud as I became invisible and tried to sneak up on Kalli. To my surprise, she turned and tackled me. *Give it up. There's nothing you can do that I won't see. We're bound together whether you like it or not.*

The moment she touched me, I lost my concentration and appeared in her arms.

Can you become invisible, too?

Kalli scrunched up her nose and squeezed her eyes shut in concentration. Her face grew redder and redder as I watched in amusement. Finally, she let out a deep breath and opened them. *I don't get it. I tried to do it the same way you did, and nothing happened.*

It was true, I felt her go through the same motions I did. To investigate, I decided to pull up her menu.

Name: Kalliphae Murphy (Edited)
Class: Pyromancer
Level: 37
Affection Level: Indifferent

Skills: Boost Magic, Amplify, Silent Cast, Mirage

Traits: Bloodline: M, Bloodline: Celestea, Enhancement: Fire, Fireproof, Heatproof, Magical Plague Immunity (Edited), MateChat [Melvin Murphy] (Edited), Inseparable [Melvin Murphy], Intertwined [Melvin Murphy], Till Death Do You Part [Melvin Murphy]

Seeing the indifferent affection level made me smile as I remembered that Lavender shielded it from me because she loved me from the beginning. Scrolling through her traits, I noticed the problem right away.

You only have the M and Celestea bloodlines.

Kalli leaned on my shoulder as she took in the menu hanging in the air in front of me. *That is strange. Let's see yours.*

Nodding, I pulled up my status.

Name: Melvin Murphy
Class: Manipulator (Unlocked)
Level: 43
Hit Points: 4,300
Mana: 51,700
Stamina: 4,300
Strength: 25
Dexterity: 25
Agility: 25
Constitution: 50
Intelligence: 85
Wisdom: 30
Charisma: 10
Luck: 20

Skills: World Editor, Manipulation, Controlling Voice, Buff (Edited), Summon (Edited), Command Attention, Formulate, Cloud Judgement, Assimilate Technology, Dark Proclamation.

Traits: Bloodline: M, Bloodline: Shaw, Bloodline: Celestea, Bloodline: Xander, Bloodline: Brent, Enhanced Regeneration, Enhanced Mana Regeneration, Absorption, Control, Shimmer, God Eye (Edited), Perfect Pitch, Mantis Style, Track Scent, Magical Plague Immunity (Edited), MateChat [Kalliphae Murphy] (Edited), Inseparable [Kalliphae Murphy], Inter-twined[Kalliphae Murphy], Till Death Do You Part[Kalliphae Murphy], Praevericator Universum, Catlike Dexterity

The first thing that came to mind was that my traits and abilities were a mess once again. While Kiki had straightened me out once, I just kept right on absorbing new abilities and not paying any attention to the menu.

Kalli said something that made me decide to take a hard look at my skills and traits, **Do you think any of those skills might help you defeat Rasputin?**

The question was, did I even know how they all worked? Focusing on each skill, I soon realized the information was there inside of my head. I just had to draw on it. For the most part, I knew what my skills did and how to use them. Since bloodlines were exempt from skill fatigue, they were safe from the purge. Next up were my regeneration traits. Losing them felt like a major loss, so I decided to keep them. Additionally, they were both traits I was born with or, at the very least, awakened with.

God Eye was a trait that I'd deleted another for. It allowed me to both see in the dark as well as through rather murky places. I was hesitant to delete it, considering I didn't know if I'd need glasses or something without it.

The first skill I decided I could do without was Perfect Pitch. While it was a memento from Stephanie and singing was fun, it just didn't serve a functional use in my everyday life.

DELETE

After that was control. It was the skill I'd gotten as a pair along with Controlling Voice. Again, both were skills I'd never used. Kalli saw I was hesitating and offered some advice, **It reminds me of the** *turn-based skill from the PING. You've never used it before, so I think we can delete them both for now. You can always add them back later if you need them.*

DELETE

DELETE

Absorption was easy enough to keep. I had a feeling that was how my siblings and I got skills from other people. Unless it was part of the M bloodline, but there was no way of knowing for sure.

A smile crossed my lips when I tried out Mantis Style. I knew Kung Fu! Kalli clapped and cheered as I bounced around, trying one strike after another.

Do you think this will work against Rasputin?

She stopped cheering and shook her head. *Only if he doesn't touch you at all.*

In the end, I decided to keep the skill. Physical combat was still one of my weak points. Next up was Shimmer. While I still wasn't adept at it, Maya had made a good case for its effectiveness. Track Scent was another worthless skill for me. While it was good for a Blood Sleuth like Mr. Bellview, it was yet another trait I'd never used.

DELETE

Plague immunity was no longer needed since we destroyed the tower, so I **DELETED** that, too. I decided to keep some of the newer traits, like the Latin one from Zofia and Catlike Reflexes.

Command Attention just felt like another control skill, so I **DELETED** that one. Formulate was an alchemy skill that intrigued me, so I decided to hold onto it. Cloud Judgment was the skill I'd gotten from Raverly. While I still had no clue what it did, it had an ominous ring to it.

DELETE

Next was Assimilate Technology. I rather enjoyed the skill I'd acquired from Joe. It made me feel like I understood technology just a little bit more than I had before. I also knew I could use the skill to put stuff together with my mind. The problem was, with manipulation, none of that was necessary. I could just edit anything I needed into existence. Ultimately, I decided to **DELETE** it.

When I looked at the last skill, Dark Proclamation, Kalli began tapping her foot. *Well? What are you waiting for?*

Wouldn't it be useful to…

She shook her head violently. *No more prophecies!*

Fine.

DELETE

With the list pruned, I decided to check how it looked.

Skills: World Editor, Manipulation, Buff (Edited), Summon (Edited), Formulate

Traits: Bloodline: M, Bloodline: Shaw, Bloodline: Celestea, Bloodline: Xander, Bloodline: Brent, Enhanced Regeneration, Enhanced Mana Regeneration, Absorption, Shimmer, God Eye (Edited), Mantis Style, MateChat [Kalliphae Murphy] (Edited), Inseparable [Kalliphae Murphy], Intertwined [Kalliphae Murphy], Till Death Do You Part [Kalliphae Murphy], Praevericator Universum, Catlike Dexterity

Kalli gave me two thumbs up. *Much better.*

It's still longer than yours.

Kalli shrugged. *What can I say, I'm not an M. At least not by blood.*

The Xander bloodline was difficult to test. For that, we had to find an unawakened to persuade to do things. Using mana on my voice to make others do my bidding felt wrong. I had a feeling it was why I never tried any of the control skills I had just deleted. We made our way outside of Celestea castle to find the busy plaza bustling with activity. Hundreds if not thousands of villagers from all over Meltopia sought refuge in the only magic city in the empire. Tents had been erected anywhere there was open space.

My first instinct was to open World Editor to add more housing for all the refugees, but Kalli held up a hand to stop me. *You haven't modified the city before. If you make any changes here, it might affect how the magic works. Why don't you focus on learning your bloodline? There are plenty of people working to make sure everyone is comfortable. You don't have to do everything.*

Taking her advice, I walked up to the first villager I saw, a scraggly man wearing a bucket helm. "Excuse me, good sir. Can I get a glass of water?"

The man stopped what he was doing to look at me. "Uh, oh, of course, Lord Melvin. Right away, sir."

Kalli giggled and tapped me on the shoulder. *You can't ask them nicely. Who in the empire wouldn't do that for you? You need to put on an illusion and demand something they wouldn't normally do for a stranger.*

She was right. I needed a disguise. Fortunately, I had a bloodline for that. Mr. Ramsey had demonstrated his specific line of magic the first time I'd met him. Then I'd gone and impersonated a troll the first time I met Esha. Deciding to try something new, I focused on an image and let my mana warp the light around me.

Kali cringed and scooted away as I felt myself get shorter. Was the magic an illusion, or did the bloodline make me more of a shapeshifter? When the man came back with my cup of water, he looked around before turning to Kalli. "Where did Lord Melvin go?"

Kalli took the cup of water and giggled. "I'm sorry, he seems to have wandered off."

The man looked down at me and asked, "Who's this little fella?"

Kalli gave me a look that was a cross between affection and revulsion. "This is one of the goblin refugees, Smellatrix."

I glared at her.

Really with the name calling?

She stuck out her tongue. *You're the one that had to go and be a goblin. Now, tell him to do something and make it good.*

Suddenly on the spot, I had to come up with a command. "Jump up and down on one leg."

He lifted one leg in the air and began to jump up and down as he awaited further instructions. "Make a noise like a dog."

The man began to bark, "Arf, arf, arf."

"A big—" I began, but Kalli cut me off.

That's enough. You can make him stop now.

I grinned and dropped the illusion. "You can stop."

The man clamped his mouth shut mid-bark, causing him to bite his tongue. That combined with his leg that was still in the air caused him to fall over backward. "My lord! Where did you come from, I didn't see you. Oh, water! I'm so sorry, Lady Kalliphae drank it. I'll get you another."

I tried to tell him that wasn't necessary, but he was gone before I could get the words out. When the two of us were alone again, I turned back to Kalli.

What advice did Lavender give you?

She frowned at the mention of the enchanter. *She says she can't help with this battle, and that it has to happen.*

Did she see the future? Anything she can tell us can be useful in the fight against Rasputin.

Kalli shook her head, frustration spreading across our bond when she replied, *She says that while she can see the future, she can't tell us anything about it. It's so annoying the way she talks. I asked her if we should get the authorities from Earth involved, but she says it will only make matters worse. When I asked what we should do, she said, "Just do what the two of you think is best." It was so annoying.*

It was my turn to frown.

I had a feeling going to her would be a waste of time. I think our best bet is going to be to sneak into Dabia and try to take him by surprise.

Kalli nodded. *We are going to need help for that. Did you talk to Orpheus yet?*

I shook my head, and we were off to Luna to check on the recovering patients.

———

We found Orpheus pacing the throne room of the castle on Luna. The ancients largely ignored the man who waited next to the portal door, not daring to enter by myself. When Kalli and I stepped out, he rushed over. "My lady! Am I too late? Have I missed the battle? What news of your parents?"

Kalli took the old man's hands in hers and said, "You're just in time, Orpheus. We are gathering people to face Rasputin as we speak. I am going to need your help to sneak into Dabia."

"Dabia?" he asked, looking confused.

Kalli nodded. "I'm afraid Rasputin has slain the king and taken the throne. He still has my parents held captive as well."

"He means to take Gaia," Orpheus said. "What of the high house? Have they made any moves yet?"

"Yes," I replied. "And he killed Maya in the process. The rest of the awakened there seem to be fleeing the planet."

"Then all is lost," Orpheus sighed.

Kalli squeezed his hand, causing the old man to look up at her. "Not all. Mel and I have a plan."

[58]

WE HAVE A PLAN?

Kalli let out a nervous laugh. ***Yeah, don't die.***

Great plan.

She stuck out her tongue. ***I think you're starting to rub off on me.***

———

We gathered in Celestea castle to go over our options. The war room with the conference table felt empty without Celestea to offer her thoughts. While Kalli's father wasn't always there, we felt his absence, too.

Seated at the table was our ragtag group of friends. Now that he was back to full health, Orpheus took his place beside Kalli. We made a pit stop at Solitair to pick up Maya and Nir so they could weigh in. With new bodies and significantly lower levels, we decided that the two wouldn't be much help in the upcoming battle with Rasputin. That, and I didn't want to lose my sister again.

Nir laughed when I brought up her level. "When you've been around longer than the System, you understand that levels have little meaning when comparing greater beings to lesser ones."

Zofia was also present, accompanied by her aide Natalya. The two of them sat huddled at the far end of the table going over notes and sifting through a box of gadgets they'd brought along.

Esha and Boombrix joined as well, even though it was decided that it would be impossible to sneak non-humans into the castle. In the end, it was the Dabian representative that was the most helpful.

Edith stood before us in her impeccably pressed uniform and said, "Dabia stands with you. We will do everything in our power to overthrow the off-worlder who usurped the throne. If you can sneak in the usual way, we will smuggle you straight to the throne room."

"No chamber pot duty this time?" I confirmed, cringing at the thought.

Edith's lip curled up into a hint of a smile but only for a moment before going back to her trademark neutral expression. "That will not be necessary. Rolfe will smuggle you through a secret corridor directly to the throne room. Once you've dealt with Rasputin, the Dabian army stands ready to overthrow his men in town."

"Do you think they can handle tanks?" I asked, wondering if the Dabians had hidden technology I was unaware of.

She shook her head. "They only have one tank, and we have ways of handling it."

"Boombrix and her sisters can make the tank go boom," Boombrix offered, a maniacal smile on her face. "Boombrix isn't afraid to sneaky-sneaky into the castle town."

Edith's lip curled up for a different reason as the tiny green goblin spoke, "I don't see how that will be—"

"Let's worry about that later," Kalli cut her off, offering a reassuring smile to Boombrix. "For now, we need every advantage we can get. As you can see, we are going into this shorthanded. We were unable to find anyone that can help us that is even remotely close to Rasputin's level."

Edith frowned. "How do you plan on beating him then?"

Should we tell her that we beat high-level people before?

Kalli shook her head at me. *No. She should already know about your defeat of Mardella. Depending on what she heard from the king, she might know how badly you were hurt in that fight. All she needs to know is that we have a plan.*

Right, don't die!

Kalli struggled to suppress a giggle. *That, and we know how he attacks. Between the two of us, I'm sure we will find a way to beat him.*

We both knew the ring was an option. Of course, it meant possibly releasing Mardella since the only other prisoners of the ring appeared to be helpless princesses. I hadn't bothered to check their level, but the odds were high that imprisoning Rasputin meant releasing Mardella, and that might mean exchanging one battle for another. Especially if she was insane.

Realizing everyone was waiting for an answer, I stood to address the room. "He showed his cards the last time we fought him. He can kill with a touch. We also know from Maya that he uses his mana to do it. That means if we can repel his mana, he can't hurt us. Kalli and I have both been working on touch-based attacks. We can thank Mardella and the ancients for that. I believe if I can get the drop on him, I can subdue him if not kill him outright. There are a few variables that come into play here. First off, we don't know if he has any other awakened with him. If he does, we will have to retreat and regroup. There is also the possibility that he has ranged attacks he hasn't shown yet."

When I stopped, Kalli took over. "We also have weapons provided by Zofia and her group that has already proven effective against him. We are hoping to use those to at least stun him long enough to give us an advantage. For any of this to work, we are relying heavily on the element of surprise. This is why we must sneak into the castle unnoticed."

"We will get you in unseen," Edith replied. "That man will execute many Dabians should you fail to kill him. I want you to bear that in mind before you go in. Failure is not an option."

I found myself nodding along with everyone else. Failure in this case potentially meant the fall of Gaia. Thinking of the tank, I was reminded of how I dealt with the last one. "Do you know where the tank is parked? I can delete it if I get within eyesight."

She shook her head. "Using your magic on it would be a dead give-away that you are in town. That is also why we haven't planned a rescue for Queen Kalliphae's parents. They are likely bait designed to capture the two of you."

Kalli shuddered and her eyes began to water at the mention of her parents. However, I felt her quickly steel herself as she blinked away the tears and replied, "Our top priority is to eliminate Rasputin. We can deal with everything else afterward."

"Agreed," Edith said, giving Kalli a nod of approval. "The next question is how many people are we planning on sneaking into Dabia?"

As it turned out, we had quite an army of people to smuggle. Zofia arranged for a group of twenty men to accompany her. From the looks of them, they were likely mercenaries employed by the TGB. I also noticed they came with more traditional weapons from Earth including guns and something that looked mysteriously like a rocket-propelled grenade.

After meeting some of the men, I turned to Zofia and snickered. "What? No Iron Man?"

She turned my look around at me with a smirk. "Would you like me to suit up?"

The funny thing was, I couldn't tell if she was joking or not. We also had a couple dozen humans from Meltopia that volunteered to help rescue Kalli's mother and father. Included in the group was Gulliver. He embraced Kalli the moment he saw her and said, "I can never thank you enough for rescuing my Guinny. Helping get your parents back is the least I can do."

The villagers didn't look nearly as battle ready as Zofia's men, but what they lacked in skill, they made up for in enthusiasm. Each came equipped with various farm tools, which I quickly edited into more deadly weapons. Zofia outfitted each with a PING and gave them a quick rundown on how to use them. I noticed she didn't pass out any regular guns but figured that was probably for the best, friendly fire being a thing and all.

———

Getting to Dabia was easy. I teleported the entire group directly under the city in the Thief's Corridor in one go. Edith snuck us up in small groups, spreading our forces across multiple homes. Unlike the last time, we didn't need safe houses that were set up specifically for that purpose as all of the townsfolk had a vested interest in liberating their city. They jumped at the chance to put up their would-be liberators.

Aside from us, the only ones left were non-humans. Boombrix danced around, cradling a wicked-looking bomb in her tiny arms. "Boombrix is ready to send the wicked humans back where they belong."

The main group went up last only after everyone else was safely hidden from the public. That group consisted of me, Kalli, Orpheus, Zofia, Gulliver, and several armed mercenaries from the TGB.

We used group chat for communication. Zofia and her people were a little apprehensive, each of them already equipped with earwigs. After trying to get them in the group, there was a lot of accidental chatter as everyone broadcast their internal thoughts, not realizing how telepathic group chat worked.

These little green men are strange.

Who said that?

The voices in my head are speaking to me again.

In the end, we decided to let them use their radios, and we would use group chat. The exception was Zofia who was eager to try anything magical. Our group didn't waste any time with safe houses. Edith marched us through alleys until we were at the familiar servant's entrance to the castle.

When Edith knocked on the door, Rolfe answered immediately, making it obvious that he was waiting for us. Gone was the look of disdain on his face. While he wasn't exactly smiling, he didn't turn his nose up at us as though we reeked of chamber pots. Edith invited him to the group the moment she saw him.

Rolfe Dia has joined the group.

He gave Edith a grim nod and said, *The staff has been confined to essential duties. Even you are not free to walk about as you like, so we need to stick to the passageways.*

Edith nodded. *That's what I expected. Do you have any information on other magic users? In the guest wings perhaps?*

Rolfe shook his head. *No, actually I was going to ask you about that. The man who killed the king and queen seems quite mad. He did bring other men into the capital but insisted they stay outside of the castle.*

Kalli stepped forward and asked, *Have you seen my parents? Are they alive?*

Rolfe's expression softened when he saw the look on Kalli's face. *I'm sorry, Your Majesty. Your parents aren't in the castle. So far as I know, nobody has seen them.*

They could be in the tank. Perhaps I can—

Kalli vetoed the idea. **It's fine. I'm sure they will turn up. We need to focus on Rasputin.**

I looked back at the group. There were more people with us than I was comfortable sneaking around for long with.

We need to get out of sight. Take us to Rasputin.

Rolfe nodded and took us to a room that looked like a janitor's closet. After moving several brooms and a mop out of the way, he pushed a tile on the wall. It sunk in, and a secret door slid open. I was mildly disappointed that special music didn't play to announce we'd discovered it.

The passage through the walls was dusty and dark but that didn't seem to bother anyone in the group. Rolfe walked with the confidence he must have gotten from many trips through the ancient walls of the castle. Kalli and I relied on the God Eye skill to see everything clear as day. Zofia donned a strange-looking pair of goggles that made her eyes seem four times bigger than normal and her mercenaries trailed close behind with their guns drawn. While Gulliver didn't have a way of seeing in the dark, he did a good job of keeping up, nonetheless.

After walking for what felt like an eternity, Rolfe stopped us, pointing to a wall with a latch on it. *Through here is the throne room. You will find him sitting on the throne. I am quite certain he is expecting you.*

[59]

WHAT DO you mean expecting us?

Rolfe froze for a second, looking back at us with a look of disbelief on his face. *You can't possibly think he doesn't know you're coming? I'm pretty sure it's the only reason Dabia still stands.*

Kalli looked sideways at me, a frown on her face. **What do you want to do?**

What could I do? It wasn't like we would gain anything by running. He would just kill more people until he got his hands on me. Part of me questioned why I wanted to save the planet in the first place. Then I thought of my mother. What would she do? She always told me to live my best life. What life would that be if I spent it running away? Then there was Kalli. This was *her* planet, *her* home. We needed to save her parents. I took a deep breath and came to a decision.

I'm going to distract him. It's me he's after. Find an opening and take him out.

Kalli tugged my shirt sleeve as I approached the wall with the latch, an urgent thought pressing against my mind. **Don't do anything stupid.**

I turned and gave her the most confident grin I could muster.

Hey! It's me we're talking about.

She rolled her eyes and forced herself to breathe. *That's why I'm worried.*

Trying not to make Kalli's fear come true, I fed some mana into the artifact wrapped around my forearm, and soon a suit of armor coated my body. The door mechanism made a clicking sound that felt like it echoed loudly through the hall when the door to the passage slid open. I waited with bated breath for any sign of movement. If anybody heard the sound, they were doing a pretty good job of pretending they didn't.

Slowly, I tiptoed through the shadows, craning my neck for a sign of Rasputin or the throne. Rolfe instructed me through group chat as I went. *Take two more lefts and the throne is straight ahead. Keep the plants between you and the throne, and he shouldn't be able to see you.*

I held my breath as I walked. It wasn't that I thought it would do any good. Every time I took a breath, I remembered Maya gasping as Rasputin's mana slowly devoured her core.

It was shortly after I began creeping through the room that I sensed Kalli slip in behind me. She pressed herself to the wall and went in the opposite direction around the other side of the room. I wanted to tell her to go back where it was safe, but I also knew she wouldn't listen.

Just a little bit farther.

I spoke more to myself than anyone else as I slid past another of the many decorative plants that lined the room in large antique vases. Through the leaves, I made out someone on the throne. It could be Rasputin. The most I could make out was the silver, black hair, and the wispy beard. Could there be two people with those features?

About halfway to the throne, I made out voices. Rasputin was talking...but to who? I stopped to listen and see if I could figure out who else was with him.

"...another day. It will be satisfying—"

Then I realized he was talking to himself. Rasputin was alone in the throne room. Some part of me realized what I needed to do, while another part screamed I was committing suicide. Kalli was quiet for once as I readied myself and stepped out into the open.

Rasputin looked up, starting to rise to his feet. "It's about time you—"

I don't know where it came from, nerves probably, but I laughed.

DELETE

Rasputin fell to the floor as the throne vanished beneath him. High above was a chandelier with thousands of crystal shards dangling from it. I focused on one of the low-hanging ones and edited it into a one-thousand-ton boulder. It snapped off the chandelier with a satisfying *pop* and plummeted to where Rasputin was struggling to get up.

The boulder kicked up a massive cloud of dust as it slammed into the ground right where Rasputin had been. I was still waiting for the dust to clear when flashes of light went off all around me accompanied by the loud cracking of gunfire. The rest of the group had managed to get in position at various places around the throne room and opened fire with a combination of PINGs and guns.

The rubble from the boulder went through a variety of transformations as multiple PING blasts struck. From the looks of things, all the PINGs had been set to animacation. Flashing rocks and what looked like ACME fireworks shot off in every direction, the dull *thuds* of the bullets more an afterthought than anything else.

The shooting stopped, and we waited in silence for the chaos to die down.

"Kekekekeke," shrewd laughter echoed from the back of the room. "You are much more impressive this time around. Finally, a worthy opponent. Now, show me, do you know how to wield that manipulator class of yours?"

I spun on him as he approached me, forming mana in my left hand to make a sword. "I know how your attack works. It's not going to work on me."

"Is that so?" he asked with a cackle, moving faster than I thought the old man was capable of.

I held the sword out in front of me while altering one of the plants next to Rasputin.

Item: Man-Eating Plant (Edited)
Components: Plant, Bloodlust
Item Rank: B

Item Level: 1
Item Owner: Rasputin

Apparently, Rasputin claimed everything in the kingdom when he killed King Thomas. Fortunately, my new man-eating plant worked as advertised and lunged for Rasputin the moment he passed it. He stopped laughing when he was forced to leap to the side as my creation snapped at his arm.

The action caused the rest of the group to come back to life and shots rang out once more. Rasputin vanished in a puff of smoke, leaving the shots to scorch the ground where he had just been.

"What else can you do, boy?" his voice echoed in the distance. I had no clue where he was. "Make this fun for me. It's been so long since I've had proper entertainment."

"Why are you doing this?" Kalli shouted from up above.

"Because I can, little girl," Rasputin replied. "Don't you know we're gods?"

I marched over to the wreckage that was the throne, knowing he had to approach if he wanted to use his skill on me. The artifact armor made me feel confident that I'd be able to withstand anything he threw my way.

The problem was, Rasputin never came. An agonized scream told me exactly what he was up to. He was picking off Zofia's men. Specifically, the ones with the guns. Standing by the throne only ensured one thing...he was going to save me for last.

It was then that I regretted allowing the TGB to leave group chat. I had no clue who was down, who was alive, or where they were. The only thing I knew was that Zofia was hidden somewhere up near Kalli and frightened yet determined. She wasn't saying anything in group chat, but she was speaking rapidly through her comms system.

Going through my options, I realized there was one thing I wanted to do. I needed to get to Kalli. If Rasputin was going to pick everyone off before dealing with me, that meant he was going to go after her at some point.

Wrapping mana around myself, I appeared at her side. She hunched over a balcony upstairs along with Gulliver, Zofia, and one of the TGB mercenaries.

Kalli pointed over the edge at Rasputin who was standing over the body of one of Zofia's men. I wasn't sure how many of her men were left, but if they were alive, none of them were moving to attack again.

"Four down," Rasputin taunted, looking up as though he knew exactly where I was.

Zofia let out a growl and threw something over the edge. I expected an explosion, but it bounced across the floor a few times before emitting an ear-splitting siren. Instinctively, I covered my ears as I looked over the balcony again. Rasputin was gone, teleported away once again.

The sound of the device was overwhelming, and I almost didn't hear it but someone screamed downstairs as Rasputin found another victim.

There! Kalli's thoughts screamed in my head, pointing toward the back of the throne room.

Rasputin towered over his victim, his bony hand clutching at the twitching man's throat. I noticed the man had a grenade on his vest, so I targeted the pin.

DELETE

Somehow, Rasputin knew what I was up to and vanished again a moment before the grenade blew up. This time, he reappeared right in front of me, his attention distracted by the explosion.

Taking advantage of the distraction, I swung the sword at Rasputin's head. He deflected it with an arm, the blade sheering off a chunk of flesh as it raked across his skin. Kalli ducked behind a pillar out of sight in the confusion. I tried to draw the blade back, but it was stuck on something.

I looked down to see Rasputin gripping it between two fingers. A twisted smile marred his face. "A mana blade? How tasty."

The blade in my hand began to warp as Rasputin did something to it. I only felt the danger at the last moment when I realized Rasputin was pumping mana of his own into my weapon, attempting to gain access to me through my summon. I immediately released the weapon, and it vanished causing him to stagger back.

Rasputin tutted at me and reached for my arm. I looked down at him in horror as his fingers closed over the black metal of the artifact armor. Should I give myself to the armor again? Let it fight for me?

His mana washed over the artifact, seeking purchase in the chinks in the armor. Then a familiar spell came from behind him.

"Pvruzth!"

Kalli screamed the word, and green flame slammed into Rasputin's back. He howled in agony and vanished again. I looked down at my hand, realizing his mana had found a way to get through the armor. I wasn't as impervious to his attack as I'd thought. Kalli noticed as well, rushing over to check on me. *We should run away.*

By that time, Zofia and her remaining men were once again shooting desperately at Rasputin. He was good at dodging the bullets and somehow had managed not to be turned into a cartoon yet. Whether that was because he figured it out or if was just good at dodging was beyond me.

I snuck back to the stairs and made my way down to the throne room.

We have to get him today. If we let him go, there's no telling how many people he will kill.

I felt Kalli sneaking after me as prepared to face off with the man. The mana blade was out of commission, so my remaining options included my ranged light magic and the ping. There was also the emotional mana but that was only if we made contact. Then there was the armor, but I feared what it would do if I let it take control.

There was another option of course. A simple way to deal with any foe. All I had to do was push mana through my ring and Rasputin would be trapped in there. Even if Mardella was released, she would be weak and disoriented, which would make her easy to kill with a gun.

Seeming to read my thoughts, Rasputin stepped out from where he was hiding. "Well, boy? Are you ready to go a round with the champ?"

[60]

I HAD to chuckle at the modern quip made by Rasputin. The thought of him sitting on a beat-up couch, eating hot wings, and watching MMA was amusing. Especially considering the stories I'd read about him in books.

We glared in silence as we circled one another. Occasionally, Rasputin was forced to teleport a few feet to avoid a PING blast, but it appeared he'd managed to kill all of the gun-wielding TGB agents.

Kalli stood a good ten feet behind him, looking for an opening to attack. While the artifact armor didn't provide the safety I originally thought it would, I felt an odd sense of confidence bubbling up inside of me. I'd beaten a vampire, a dragon god, and Mardella. As far as Rasputin was concerned, he was just another rung on the ladder of baddies I had to defeat on my way to the top.

Rasputin lunged, dragging me out of my headspace as his bony fingers latched onto my wrist once again. He didn't even notice the jagged barbs on the artifact armor that dug into his skin. I felt his mana as it seeped through the armor and tried to invade my body. It was impure and felt gross. I'd experienced many different types of mana, but his was putrid.

My mana flared within me, forcing the invading mana from my

THE ACCIDENTAL CORRUPTION

channels while at the same time striking Rasputin in the chest with quick jabs from my free hand. He choked and staggered backward, releasing me from his grip. I pressed the advantage, feeling a sense of satisfaction that I'd been able to repel him. While my left wrist still felt numb, the sick mana hadn't found a path to travel to my core.

Rasputin recovered quickly and lunged at me once again, this time going directly for my chest. I instinctually knew his goal was to find a more direct path to my core where his mana could do the most damage. Unlike Mardella's magic, which my bloodline could withstand, we already had proof that Rasputin's was fatal once it touched the core.

This time when he laid his hands on me, I was prepared and grabbed his wrists. I felt the cold metal of the ring rub against his hand and had a momentary urge to use it on him, but it passed when I realized I could beat him the old-fashioned way.

After prying him away from my chest, we had an internal battle with both of our manas surging and slamming into each other. Both of our bodies shook from the sheer force of the mana we were expending. With nowhere to go, the mana escaped in brilliant flashes of light and dark, making it seem to anyone watching as though night was threatening to overwhelm the daylight by snuffing it out. Unsure of what emotion to choose, I stuck with the one I'd chosen to defeat Mardella's curse, curiosity.

It wasn't an ideal emotion as it was the last thing on my mind in a life-or-death situation. I still remembered what happened to Maya's old body and had no desire to experience it for myself. Not even for the sake of science.

Just when I thought we were going to be stuck in a stalemate, a flash of golden light lit up the room, and Rasputin stiffened. I slowly disentangled myself from his fingers to see what was going on. Zofia emerged from the shadows and walked up to the man. In a cold voice I'd never heard from her, she said, "On your knees. Now!"

To my surprise, he obediently fell to his knees. Zofia smiled and looked at me for confirmation. When I nodded, she leaned closer to Rasputin and whispered, "Kill yourself."

CRACK!

Rasputin's backhand sent the small woman flying across the room until she collided with the far wall and crashed to the floor and went still.

Rasputin slowly climbed to his feet, glaring daggers at me. "That almost worked. If your little friend hadn't hesitated, she might have actually pulled it off. If she isn't dead already, I'll make sure she pays for that once I'm done with you. Now, then, stop struggling and give up your soul."

The confidence I had was suddenly gone as I stared at the lifeless form of Zofia bleeding slowly onto the hard floor. Rasputin reached out a hand to grab me when a club crashed down hard on it. The bone cracked, causing Rasputin to wince in pain. It was the perfect opportunity to strike when Rasputin turned to find Gulliver readying another blow. I watched the old man excitedly, hoping an adult would handle my battle for once.

Rasputin was ready for the second blow. He deflected it with his good arm before grabbing the old man's throat. It was over before I had a chance to react. I watched in horror as the light drained from Gulliver's eyes. Satisfied that his perverted spell worked, Rasputin discarded the man's corpse and returned his attention to me. "Now, where were we?"

I screamed in fury for both Zofia and Gulliver, imagining his daughter when I told her I'd failed to protect her father. We clashed again in an explosion of mana that seared the walls and columns around us. Red carpet leading to the ruins of the throne frayed and smoldered beneath our feet.

After a while, we both tired and staggered away from each other. Rasputin wheezed and cackled as he taunted me again, "You lack the conviction to do what is necessary. It's a shame really. You could have had potential. Now, you will only live on as part of my legacy. I will be the first to meet Father."

"Where are Kalli's parents?" I asked, anxious to stall while I planned my next attack. Was it time to finally use the ring?

To my surprise, Rasputin vanished. I looked around, finding no sign of him in the throne room. Kalli also peeked her head out of where she'd been hiding in an attempt to locate the old man. Just when I thought we were going to have to scour the castle for him, he reappeared holding a bag.

Dropping it at my feet, he grinned maniacally. "I'd almost forgotten your gift. Go ahead. Open it, I'll wait."

Not taking my eyes off Rasputin, I bent down and scooped up the bag. It was remarkably heavy, and whatever was inside was staining it a very grotesque color. The stench of rot made me retch the instant I opened the bag. Lifeless eyes peered out at me, and I quickly twisted the bag shut, praying Kalli didn't see through my eyes.

"No!" she screamed, charging out from behind a pillar in a blind rush toward us.

Rasputin whooped like Christmas had come early as he rounded on the girl with a sadistic grin. Kalli splayed both hands out and screamed, "I am going to erase you!"

"Pvruzth."

"Pvruzth."

"Bvoomzt."

While I knew Kalli had increased the size of her mana pool, I'd never seen her actually call on it before. Green flames erupted from the artifact in waves, washing over Rasputin, and charring his skin instantly. Still, Kalli wasn't satisfied. She followed up with a massive green fireball that threatened to take Rasputin out and me along with it. We both dove out of the way as the blast went through the wall as if it wasn't there. Additional explosions erupted from deeper into the castle in the wake of the blast.

I looked up to see Kalli bent over, panting. Clearly, she'd used all of her mana on the attack. I looked over at the ground where Rasputin had fallen. Aside from a scorch mark on the ground, he was nowhere to be found.

Cursing myself, I climbed back to my feet to see if I could help Kalli, who was struggling to stand after expending all of her mana. In the distance, Rasputin howled and plummeted from the second-floor balcony. What looked like a ninja jumped down after him, a tiny dagger in hand.

What turned out to be Orpheus shuddered when Rasputin grabbed his ankle. He tried desperately to free himself before collapsing to the ground. I raced over to the spot where Rasputin lay panting, but he vanished again. Looking down at Orpheus, I could tell he was in pain. There wasn't much to do for him at the moment and I needed to protect Kalli, so I turned to make my way back to her.

WHAM!

Rasputin appeared out of nowhere, tackling me to the ground. We wrestled for a few moments, each trying desperately to get on top. His skin was still smoking with blisters all over his body from where Kalli's attack had landed. The artifact armor ripped chunks of skin off his lanky arms every time I grabbed him. He fought through the pain, a look of insanity in his eyes. Somehow, we ended up clutching each other's arms again. I thought of the ring and hesitated yet again. Would it be fair to release Mardella into such a mutilated body? Could anyone other than Rasputin survive like that? Would I want Rasputin in my ring every time I went there?

He sensed my hesitation and laughed. "I'm surprised you've lived this long with an attitude like that. You lack what it takes to survive as an M. Consider this a fav... Urk!"

His word got cut off as Kalli grabbed him from behind in a head-lock. Tears ran down her face as she strained with all her might to choke the life out of him. No, that wasn't it. She wanted to snap his neck.

Kalli...

My words were lost on her ears as she continued to strain, agony and exhaustion etched across her face. Rasputin wasn't giving up without a fight. Using strength I didn't know he had left, he peeled me off and stood slowly, carrying Kalli on his back like a baby.

Fear replaced hate in her eyes as he reached back to grab her. I lunged forward in an attempt to save her but then something strange happened...

...Kalli exploded.

The force of the blast blew both of us off our feet. I crashed into the ground and rolled several times before coming to a stop. Pain shot through my body as my enhanced regeneration struggled to compensate.

Kalli!

Whatever she'd done had been extremely violent. There was no response from her through our connection. I couldn't sense her, which made me want to drop everything and teleport to her side. The only problem was, I couldn't yet. Not while Rasputin still lived. In the distance, I saw him move as he groaned and struggled to get up.

Gone was the sinister laughter. It was replaced by grim determination as he concentrated his remaining energy on the task at hand. That was to kill me. I was done with self-doubt. The thought that my inaction caused Kalli harm was too much to bear.

I marched with purpose over to Rasputin. One of us was going to die, and we both knew it. The idea of using the ring wasn't enough anymore. He looked at me as I approached. "Your eyes. They changed."

I didn't know what he meant, and I didn't care. I was going to beat him at his own game. We reached out to each other, knowing full well that only one of us would survive the embrace. The moment our hands touched, I let go of everything. All the hate, rage, and fear I felt the moment Kalli vanished from my mind melted out of me and into Rasputin. He trembled as his mana was overwhelmed by the sheer volume of mine.

At that moment I felt like the artifact armor. My vision blurred in a thick red haze as I let the raw emotion overwhelm me. I knew it wasn't the armor doing it. It was me. Something snapped, and I let myself turn into something I didn't recognize.

Rasputin put up a good fight, his mana washed over me, desperately seeking admittance so he could find my core and crush it. When he got to my mouth, it gave me an idea. While my mana was flooding into his body, I was nowhere near as good at killing with it as he was. For all I knew, it would take days to whittle away at his core. However, the fleshy parts of his body were another story. I didn't have my mana blade anymore, but I did have something that was very good at doing damage and I knew exactly how to control it.

The armor protecting my body melted away from me until it was a living ball of liquid. I then directed it into Rasputin's open mouth. His eyes bulged when it made its way down his gullet. I held him tightly as the artifact had its way inside of him. Rasputin twitched violently in my arms as his internal organs were eviscerated by the armor.

I looked him straight in the eyes as I watched the life fade from them. Only then did I drop his lifeless body to the ground. After staring at the corpse for a moment, I stopped to take inventory of the wreckage around me, and my thoughts turned to Kalli.

Kalli! Where are you? What did you just do?

There was no reply. I wanted to teleport to her but again, there were injured people around me. Kalli would kill me if I teleported to her without checking on them. As I'd feared, Gulliver was dead. Rasputin had used his soul magic and destroyed his core. I pushed my mana inside him to be sure before quickly moving on to Zofia.

She was luckier. While she was mortally wounded, it was something I could heal with my magic. I quickly mended bones and repaired ruptured arteries before moving on to Orpheus. While Rasputin had invaded his body with that rancid mana, he hadn't quite made it to his core before the contact was broken. I wasn't sure if he would survive, but at least he had a chance. Half of the TGB mercenaries were lucky and still alive. I quickly did what I could for them but decided I could wait no longer and teleported…

———

While I was supposed to end up at Kalli's side, I found myself in a very strange place. I rested my hand on an empty pedestal and whispered to myself, "Is this a dream?"

THANK YOU FOR READING ACCIDENTAL CORRUPTION

We hope you enjoyed it as much as we enjoyed bringing it to you. We just wanted to take a moment to encourage you to review the book. Follow this link: The Accidental Corruption, to be directed to the book's Amazon product page to leave your review.

Every review helps further the author's reach and, ultimately, helps them continue writing fantastic books for us all to enjoy.

ALSO IN SERIES:
The Accidental Summoning
The Accidental Education
The Accidental Contract
The Accidental Corruption
The Accidental Origin

———

Want to discuss our books with other readers and even the authors? Join our Discord server today and be a part of the Aethon community.

Facebook | Instagram | Twitter | Website

You can also join our non-spam mailing list by visiting www. subscribepage.com/AethonReadersGroup and never miss out on future releases. You'll also receive three full books completely Free as our thanks to you.

Looking for more great LitRPG?

Reincarnated in a new world where survival of the fittest reigns supreme. If waking up in a new world isn't bad enough, Hestia starts her new life as a small, newborn dragon in a hostile forest filled with vicious monsters. With status screens obscuring her vision, her first task is to escape two hungry kobolds wanting some grilled lizard for breakfast. Equipped with fragmented memories from her past life and the game-like mechanics of her new reality, Hestia must face trials, beasts, bosses and more as she grows in size and power. She is determined to find civilization. For nothing will stop her from fulfilling her one true desire: to become an Idol. Don't miss the adventure of a lifetime in this new LitRPG Series about an underdog rising up to be the idol her new world didn't know it needed. Hestia may start small, but one day her power will match her determination.

Get Awakening Now!

———

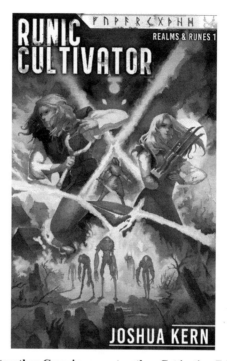

Train together. Grow in power together. Get justice. Erik once lived a simple life as an herb grower in a forest. But it was never meant to last. Now, he and his betrothed, Ainsley have been training tirelessly to get revenge on the men who murdered his mother. They have come far since those young, early days. Cultivation of the body, and the spirit, of the power within, and how to fight as a team. That is what their teacher has drilled into them day in and day out for the last few years. It's time for Erik and Ainsley to leave the safety of the forest and to begin their own journey, one that will take them across the realms on a path to justice. Can they make it? Are they strong enough? Find out in the start of a new Cultivation LitRPG Series from Joshua Kern, bestselling author of The Game of Gods.

Get Runic Cultivator Now!

———

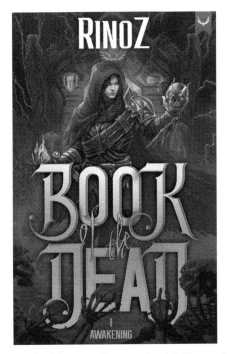

With one touch of the stone, Tyron receives his Class and his life changes forever. In an instant his bright and promising future as the scion of two powerful Slayers is torn apart and he must make a decision. Will he allow his Class to be purged from his soul, or will he cling to it, abandon all that he knows, and rise to power? Don't miss the start of the next hit LitRPG series from RinoZ, the author of Chrysalis. Book of the Dead takes on all aspects of Necromancy headfirst, from the tactical manuevering of skeletons, to what it's like spending so much time amongst the undead.

Get Awakening Now!

For all our LitRPG books, visit our website.

Made in the USA
Columbia, SC
22 October 2024

09b4722a-956f-4b06-adfb-a8004c7e02a8R01